The
SHADE
TREE

GUERNICA
PRIZE
3

Canada Council **Conseil des Arts**
for the Arts **du Canada**

ONTARIO ARTS COUNCIL
CONSEIL DES ARTS DE L'ONTARIO
an Ontario government agency
un organisme du gouvernement de l'Ontario

Canadä

Guernica Editions Inc. acknowledges the support of the Canada Council
for the Arts and the Ontario Arts Council. The Ontario Arts Council
is an agency of the Government of Ontario.
We acknowledge the financial support of the Government of Canada.

The SHADE TREE

THERESA SHEA

GUERNICA
EDITIONS
TORONTO • CHICAGO • BUFFALO • LANCASTER (U.K.)
2021

Michael Mirolla, general editor
Julie Roorda, editor
David Moratto, interior and cover design
Guernica Editions Inc.
287 Templemead Drive, Hamilton, (ON), Canada L8W 2W4
2250 Military Road, Tonawanda, N.Y. 14150-6000 U.S.A.
www.guernicaeditions.com

Distributors:
Independent Publishers Group (IPG)
600 North Pulaski Road, Chicago IL 60624
University of Toronto Press Distribution (UTP)
5201 Dufferin Street, Toronto (ON), Canada M3H 5T8
Gazelle Book Services, White Cross Mills
High Town, Lancaster LA1 4XS U.K.

First edition.
Printed in Canada.

Legal Deposit—Third Quarter
Library of Congress Catalog Card Number: 2021933082
Library and Archives Canada Cataloguing in Publication
Title: The shade tree / Theresa Shea.
Names: Shea, Theresa, author.
Description: First edition. | Series statement: Guernica prize ; 3
Identifiers: Canadiana (print) 20210140038
| Canadiana (ebook) 20210140100 | ISBN 9781771836296 (softcover)
| ISBN 9781771836302 (EPUB) | ISBN 9781771836319 (Kindle)
Classification: LCC PS8637.H42 S53 2021 | DDC C813/.6—dc23

But we clung to the belief ... that our white skin made us "better" than all other people. And this belief comforted us, for we felt worthless and weak when confronted with authorities who had cheapened nearly all we held dear, except our skin color. There, in the land of Epidermis, every one of us was a little king.

 —**Lillian Smith**, *Killers of the Dream*

We are well advised to keep on nodding terms with the people we used to be, whether we find them attractive company or not.

 —**Joan Didion**

*To my mother, Sharon Shea, for attending
the March on Washington
with her two daughters.*

I was three months old.

Gideon jumped from the wagon and ran for the woods; small knives jabbed his lungs and sides. *What have you done? What have you done?*

Terror and elation ran like wild dogs through his veins. It had felt so good to stand behind Old Man Yates in the wagon bed and bring that branch down hard onto his white skull. The reverberation had rattled up Gideon's forearms and through his locked elbows. He'd watched with amazement and relief as the old man fell like a fat bird from its perch.

All his life white men had been turning their backs on him, so sure of themselves. Incredibly, until this moment, he'd kept his rage reined tight.

Adrenalin added speed to Gideon's legs. He wiped sweat from his eyes and headed towards the swamp. The dogs would lose his scent in water, but the alligators would pick it up. He'd have to be careful. Predators were everywhere.

He screamed his wife's name inside his head. *Sliver! I'm sorry, baby. I couldn't help it.*

Tears mixed with his sweat. He knew how she'd respond. *Couldn't help it? Are you a puppet? Who's pulling your strings?*

That's what she said to the kids when they claimed innocence. *What kind of a person do you want to be?* she'd ask them. *Every day you'll have decisions to make, and you'll either move closer to that person or farther away. Think on it!*

But he'd done it for her, and for his daughters who would one day catch Old Man Yates's eye. And for all the stories he'd heard and the acts he'd witnessed. Would Sliver understand that? The old man had had it coming all right. But who would suffer now?

He pulled his shoes off and held one in each hand. The water was warm at the bank. Gideon plunged in and tried to keep his speed up and his noise down. He'd never ventured far from the Yates's before. He'd never had cause. But he knew about the fishing spot around the bend that the sheriff and some of his boys visited. Travelling at night would increase his chances of getting away, but he couldn't wait for darkness. He needed to put some distance between him and the old man. Was he dead or only injured? If he was alive, he'd know who'd swung the branch. And if he was dead, well, that's why Gideon was running.

A fish jumped nearby and landed on its side with a splash. Gideon almost left his skin from fright. The sawgrass marsh stretched far to his right. To his left, small islands of trees formed a hammock over the water. Full sun or shade? He chose the shade and waded left.

A water strider skimmed the swamp's surface towards a dead insect floating. Just before it got there, a fish swallowed it up. Or was it a bullfrog? Either way, it was a bad omen. Gideon assessed his chances of survival and didn't like the outcome, but he had no time to panic. He lifted each foot from the muddy swamp bed that tried to suck him down and repeated that action. He focused on the patience and determination he'd once had when teaching himself to juggle. Again and again he'd thrown oranges into the air. Two at a time was easy. Three took more practice, the results so slow to come. Then four. And finally he could juggle five at a time, oranges revolving in a circle, spaced perfectly and in time around him: Gideon, creator of his own universe.

And he and Sliver had peopled that universe with children. To what avail? His arms were empty now.

I did it for you, Sliver. For the kids.

His foot squelched as he pulled it from the swamp bottom and continued his forward motion.

I'll send for you. Don't you worry now. You'll be hearing from me soon. Real soon.

Yes, he nodded to himself. Once he got to the county line, he'd hitch a ride North. That was the only direction to choose.

I'll send for you, baby.

He began to cry. Sliver was pregnant with their fifth child. What if they hurt her? Or his children? Seth, the eldest, was only eight.

Old Man Yates had taken his hat off to wipe his brow. He'd presented his bald globe to Gideon as if it was a gift. It had felt so good to swing, but he hadn't thought it through.

A wooden bridge appeared in the distance. He detoured away from it. Bridges were dangerous. He'd found a rhythm and picked up speed. The sooner he got away from here, the sooner he could send for his family.

Go, go, go. He timed each stride to a story he was writing on freedom. *Soon, soon, soon.*

What was that?

He stopped and held his breath. Voices.

They came from the fishing hole. He listened harder. Just voices. No dogs. He dropped low in the water and moved closer to the bank, near the tree roots that offered a protective shelter.

He tucked into the bank and waited. He'd wait all day if he had to. He was good at waiting.

PART ONE

1930—1935

CHAPTER 1

The summer of 1930 was long and hot. The wind blew from the Atlantic on the east and from the Gulf of Mexico on the west and fanned the leaves of all the trees and flowers and orchards and gardens on the narrow Florida peninsula.

Ten-year-old Mavis Turner had to agree that her sister Ellie was right: nothing much happened in their days. They did their sewing, some needlepoint when forced to, and whatever other chores their mama saw fit to delegate, depending on the season and their finances. The better the harvest, the fewer chores the girls did in the house because they could get darkies to do them instead. It was a kindness getting them to do work. That's what their daddy said, because they always needed money and didn't know how to take care of themselves. He said they were dark because they rolled in their own dirt, adding that even animals didn't dirty their own nests. Mavis wondered if he'd seen Ellie's room lately.

She swung on the porch swing and looked out over the citrus grove. At the high arc of the swing she saw the rows of orange trees perfectly spaced apart that went on for acres. At the low arc of the swing, all she saw was the front row. Lots of trees; not so many. Lots of trees; not so many.

Ellie appeared from behind the barn and walked slowly towards the house. Every hair was in place. The pleats of her dress hung with sharp edges. Her sister had been given more than her fair share of beauty. Older by three years, Ellie had probably taken some of Mavis's without even asking. She was greedy like that. Mavis got tired of hearing the men in town predict Ellie would be the most beautiful girl in Neelan Junction. She especially didn't like it when they said it in front of her, as if she was invisible.

Ellie threw herself down beside Mavis and the swing went all sideways for a minute until settling back into a normal rhythm.

"What were you doing out by the barn?"

"Minding my own business," Ellie said.

"Well, as long as you're not minding mine."

"You're too young to have business to mind." Then Ellie groaned and made a face, nodding towards the courtyard.

Mavis turned to see the midwife walking around the back of the house.

"Why doesn't she take the other path?" Ellie said. "I don't need reminding that we're poor. I liked it better when Doc Wilson came for Mama's babies. What's she doing here anyway? The baby was born last week!"

"Sliver's probably just checking to make sure the baby's feeding alright."

"Sliver, huh? You're on a first-name basis?"

"Mamie told me her name. It suits her. She's thin and dark, like a sliver. You learn a lot by asking questions. You should try it sometime. Plus, you should be grateful she's here. At least Mama's baby didn't die this time."

"If that means she'll stop having them so the midwife stops coming, then I'll be grateful."

Samuel crossed the courtyard pushing a wheelbarrow filled with pruned branches and headed to the barn. Mavis waved.

"If Mama sees you waving at Mamie's boy, there'll be trouble. Didn't she tell you to stay away from him?"

Mavis nodded. "But she didn't listen to the whole story. Samuel was only carrying me because I fell down and hurt myself."

They had been throwing rotten oranges at the back of the barn. Once she convinced him they wouldn't get into any trouble because the rotten fruit was useless, he threw hard and the oranges exploded on impact, sending pulp and juice flying everywhere. When they finally tired of the sport, they ran back to the house. Mavis tripped and fell hard, taking a few layers of skin off one knee. Blood boiled up out of the wound and she'd cried out in alarm. Samuel doubled back, picked her up, and ran to the kitchen door to get Mamie's help. Mavis had her arms wrapped tight around his neck to keep from falling when her mama came out of the house and started screaming for them to stop. It didn't matter how much Mavis tried to explain, her mama was adamant that she not play with him anymore. That had been about six months ago, and she still missed him.

The swing moved through the heat and made its own breeze in the still air.

"Samuel's lucky nothing else happened to him."

"Why?" Mavis asked. "He was only trying to help."

"Did Missy tell you what happened at Slew Town?"

Missy Richardson's daddy owned the turpentine still. Slew Town was where all his workers lived. That's also where the prisoners were sent. It was the great threat held over all the children of Neelan Junction: *If you don't behave, you'll end up in Slew Town.* It didn't matter that only negroes lived there. There was a first time for everything.

"No. What happened?"

"There was a boy there nicknamed Whitey because he'd worked with turpentine so much that the black washed from his hands. Missy claimed that's how the pitch turned black, by sucking Whitey's darkness straight from his skin. One by one his fingers turned white, first at the tips and then moving up to the knuckles." Ellie held her hands up and wiggled her fingers dramatically like they were spiders. "And then his entire hands, and then his wrists. Before long, he was white up to his elbows. Missy said if a door opened and a hand reached in, nobody would know it was a darky." Ellie smoothed the folds of her dress.

"Is that it?"

"Are you sure you want to hear more? You don't seem too interested."

"Yes!" Mavis hated how Ellie got her excited about something and then acted as if it wasn't worth telling.

"Okay, well, Missy's brother said if the bleaching kept on, Whitey would one day be all white."

Now Mavis knew it was just another one of Ellie's made-up stories. "That's ridiculous."

"Is it?" She shrugged. "Anyway, we'll never find out. He was found yesterday floating in one of the vats. His eyeballs had disintegrated. Turpentine does that, you know."

Mavis imagined gaping eye sockets and shuddered. Why did Ellie tell her these things?

"He was only thirteen," she added. "Same age as me."

"So he drowned?"

"You could say that. Except Missy said his ankles were tied together."

"Why would he go swimming with his ankles tied together?"

"He wasn't the one who tied them, stupid."

Well then who did? Mavis hid her confusion and pretended to know. "I don't believe you."

"Suit yourself. Ask Missy next time you see her."

Just then, a cat darted across the parched grass towards the barn with a mouse dangling from its mouth. Mavis loved cats. She jumped up and followed it, but by the time she wrenched the barn door open, the cat was gone, and she was alone. Ellie hadn't followed.

The air was even more heavy, humid, and close inside. She stood still to catch her breath. Dust particles danced in the shafts of sunlight shining through the gaps in the wood. Her palms had dirt melted into both lifelines like the black veins in shrimp that had to be removed before you ate them. Her brother Jimmy said the black stuff was poop, but boys were always saying disgusting things. What did he know, even if he was fifteen?

Hay rustled overhead in the loft, a silky whisper. Mavis climbed the ladder. The temperature changed at each rung. *Hot, hotter, hotter…*

An engine started nearby—the tractor her father had bought when he still could afford to. Or maybe the sound had carried from the Yates's property that buttressed against theirs. They had enough money to buy whatever modern equipment they wanted. Or so her daddy said. He'd been happy with his tractor for a day or two before Willis Yates bought a new one, and then all her daddy noted was the rust on the bolts holding his tractor together.

Mavis stepped off the ladder and listened for the rustling sound. How patient she could be. She listened and followed and moved and waited and eventually discovered a nest of kittens behind a stack of old hay bales. *One, two, three... seven!* Tiny things with a sparse coating of fur and eyes sealed tight. The mama cat hissed, and Mavis slowly backed away. The writhing mass of new life sent a thrill through her. She was the only one who knew they were there. The secret was sugar on her tongue.

Ellie was gone from the porch swing when Mavis ran back. In her excitement, she didn't note the paint peeling in thick strips from the west side of the house that got the most light, or the softness of the wood on the second step up to the back door when her foot landed on it, or the extra heat as she ran through the kitchen past Mamie at the stove and eased her way soundlessly up the stairs to not wake the new baby. But there was no need to be quiet. The baby was crying, and her mama was calling out Ellie's name.

Mavis knew she'd find her sister hiding in her closet, hoping someone else would answer her mama's call. Sure enough, Ellie sat cross-legged on her closet floor, brushing her long dark hair that was so shiny it was almost blue.

"Mama's calling you."

"You go."

"She's not calling me." Mavis folded herself into the closet and left the door open a crack, so they'd have some light. "Guess what? I found a litter of kittens! There's seven of them. Up in the hayloft behind the rotted bales."

"Well, call *The Neelan News*. I'm sure no one's seen anything like it before."

The sweetness on her tongue turned sour. "Must you ruin everything?"

"You know I hate cats and their sandpaper tongues."

Mavis left the closet. "Mama's still calling for you," she said through the closed door. "I'm going to tell her you're hiding on purpose." It was worth sacrificing her own freedom if that meant getting back at Ellie.

That's likely why Ellie told their father about the kittens when he returned to the house before supper.

It was only by luck that Mavis saw him carrying the burlap sack and heading for the creek, the mama cat mewling at his heels. She ran after him, taking two strides for his one. *What was in the bag? What was he going to do?* She begged to keep one. Just one. *Please?*

Finally, he stopped. "One!" His face contorted into an ugly shape because he was doing something he didn't want to do. But if Ellie wanted one, he wouldn't be mad at all. He'd likely let her keep two because he loved her the most.

He opened the sack. "Hurry up. I haven't got all day."

She stretched on tiptoes, reached in, felt for a leg, and pulled. A kitten emerged, its pink flesh stippled with black fur. She recoiled from its newness and dropped it on the ground. The mama cat grabbed it by the scruff and ran back to the loft. Mavis followed her, in case she changed her nest, and her daddy disappeared with the remaining kittens.

Mavis named her kitten Lucky, because he was lucky she saved him. When she could get him from his mama, she carried him around in a homemade sling, just like the darkies carried their babies.

"*Lucky this and Lucky that,*" Ellie mocked a few days later at breakfast. "If you love that cat so much, you should go to the creek and rescue the other ones. Clem Fitzhenry said they can breathe underwater when they're young, but they lose that ability over time. He once saved kittens that had been submerged for almost a week."

Clem was smart in school. Could it be true? Hope bloomed behind her ribcage, but Mavis hesitated. Ellie enjoyed making her look foolish.

"It might already be too late," Ellie said.

"Why didn't you tell me sooner? Will you come?"

"No. You know I hate cats."

"But won't Daddy be mad if I save them? He says there's already too many."

"Not if he doesn't know. When's the last time he was up in the hayloft?"

When he took the kittens.

Now that she knew the kittens might still be alive, Mavis had to go see. She took Lucky back to his mama. Behind the barn, four ne-groes were digging in the dirt. She didn't recognize two of them, but there were always some just passing through, trying to make money to get somewhere else. She took the shortcut past the twelve shacks that housed half-a-dozen families, a few couples, and some migrant pickers that rotated through. She passed the worn path that led to the giant shade tree that cast long shadows in every direction. She arrived at Sugar Creek short of breath and saw the sack partially submerged mid-stream and held down by a large rock in the current that lacked urgency. Mavis took her shoes and socks off and waded in. Right away, her feet went partially numb, which was good because she couldn't feel the sharp edges of the rocks. It took a few pushes to move the big rock, but she was determined. She freed the waterlogged sack and carried it to shore. "It's okay," she said. "We're almost there." Lucky's brothers and sisters would be so happy to see her! She readied her apology for making them wait. She'd only just learned that kittens could breathe underwater. There was so much to learn in life.

Her hands shook as she untied the cord and tipped the contents onto the grass.

The first kitten gulched onto the bank with a soggy *thud.* The rest followed in a gush of muck and gore and stench. Mavis's breakfast rose from her stomach and filled her mouth. In her haste not to vomit on herself, she planted her foot in the pile of decomposing bodies that were cold and slippery, and they burst beneath her weight like overripe melons.

She fell onto one knee and vomited until only dry heaves shook her body.

Then she started home, sobbing and furious.

She imagined Ellie putting one hand to her heart and laughing. *You didn't actually* believe *the kittens would be alive, did you?*

She hated Ellie.

Hated. Hated. Hated her.

CHAPTER 2

Mavis returned to the house and pretended not to see Ellie on the porch, fanning herself and acting like she didn't know she looked pretty.

Bits of vomit clung to the hem of Mavis's dress; rage and self-pity boiled inside her and made a foul stew. She wanted to hurt something or someone.

The kitchen screen door banged shut behind her. She'd forgotten her shoes and socks at the creek. She'd send someone for them.

Mamie turned from the sink and tried to hide her shock. She wiped her hands on her apron and opened her arms. Normally, Mavis would have thrown herself into that embrace, but she pretended the cook wasn't there. She wanted to keep her rage sharp both to use against her sister and against herself for being so stupid. She ran upstairs to her room. She didn't need Mamie. She didn't need anyone.

Mavis's resolve to never speak to her sister again for as long as she lived wavered in the days ahead.

She had nothing to do and no one to do it with.

She visited Mama and her new baby sister Gertie and asked if she might play with Samuel again. Her mama got mad when Mavis tried to reason with her. And she got madder still when Mavis asked if Samuel's skin was getting lighter like that boy Whitey in Slew Town. Did Samuel work with turpentine? Was that why his skin wasn't as dark as Mamie's? Her mama turned red in the face and said Mavis shouldn't listen to Ellie's nonsense.

Bored still, Mavis went out the back door and visited the four little white crosses not far from the vegetable garden that marked where her siblings' remains had been buried. Ellie said they were remains because the babies hadn't fully formed. She said they'd been planted near the garden like seeds, to see if they'd grow more. She said that any time, one of them could ripen and become a sister or brother. She said if Mavis heard any crying in the night, it was likely one of the babies come to life and Mavis should run out with a blanket.

A bead of sweat rolled down the middle of her back like a teardrop. Why was it always so hot? She sat beside the crosses in the grass and told her dead siblings she was sorry they didn't get a chance to live, especially since they'd have been better siblings than Ellie who thought telling stories was different from lying. Jimmy didn't have time for Mavis, and his friends were all boys. Gertie was too little. In truth, life was often dull and uneventful, she told them, so maybe they weren't missing out on much.

A ladybug landed on her arm. She put it on one of the white crosses and enjoyed the colours. Ladybugs were helpers; they could clear a grove of aphids and mealybugs in no time.

Gradually, Mavis's circles around Ellie become smaller and smaller until one day she came close enough that Ellie called out: "You can braid my hair with yours if you want."

"Really?" Ellie had always said no.

"Really."

"I'll get my brush!"

In the high humidity and heat, the sisters sat side by side on the porch swing, tucked tight with their thighs touching. Mavis pulled all their hair together between them with her left hand and used her right hand to brush it, joining her mousy brown strands with Ellie's shiny black ones to form a single, thick mass.

The front courtyard was busy with workers moving from the barn to the groves and back. "Samuel looks different lately, don't you think?" Ellie asked.

"How do you mean?" Mavis smoothed the hair and divided it into three sections.

"I don't know. Like less of a boy, I guess, and more like a man."

She and Ellie had spent hours in the kitchen playing with Samuel when they were young. He had been so painfully shy. Ellie had made it her mission to make him laugh. *Look at me,* she'd say, her voice playful at first and then exasperated when he didn't do what she wanted. Finally, he'd turn, and she'd have her fingers up her nose, or her eyes crossed, and he'd laugh and laugh. Then the laughing got easier until every time he looked at Ellie he laughed, which she didn't find funny, so the game stopped.

"Well, he's older than you," Mavis said.

"Why is he going into the barn again? He was in their yesterday, too."

Mavis braided the pieces over and under and over and under. "Why wouldn't he? Stop moving."

"Because he doesn't have anything to do in there."

"How do you know? Maybe Mamie sent him on an errand. Sit still. I'm almost done." Mavis tied the elastic to the bottom and smoothed the weave with her hands. The thick plait hung over their shoulders between them.

"Look! It's so beautiful."

Ellie turned her head to appraise it and Mavis's head turned too. Then Mavis turned her head and Ellie's followed.

"Ouch!"

Mavis laughed.

A young, light-skinned negro came out of the grove and joined Samuel by the barn.

"Look," Ellie said, laughing, "it's our half-brother!"

"What are you talking about?"

"The mulatto. He's even lighter than Samuel. He looks like Daddy, only dipped in pitch."

Just then, their mama called out. Ellie jumped up to hide and Mavis jumped to keep her scalp from ripping off. "Ow! Sit down!"

The pain subsided as soon as they sat.

"Undo it," Ellie hissed. "Hurry!"

Mavis's fingers were slow because of Ellie's impatience.

Their mama came out onto the porch. "There you are, Ellie. Where have you been all morning? I need your help."

"I can't help. Mavis has me tied up."

"Well, Mavis can untie you. I don't know where you find time for games."

Mavis unbraided as fast as her fingers allowed while their mama issued a list of instructions and then went back inside.

"You'd think I was one of the darkies, having to do chores. It's not my fault Daddy keeps selling off land. Where does the money go? Everything here is an eyesore and falling down around us. I was the only girl in school this year who didn't have a new dress."

"I didn't have one either."

"Does everything have to be about you?"

Mavis finished unbraiding and Ellie stalked off towards the barn.

"Mama wants us in the parlour."

"She wouldn't have found me if it hadn't been for you. Tell her I'll be there soon."

Mavis knew that meant not at all. Which meant Mavis would have to work twice as hard to make it up to their mama.

Sure enough, Ellie didn't show up again until supper time.

Daddy asked God to bless them for what they were about to receive and then grabbed his fork. The fried catfish snapped in his mouth when he bit down. He chewed for a moment and then stopped to drain his glass. He asked Jimmy if he'd heard about the negro going around asking neighbours for charity. "It's not right."

Mavis knew the speech almost by heart.

"Folks in Neelan Junction take care of their own. Not like the damned government, profiting off the hard work of people in the South. All those men sitting in Washington, wearing cotton clothes and smoking tobacco and thinking those things materialized out of thin air."

Mamie came in with a decanter of whiskey and set it on the table as the speech continued.

"Times are hard. There isn't enough for my own family let alone anything left over to share, and even if there was, it wouldn't go to some darky passing through. Shake him upside down and let's see what falls from his pockets."

"Do you think he'll come here?" Ellie asked, beaming. "I hope so."

"And what have I always told you?" He smiled at his eldest daughter.

"That I can have whatever I want!"

"That's right. Because why?"

"Because I'm your best girl."

"Because why?" He cupped his hand to his ear.

"Because I'm your best girl," Ellie said louder, laughing.

"That's right, and my prettiest girl, too. No one holds a candle to you, so if you want him to come knocking, then I hope he does."

Mavis pushed her food around her plate, using the grits as a wall to keep the fish juice from finding its way into the collard greens. She didn't care she wasn't her daddy's prettiest girl if being prettier meant thinking more about being pretty. But because Ellie wanted the negro to come knocking, Mavis decided that she didn't. Ellie too often got her way. Plus, her daddy killing the kittens still felt close. He hadn't noticed that she'd been ignoring him since then, which only served to confirm that she didn't much matter to him. He had Jimmy, his first-born, and then Ellie, his first daughter. When Mavis came along, she was just another girl, and a less pretty one at that. And then there were a lot of dead babies until Gertie.

Thinking of the dead babies reminded her of the baby remains planted next to the garden. Suddenly her collard greens turned her stomach, but then she wondered if the white crosses were only symbols. Maybe her daddy had carried her siblings' remains to Sugar Creek in burlap sacks and walked away before the cold water had time to close over their unfinished forms.

CHAPTER 3

The negro came knocking on a Sunday when the sisters were having breakfast.

Ellie got to the kitchen door two steps ahead of Mavis and flung it open.

He was thin as a blade of grass, and his eyes held more moisture than a storm cloud. He was barefoot and unwashed. Mavis could see his darkness through his threadbare clothes. His name, if anyone had asked, might have been Desperate. But she didn't ask. The Turners weren't in the habit of asking darkies questions; they were in the habit of telling them what to do.

A look of surprise crossed the negro's face, as if asking why a white girl, dressed in her church finery, was answering the kitchen door. He didn't have time to catch himself before he looked Ellie full in the eyes. "Excuse me Miss, can you spare some food for a starvin' man?"

Ellie clutched at her face as if he'd thrown turpentine. Jimmy always said if a darky looked you right in the eye that you'd drown before your next birthday. But Jimmy said all kinds of stupid things. Was Ellie going to drown? She was too good a swimmer for that to happen, wasn't she?

"Daddy!"

Mamie put a hand on Ellie's shoulder. "Quiet, now. You leave your daddy be."

But Ellie wriggled free and ran, blinking as if to extinguish the fire. "Daddy, Daddy!"

"Wait for me!" Mavis raced after her, down the porch steps and across the yard to the path that led to the gate by the west grove where their daddy was working.

"He's here, Daddy," Ellie cried, and when she got close she fell into his arms. "He knocked and then reached through the door and tried to grab me!"

Daddy held Ellie close for a moment.

"I was so scared!" she panted. "I'm sure I'll have a bruise."

His jaw tightened. He took out his handkerchief and wiped his brow. "He touched you?"

"Yes."

His face got all mottled and twisted, and he headed to the house.

"He never touched you!" Mavis said. "Why did you say that?"

Ellie adjusted her hair and looked at Mavis as if she had a lot to learn. "Because I felt like it."

Mavis trailed behind and heard her daddy invite Desperate to sit on the back porch. He told Mamie to get their visitor a piece of bread and a glass of milk if he wanted it. She spread butter thick on both sides and sprinkled sugar on top even though she wasn't supposed to use sugar on bread.

Desperate thanked them for their kindness. He closed his eyes as the goodness melted in his mouth. He might as well have still been chewing when Sheriff Thorpe showed up in his big hat, a swollen cigar clamped in the left side of his mouth, and arrested Desperate for stealing bread. Then Desperate's eyes started to leak, and Mavis wondered if Mamie had added spice to the butter. She was always adding extra spice to things.

Things happened fast after that as word spread.

By midday, the whole town had arrived. Sandra Strome wore the ribbon in her hair that Ellie coveted. Dorrie Brantford, the banker's daughter, stood beside Sandra. Strolling to join the two was Betsy Hargraves. She was twelve and still waiting for her two front teeth to grow in. She could poke the tip of her tongue out of her mouth with her jaw clamped tight. Then Ellie's best friend Jessica Calder joined the group. Also swelling the crowd were Susan King, Leona Smith, Posey Jones, and Pearl Wilson. Town girls, happy for an outing. Anybody who was missing wasn't worth mentioning.

The larger the crowd became, the worse Mavis felt. They had come because of Ellie's lie.

Mavis went to find Mamie. The cook's face was set hard.

"Go on back outside. I got no time for you."

Why was Mamie mad at her? Standing at the kitchen door, Mavis saw Ellie surrounded by her friends. She had changed from her nice church dress into her nicer church dress. She pantomimed her near-death experience at Desperate's hands, tilting her head back and rolling her eyes, *No, no!* Then she clutched at her face and pretended she was blind, flailing her arms about in the air. The girls laughed and looked around to see if any boys were watching.

A wagon arrived and Mrs. Dumfrey, whose husband owned and ran *The Neelan News*, climbed down carrying her famous lemon cheesecake on a platter. Then Mayor Humphreys arrived with his wife and daughter, Claire, who waved and smiled and clapped her hands.

Ellie stood beside their daddy now, holding his hand and smiling. A new and unwanted thought popped into Mavis's head: Ellie wasn't the only liar; her daddy was a liar too.

⌐ Down by the pond by the mill, Mavis's Great Grandfather Turner had planted an oak tree when his first child was born.

Five decades later, the tree threw shade eight fathoms deep. Everyone called it the shade tree. One branch had been stripped of its foliage. It stuck out naked and strong over a patch of well-trampled grass. Sometimes the children hung a rope swing there. Sometimes the Turner men hung game. And sometimes they hung negroes.

By the time the sun was at its midpoint in the sky, when a body can turn in any direction and not cast a shadow, the men led Desperate to the tree. His wrists were tied behind his back. Sheriff Thorpe lowered a noose, snugged it around Desperate's neck, and threw the excess rope over the naked branch.

Ellie stood next to their daddy, her lie locked safe in her chest.

Why hadn't Mamie come out to say Desperate hadn't stolen any food?

Mavis walked over to her daddy and pulled on his sleeve. He didn't respond. She pulled again.

"What?"

She was scared but pushed through. "He never touched Ellie, Daddy. She lied. And he didn't steal any bread either. You told Mamie to give him some."

"I can't hear you. Go find your mama."

The sheriff pulled out the slack. "Are you ready, boy?"

Desperate kept his eyes low and didn't say a word.

A fish hawk flew overhead, towards the swimming hole — it would be quiet there now. All the children were here. Mavis wished she could join the bird.

"I said, *are you ready, boy?*"

Desperate's lips moved but no sound came out.

The crowd had grown. Mr. Irwin had arrived, from the blacksmith shop, with his wife and daughter. Mr. Worthington, who owned the construction company, arrived with his wife and son, John. Mr. Hughes stood nearby, his tailor tape still looped around his neck. Leon Mays, the teacher, was standing beside the banker's wife. Mr. Jones stood with his children, Ledger and Posey. Postmaster Skinner was in conversation with Mrs. Irwin, who laughed and put her hand over her mouth to hide her buck teeth. Old Mrs. Stykley pushed her way to the front of the crowd. She had recently finished a quilt for Mavis's newborn sister, Gertie.

"Is the preacher here?" Mavis's daddy called out.

"Not yet," someone yelled. "He's coming."

"Well, maybe if he's here in time, he can preach about how stealing is a sin."

A chorus of approval rang from the crowd. The circle narrowed as people pushed in for a closer view.

"Come on, Turner," a man yelled. "We haven't got all day!"

"Sure we do. It's the Sabbath!" He leaned on the rope until

Desperate's feet came off the ground; then he secured it. The crowd cheered.

Posey came and stood beside Mavis. She peeled an orange fresh from the tree. In the sun's rays the juices spurted like mini fireworks.

"Watch your eyes," Posey said. "Did you ever get orange juice in your eyes?"

Mavis nodded. "It hurts, doesn't it?"

Jimmy grabbed a stick, walked towards Desperate, poked him a few times as if testing the doneness of meat, gripped it like a baseball bat, and swung with all his might.

Desperate let out a muffled cry, and Jimmy wound up again. Then he passed the stick to his best friend John. Ledger was next. Soon, a line of boys stretched long, with Danny Thorpe, the sheriff's boy, cutting repeatedly into the front of the line and the other boys letting him.

Off to the side, the women had laid out a large blanket for the food. There was fried chicken and watermelon and biscuits and homemade pie and salads and lemonade. Preacher Heath arrived and said grace. By then, Desperate was past the point of hearing, so he didn't get the sermon on stealing that Mavis's daddy thought he deserved. The women called everyone to eat before the ants and wasps spirited the food away.

Afterwards, the beating continued. Every now and then someone came up with some new way to hurt Desperate, and the crowd's approval was unanimous.

"Have a turn, Mavis," Ellie said, holding out a stick.

She shook her head. What if it was Samuel who'd wandered into a group of strangers and was hung from the branch? Did Desperate have family somewhere? People who loved him? Maybe he had a younger sister who'd wonder what happened to him when he never came home.

"Suit yourself. And you'd better hurry if you want a piece of Mrs. Dumfrey's lemon cheesecake."

"I already had one."

Her daddy looked around. "Has anyone seen Clyde McCall?"

"Over here!" Clyde raised his arm. He was setting up his tripod and camera. "Who wants a picture?"

Shouts filled the air and a dozen hands shot up.

The photographer arranged the children next to Desperate's body and told them to keep still. The lemon cheesecake curdled in the back of Mavis's throat. She swallowed hard.

"Smile!" Clive prompted.

They turned their best selves to the camera and froze. Afterwards, if they had a coin in their palm, they lined up individually for a souvenir photo with the body.

Ellie took the coin she'd been given and went to the front of the line. She swatted at flies and stood beside the battered corpse. Emboldened, she reached out a hand and touched Desperate's pant leg.

"Ellie Louise, don't you dare get blood on your dress!" her mama called out.

Ellie pulled her hand back. "Mavis, come get a picture with me."

Mavis shook her head.

"I'm not asking. Come on!"

Mavis heard the command in Ellie's voice and thought she had no choice but to obey.

Desperate's feet had toes missing. Only one arm remained attached to his body. The other was nowhere in sight. Maybe a dog had carried it into the woods. Or maybe one of the boys had claimed it. In the dirt below, blood-crusted fingers were scattered like dug-up roots.

"Smile!" Mr. McCall said.

Ellie elbowed her and Mavis smiled, holding it for as long as she could. The smell of blood and dirt mixed together for an awful mud pie. Could the sun get any hotter? The curdling in the back of her throat escalated. Any second now, she was going to be sick.

Desperate. She played with the name to distract herself. *Don't be Desperate. I'm not Desperate.*

She gazed around at her friends and neighbours and felt squeezed to death by loneliness.

And then the dishes were scraped and packed, the crowd dispersed, and it was an ordinary Sunday again.

The sisters watched the last of the wagons roll away.

"Do you still think I'm going to drown?" Ellie asked.

"I doubt it."

"Well, I'll stay away from the swimming hole for a while, just in case."

The sun was a ball of flames.

After a while, Ellie sighed and broke the silence: "What are we going to do now?"

CHAPTER 4

For most of her life, Sliver Lanier had been called the midwife, as in, "get the midwife," or, "we need the midwife," or, "thank God, here's the midwife."

She'd arrived in Neelan Junction in 1900, thirty years earlier, when her daddy, blinded by grief and shock, had packed his three children into the wagon and crossed the state line from Georgia into Florida. He left God behind when he crossed that line too. All that singing and praying and believing in church hadn't done a damn thing for him or for his people. It just made them accept their lot. He was done with the lie. His sister Harriet had told him to come. She worked for the Yates's, who owned one of the largest orange groves in Florida. It was a big harvest that year. Harriet said they always hired extra pickers during the peak season. If he got there soon, maybe they would take him on. They'd rather hire kin than use the convicts and drifters from Slew Town.

Sliver was fifteen years old. When the wagon finally pulled into the Yates's front yard, all she saw was ladders perched against the trees. Was that to be her job? She was afraid of heights; there was no way she was climbing up a ladder to pick oranges. She'd do better by using all her might to shake the trunk and make the fruit fall. Luckily, her Aunt Harriet needed an extra pair of hands to help out wherever she was needed—in the kitchen, in the garden, in the laundry, in the here and now. There was no shortage of things to do. And when Aunt Harriet bragged to the others working there and on neighbouring land that

Sliver used to help her mama deliver babies, people came knocking sometimes and asked for help.

It was mostly black babies Sliver helped bring into the world, the newborn flesh an extension of her own dark hands, but sometimes she birthed white babies if their parents had no money or were too cheap to pay a regular doctor. That's how she'd ended up birthing Mrs. Yates's son Willis, because Old Man Yates was too cheap to pay for the town doctor to make the house call. Mrs. Yates never did forgive her husband for that, but he didn't care. He never gave any thought to pleasing his wife. He just wanted her to go from being a heifer to a cow, and it didn't matter who was on hand for that transition. Sliver's mama said childbirth was God's cruel joke on white women. They were used to being high and mighty and delegating unwanted jobs, but no amount of privilege could spare them from going through that labour themselves. Despite the primping and bossing they did in the rest of their lives, they bore babies just the same way as black women did: They opened their legs.

Sliver walked along the hard dirt path that connected the Yates's property to the Turner's and enjoyed the sun's heat on her skin. She could tell when she'd crossed into the Turner grove because the trees weren't pruned as nicely as those in the Yates's. The damage from the Okeechobee Hurricane two years earlier was still plain as day on the Turner land. Broken tree branches were piled willy-nilly. Some branches hung from the trees, partially ripped like hangnails. Every trip she made to the Turners, she stepped over debris, and each time she scolded herself for not clearing a path. But why make more work for herself? It wasn't as if Mrs. Turner was ever happy to see her. After losing four babies, she might show some appreciation for Sliver's skills, but the woman couldn't see past her own prejudice. Sliver said her *yes Ma'am* and *no Ma'am* and kept her opinions to herself. White folks was bad enough, but poor white folks was worse. They hated negroes even more, if that was possible, so they were more dangerous. Once she knew the baby was gaining weight, Sliver would stop coming. It was no business of hers that the Turners couldn't afford a doctor, and she didn't give a hoot that they didn't have a wet nurse either. Nursing a child wasn't a punishment.

Sliver well remembered the tingling sensation when her milk let down and the sweet milky scent that came with a sweaty newborn at the breast resting peacefully flesh on flesh, and watching that baby fall asleep and slowly, slowly, losing suction until *pop*, her nipple suddenly appeared. She missed those days. This was Mrs. Turner's fourth baby that had lived, but she was only now learning how to nurse one. The wonder of it. Mrs. Turner said she'd figure it out on her own. She had nothing to learn from a negro. Except she didn't say negro.

Sliver walked by the shacks and nodded at the children playing nearby. She knew each and every one of them; nobody loved a midwife more than a woman who'd had a midwife's tending. That was a life-long love affair.

A black man left one of the shacks at the end of the row, slamming the door twice to see if it would stick before giving up. She didn't recognize him but nodded as he passed. Staying here was a step up from Slew Town, except Master Turner changed the rent all the time, sometimes mid-month, depending on his own needs. When people couldn't pay the extra sum, they were turned out. Nobody ever got a refund, and sometimes a new tenant was in place by the following day.

She passed Mamie's small shack. It had flowers in front and curtains in the window. When she was home, good cooking smells wafted out, but not today. Jimmy Turner exited a shack two doors down. Sliver pretended not to see him and kept her eyes down as if looking for snakes.

The big house was up ahead. The older Turner girls were on the porch swing doing what looked to be nothing. Sliver didn't envy free time. Having nothing to do would just set her mind to dwelling on the past, and that was like sticking her finger into a wound and encouraging infection. Once something was done, there wasn't much she could do about changing it. She'd learned that lesson in Georgia when she was ten years old and those white boys had knocked her down with their wagon. Her left foot had got twisted up under a wheel when she jumped out of the way, and she'd fallen into the ditch with her mouth wide open and screaming.

The boys didn't care about her pain. One of them leaned over her and put the toe of his shoe into her ribs to make sure she was listening. *This ain't the North. Tell your daddy it's time to pack up.*

Then they drove off laughing.

Sliver had stayed in the ditch with her leg twisted at an unnatural angle and had ridden out the pain while waiting for someone to find her. She'd counted to one hundred and then backwards to zero over and over again, until one of the field hands found her and took her home. Her eyes stayed dry until she saw her mama, and then the tears flowed. People did that—held on to their pain until they were in the presence of love. She'd seen it countless times in her life—a person's stubborn refusal to cry until a loved one arrived. Until it was safe.

Sliver asked what those boys meant about the North, and her mama said it was a place where negroes could own their own business and not be bossed about or have their belongings taken or destroyed.

"Then why don't we go there?"

"Because not every plant can successfully be transplanted. Our roots run deep here. This is our home."

And it remained their home for another four years until her mama was killed. Then it was a place they needed to get away from.

Sliver's leg had never healed properly. When she was tired, she had a noticeable limp. She was the kind of child her son Charlie would have brought home for healing.

She was at the Turner's back door before she acknowledged the real reason for her visit: She wasn't here for Mrs. Turner's baby; she was here for Mamie. The news of that poor man's lynching hadn't taken long to travel.

Mamie stood at the counter, cutting up vegetables. Her eyes were swollen. The two women put their foreheads together, and Mamie cried some more telling the story. Nobody knew who he was or where his people were. There was no body to claim.

Sliver waited until Mamie had dried her tears before asking who lived two doors down from Mamie.

"I don't know. They're new. They showed up with the rest of the pickers and stayed when Beulah and her family moved on."

Sliver's two brothers had also moved on as soon as they were old enough, joining the great migration to the shipyards, planning to one day go north. They'd left together, but she hadn't heard from them again.

"Do they have a daughter?"

"Yes. Cadence. Why?"

"Jimmy came out of there just now."

Mamie pursed her lips and nodded. She'd let Cadence's mother know to watch out.

"Let me help with the cooking," Sliver said. "What do you need?"

They worked side by side, talking and comforting one another. They shared notes on the negro's death, then they moved on to discuss the ones they loved and the ones they worried about. In that manner, the afternoon hours passed quickly, and it was soon time for Sliver to leave.

She didn't like it here. The Turners had airs without the means. Their fortunes had fallen, yet they acted as if nobody knew. If the girls on the porch swing weren't already rolling up their sleeves to help with the work, then they would be soon. She wouldn't put it past Mr. Turner to have lynched that man as a means to maintain his status. From what she'd heard, everybody in town had showed up, even the mayor, and the Turners were the ones to provide the entertainment. It broke her to know that was likely the truth, but she'd gotten used to putting herself back together again.

She said her goodbyes to Mamie and told her to stop by any time. Everybody knew where to find the midwife.

Sliver was a light sleeper.

She was always on guard.

CHAPTER 5

Outside her bedroom window, Ellie watched Jimmy saunter across the yard, drawing deeply on a cigarette. He'd been spending time with one of the new negroes. Ellie had seen him with her before. Or maybe he was coming from town. He was free to come and go on his own, whereas Ellie required permission or a specific reason to go to town. She felt like a prisoner, but she hadn't committed any crime.

It also wasn't fair that Jimmy could smoke openly. She'd been dying to try it herself and hoped her brother hadn't noticed the missing cigarette she'd taken while he slept. If she *did* enjoy it, she'd make sure to marry a man one day who could buy her a gold cigarette case, one like the banker had. She'd seen the sun glint off Mr. Brantford's as he casually slid it into his suit pocket.

She slipped quietly past her mama's bedroom, down the stairs, and out the front door. Her feet noiselessly took her to the barn. The door still hung crookedly on its hinge. Before the hurricane that wiped out most of the orange grove, things had been repaired quickly. How long ago that seemed. It took some effort for her to wrench the door open. Wasn't anyone going to fix it? Ellie couldn't recall the last time anyone had put fresh flowers in her bedroom, and she wasn't about to do so herself. The point was to have someone do it *for* her. She didn't want to become like her friend's mama who cut flowers in her own garden and then pretended someone had delivered them.

Ellie turned to be sure Mavis hadn't followed, wedged the door closed behind her, climbed the ladder to the loft, and sat on a hay bale.

The steady hum of insects was amplified in the dull heat. She fanned the air in front of her face, hoping to dry the slight sheen of sweat on her forehead. She lifted her hair off her neck and chastised herself for not putting it up before coming out. She closed her eyes. *Once upon a time there was a beautiful young woman who didn't know that good fortune was right around the corner.*

When she opened them, she was still in a hayloft.

Jimmy's cigarette was slightly crushed from being stuffed in her bodice. She re-worked its shape with her fingers, struck a match, put a flame to the end, inhaled, and coughed until her eyes watered. Oh, but it tasted awful! A spark dropped onto her dress and burned a tiny hole in the material. Ellie beat at her chest to put it out. Where had the match gone? Had she blown it out? It wouldn't do to start a fire. She looked around her but didn't see any smoke.

When she finally stopped coughing, she inhaled a shallower breath. That was better. Determined, she kept at it. By the time the cigarette burned down, her eyes had stopped watering and she imagined she looked casual, like a lady should. *The way she exhaled indicated she had something far more interesting to do in another room. How generous she was to give her time.*

Ellie lifted her chin to portray the image she imagined and stubbed out the cigarette. She needed more practice.

The barn door squealed open and someone came in whistling. Ellie stood up soundlessly and held her breath. Mavis didn't know how to whistle. Was Jimmy coming to get his cigarette back? She tiptoed to the ladder and peered down. Samuel stood below with a shovel in each hand. The crown of his head had a little naked white spot from which his hair whorled. From here, she couldn't tell if it whorled in a clockwise or counterclockwise direction, nor could she remember what either one meant. She'd known that once, something about a person being more likely to be right-handed if his hair whorled in a clockwise direction. Or was it highly sexual? It was one of those useless bits of information she'd found interesting at one point and thought she'd never forget. She didn't until this moment know if negroes had that spot on their heads. Their hair was nappy and not silken, so maybe it wouldn't fall. And even now, she couldn't be sure if she'd seen it or wished it from the distance.

Samuel was alone.

That meant she was alone with a black man. Or boy. That was forbidden.

Ellie didn't want him to do something embarrassing, believing no one was around to see him, so she cleared her throat.

His head jerked up like he'd been shot. She saw his face, upside down, lips where his forehead should be. His eyes two white mouths gaping.

"It's just me," Ellie said. "Don't be scared."

"I'm not scared."

"Liar." She'd seen the fear in his eyes before he knew it was her. She turned around and began her descent, holding her skirt to her legs so she wouldn't expose herself when he tried to look up it. By the time she reached the ground, he was gone. Was he afraid of her? The idea sent a thrill through her body. Should he be? Oh to have that kind of power.

Had her mama forbidden her daughters from spending time with Samuel because she knew of the stirrings that would start in their bodies? Ellie felt it already. Mavis would soon too, a desire that started like a spark in the midsection and spread. A desire that good girls were supposed to ignore and deny, even if smoke was coming out of their ears.

Her mama never should have let them play together in the first place if she didn't want them developing *familiarity*. Sometimes Ellie wondered if Samuel ever missed them. He probably missed Mavis because she was nicer to him, but it wasn't Ellie's fault. She'd been given beauty. Mavis had gotten kindness. Ellie wouldn't trade one for the other.

Samuel's quick disappearance suggested there was a reason for him to flee, which was tinder to her imagination. If she placed the tip of her tongue on his skin, would it be sweet like chocolate? And if he placed his on hers, would it be rich like cream? If she applied herself, could she lick his colour right off like the turpentine had pulled the colour from Whitey's skin? Of course not. Now she was being ridiculous. *The salt from her tongue dissolved the pigment ...* She smiled at her wild imaginings.

It was cooler on the ground than in the loft but not by much. She lifted her arms and hoped the round sweat marks beneath her armpits would dry. Her mama said you could tell the difference between a lady and a peasant by the amount of salt dried into their dress fabric. Ellie kept her arms up to get some air into her armpits. Her mama would smack her if she ever said that word out loud. *Armpit.*

Avocadoes had pits. Stone pits. Like peaches. Pits that would break molars. Lots of fruit had pits. That's how you knew a fruit from a vegetable. Or was it seeds? Mamie would know.

Ellie was tired of the heat and the dust. She hauled the barn door closed behind her, flinching as it squealed like an animal in pain. Samuel had fled before she could tell him not to. Next time, she would be ready. She would tell him to stay and wait for her, and he would have to listen. He would have to do what he was told.

CHAPTER 6

A year passed. Mavis grew three inches.

Another year passed, and Mavis grew two more. How did a body know when it didn't need to grow anymore? She wasn't like a tree, that kept reaching or blossoming. She had an end point when her bones would simply stop pushing outwards. She hoped it would be soon because she didn't like being clumsy. She wanted her body to do what she told it to do, not trip over feet that had changed size.

It was 1932. She was twelve years old. Childhood was receding. She went to bed, and she woke up. The moon rose and the sun set. The tides rose and the tides fell. That's why Mavis believed in God, not because the preacher said she should but because of the changing seasons and the trees bearing fruit after they'd flowered and perfumed the air. It couldn't all just happen by itself, could it? *Something* had to be in charge, and she was glad it wasn't her daddy given how poorly he managed things. Running the seasons was too big a job for humans to manage. There was too much scheduling to keep track of. Plus, who would ever agree on what kind of weather was needed when?

We want it to be sunny for the picnic on the weekend.

No, we need rain for the crops.

The annual harvest dance was just two weeks away. Mavis looked forward to its arrival simply so it could pass and be in the future again. Ellie said Mavis needed to be more interested in dresses and hairstyles and boys and dances, but for Mavis a good night at the harvest dance would be standing against the back wall and being invisible.

Her mama had just birthed another baby that she named George.

The midwife had showed up for that birth, too. Ellie said it was awful to think of her own parents doing what needed to be done to make babies. Disgusting even. Mavis had said *la la la la la* and plugged her ears not to listen. Now baby Gertie couldn't be called baby Gertie anymore because there was a baby George.

Mavis lay on her stomach on Ellie's bed, her chin resting in her hands, her knees bent and feet in the air.

"Tell me which dress looks better, okay?" Ellie wriggled out of her everyday dress and threw it over a chair. "Did I tell you what Mr. Jones did last week when I was in town?"

"No. What?"

"I went into his store to look at some cloth because Claire was bragging about her new dress."

"The mayor's daughter has to look nice."

"And I don't?" Ellie pulled a dress over her head. "I knew I couldn't buy anything, but I asked Mr. Jones to show me something nice, and he flushed red as a rooster's comb. He disappeared in the back and came out carrying a bolt of cloth. He spent the next five minutes stuttering about how nice I would look in it. I believe he is blinded by my beauty."

"Sounds like he's just tongue-tied." Mavis felt it her duty to keep her sister right-sized. "Was Posey there?"

"No, but Ledger came out to make sure I'd be at the dance."

Mavis snorted. Ellie miss a dance? "He doesn't know you, does he?"

Ellie finished doing up the buttons and twirled in front of the mirror. "How does this look?"

Lucky purred in Mavis's lap. His black fur was silky beneath her palm as he kneaded his claws into her thighs. Pain. No pain. Pain. No pain. Sometimes he dug his claws in deep, and just when she was about to cry out, he'd pull them in again, as if he knew exactly the threshold of her pain, or as if he was trying to expand it.

"It's nice."

"*It's nice,*" Ellie mocked. "If I'm the only one there without a new dress, I'll kill myself."

"I won't have a new dress."

"You don't count." Ellie flopped onto her back beside Mavis. "One day I'm going to move to a big city and be a clerk at a fancy department store. I'll get a big discount on purchases, so I'll dress up every day and wear silk stockings and makeup and have someone do my hair nice and fancy. And a rich man will come in one afternoon to buy something for his mother, or his wife, I don't care, and I will flirt with him!"

"Ellie!"

She laughed. "And he'll fall head over heels in love with me."

"He'll fall alright. I thought you wanted to be a nurse and travel overseas to help wounded soldiers."

"I'm over that now. Plus, I don't think I'm the nurturing type. I almost threw up changing George's diaper!"

They laughed and held hands.

"I never thought I'd see the day when I'd have to do something like that," Ellie said. "And if you tell anyone, I'll never forgive you. I washed my hands for ten straight minutes after, thinking of the embarrassment of finding dried poop under my nails."

"Once upon a time there was a girl named Ellie, whose hands were awfully smelly ..."

"Stop!"

The bed shook as they laughed.

The heavy curtains were drawn to keep the heat out. Dust danced in the shafts of light where the curtain gaped from the wall. When they finally stopped laughing, Mavis's eyes felt heavy. If she closed them, she'd be asleep in no time.

"I just want something *interesting* to happen," Ellie said. "I'm tired of the same boys and always going to the same dances. There's almost never anyone new!"

"New isn't always better."

"No, but it's at least *different*." Ellie grabbed Lucky by the scruff, plopped him down on the bed, and put her palm on Mavis's belly. "One day, a fire is going to start inside your body, right here." She pressed down and rubbed hard as if the friction could create a flame. "And it'll get so hot you'll think you're going to die. And there's only one thing that will put it out."

"Water?"

Ellie ignored her. "You're going to need a man to put out that fire."

Well, *that* wasn't news. If the barn caught fire, Mavis would want the men to put it out.

"A naked man."

Mavis burst out laughing.

"You laugh now," Ellie said, standing and returning to the mirror. "But you'll understand one day. When you're older."

"I hate when you do that. So, in three years I'll understand?"

"For you, maybe it will take longer."

"Ellie!"

"Well, if you're so smart, have you figured out yet why Samuel's skin isn't as dark as Mamie's?"

Mavis had given it some thought. Ellie's hair was darker than hers. People weren't all the same. Animals, too. Dogs from the same litter had different markings. Some had thicker coats, and some birds had longer tails.

"You asked me, remember?" Ellie said. "Do you have any idea what I'm talking about? Well, I'll tell you. Are you ready?" She paused for dramatic effect. "The light-skinned ones come from a white person doing the deed with a coloured person." Ellie grabbed Mavis's wrist to get her attention and leaned close. "Imagine skin so salty you could roll a cob of corn on it and never have to reach for the shaker."

Mavis jerked her arm free and rolled off the bed. "You're crazy." She ran out of the room, down the stairs, and onto the porch where the air, while still hot, felt more fresh.

Ellie followed on her heels. "You know what Mama says about men." She did a good impersonation: *"Men are animals. That's all you need to know."*

Her daddy said *negroes* were animals, but her mama said *men* were animals. So who was the animal? Black men? White men? Men in general?

"And Mama ought to know," Ellie added, "because she said she was done having babies after Gertie, but now she has George."

"You're too hard on people, Ellie."

"Says who?"

"Says me."

"Well then it must be true."

A breeze rustled the leaves on the trees, and the girls instinctively turned their faces towards it. The big harvest was almost over. Most of the oranges had been picked and shipped. Already, the number of workers in the grove had begun to diminish.

"It would be easier if we were self-pollinating," Ellie said, "like the orange trees."

"What are you talking about?"

"They don't need bees to move the pollen. Jimmy told me. They fertilize themselves. They don't have to *copulate* at all."

"Of course, they don't!"

"Isn't that a funny word? *Copulate.* Say it."

"No."

"Come on. *Copulate.*"

Mavis did just to make her sister stop. "There. Are you happy?"

"No. If Mama doesn't want babies, she should just drink some of Mamie's mixture. Then that midwife wouldn't have to be lurking about all the time."

"I told you her name is Sliver, and she's not lurking."

"Well *she* probably told Mamie how to make it, seeing how she knows all about babies. I've seen what Mamie boils up on the stove sometimes. Once, I saw her grinding up ants. Ants! Can you imagine ants crawling around your insides? Mixed with lilac and mustard and roots and whatever else Mamie has on hand?" Ellie shivered.

"How would ants get into your insides?"

"Oh Mavis. You're lucky you have me to explain things to you."

The sisters dropped into the swing and Mavis pushed off: *Lots of trees; not so many. Lots of trees; not so many.*

"I wish I was a boy," Ellie said.

Mavis snorted. Jimmy and his friends hung over the bridge railing to see whose spit could string out the longest. "Boys do dumb things and think their smallest efforts are cause for celebration. What about that woman we read about in the paper? The one who flies airplanes?"

"Amelia Earhart?"

"Yes. What did she do again?"

Ellie rolled her eyes. "She flew non-stop across the Atlantic."

"Well, I should *hope* it was non-stop, unless she wanted to land in the sea. She must be famous if they wrote about her in Neelan Junction. Imagine being the first woman to do something."

"She's an exception," Ellie said. "Most women don't do anything out of the ordinary."

"What about Annie Oakley?" Mavis pretended she had a gun in each hand and was shooting things out of the sky. "She got to perform for the Queen."

"Again, an exception, and I'm not going to run off and join some travelling show. Jimmy can go into town on his own whenever he wants. And he could get on the train and travel, and Daddy would let him as long as he promised to come back. But I'll never go anywhere but to school and to church and to town."

"If you were a boy, you wouldn't be beautiful."

"What does being beautiful get me now? Daddy's just going to use it to marry me off to someone with money. There aren't a lot of options. I'm afraid it might be Willis Yates. He's not at all handsome, and he's seven years older than me. If I was a boy, I'd have more say in who I married." She ran her hands through her hair and fluffed it up. "I'd want my name to be Randall. Doesn't that sound nice?" She stared across the yard as if something regal was in sight. "Or Randy for short." She smiled and raised her eyebrows up and down to indicate arousal.

Mavis was trying to reconcile her mama's belief that men were animals with Ellie's and her friends' desire to attract them. "If men are animals, what are women?"

"Women are birds because they often have to take flight."

"But couldn't they be some other kind of animal and just run? Like a deer? Deer are fast."

Ellie shook her head. "Men hunt deer. Birds get to go into the sky. Women have to be able to go where men can't go."

"But men hunt ducks and geese ..."

"Yes but travelling by air makes it harder for men to track you. Even an experienced hunter couldn't follow that trail."

"Maybe Hunter could be your last name: Randall Hunter."

Ellie considered it. "I like it. But I'll never be free and neither will you. Women are owned first by their fathers and then by husbands. It's the law."

"Oh, you're a lawyer now?"

"When you marry a man, you become your husband's property, and you have to do what he says. Ask Mama if you don't believe me. That's why women are birds, because it helps them to believe in their own freedom. Do you know what kind of bird you are?"

Mavis shook her head.

"You're a gull."

Gulls got to stay close to water. They kept themselves clean.

"Do you know *why* you're a gull?"

"Why?"

"Because you're gull-ible." Ellie folded at the waist and laughed.

There were worse things to be than a gull. Like a vulture. Or a turkey with its wattled neck.

"If you spent less time following me around and more time watching what goes on around here," Ellie said, "then maybe you wouldn't have to ask so many questions. Come on." She jumped up so the swing went in a jerky sideways motion. "Let's go see if Mamie has anything to drink."

Mavis's stomach dipped and rolled as she adjusted herself to the sudden change in motion. She waited until the swing straightened then followed her sister inside.

CHAPTER 7

All eyes turned towards Ellie when she walked into the dance hall. Her peripheral vision was exceptional. She straightened her back and adjusted her posture so that her bosom was more pronounced.

Mr. Wynn, the barber, nodded as she passed. He opened and closed his mouth, but no words came out. Then he turned away to hide the colour rising in his cheeks. Ellie knew she had caused his tongue to tie, and the image of his thick muscular organ trying to knot itself behind his closed teeth made the corners of her mouth curl. She put the tip of her tongue against the ribbed ceiling of her mouth and rubbed it lightly back and forth and felt the tickle rise in her nose like she might have to sneeze.

Mr. Everett, the undertaker, had one leg bent behind him, the sole of his boot on the wall. She walked a wide circle around him. His hands touched dead bodies. She didn't like to think of them on her body even as his gaze showed him busy with imagining it.

John Worthington filled her dance card more than any other young man. His father owned the construction company in town, which had expanded in the years since the hurricane's destruction because everybody had something to rebuild. His cuffs weren't frayed. He smelled of store-bought soap, and his blue eyes and dimpled cheeks weakened her knees. *Ellie Worthington.* She had written the name out when she was bored in school, using small hearts to dot the i's. As the eldest son, John would inherit the construction company one day. He'd have ample sums to buy her a gold cigarette case and take her on trips, something her mother had wanted to do but her father had never got around to and now couldn't afford.

The music switched to a slower tune and John reduced the space between them. His hand felt hot in the small of her back. Was her dress soaking up his sweat? She only had one good dress. She couldn't afford to have the fabric ruined. And what was he saying, anyway, as he guided her around the dance floor? Did he think her so dull that he could only discuss the weather? In between his bursts of conversation, he breathed through his mouth. Ellie only did that when she didn't like the smell of something. Was her breath bad? Were her underarms not fresh?

The song ended and John took her back to her table. He looked over towards his friends, and Ellie felt the irritation of knowing he wasn't as smitten as he should be. But never mind. Ledger Jones was walking her way. Ellie greeted him effusively to let John know she wasn't beholden. Ledger's teeth were straight and unstained. Such a contrast to so many of the men whose teeth protruded, overlapped, were discoloured, or were missing entirely. If only he was taller. A short man didn't make her feel petite. But Ledger made up for his diminutive stature by having a large wit. When they danced, he commented on all the dancers individually and made up nicknames for them: Club foot. Pin head. Noser.

"Well, I wonder what you'd call me?" Ellie said, as she laughed and enjoyed his banter.

He leaned close. His breath smelled of whiskey. "Luscious," he whispered slowly, drawing out the *sssss* like a snake. Then he pulled back and smiled his perfect smile. "Or flawless. Which would you prefer?"

She raised her chin ever so slightly. "Either one will do." He put extra pressure on her lower back, and she stepped into his body a fraction more.

They slowed down as the song came to an end. Another one was about to begin when someone interrupted.

"May I have this dance?"

The voice came from behind her. Ellie's curls swung as she turned to see who had spoken.

Willis Yates.

His ears stuck out from his head. His nose was hawked. His lips were meaty and full, and his hair was blonde and almost invisible on his pale scalp.

Ledger bowed, kissed her hand, and then made a show of transferring it to Willis.

A real man would never let a woman go so easily, Ellie thought, but Ledger had already put her hand in Willis's. Her mama had told her it was just as easy to marry a rich man as it was to marry a poor one. The choice was a sign of intelligence. But was it too much to hope for a man who was rich *and* handsome?

Dancing with Willis after Ledger was like moving from silk to wool. He was heavy on his feet; his hands were damp, and there was a sheen on his forehead that made Ellie wonder if he only ate fried food. But he had money, and the way he fawned over her suggested new dresses and a gold cigarette case could be in her near future if she wanted.

"Are you enjoying yourself?" he asked.

"Yes." At the back of the room, John was talking to Betsy Hargraves, who was wearing the same dress she'd worn to last year's dance. Ellie wasn't fooled by the new sash. Then Posey Jones, Ledger's younger sister, took John's hand and led him to the dance floor. How brazen! Mavis waved from where she was standing camouflaged against the back wall and feigned as if she was yawning. No one had asked her to dance and likely no one would she was that invisible.

"My orange grove had the best yield ever this year," Willis said.

"Yes?" Ellie tried to look interested. Had Posey made her own dress?

"And I expect better for next year."

Ledger was talking to Jimmy now. Sandra Strome joined them and said something that made them both laugh; then they all looked at Ellie and smiled. She felt her face flush.

"... and buy the next grove."

"I beg your pardon?"

"I said next year I'm expanding the grove again. I'm in charge, you know." He grew an inch or two, and Ellie recalled his daddy had died when he was just a baby. Before that, Willis's grandfather had bought up a number of groves after the great freeze of 1894. *Robbed people blind,* according to her daddy. *Took advantage of their misfortune.* Ellie remembered wishing her daddy had been smart enough to do the same thing, even if it was before his time.

Willis talked about new methods that would one day let orange growers freeze the juice they produced so it could be shipped anywhere. "That'll put an end to wastage from oranges rotting when the crop is larger than the demand." With careful planning, Willis said, he could have the biggest citrus grove in the entire state of Florida, maybe even in the country.

A white ball of saliva had gathered at the middle of his lips and stretched as he talked. And talked. Would he never stop? Surely there was a girl at the dance who would find him interesting. Ellie kept her face neutral and thought if he was an animal he'd be a big hairy dog, latched onto one of her legs. She couldn't help but smile at the image, and Willis took that for a sign of encouragement.

"As my mama always says ..."

"Excuse me, Willis, but I'm feeling a bit tired. Do you mind if I sit down?"

"Yes. Forgive me. I should have asked if you needed a rest. You've been on the dance floor all night." He led her to a chair.

"Thank you. I'll be fine now." She willed him to go away.

He sat down. A burst of noise drew her attention to the door: the sheriff's son and a group of his friends had just arrived. Danny Thorpe scanned the room. His eyes passed over her without stopping. He needed glasses.

Willis started in again about his future plans for his grove and the sweetness of his oranges.

"I'm ever so thirsty," she interrupted.

"I'm sorry. I should have asked." His face flushed and he hurried off to get her something to drink.

Ellie smoothed her dress and counted slowly to five. Nobody needed to see that she was making an escape. It had to look entirely planned. Three ... Four ... Five.

She stood up and sauntered slowly across the room.

All eyes turned towards her, and she pretended not to notice.

⌐ Her feet were still sore from dancing two days later when her daddy called her into the study and gestured for her to sit in the chair opposite his desk.

"Hear me out fully before you speak." He folded his hands on his desk and cleared his throat. "Willis has made his intentions known." He held up his hand to stop her from interrupting. "You know that I've always been proud of you, and today I'm even more proud for what you can do for this family. I agreed to the union because he'll be able to give you a better life and help us too. We still have some things to work out, but ..."

"Daddy, I'm too young to be married!"

"I know. The wedding won't happen right away. I just promised your hand."

She saw Willis's moist face and his eager eyes. She recalled the irritation she'd felt when he'd kept apologizing. "No. Tell him no."

"I'm not asking what I should do, Ellie. I'm stating a fact. You will marry Willis."

She shook her head. "All my life you told me I didn't have to settle for things. You said I could have whatever I wanted. Well I don't *want* Willis."

"He has money, Ellie. Lots of it."

"What about John Worthington? He has money."

"Not like Willis he doesn't. Come on, Ellie. Be practical. Willis is building you a new house to set you up nicely in. You should have seen how happy he was!"

Her daddy wanted her to think he'd done her a favour. That he was watching out for her when, in truth, he was only helping himself. He'd run out of parcels of land to sell. Now he was turning to his daughters. "How much money? Did you decide on a sum for what I'm worth?"

He turned red in the face and leaned across the desk towards her. "How dare you talk to me like that? You will marry who I say, when I say. And you will marry Willis Yates. Do you understand me?"

She stormed from the study with the proof that her daddy had never loved her. If he'd worked harder, none of this would have happened. She wasn't going to bail him out. It wasn't fair that she be sacrificed. Why couldn't he sell Mavis instead? It wasn't Ellie's fault that she was more beautiful and could collect a larger sum.

She left the house and started walking. *How dare her daddy promise her hand? Was she to have no say in her future?* She passed the shacks and took the worn path past the shade tree. Before long, she was sitting on the bank of Sugar Creek, listening to the water trickling over rocks, and experiencing the full weight of her predicament. Such build up she'd had, imagining a life of freedom and fun, such a monumental let down to have it determined for her.

What had her father bartered for? How much would he gain? How easily she'd be transferred from her father's inventory to Willis's. And what would Willis's be? Four hundred acres, sixteen horses, thirty chickens, fifty negroes, and one wife. Soon enough he'd want to add children to that list.

She took her shoes off and submerged her feet in the water. For a brief moment, the coolness of liquid between her toes calmed her, but just as quickly her anger returned. She didn't want the house Willis was building for her. She'd never be happy in it. She'd pray for lightning to strike and burn it down, but she couldn't leave her fate up to the weather. If she had to, she'd wait for a storm, slip through the darkness, soak a rag in turpentine, stuff it into a bottle, light it, and throw it into the house.

Couldn't Willis tell she didn't want him? That she would always be unwilling?

If she were an animal, she'd be a badger, backed into a corner and fighting tooth and nail for her life.

She wouldn't marry Willis Yates, no matter what her daddy said. She wouldn't.

The conviction grew.

And she wasn't a badger, she was a bird. And she'd spread her wings and take to the skies. Hadn't she told Mavis women were birds? All she had to do was plan her flight.

CHAPTER 8

Sliver opened her eyes and stared up at the ceiling, listening. A pink glow from the window indicated dawn, as did the bird song. God's choir. Oh to wake up as cheerful as the birds! Their joy likely came from being exactly where they were, in the present, not foraging in memories or thinking about what might come, just singing for the right-this-minute. She was jealous because her mind didn't work that way. If it was split into sections, a large portion was devoted to the past. Mornings were often when she did her visiting there. And this morning, she was swamped by memory.

She remembered plain as day seeing the Yates's house for the very first time. It was two storeys high with a wrap-around porch freshly painted and blindingly white. In fact, Sliver would always remember the colours of that moment: the white, white house, and the oranges brilliant in the sun's yellow rays and clustered against the green leaves with pockets of blue sky peeking through where the branches were particularly heavy and weighed down. She hadn't known as many colours in Georgia.

A dark-skinned boy standing at the top of a silver ladder leaned against a tree at the far edge of the yard, a boy not much older than she was, his shirt damp against his back, his skin shimmering with a light sweat in the heat. He pulled oranges from branches like he was plucking stars from the sky. He was not yet a man but soon. He must have felt her eyes on him, or he had heard the wagon arrive and was curious to see who was in it, because he turned towards her and their eyes met and stalled. The great metronome of life missed a beat. And in that stalled yet heightened moment, the grief and injustice she'd packed tight and stored for safe keeping shifted just enough that a thin ray of light pierced through to suggest the storm she had been weathering would soon come to an end. What had been heavy and hard to carry became suddenly easier to bear.

The boy dropped to the ground, picked up some oranges that had fallen, and threw them in the air—one, two, three, four, five. They arced in a perfect circle above him, arriving and leaving his hands only to arrive and leave again like magic. Sliver heard laughter and turned to see her two younger brothers smiling. A pocket of joy opened around them. He was performing for her, and her heart that had only beat grief in the past few months altered its rhythm. And just like she knew the sun would set that evening and rise the following morning, so too did she know she would marry the boy who made oranges dance in the sky.

She learned his name was Gideon, and in the days following, she whispered it to herself. *Gideon. Gideon.* She could even say it without moving her lips, so no one knew of her obsession. *Gideon. Gideon.* If he was the good thing to come out of all the grief that had brought Sliver here, then so be it. Her mama loved her. Her mama had brought Gideon to her. That's what she told herself when she closed her eyes and saw oranges circling in the air. That helped to erase the image of her mama dead and suspended.

Gideon helped to ease her pain, and Sliver, in turn, was able to ease her daddy's and her brothers' grief too. Somehow, they had all survived the tragedy they had known was coming but hoped would never arrive. Yes, their family had done well for themselves, but it hadn't come to them without hard work. *Who did they think they were?* Human beings wanting to live a decent life, that's who. How was that more of a crime than the killing?

She and Gideon circled each other for a year, drawing closer and closer in their slow mating dance until one day Gideon's mouth finally found hers. He tasted like citrus; he smelled like it too. He had a bright, tangy scent like he rubbed oranges all over his flesh and even into his armpits. She buried her nose there and breathed deep.

They married when she was seventeen and moved into a small shack at the very edge of the south grove. Housing for the negroes at the Yates's was divided into four clusters determined by what grove they worked in: north, south, east, or west. Each cluster had roughly ten shacks, and each had its own garden to feed the families. Given the size of the grove, the numerous work areas and jobs needing to be done, and the distance between the clusters, sometimes weeks would go by without any visiting going on. But everybody knew everybody else; there were rarely any vacancies for the migrant pickers to fill. They had to find their own housing in whatever makeshift place they found—in a tent in a field, at the Turner's, or in Slew Town paying high rates to Reggie Richardson for a cot.

Sliver and Gideon's was the last shack in the south quadrant when taking the path from the main house, but the first shack for those coming from Slew Town, which was a blessing because, if they were coming for the midwife, it was usually an emergency.

It wasn't long after marrying that Gideon put his ear to her swell to listen to his own baby ripening.

⚬ Sliver slept like the dead in early pregnancy. One night, someone's hands shook her awake and she bolted upright in fear, surfacing as if she'd been underwater too long and desperately needed oxygen. Gideon's face was right there. *I'm sorry, baby, but you're needed in Slew Town.*

Word had spread about her midwifery skills. Too many women died in childbirth there. Sliver was a hope some were afraid to reach for because sometimes it was better to wish someone could help than to have someone show up and fail.

Gideon lit a lamp. She dressed quickly.

Outside, a young man named Callum bounced from one foot to another, panic and dread evident in his eyes and the set of his mouth. He motioned for her to follow and set a quick pace. Sliver shouldered the supply bag that had once been her mama's and walked quickly but carefully because of the extra cargo she carried in her belly. She had been hired to help her Aunt Harriet with chores; delivering babies wasn't part of her work, and she began to prepare herself for the exhaustion of the morning's early start.

Darkness pressed in from both sides of the road, humidity a heavy pelt. There were ditches beside the road here, too, which reminded her of Georgia and trouble that could always be present. When it rained really hard here, the ditches filled with water deep enough for drowning. Turtles barely needed their legs for walking, and more than once she'd mistaken a turtle's shell for a skull and felt afraid.

Callum stayed ahead, always ahead. Sliver's dress stuck to the small of her back. Her limp arrived too soon.

As she walked, she remembered Gideon's history lesson. In the late 1800s, someone had taken a knife to a longleaf pine and dug in deep—maybe carving initials of love—and from that trunk a golden sap had flowed like syrup. And that sap, when collected and boiled and handled this way and that became tar, pitch, and turpentine. And all those wooden boats with hulls big as cliffs could be patched and sealed with the product of that great tree. The only thing required was human labour. Convicts. Black hands to toil in Florida's twin industries, orange trees and pine trees, citrus and turpentine, living side by side.

Slew Town.

The sap ran from early spring through to October. Wooden barrels were lined in rows as neat as the orange trees at the Yates's but less beautiful and certainly not as fragrant. Sliver didn't know on that first visit that Reggie Richardson, who owned the turpentine still, also ran Slew Town. She didn't know that Sheriff Thorpe supplied the still with labour by arresting black men and forcing them to work for the freedom they never could afford. She'd heard stories about the place and now was finally going to see it firsthand.

Sliver's eyes began to water as they got close. Breathing burned her nostrils. She wiped at her nose to stop it from running, but it kept on.

"You get used to it," Callum said. "It just takes time."

He led her to a shack that looked exactly like the one not more than an arm's length away. It sloped dramatically to the east where the sky in a few hours would begin to brighten. Sliver imagined the furniture all slid up against the east wall, but she quickly adjusted that belief when she went inside. There was hardly any furniture to speak of. Life at the Yates's certainly had its challenges, she reminded herself, like worrying about her brothers climbing ladders and reaching for the sky, but she'd take citrus over turpentine any day.

A girl lay on her back on a thin mat on the floor. Even with burning nostrils, Sliver smelled the signs of a long internment: sweat, blood, and other bodily fluids. She felt for a pulse at the girl's wrist. She was barely alive.

A voice spoke behind her and Sliver jumped. The woman introduced herself as Callum's mother, Hany, and explained the details: Bess was Callum's wife. She was sixteen; this was her first child. Labour had started two days earlier. Things progressed normally at first, slowly, but normally. But then things just stopped. "It's likely too late," Hany said.

"We got to at least try," Callum said.

"I need some water," Sliver told Hany. "Now."

The woman left. Silver knelt down and put her hands on Bess's globe, feeling all around.

A well must have been close by because Hany was back fast with a bucket. "There ain't no hope," she muttered again, looking at her son with sad eyes.

Sliver needed them gone. She didn't need anyone's opinion and what she had to do didn't require witnesses. "Go ask someone for some clean rags."

"We ain't got none," Hany said.

"Then go get some fresh air." She gestured toward the door. "And don't come back inside until I call you."

She had turned many a baby in her day. Her mama had been a good teacher. When Sliver was a child, her small hands could sometimes reach places her mama's couldn't. *Listen to me, Sliver. Listen good. My voice are your fingers. Understand?* And Sliver would close her eyes and pretend her hand belonged to her mama who just needed to talk out loud to tell it where to go.

Now her hands were bigger, and her mama hadn't been beside her for some time, but Sliver still carried her teachings.

Bess lay mostly senseless. Her light had gone dim. Sliver rolled up her sleeves, washed her hands, and said a silent prayer.

She entered Bess's body, and pretended her fingertips were eyes. The baby's head had lodged sideways in the pelvis, its ear at the cervix as if wanting to hear the outside world before seeing it, but the extended contractions had almost fused the skull into place. She felt around the edges. Where was it stuck? Sliver used her hands, one on the inside and one on the outside, and slowly, slowly managed to reverse the baby's forward motion, taking time to ensure its neck didn't snap until finally she had adjusted the baby enough to re-start its journey. Bess moaned but didn't regain consciousness. Thirty minutes later, Sliver's arms were so weak she could barely hold the child that slipped into them. When she called Callum and Hany back inside, Bess was awake, and her son was at her breast.

Sliver crawled to the opposite corner of the shack, where a weak light peeked in through the warped wood, and put her head down on the floor. Mosquitos hummed all around her, but she was too tired to swat them away. She didn't ask for a thing because there was nothing to ask for, and she fell headlong into sleep before waking in time to return home to work.

Five months later, she and Gideon welcomed their son Seth. Even though Sliver had attended many, many births, he was a miracle to her, right away making the world a better place.

Thankfully, her daddy got to hold his grandson before his own heart gave out having been too busted up to mend. He died a week later, knowing Seth's life would replace his own life on a planet both filling with and emptying of people. Aunt Harriet helped put him to rest as Sliver cared for her son.

Her belly swelled again and again in the years ahead. Gideon talked to the babies inside, sang to them too in his deep voice, and asked them to send messages. *Tap once if you're a girl.* Then he'd watch her belly for a foot or a fist. And even though she told him he was crazy, he guessed right every time. Except for the last time.

⤳ Sliver made regular visits to Slew Town in the days and months and years that followed her arrival and tried to alleviate the hardships she found there. She learned that half the 'convicts' had been picked up for walking on the wrong side of the road, for vagrancy, for asking questions, for showing up. The other half were there because the still gave them a place to live and food to eat. That their wages would never cover their debts was a given. They looked to the roof over their heads, even if it sagged and leaked, and were grateful for a door to close on a house they felt was their own, even if it wasn't. Sliver learned a black man getting arrested for nothing at all could happen in Florida, too. If a negro rebelled in any way against custom, he was subjected to cruel punishment and often death, and sometimes the rules changed as quickly as the weather. She wondered if maybe her daddy's wagon should have pointed north instead of going deeper into the south. Except she'd found Gideon. That's why she'd come, but that didn't mean they needed to stay.

"Where's your man?" Sliver asked whenever she delivered a baby in Slew Town.

The answer was often the same: "I ain't got no man."

That was like a watermelon saying it didn't have any seeds. Sliver finally stopped asking. By then, she knew that Reggie Richardson made money off more than just turpentine. He took bets on fights between black men, he rented black women out by the hour or by the night. Everything had a price tag on it. Everything was for sale.

The more she learned about the place, the more she wanted her brothers to move away. The distance between the Yates's and Slew Town wasn't far enough to give her comfort. There was work in the shipyards in Fort Lauderdale. Aunt Harriet's own son had gone. They should go too. Maybe things would be better for them in a city.

Sliver was a frequent visitor to Slew Town because the babies kept coming. And she got used to finding small offerings outside her home — a head of cabbage, a freshly caught fish, bone buttons, colourful bits of yarn or cloth — gratitude for her care.

And when she showed up at work without having had any sleep, she learned to hide her fatigue so Mrs. Yates wouldn't berate her by saying, *I don't pay you to deliver babies, do I?*

Sliver stretched in bed and stared up at the ceiling. The birds were particularly loud this morning and her memory was a fast tide. Was a change in the weather coming? She sighed long and deep and exhaled slowly. What she would give to go back to those early days with Gideon stretched out long beside her, babies curled all around them in bed, and the sweet scent of breast milk in the air. How long ago that seemed.

She swung her legs over the side of the bed and sat for a moment to let any dizziness pass. Then she thought about her day and knew she would start at the garden. When Gideon had disappeared, the garden had saved her. Hands in the dirt. The seed gently placed, covered, and nurtured.

All the care that went into the tending of children and men and gardens.

All her babies: boy, girl, girl, boy.

And then, Charlie.

She had never expected Gideon to leave her first. That pain felt fresh again this morning. She would put some dirt on that memory and try once again to bury it.

CHAPTER 9

Mavis pierced her breakfast egg with a fork and the yolk bled onto her toast. She sprinkled salt on top and watched it melt into the yellow. Mamie cooked eggs to perfection, even on laundry day when she complained she had enough to do without spoiling Mavis by catering to her needs.

Ellie came in and asked for toast. It was her last breakfast as a sixteen-year-old because the following day was her birthday.

"Are you going to be any different tomorrow?" Mavis asked. Ellie normally loved her birthday, but since being promised to Willis, the excitement had disappeared. Getting older just brought her closer to a future she didn't desire.

Ellie shrugged. "I don't know. Am I?"

"Maybe you'll be nicer to your sister."

"I'm nice enough to Gertie." Their younger sister was almost four. And baby George was already two.

"I meant to me!"

"I'll be nicer if you're less irritating. Can you do me a favour? It can be my early birthday present."

"What?"

"I lost my purple hair ribbon. The one you love so much."

Mavis knew the one.

"I last had it out by the barn. Or maybe by the watering hole. I can't remember. Can you look for it?"

"Why would I?"

"If you find it, I'll let you keep it if I can borrow it from time to time."

"Really?" The generous side of Ellie didn't come out often. Mavis knew the ribbon would be pretty in her hair.

"Really."

"Okay." She pushed her toast crust over the plate to soak up the remaining yolk and then ran outside. The sheets on the line were wedding dresses at a dance.

At the barn she lifted buckets and tools and even went into the pen where the new piglets rooted, looking for a flash of purple. Then she went inside the barn and even climbed into the loft. Then she couldn't remember if Ellie had told her to look at the watering *hole* or at the watering *pump*. The pump was closer than the hole, but the hole made more sense than the pump. She wanted that ribbon, but she didn't want to spend all day hunting for it, so she went back to the house to ask her sister for more details.

Ellie wasn't on the porch swing.

She wasn't in the kitchen.

She wasn't in her bedroom or in her closet or standing in front of their mama's mirror admiring herself.

Mavis descended the stairs soundlessly and felt the air stir as if a body had just passed through. She followed the air current, turned the corner, and saw a flash of white down the hallway. Ellie. She opened her mouth to call out, but her sister disappeared into the parlour and closed the door so carefully that Mavis thought she must be playing a game. Mavis crept down the hall on the balls of her feet, turned the doorknob as quietly as possible, and pushed.

It was locked.

She put her ear to the door and heard a rustling on the other side and a murmur of voices. She grinned and almost laughed out loud. A secret rendezvous. Now she understood why Ellie had sent her off. She retreated to the staircase and sat down to wait. Who would come out? Ledger? John? Not Willis Yates, she was sure about that.

Mavis imagined all kinds of scenarios with glee as Lucky wound his way around her ankles and purred. She scratched a mosquito bite on her leg until it bled. Then she licked her finger and pressed it against the bleeding to make it stop. Then another bite on her other leg began to itch, and she switched her attention. Suddenly her entire body itched, and she gave herself a quick scratching all over with both hands.

Her excitement to discover who was with Ellie turned to irritation as the minutes passed. What was going on in there? And why was it taking so long? She thought about leaving, but her time would be wasted if she gave up now.

The house was quiet. Her mama had taken Gertie and George to tea at the neighbours. Lucky was an engine purring in her lap. Mavis thought about her breakfast egg, perfectly salted, and wished she could have another. She was about to give up her post when she heard the doorknob rattle and the key in the lock. She backed into the stairway before the parlour door opened. If Ellie walked towards the stairs, Mavis would be discovered. She held her breath and waited. Then she peeked around the corner to see Ellie smoothing her hair and skirt and walking in the opposite direction, towards the kitchen. The parlour door remained open.

Mavis counted to ten and walked down the hall. She put her hand on the doorjamb and looked inside the room. Samuel was arranging wood into neat stacks beside the fireplace. Mamie's boy wasn't a boy anymore. His shoulders had broadened as if they knew he'd have a heavy burden to carry. She wanted to say 'hi,' but something told her not to. Was he okay?

She retraced her steps and went upstairs. The game wasn't fun anymore. Ellie hadn't lost her hair ribbon at all. And now Mavis had a secret she didn't like and didn't want.

Why did you lie, Ellie?
Because I felt like it.

She lay on her bed and heard Mamie outside, calling on someone to help her get the sheets down so she could hang more laundry. They might not have new dresses anymore, but they still had clothes that needed washing.

After the parlour incident, Mavis kept her secret about Ellie close, waiting for the perfect time to reveal it. But the days came and went and the opportunity to lord something over her sister never presented itself.

They attended school and church.

The trees blossomed and bore fruit as the seasons changed.

Before Mavis knew it, a calendar year had passed since Lucky had warmed her lap on the stairs. She watched enough to know Ellie still met with Samuel. In fact, her sister had changed. When Jimmy's friends visited, Ellie no longer tried to catch their eyes, and because she no longer flirted, there was no game to play, and the young men eventually quit trying to play it with her.

Sandra Strome set her eyes on Jimmy, and the sisters endured her increased presence at the house.

One by one, the young men of Neelan Junction quit paying attention to Ellie Turner, except, that is, for Willis Yates. His house was almost finished.

One afternoon in the heat of the harvest, Ellie gestured from the porch towards one of the workers. "Who's that?"

"Who's who?" Mavis asked. The yard was busy. Every tree had a ladder propped against it and a man's weight pushing the pronged feet into the dirt. Branches heavy with fruit soon reached higher as they were relieved of their weight.

"The one with the basket on his head. How on earth can he keep all of those oranges balanced?"

The oranges were stacked in a pyramid that extended above the basket's rim.

"Imagine standing beside him and taking the oranges out, one at a time," Ellie said. "Do you think he'd get taller as his basket got lighter?"

"Maybe he's standing as tall as he can right now, so the oranges won't fall out."

"I think he'd get taller. What's his name? Is he new?"

"I don't know. He might be Jedediah."

"Jed-a-who-a?"

Mavis laughed. "Jedediah. I heard Mamie telling someone there were new workers here." If that was him, she also knew he had a wife and kids.

Jedediah emptied his basket into one of the large wooden boxes beside the barn and went back to fill it again. The shadows on the ground changed as the trees were relieved of their cargo.

Lucky jumped onto the swing and tried to get into Ellie's lap, but she pushed him away, so he settled in Mavis's.

"I'm so bored I could die," Ellie said.

"There are worse things to die from. Like planning your wedding."

"Don't even mention that." Ellie rubbed her scalp furiously with both hands so that her hair fluffed like birds' feathers when they shook themselves after dipping into water.

"Do you want to know a secret?" Ellie asked. "You have to promise not to tell."

"I'm good at keeping secrets. I know something about you that I've kept secret for some time now."

Ellie raised her eyebrows. "You do? What?"

"I know about you and Samuel in the parlour."

Ellie's face froze for a second. Then it changed shape as it twisted. She leaned so close that Mavis felt the heat of Ellie's breath on her cheek. "If you ever, *ever* mention that again, to me or to *anyone,* I will disown you." She stood up and started for the door then turned back. "Better yet, I'll drown your cat." The house door slammed behind her.

Mavis hugged Lucky tight. How stupid to have wasted her secret by giving it up so easily. Was Ellie going to tell her about Samuel? Was that her secret? Mavis should have waited. She would never know now. Ellie was good at nursing grudges. That's the only kind of nursing she excelled at.

It wasn't fair that Ellie had chastised her for not noticing anything, but when Mavis *did* keep her eyes open and noticed things, Ellie told her to mind her own business.

Mavis spent the entire month of July with her eyes open and was amazed by what she saw. What business did her daddy have in Mamie's shack in the middle of the afternoon? He didn't stay in there for long, and when he emerged, Mavis knew she shouldn't mention that she'd seen him there. And was that John Worthington hanging about, mooning after Mamie's daughter Faith? And what on earth was Jimmy doing coming out of Cadence's shack?

Mavis threw all her observations into a big basket and put the lid on it. As the basket filled, she couldn't ignore the contents, and she took them out, one by one, and placed them beside what she'd been told or what she knew to be true and held them up for examination. That white men were superior because they were not ruled by their base instincts. That black men could not control their sexual appetite. That white women's sexual purity needed to be protected. That black women enjoyed their bodies too much. That it was against the law for the two races to mix.

But why, then, were there so many different shades of black?

And Ellie hardly needed protecting! Samuel did.

Mavis had also seen Ellie under the poplar tree near the dirt path that led to the shacks as if she had a reason to be there. Why had she asked after Jedediah? Should Mavis tell her he had a wife and kids?

Mavis sifted through her information alone, looking at it from a variety of angles, depending on the day, and coming up with different interpretations. At church, the preacher talked about charity and forgiveness as if he practised both himself, but Mavis remembered the look of greed on his face as he pushed forward to claim the last piece of Mrs. Dumfrey's lemon cheesecake at the picnic that wasn't a picnic at all, as if nothing out of the ordinary was happening around them.

CHAPTER 10

Ellie left the house by the kitchen door and headed past the garden. Beside it, the late morning sun cast shadows off the four white crosses onto the green grass. If she had her way, she'd pluck and discard them as if they were weeds. It was morbid having to think on death every time she saw them, especially so early in the day.

She crossed the open area and walked up the small rise. From there, she could see the negro quarters and the various sheds that housed tools and equipment: now, it was a hive of activity, but it wasn't always. Extending the hive metaphor, she imagined she was the queen in charge of overseeing her worker bees. And the worker bees were there to care for her, always. That was the law of nature, that the queen be cared for. That the workers do what they were told.

She surveyed the area, judged the distances, and calculated. Ellie's teachers had always said she was clever, but they didn't mean it as a compliment. How did a girl so easily find her way through mathematical formulas? A woman didn't need that skill. But Ellie's mind naturally gravitated to calculating odds. For example, what were the odds she'd get caught with Samuel in the parlour? Or Jedediah in the shed? And what were the odds she could get out of marrying Willis Yates? Or make lightning strike the house he was building?

The first time she'd arranged for Samuel to be in the parlour, her heart had nearly burst from excitement. How could she be so bold? And the look on his face when she'd locked the door! *Undress me*, she'd said. It was supposed to be an invitation, but it had come out as a command, and he'd looked at her with the same fearful eyes she'd seen in the barn that day when he hadn't known she was there. How quickly her excitement had turned to irritation. Did she have to talk him into it? Wasn't he supposed to be crazy for white women? She was Ellie Turner, the most sought-after girl in the county, offering herself to him. Did he not recognize his good fortune? She hadn't planned to say she'd tell her daddy if he didn't do what she wanted, but his reluctance forced the words from her. He had spoiled what might have been an enjoyable moment.

Worse still, Samuel's interest in her hadn't increased. He only did what he was told because he had to, not because he wanted to. And afterwards, he hurried off as if she was a chore he was happy to have completed. That stung. She'd expected him to love her.

Something moved beside the barn and caught her eye. John Worthington came into view with ... with ... who was he with? Mamie's daughter? Was he courting Faith? She snorted. As if he could.

"Hi Faith," she called, waving. Faith looked relieved for the interruption and ran off. Ellie gloated, but then John threw her a look of such loathing that she almost stumbled. Who did he think he was to look at her that way? And on her property! He was no better than she was.

"You come here to visit Jimmy or don't come at all!" She didn't yell very often, and it felt good.

John laughed to let her know he didn't take instructions from women. As he walked off, he called over his shoulder, "Say hi to Willis for me." Then he laughed some more. "I hear he's working on your house right now."

She wouldn't give him the satisfaction of seeing her cry, so she bit her lip and turned away as rage boiled up inside her. To be so excluded from determining her own life! She ached for a way to have some control. It wasn't fair that her daddy got to write her life story just because she was a woman. That he lacked imagination was even worse as it meant her life would be tedious and dull. She hated him for that, and she hated that she couldn't change his mind.

But he couldn't control everything about her.

Ellie could be patient when she needed to be. And in the days and months to come, while the girls from town batted their eyes and flirted with the local boys, Ellie was able to remain aloof because Samuel, timid though he was, eased her desires. His was the hand that took the whistling kettle off the flame. His was the hand that offered a reprieve to her longing, but she knew she guided that hand, and she wanted more.

She imagined the humidity on Jedediah's flesh was like the fancy glaze on a fine bit of baking. She'd always had a sweet tooth. Her hunger grew, and she began to chart his movements.

Ellie noted the distance from the dirt path to the tool shed. She surveyed it from different angles and calculated who could see what from where. Jedediah appeared to be the only one who ever went into the shed. How long did he spend when he was in it? How often did he go there? Where was her father now? Her brother? Mavis? Who else might catch sight of her skirt disappearing? And what excuse might she have if discovered when entering or leaving the shed?

The day arrived when her research required testing.

Mamie raised an eyebrow when Ellie arrived earlier than normal for breakfast.

"I couldn't sleep," Ellie said. "So I thought I'd go for a stroll."

"Mmm hmm," Mamie said, "cause you always get up early and go for a stroll. You want me to let Mavis know where you'll be?"

"No. I see enough of her. And by the way, John Worthington is hanging around your Faith." She enjoyed the look of surprise on Mamie's face. That would teach her for being cheeky.

Ellie finished her food quickly and left. She walked barefoot at a measured pace through the dew-damp grass and enjoyed the moisture between her toes. When she got to the top of the rise, she hiked her skirt and ran for the tool shed. If a black person could move without being seen in the dark, she hoped her white skin afforded her a similar invisibility in the daylight.

The door squeaked when she opened it. She flinched at the noise and quickly stepped into the dim light. She tried to catch her breath. If she crouched down, no one would see her through the dust-streaked window. Her heart hammered for all the world to hear.

She waited.

And waited.

A wasp circled persistently. Her legs began to cramp. Sweat beaded her upper lip. She pulled her heavy hair into a makeshift bun and felt the coolness at the nape of her neck. Mosquitoes whined all around. She smelled rust, dirt, rotting wood. Then she heard someone humming and held her breath. The sound came closer. The shed door opened, and Jedediah's silhouette filled the doorframe. He stepped inside, rooted through some equipment, found what he wanted, and left. How quickly the door swung shut behind him without Ellie working up the courage to speak.

All that build-up wasted. She waited a few minutes for her pulse to slow and then slipped out of the shed hot, stiff, itchy, and irritated. Mosquitoes had feasted on her flesh. For what? Nothing. She had miscalculated, expecting Jedediah to spend more time in the shed.

She waited a few more days, wrote a script, memorized her lines so she'd be ready, arrived early at breakfast again, and made her way back to the shed. Her daddy's words repeated in her head: *you're my best girl. You can have whatever you want.* Once, she had thought that was a good thing; now she knew it was more important to be able to state what she *didn't* want, because she didn't want Willis, but nobody appeared to be listening.

What did she want? Clearly it wasn't just money, because Willis had that. No, if she had to articulate it, she wanted pleasure. She wanted her body to sing. She wanted simultaneously to be in control and to lose control. She wanted to live as she pleased.

The shed door squeaked again when she went inside. The wasp circled again. Was it the same one, endlessly orbiting because it couldn't find its way out?

She didn't have to wait long before the door opened. As soon as it closed behind Jedediah, Ellie stood up immediately from her hiding spot. "Don't leave."

He jumped from the shock.

She took a few steps forward, gripped his arm, and recited her lines. "Don't go. I won't tell anyone you're with me unless you leave. And if you do, I'll tell my daddy."

She wanted him to want her because she was beautiful, not because she could have him killed. She wanted to be the one to say if and when it was over.

"I don't want no trouble, Miss."

"Neither do I."

Flies batted against the windowpane, marking time.

She stepped into his shadow until her own disappeared.

CHAPTER 11

Spring arrived, and the scent of yellow jessamine perfumed the air as tropical rains fell and the mists danced from the moist ground and dissolved into the humid air. In mid-April, white bows blossomed on the grove trees and promised thousands upon thousands of gifts.

Mavis was surprised one Sunday to find Willis Yates seated at their supper table. Ellie's face turned a series of colours during the meal even as she tried to appear unshaken. She only spoke when spoken to, and even then she answered curtly. When the meal was finished and the men went off to the parlour, the two sisters made a quick escape before their mama could scold Ellie for her bad manners.

Ellie took the stairs two at a time and made it to her bedroom first. "I do not *want* to marry Willis!" She paced from the door to the window and back. "Did you *hear* how loudly he chewed? Imagine having that irritation at every meal. And Daddy didn't even tell me he was coming!"

"Would it have made a difference?"

"Yes, I could have feigned illness!"

"That's likely why he didn't tell you. Have you tried talking to Daddy again? You've always been his favourite. Maybe if you keep trying ..."

"He won't listen! He actually put his hands over his ears and sent me away last time I tried. I told you: we are Daddy's *property*. It's like we're his crop to sell. If he wants to make money off of us, he will. If you haven't noticed, this place is falling apart around our ears. It's a simple equation: Willis has money and Daddy needs some. Willis wants a wife and Daddy has a daughter he wants."

"Then why hasn't a wedding date been set?"

"Because Willis is building me some kind of fancy house. So it's taking time, thank goodness. But maybe it's done now and that's why he was here. I've been praying for lightning to burn it to the ground."

"Well, I don't want you to marry and go off. What if we ran away?"

"How? Do you have money hidden somewhere? I know I don't. It must be calming to have so much empty space between your ears."

"Don't take your frustration out on me. It's not fair. I'm only trying to help."

"There's not much fair in life, Mavis. The sooner you get used to it the better."

Clearly something had changed in Willis's timeline, because when Mavis came downstairs for breakfast a few days later, she found Jimmy answering the front door.

"Morning, Willis. What brings you out this time of day?"

"I came to talk to Ellie."

"Showing up unannounced first thing in the morning might not be the best time to visit a woman." Jimmy stepped back and gestured him in.

"Are you short of pickers?" Willis asked.

"Why?"

"I couldn't help but notice how much fruit is rotting on the ground. The wasps are thick as tadpoles in the pond."

"We're not selling any more land right now, if that's what you want to know. What brings you here?"

"The house is finished. I came to tell Ellie the good news. I decided I couldn't wait."

Jimmy turned. "Can you go tell Ellie Willis is here?"

Mavis ran upstairs but found Ellie's room empty. She came back and told them. "Maybe ask Mamie where she is."

They walked into the kitchen.

"Have you seen Ellie?" Jimmy asked.

"She already ate and went out," Mamie said.

"That's a switch. Come on, Willis. I guess we have to go find her."

Mavis stayed behind for breakfast.

"Do you really not know where your sister is?" Mamie asked.

"No. Do you?"

Mamie divided a ball of dough into four sections and began to shape them into loaves. "Miss Ellie ain't got no sense, so you've got to have it for her. I'll poach you an egg as soon as I'm done here. I just need a few minutes."

Mavis went outside and watched Jimmy head towards the barn. Willis appeared to follow a set of footprints visible in the dew that led up the rise. He got to the top and scanned the area. Suddenly he let out a yell and disappeared.

Mavis's insides turned liquidy. Something bad was about to happen. She should have told Willis Ellie was sick in bed.

She heard more yelling. Then Willis appeared at the top of the hill dragging Ellie by the arm. Mamie came out on the porch to see what the commotion was. Then Mama came out too, baby George clinging to her leg.

Jimmy ran back from the barn. "What the hell's going on?"

Willis's face was distorted with rage. He dragged Ellie across the yard and threw her at Jimmy's feet. "Your whore of a sister's been lifting her skirt. I saw her coming out of a shed." He could barely catch his breath.

"Call your father," Mama told Jimmy. She took George's hand and Mamie's arm, to steady herself, and went inside before hearing any more details.

Ellie tried to wrench her arm free, but Willis had a firm grip.

"Leave her alone!" Mavis yelled. "Ellie's allowed to go wherever she wants here."

Jimmy looked from Willis to Ellie and back. Mavis saw family loyalty battle with financial necessity. "Is it true?"

Ellie's head hung down. Her hair curtained her face.

Jimmy shook her by the shoulders. "Answer me. Is it true?"

"He made me," Ellie sobbed.

"She's lying," Willis spat. "You didn't see her leaving the shed!"

Ellie scrambled to her feet and grabbed Jimmy's arm. "Don't tell Daddy. It would kill him!"

"Who was it?" Jimmy's face was as red and distorted as Willis's now. He shook Ellie by the arm. "Who?"

"Jedediah," Ellie whispered.

"Who?" he yelled.

Her voice came out funny from the shaking. "Jedediah."

Jimmy pushed Ellie down in disgust. "Come on, Willis. Let's go get my daddy."

"NO!" Ellie lunged for his arm. "Jimmy. I'm begging you. PLEASE!"

He pushed her away. "It's too late for that." Then, as if realizing she might disappear, he grabbed her arm and told Willis to get the other one. "We'll lock her in her room."

Mavis tried to block their way but was pushed aside. Maybe if Willis hadn't been there, Ellie could have talked her way out of it. But he was the witness that required them to take action. Ellie had been promised to him, so Willis had some right to be here. His visit had set everything in motion. Worst of all, he hadn't even been invited.

Mavis followed them as they dragged a struggling Ellie upstairs, threw her into her room, and locked the door. Jimmy slipped the key into his pocket. Then they thundered down the stairs and out the front door, slamming it behind them.

Mavis was alone in the sudden quiet. Her heart pounded in her ears. She crouched down outside Ellie's door and slid her fingers under it. "Ellie?"

A few seconds passed before Ellie's fingers laced into her own. "Mavis. Listen. You've got to get to Daddy first. Tell him I didn't do it. Okay? Hurry! Willis is lying."

"I'm scared Daddy won't listen to me."

"Where's the key?"

"Jimmy took it with him."

She could hear voices outside growing louder.

"Ellie? What should I do?"

Then footsteps on the porch.

"Ellie?"

Then feet pounding up the stairs.

Mavis stood up and tried to block the door. "Daddy, wait. Willis is lying. Ellie didn't do it."

His teeth were clenched so hard it was a wonder his molars didn't shatter. "Get away!"

And she did, like a dog kicked and beaten. She slunk down the hall and waited until her daddy came out and sent Willis in, saying, "She's yours now. I don't care what you do to her."

Father and son walked away, and Willis went into Ellie's room.

Mavis crept closer to the door. She heard raised voices, scuffling sounds, and Ellie crying. Willis was hurting her. Why didn't her daddy stop it?

She paced the hallway for what seemed like hours. Willis finally came out and knocked into Mavis as he passed. He no longer had to be nice to the Turner girls.

The door was ajar. Inside Ellie's room, a dead animal lay in the middle of the floor. It was shiny and black and curled into itself. Mavis poked at it gingerly with her toes. It was Ellie's hair.

Her sister lay in bed, her back towards the room. Her naked skull looked small without hair to give it extra volume. Patches of scalp showed through here and there unevenly.

"Ellie? Are you okay?" She reached out and touched her shoulder, but Ellie pulled away. "It's me." In spite of her resolve, Mavis began to cry.

"Go away," Ellie said.

Mavis shook her head, even though Ellie couldn't see her. "It will grow back. Don't worry. I'll massage oil into your scalp, and your new hair will be so shiny that people will squint when they look at you."

Ellie didn't respond.

"I hate Willis. Wait until I tell Daddy what he did to you."

"It was Daddy who cut my hair. Willis did this." She rolled over and removed the bedsheet that she'd held firmly against her face.

Jagged cuts crisscrossed her cheeks and seeped blood.

Mavis's hands flew to her mouth.

THE SHADE TREE · 73

"It's bad, isn't it?" Ellie started to cry while trying to keep her face still. She winced. Tears ran into the fresh cuts. "How bad? I'm afraid to look."

Mavis steeled herself and leaned it for a closer look. Bits of pink flesh showed at the edges of the cuts where the skin gaped. And it wasn't just one cheek: both had been cut and were beginning to swell.

"He had a knife, and he pinned my arms down and held it to my face. I didn't think he'd do it." She wiped at her tears. "Oh, it hurts. It really hurts."

"Shhhh. It'll be okay. It looks worse because it's fresh. And it's starting to swell. I'll get a fresh cloth, okay? Don't touch your face. I'll be right back."

She ran to the kitchen and asked Mamie for a cloth and some ointment.

"What for?"

"For Ellie. Willis cut her face. It's horrible. Do you have something that will keep scars from forming? Hurry!"

When Mavis returned, Ellie hadn't moved. Mavis soaked the fresh rag in water and held it firmly to Ellie's cheeks, dabbing gingerly while applying slight pressure to pull the ends of her skin together.

"It feels like my face is on fire."

"Shhh. Try not to talk." Mavis kept the pressure on until she was satisfied the bleeding had stopped. Then she applied some of Mamie's ointment. It smelled like fresh fields or flowers past their prime.

"What's that?"

"Mamie said it was good for cuts."

"It's nice and cool."

"She said it would help with scarring."

From downstairs, her daddy bellowed Mavis's name.

"Don't go!" Ellie gripped her wrist.

He yelled again. It was not a tone to ignore.

"I have to, but I'll be back as soon as I can." She kissed Ellie's hand and ran.

Her parents were in the parlour. "Sit down, Mavis, and listen good," her daddy said. How weary he looked as he rubbed his hand over the bristles on his cheek. "After this morning's events, Ellie's name is never to be spoken in this house again. Do you understand? I have four children now — Jimmy, you, Gertie, and George."

"But she's my sister."

"She *was* your sister."

"And she's your daughter!"

"Not anymore."

Her mama sat white-lipped in a straight-backed chair. The slight upward tilt of her chin indicated she agreed with her husband's decision.

"God knows why, but Willis still plans to marry her," her daddy said. "Ellie's to be moved to the Yates's as soon as possible."

"You haven't seen what he did to her. You can't make her go now!"

His hand slammed down on the table. "Whatever happened to her is her own fault! She brought it on herself."

Mavis saw Ellie's bald head, her cut cheeks, and the swelling that threatened to swallow her blue eyes. They had done that to her — her daddy, Jimmy, and Willis. They had done that. "But …"

His hand slammed down again, and Mavis cowered. Just because her parents were unified in their decision didn't make it right.

"You are in charge of Gertie and George until Ellie's departure," her mama said. "Go to them now. They are waiting with Mamie in the kitchen."

She stared at her parents. How defeated they looked. How exhausted. Ellie had worn them down. Even being the favourite child wouldn't save Ellie. Now Mavis understood that love was only good for as long as someone agreed to love you. Before this moment, she had believed that families were the place where that love kept going. But that wasn't true. Love was bound by a host of conditions. If only she and Ellie could run away together … There had to be some way for that to happen.

CHAPTER 12

Ellie's heartbeat resided in her cheeks. The engine that pounded blood through her veins roared in the wounds on her face. *Oh. God. It. Hurts. Oh. God. It. Hurts.*

She dozed on and off, trying to comprehend the morning's events. Suitors *never* came first thing in the day. How could she have planned for that? Still, could she have made Willis doubt what he'd seen instead of encouraging his anger?

They had struggled. He got her on the ground and sat on her, using his knees to pin her arms. His weight was crushing. He held a knife over her cheek. If she'd apologized, maybe things would have gone differently. If she'd sweet-talked him into thinking she somehow loved him, maybe he would have behaved better. Instead, her anger made her defiant. How *dare* he think he owned her!

Willis's breath had been hot and smelled like cabbage. He was inches from her face when he hissed, "My mama says you think you're too good for me."

She couldn't help herself. "Your mama's right."

Pinned beneath his heft, her only weapon was words. "Jedediah's more of a man than you'll ever be."

"Not for long."

The blade sliced through her flesh with ease. She remembered thinking: *How strange that skin can hold in so much and give way in an instant.*

The smell of Mamie's cooking woke her. She must have dozed. She was hungry. Cutlery clinked on china downstairs for the noon meal, but nobody came for her. Why hadn't Mavis returned?

Shadows lengthened on the floor as the afternoon passed. Soon, darkness overpowered the remaining light. Her head ached from crying. She dabbed at her cheeks; it was difficult to cry without scrunching up her face, but she tried, staring at the ceiling and letting the tears roll down to fill her ears. She lit a lamp on her bedside table and reached for another rag, thankful that Mavis had brought quite a few.

Gradually, the evening wore on and the house noises subsided. One of the dogs barked out by the barn. An owl hooted nearby. The wind picked up and gusted through the trees. At some point, Ellie heard the floorboards creak in the hallway. She tensed when her door opened. In the dark it was hard to make out who was there. Was it her mama? Why didn't she speak? *Help me.* "Mama?"

"How *could* you?" her mama spat. "You never did know how to think about anyone but yourself, did you?"

"Mama please ..."

"It's too late for your begging. Do you have any idea what you've done? You have destroyed your father and the Turner name. Willis insists on marrying you. I can only think he wants to publicly embarrass us, keeping you where everyone can see you, but I'll have none of it."

Something sailed through the air and landed on the bed. Ellie reached for it: a small velvet pouch filled with coins.

"I want you on the night train. Your daddy won't know you're gone until later tomorrow. I won't have you living anywhere nearby and reminding us of the shame you've brought on the family."

Where had her mama gotten the money? Wouldn't she be in trouble for giving it away? Or was this her way of saving Ellie from a marriage she didn't want? Maybe she *did* still love her.

"You are no longer a member of this family. You are never to contact any of us again, and you're to leave Mavis alone. Do you understand me?"

There was no love in her voice. Ellie nodded.

"Never," she repeated. "A wagon will be waiting out front in an hour. Be ready." She closed the door and retreated down the hall.

Ellie didn't have any tears left. She gathered a change of clothes.

Fresh undergarments. Some toiletries. Mamie's ointment. Now what? Her mama hadn't said where she should go. What would Willis do when he discovered his bride-to-be was gone? It made no sense that he still wanted to marry her after what he'd done.

If Mavis came to her room right now, Ellie decided she'd use half the money to bring her along. Her mama had forbidden her to speak to Mavis, but Ellie couldn't control if Mavis spoke to her. *Please, Mavis. Wake up. Please come see me.*

Mavis did not come.

Too soon, the wagon rolled up outside. Ellie penned a quick note. She wasn't really breaking the rules because she was leaving her sister alone.

She tiptoed down the hallway, slipped the note under Mavis's door, and descended the stairs. She'd wrapped a scarf around her head to hide her sheared hair. With the leftover material, she'd made a make-shift veil that covered her injured cheeks. One hand held the scarf tight against her face, and the other held her small bag of belongings. She said a series of goodbyes in her mind. *Goodbye Mama. Goodbye Daddy. Jimmy, Mavis, Gertie, George. Goodbye Mamie.*

The citrus grove and Neelan Junction were her entire world; but that world had proved to be too small for her.

Samuel helped her into the wagon and tried not to look shocked by her shrouded appearance. Ellie clutched her bag to her chest as the wagon jolted forward.

The night air was lush with scents. A half-moon lit their path. Shadows of tree branches looked like arms reaching onto the road. At the wooden bridge that spanned Sugar Creek, the horse stopped abruptly and refused to move. Samuel jumped down and grabbed the horse's bridle, talking soothingly and leading it forward.

Halfway across, Ellie saw two ropes looped to the railing, three feet apart.

"Samuel?"

He turned.

She pointed to the ropes.

He nodded but didn't speak.

She'd given little thought to Jedediah's predicament. "Why are there two ropes?"

Again Samuel didn't reply.

"Who else is down there?"

They were at the end of the bridge now. Samuel got back on the wagon. "His wife, Delia."

Ellie forced her spine to stay straight as the horse began to trot again. His wife hadn't done anything, and Jedediah had only done what he was told. *I don't want no trouble, Miss.*

A cloud obscured the moon and for a moment Samuel disappeared on the bench before her.

"Samuel?"

"Yes?"

"I never meant for anything bad to happen."

"I know."

"You believe me, don't you?"

"I do."

His back stayed straight. A moment passed. He turned so she could see his profile. "Did you tell anyone about me?"

She hadn't, but that was only because nobody had asked the right question. If her daddy had said, *who else?* she would have offered his name on a platter in the hope of saving herself. "No. I didn't tell anyone. I would never do that to you."

━ She heard the train before she saw it. The whistle was familiar. Sometimes, when the nights got cold and there was the threat of frost, the night train sat at the station and blew its whistle repeatedly as a signal for the men of Neelan Junction to tend to their groves. Light fires. Pile dirt or sand at the base of all the trees. Save the oranges. Always, save the oranges.

"Where will you go?" Samuel asked.

"As far away as my money can take me. Wherever that is. You should visit me some time." It was just something to say. They both knew it would never happen. "I hope you won't get into trouble for taking me to the station. Because it was Mama who asked you, right?

Make sure you say it wasn't my idea if anybody asks." Maybe her daddy, in time, would forgive her. She was his best girl. He'd miss her terribly, wouldn't he?

Mr. Calder sold her a ticket to Fort Lauderdale and asked why she was all covered up in this heat. Ellie didn't respond. She knew how quickly he'd tell people what he'd seen. She wasn't about to give him more information. He took her bag and helped her up the steel stairway.

The few passengers on board were asleep. She found an empty seat by a window and claimed it.

Almost immediately, the train lurched forward. Ellie's cheeks throbbed. She reached a hand under her scarf and touched her left cheek. It came away sticky with blood.

She rested her forehead against the cool window and imagined putting her cheeks to the glass and rolling her face from side to side. It would feel good, but she'd make a mess. Plus, who knew when the window had last been properly cleaned.

The train soon moved at a steady, rocking speed. The conductor took her ticket and gave half back to her without raising an eyebrow.

Under different circumstances, how freeing the train would feel with its magnificent gait. Under different circumstances, leaving Neelan Junction would have been cause for celebration.

How dare Willis show up unannounced!

This very morning she had still been herself. She had just left the shed and stepped into the sunshine. Jedediah's salt was drying on her lips.

She heard Willis's bellow again — part pain and part rage. Primal.

He should have been the one to swing for what he did to her.

Not Jedediah, and certainly not Delia. Willis. Rope burn around his neck. A bright red collar. Ellie would stand beside his body and wait all day for the photographer to show up.

Right now, Mavis was asleep in her bed, twisted in her bedclothes, unaware of her sister's departure. *Women are birds, Mavis, because they have to take flight from time to time to believe in their own freedom.*

Ellie put her hands together in her lap and made the motion of wings in flight. *Look at me, Mavis! Look at me go!*

The window in the darkness was a mirror. Instead of seeing the scenery pass, she saw her shrouded self. She had to close her eyes to see the Florida landscape in her mind: the spiderwort and wild mustard; the holly berries in autumn and winter, bright lamps in the half-light; the oleanders and dogwoods; the rattlesnakes and toads and snails and turtles; the blossoms on the orange trees, so fragrant in their delicate beauty.

She had miscalculated. But was it her fault she'd taken what she wanted, just like her father and Jimmy had? Was it her fault she'd followed in their footsteps or been born female?

The night was pitch-black, the air salty.

She had loved this landscape, but now all it represented was the lust and longing and rage that had brought about her flight.

CHAPTER 13

In the late evening hours of an August night in 1935, Ellie Turner stepped into the humid air of Union Station in Washington, DC. Only her eyes showed above the scarf that shrouded her head and was pulled tight to her face to hide her recent disfigurement.

She stared at the high domed ceiling, amazed that so many lights could be held in place like constellations. Such a far cry from the wooden platform with the single bulb at the station back home.

She moved with halting steps, unused to walking in a crowd. Seeing her now, no one would know that Ellie Turner had once moved her body as if it were silk, putting one foot directly in front of the other to accentuate the fluidity of her hips. Men had lost their train of thought and adjusted themselves in their trousers when she walked into a room, but that wouldn't happen anymore.

Ellie smelled her own sour breath against the damp scarf that covered her mouth. Oh for a bed to lie down in. She scanned the faces in the crowd; too many of them were dark. She stepped into the empty waiting room, put her bag on the floor, and sat down. The hour changed to 11 p.m. She let the scarf fall from her face and breathed the air freely for a moment. Her skin had tightened around her wounds; it was hard not to scratch at the newly forming scabs.

Her only plan had been to get away from Neelan Junction. What was she supposed to do now? She couldn't spend the night in the train station.

An older couple entered the waiting room and sat down a few seats away. They were well dressed. The woman looked at her as if Ellie might have stolen something. Ellie pulled her scarf up. Nobody knew who she was here. She stepped into the stream of people headed to the main entrance, disoriented by how quickly everybody moved and how freely the coloureds mixed as if they were allowed.

Fresh air blew in from the entrance and she followed it. Had Willis discovered her escape yet? That she'd thwarted his wedding plans was the only solace she had, and she clung to it to maintain her accustomed sense of privilege.

Taxicabs waited in a line outside the station. In the soft rainfall, a streetcar rattled by. She'd only ever seen one in a magazine. How did a person get on it?

She didn't know where she was going or how to get there. A white woman saw her distress and asked if she needed help. She directed her to a line of taxis and said a driver could help her. Ellie was grateful.

Once she was in the backseat of a taxi, her nerves calmed instantly. The driver was in charge of her now. She'd requested he take her to a modestly priced accommodation of good standing that catered to women. She had to repeat herself twice before he understood her. An accent? She didn't have an accent. He was the one who was difficult to understand!

Streetlights illuminated the unfamiliar city. Limestone spires stabbed the sky. Buildings reached higher than any she'd ever seen. So many windows. So many doorways. And despite the late hour, lots of people were still out on the streets.

In less than ten minutes, the cab stopped in front of a two-storey wooden house with a narrow front porch and a sign that said Rooms for Rent. It looked like one of the rundown homes on the poor side of Neelan Junction, but maybe it was nicer on the inside; she had asked for 'modest,' and she couldn't afford to be picky. Plus, she was exhausted. She desperately needed to sleep. She paid the driver and let him carry her bag to the front door. If she could, she'd have climbed into his arms and let him carry her too.

Who would take care of her now?

The rain had softened to a mist, and it settled on Ellie like a butterfly lands on a leaf. At another time, she would have enjoyed the fresh night air and the coolness on her skin, but her nerves were too frayed. All her life her daddy had railed against the government's laws that kept the south in chains. All her life she'd imagined a big white house with politicians going in and out like ants visiting the hill. If her father hated the government so much, as he now hated her, then maybe she'd be safe here. That's what she'd thought when she'd arrived in Fort Lauderdale and purchased another ticket.

The taxi driver left without waiting to see if she got inside safely.

A sudden gust of wind set the tree branches on the boulevard in motion. Back home, the owls would be diving for field mice, their wings silent in the plunge. What birds took to the sky here? White paint pulled away from the wood on the rooming house; she didn't like the look of this place at all.

Inside, the entrance was empty save for a small table against the wall that held a few envelopes—mail for the guests. Lace curtains that had once been white were now a worn yellow and covered a small window. The only thing that kept her from turning around and leaving was the vase of fresh flowers on the counter, colourful and fragrant amidst their dull surroundings. Someone cared about the place.

Ellie rang the desk bell, and a thick-waisted woman eventually appeared from behind a closed door.

She eyed Ellie's scarf-covered face with suspicion. "I run a respectable place."

"That's why I'm here."

The landlady made her pay upfront for the week before leading her to a small room off the main hallway. The bathroom was down the hall, but there was a washbasin on a table beneath a mirror beside a single bed on which two towels were folded. The room was half the size of hers back home, but it appeared to be clean. It would do for now.

Ellie put her bag down, took the basin to the bathroom, filled it with warm water, returned to her room, and locked the door. She draped one of the towels over the mirror. With trembling hands, she cupped water and brought it to her face again and again until the scabs softened, and her face became pliable. Then she applied some ointment to ease the dreadful tightening. Once the wounds healed, maybe the heat would leave her face. And maybe the scars wouldn't be so bad. Maybe Mamie's lotion really would reduce scarring.

She undressed and fell into bed. She had never been so exhausted in her life. Closing her eyes was a great luxury.

⌐ Days passed. Ellie only left her room to use the bathroom and to put the food tray outside her door. Each morning, she washed her face and applied ointment and was grateful when the itching subsided. After a week, she gathered the courage to remove the towel from the mirror. She used to love mirrors. She'd spent hours staring at her own beauty. People said her mother had been beautiful once too, but after so many pregnancies, a softness entered the body and made it slack, a quality not attributed to beauty. If having children did that, then Ellie didn't particularly want any.

She took a deep breath, faced the mirror, and began her inspection. Starting at her forehead, she was relieved to find it unchanged. Her hair had begun to grow back. It looked like the soft, dark pelt of an otter—a stark contrast against the pearly whiteness of her skin. She moved her gaze a little lower until she met her eyebrows. They were still finely arched and delicately lined. Her eyelashes remained long and nicely curled, her eyes still a clear and arresting blue. She held her gaze, took another breath, and exhaled slowly. Maybe it wouldn't be as bad as she imagined.

The first scar ran from the bridge of her nose over to her right cheekbone, jaggedly through the middle of her cheek, then down to her mouth. The scar was plump, as if an earthworm had been dropped onto her cheek and languished. The scar on the left side of her face consisted of four fairly straight lines that could have been a letter in the centre of her cheek. Even with the reversed image, the letter was the same: W. For whore, no doubt. Then she thought again: no—for Willis. He had marked his property.

She lifted her hand to her face and realized the mirror had reversed things. Her right cheek bore the W. Her left the jagged gash. It was where he had started.

The image before her was devastating. It was far worse than she'd expected. No amount of ointment would make the scars disappear. Who would have her now?

She climbed into bed, pulled the covers to her chin, and cried.

A pounding headache woke her. She lay there assessing her situation. She'd paid for the week at the rooming house, thinking she'd have time to heal, but she didn't have enough to cover another. Now what? With her disfigured face, no one would hire her as a clerk in a fancy department store, as she'd once hoped, or as a teacher. And what mother would introduce Ellie as the new tutor? She sucked the inside of her cheek between her molars. Perhaps she could become a maid. Nobody cared what a maid looked like. But it was beneath her. She'd rather die.

She had borrowed a needle and thread from the landlady and designed a veil using a piece of cloth and sewing loops at both ends that fastened over her ears. It hid her scars, but it also drew attention that she had something to hide. People would still stare. She had once welcomed and even expected people to stare at her, but this kind of staring was one of curiosity not admiration.

She wished Mavis was with her. And Mamie to cook and clean for her. And even Jimmy, who had once had friends who'd worshiped her.

The life she'd once scorned now seemed enviable.

She had never been so lonely in her life.

Another day passed.

She had enough money to pay for two more nights of lodging when a knock sounded at her door. Had the maid returned so soon? The room had already been cleaned.

The knock came again. It was a gentle knock—an apology for the intrusion.

Ellie put on her veil and opened the door.

PART TWO

1935—1940

CHAPTER 14

At fifty years old, Sliver had lost track of the number of babies she'd brought into the world. These days, she spent as much time tending her gardens as she did tending to babies. Both gave her pleasure.

She stretched her arms over her head in the sunshine to ease the tension in her lower back. Then she wiped the sweat from her brow and looked at the sizeable pile of weeds she'd already pulled at the house garden. Waiting until the weeds got to a certain height helped to make sure she got all the roots. Weeding prematurely was like trying to pull the placenta before the baby came out: useless.

Sliver's tongue felt thick in her mouth. Some water would go down good. She turned to get some from the barrel beside the garden and saw a cloud of dust rising above the distant fields, kicked up from the dirt road and fouling the air all around. The cloud was moving fast, so it had to be a car, not a carriage.

The screen door slammed at the house and Mrs. Yates came onto the porch. She stared at the dust too. Sliver put her hoe down and walked over before she was called. It was a tiny thing, doing ahead of time something she knew she'd be asked to do; it made her feel more in charge of her life.

"Do you think it's him?" Mrs. Yates asked.

"Could be." Sliver shifted to take some weight off her bad leg.

Willis had disappeared ten days earlier without telling his mama where he was going or for how long. He'd never done that before. A few days ago, some women from town dropped by to congratulate Mrs. Yates, and she had pretended to know what for.

"Have you seen how it's been written up in the paper?" Mrs. Hargraves asked.

"I haven't had a chance to read it yet," Mrs. Yates replied. "I've been so busy today."

Busy doing what? Sliver thought. *Being taken care of?*

The women opened *The Neelan News* to show her the headline: *Citrus Baron Willis Yates Marries Ellie Turner.*

"Oh that," she said. "I thought you meant something new."

Sliver admired how quickly Mrs. Yates covered her own ignorance. There was no way she'd let the town ladies know something about her family that she didn't know. But Master Willis a citrus baron? Sliver caught a laugh in her throat. Wait until she told Mamie: white folks just loved giving themselves titles.

"Did you know about this?" Mrs. Yates asked after her guests had left.

Sliver skimmed the article. It said Ellie had been disfigured by a crazed negro. Willis had been at her house when the attack occurred. It said he'd already asked for her hand, prior to her disfigurement. *I've always loved Ellie,* he told the reporter. *And I will love her still.*

"No," Sliver said. "I didn't know." She didn't know about the wedding, but she knew what had led to Miss Ellie leaving. Mamie had told her the story about Miss Ellie being caught with Jedediah. The article didn't mention that he and his wife ended up dead. That made three dead negroes because of Ellie — that poor man who got lynched years back, and now Jedediah and his wife. Mamie said she had a hard time being nice to Miss Ellie. *She don't think about nobody but herself. I don't trust her one bit, the way she appears and disappears without a sound.*

The dust cloud continued to approach.

If Sliver was writing the newspaper story, she'd write it differently and make sure to mention that the murdered Jedediah and Delia left behind three children. Apparently Delia had clung to her husband so tight, that the men had taken her with him. Sliver's eyes still burned thinking about those kids having to go live with their aunt in Slew Town.

"They married her off because they needed money," Mrs. Yates spat. "And my Willis was dumb enough to go ahead with it."

"Who did?"

"The Turners. I told Willis that Ellie was no good. I saw the way she flirted with all the boys at church and stared at herself whenever she saw her own reflection, but he was set on marrying her." She squinted at the dust's movement as if watching a tornado and trying to decide when to get into the storm cellar. "I know my Willis is a better man than his father, but like so many men, Willis uses the wrong organ to do his thinking."

Sliver hid her surprise at Mrs. Yates's crass confession. Was she supposed to respond?

"I know more about my husband's activities than I ever made out," she added. "Let me just say I did not enjoy being his wife."

For good reason. Old Man Yates had humiliated his wife every chance he got. Like calling in the midwife instead of the doctor. Sliver had seen Mrs. Yates's lower parts on full display when she helped bring Master Willis into the world. Mrs. Yates hadn't spoken to her for years afterwards because of her own embarrassment at being so fully seen.

The dark cloud turned up the driveway. *There goes my garden,* Sliver thought, imagining the dust settling onto her cucumbers and tomatoes.

A car materialized from the dust cloud and pulled to a stop in front of the house. Thankfully, the breeze blew the dust away from the porch. Master Willis stepped out of the driver's side, opened the back door, reached a long arm inside, and pulled out a woman with a black scarf covering her head and face and a black skirt that near touched the ground. He led the pillar of doom to the bottom of the porch stairs.

"Mama, I would like you to welcome Ellie to our home. She's Mrs. Willis Yates now."

Sliver's skin was damp from the heat. She stared at her hands and watched the dust melt into her pores even as the air temperature suddenly dropped. She couldn't tell if the unexpected coolness came from Master Willis's new wife or from Mrs. Yates, who looked at Miss Ellie as if she'd found something dead on the side of the road.

"Why is her face hidden?"

"She has sustained some injuries," Willis said.

"So it's true?" She turned to the new bride. "Show me."

Miss Ellie didn't move a muscle. Her eyes didn't blink.

Sliver wanted to leave but didn't want to draw attention to herself.

"Show me."

Willis waited a moment and then reached over and pulled the scarf from his wife's head.

Miss Ellie looked like a little bald bird with fuzz growing on her head. And her face looked like a nest of twigs. She'd been cut alright.

The corners of Mrs. Yates's mouth turned up ever so slightly. She wasn't going to laugh, was she?

"Mama? I asked you to welcome Ellie to our home."

The wind rustled the weeping willow by the porch. Sliver wondered if it was a snake she heard and not a tree.

"Mama?"

The sun went behind a cloud, and in the sudden shade they adjusted their eyes.

Mrs. Yates looked from Miss Ellie to Willis and back again and shook her head. "Now you've thrown the Devil against the wall," she said and turned away. The screen door slammed shut behind her.

Sliver stood stock still, hoping her presence had been forgotten.

Master Willis stared at the door, disappointment and anger visible in the set of his mouth. He took Miss Ellie by the elbow and walked her like an invalid across the courtyard to the new home he'd laboured on for close to two years, sparing no expense, in preparation of welcoming his new bride. The one his mama had just cursed.

"Don't just stand there," Willis called over his shoulder. "Bring our bags."

It took Sliver a moment to realize he was talking to her. She looked around and discovered she was alone. Normally the sight of a car drew a crowd, but not today. Even the birds had grown silent.

Sliver opened the trunk of the car and pulled out two suitcases. The sun reappeared from behind a cloud. Had she imagined the sudden halt in life's motion?

She crossed the courtyard, climbed two stairs to the porch, and put the suitcases down at the front door. Master Willis had hung a porch swing to the right of the door just like the one at the Turners' house. Although it sat empty, it swung quietly now on its metal chains. The hair on the back of her neck stood up. Sliver took her imagination in hand and backed down the stairs, not wanting to turn her back on the door in case it suddenly burst open. Then she backed across the small courtyard until she was at the main house where she'd started. If the car wasn't still parked where Master Willis had left it, Sliver might have thought she'd imagined the entire thing: him arriving with his new bride; her covered in a dark scarf; Mrs. Yates taking that scarf down and sneering at what lay beneath it because she'd been denied a proper wedding celebration and a proper bride.

Folks get damaged over time, Sliver thought. *Even white folks.*

The sound of metal hitting metal interrupted her thoughts. That'd be her boy Charlie, the best blacksmith in the area, forging horseshoes in the barn. He'd been put on this sweet earth to care for others. He was tender from the start. Once, he'd brought home a baby fox that was near dead, one of its legs still caught in a trap. All Sliver could think about was rabies, but Charlie just focused on saving its life. He got some rubbing alcohol from the barn, asked Sliver to wrap towels around her hands and hold the fox's head down. *Don't worry,* he said, *he's so weak. I'll be quick.* Once he got the trap off he'd poured alcohol on the wound before the fox got away. Sliver's heart still jumped thinking about that crazy healing. Charlie swore he saw the fox a few months later, not limping at all. And maybe he was right. All Sliver knew was, whenever someone had trouble with a lame horse, Master Yates sent Charlie over to set things right.

She stopped at the garden to see how her plants had fared. The dust was barely visible. She rubbed small circles on her face around her eyes to make sure any dust there would be absorbed, thinking it might fill in some of her wrinkles. In childhood she'd learned to keep her face impassive, to not show shock or alarm, fear or joy, but still, grief and worry had etched its design onto her face over time.

It was the fall of 1935 when Master Willis brought home his new wife, and even knowing what Mamie had told her about Ellie—that she moved in and out of rooms quietly, never making a noise; that she was used to taking what she wanted and not caring about the out-come—even knowing what she knew, Sliver could not have predicted what lay ahead.

CHAPTER 15

Ellie pulled a store-bought cigarette from her case and put a match to the end. Then she tossed it onto the bed and watched it bounce. It was her wedding present. Gold, like she'd wanted. Willis had her initials engraved on it in fancy script, to surprise her: *ELY*, for Ellie Louise Yates. She would have preferred the case to be blank, or just to have her first two initials engraved in it. The T was the name that had shown she belonged to her daddy, but the Y now showed she belonged to her husband. And ELY was a boy's name. She wouldn't be in this predicament if she'd been a boy. Already she understood if she wanted something, she had to take full charge of it to avoid disappointment.

The new house Willis had built for her was the nicest house in Neelan Junction, she was sure. Only she wouldn't admit it to him. All the doors opened and closed without rubbing or sticking; if she dropped something on the floor, it didn't roll into the corner; and the windows had screens on them to let the air in but to keep the bugs out.

She had to admit that her living circumstances had certainly improved. A brand new house? With paint so fresh the smell still lingered? If only she hadn't had to marry Willis to make that happen.

The bedroom was on the second floor and looked out the front of the house. She blew smoke out the window screen and watched the activity below. There were more workers here than at home, which made sense because Willis had more trees and land. He'd bragged about how much he owned, but she hadn't paid attention. He had money; she didn't care how he got it.

At breakfast, Willis had emptied half a pot of honey onto his toast.

She watched his knife go into the pot again and again, transferring crumbs. She made a note not to use that pot for her tea. She almost asked if he wanted some toast to go along with his honey but didn't want him to think she was interested in having a conversation. She talked in her head instead. Her own company was preferable, and when she got bored, she imagined conversations with others.

She saw someone in the garden, to the left of the main house, bent at the waist. It was the midwife, wasn't it? What was her name again? Slipper? Ellie had almost been glad to see her when Willis hauled Ellie out of the back of the car. The midwife reminded her of home, which reminded her of Mavis, which in turn made her sad.

She blew another stream of smoke through the screen. The midwife reminded her of poverty, too, and the embarrassment of not having a new dress. Why was the midwife here? Old Lady Yates was well past her prime.

Her hand trembled as she brought the cigarette to her lips and recalled the midwife witnessing her humiliation on the porch the day before. She'd like to throw Mrs. Yates against the wall. The Devil? Indeed.

The breeze carried her cigarette smoke and pulled it apart and melted it like cotton candy. Did the midwife smell the smoke in the garden? Ellie was home but not home, in Neelan Junction but far away. If she could get Mavis to move here, she might be alright. Was her daddy sorry for what he'd done? Did he miss her? Her mama must be mad that Ellie had come back, but it wasn't her doing. Willis had come for her.

The double bed with its dark brown wooden headboard took up most of the room. Willis said he'd had it built special, to last, as if the idea of being in it with him was a pleasant one. She was here against her will. He must know that. Yes, she'd collapsed in seeming gratitude when he had arrived at her rooming house, but only because after she'd surveyed the irreparable damage to her face, and after she'd sifted through the available jobs for women—all of which involved being *seen*—death had been her only option. She'd already begun to wonder how close the nearest bridge might be.

When the knock came, she'd expected the maid. It was a shock to see Willis there; he caught her before she fell to the ground.

"How did you find me?"

"A good private investigator is worth his weight in gold," Willis boasted. "The station master said you had your head and face covered with a scarf when you left Neelan Junction. You were easy for people to remember."

Well aren't you clever? Even then she had replied inside her head because she didn't trust Willis to recognize sarcasm. He'd likely think she was complimenting him.

After they'd married and were journeying back to Neelan Junction, she'd bluntly asked, "Why did you come for me? After what you knew, I don't understand why you still wanted to marry me."

It hadn't taken him long to answer. Clearly he'd rehearsed his reply. "Because I always get what I want."

So do I, Ellie thought. Then she realized she had to change the tense. *So did I.* She hadn't wanted to be Mrs. Willis Yates. Willis had ruined everything. Plus, he was wrong. He hadn't gotten what he wanted. He'd wanted the beautiful Ellie.

There was no ashtray in the room. She dropped her cigarette on the new wooden floor and turned the toe of her boot back and forth to make sure it extinguished. The maid would bring an ashtray soon enough if Ellie kept using the floor. Mona. Yes, that was the maid's name. Short for Ramona? She didn't really care.

Had her mama heard she was back yet? Would she visit? Had Mavis heard? Ellie had so many stories to tell her, big city stories.

Out the window, the midwife put her tools in the small shed beside the garden before disappearing behind the main house. She walked with a slight limp. Damaged goods. Ellie had something in common with her now.

She picked her cigarette case up off the bed, let it drop, and watched it bounce. Then she did it again. And again. Would life always be so dull?

She missed Mavis.

What on earth would she do with her days?

CHAPTER 16

Trying to keep a secret in Neelan Junction was like trying to keep the barn cats from having kittens. When Mavis arrived downstairs for breakfast the day following Ellie's return, Mamie put her plate down and whispered into her ear: "I got news: Ellie's back. She married Willis and is over at the Yates's."

Mavis's mouth dropped. "Really?"

Mamie nodded.

"Since when?"

"Yesterday."

"How do you know?"

"Sliver told me." Then she handed Mavis *The Neelan News*. "And it was in the paper. Yesterday."

Ellie married Willis? After what he'd done to her? "Why? She doesn't even like him."

"I'm just reporting the facts."

Mavis glanced at the article and jumped up. "I'm going over there right now."

"No, you're not. Eat your breakfast. Sliver said no one's allowed to see her. I don't think *Old* Mrs. Yates has accepted having a *young* Mrs. Yates yet. They need some time to get settled before people can drop by."

"Says who?"

"Says Sliver."

"She's just the midwife."

"There's no such thing as 'just the midwife.'"

Mavis finished breakfast and ran to her room to re-read the letter Ellie had slipped under her door the night she'd disappeared.

Dear Mavis,

Mama gave me money and told me to get on the train for the shame I've brought on the family. I believe I have been officially disowned. Likely leaving is for the best, as I'd rather die than marry Willis. Especially now, after what he did to me. When I get settled, I'll send for you. But don't tell Mama. She said I'm never to contact you. Ever. You can have all my clothes and whatever else you want that's left in my room. I plan to buy new things once I'm established — new everything! Big city things. Fancy things. I'll send for you, okay? Hopefully soon.

Love,
Ellie (XOXOXO)

There would be no big city adventure. Ellie had flown the coop but ended up right back where she'd started, except for right next door. Mavis could unpack the travel bag she'd stowed in her closet for a quick escape. She had to admit it was a disappointment. Still, she couldn't wait to see her.

Preacher Heath delivered sermons every Sunday in Neelan Junction, and the majority of families in town attended church. Mavis had fallen asleep during his sermons more times than she could count, but since learning that Ellie was back, she couldn't wait for Sunday to come. Church was likely the safest place Mavis could visit with her sister without getting into trouble. It was neutral ground.

The church stood on a corner lot at the east end of town. It was a small wooden structure painted white with a dark green trim. A modest spire topped with a gold cross jutted towards heaven. The family wagon pulled up outside. Mavis wore a scarf over her hair because of the wind. September in Florida often brought tropical storms that could turn into hurricanes. Sometimes the storms that seemed to be travelling directly towards Neelan Junction ended up veering off at the last minute and not making landfall at all. The storms her daddy prepared for often didn't show. He said it was the ones you didn't expect that hurt the most.

Mavis took her spot in her family pew, third row from the front, and waited. The pews had been designated according to standings. The first pew was for Mayor Humphreys and his family. The second pew was reserved for Sheriff Thorpe and his family. The Turners had been in the third pew for decades, a marker from the time when they'd enjoyed better days. Their pew, they knew, should now go to the Yates's, who occupied the fourth pew, but her daddy said he'd never move unless forced to.

Ellie was nowhere in sight.

Mavis looked around nonchalantly as if she didn't care who was in attendance, yet her heart jumped when Mrs. Yates arrived. She was alone. No Willis. No Ellie.

Mavis felt the old lady's eyes bore a hole into the back of her head. What was she thinking as she stared at the Turner family? That Mrs. Turner's new hat was bought by her son's money? That the Turners had found a way to stay afloat at her son's expense? That Ellie didn't deserve to have married the richest bachelor in Neelan Junction? Oh, but he was no gentleman. Mavis knew what he'd done to Ellie. Even if she were to tell everyone it was Willis who'd cut her sister, who would believe her? *The Neelan News* had called him a hero for marrying poor disfigured Ellie who would no longer have any prospects. Such a good man, they lied. And such a shame about Ellie. She'd been a beauty alright. Willis must really love her.

Well, if he was so great, why wasn't he in church?

There was nothing unique about the preacher's sermon that day. He spoke about forgiveness and charity, and Mavis tried to keep her eyes open.

Finally, the sermon ended. Mavis had made sure to sit on the outside of the pew. She stood abruptly and made her way outside, in case somehow she'd missed Ellie. She watched everyone leave the building. Mrs. Yates walked towards her carriage. A black man helped her up and took the reins. Who was he? She'd ask Mamie. If she didn't hear from Ellie by next week, maybe Mavis could send a note with him.

⌐ Monday passed. And Tuesday. Mavis told herself she'd hear from Ellie on Wednesday, and she kept her eyes and ears open for any clues, but none came. Then Thursday passed, and Friday. The wait was unbearable, having Ellie so close and yet so far away. On Saturday, Mavis got a sheet of paper and a pen and started a note.

> *Dear Ellie,*
>
> *I'm so glad you're back. I waited for you at church, but you didn't come. I've missed you more than anything …*

She put the end of the pen in her mouth and imagined Ellie smiling and asking, *more than what?*
More than the bees miss their flowers.
More than …
She added a few more things in her list to make Ellie laugh.
On Sunday, she carried the note to church and made sure to sit at the end of the pew again, so she could bolt for the door well ahead of Mrs. Yates once the preacher stopped droning. Mavis had asked Mamie who drove Mrs. Yates to church, and Mamie said it was likely the blacksmith.
"What's his name?"
"Charlie. Why are you asking?"
"No reason."
The Yates's wagon was parked in its usual spot beneath a tree with passable shade. The blacksmith sat with his shoulders hunched to fit into the white cotton shirt that pulled dangerously at the seams as if it was made for another body, which likely it was. As soon as Preacher Heath finished, Mavis ran to the wagon and pressed the note into Charlie's palm. "I can't explain, but get this to my sister, Mr. Yates's

new bride." She stepped away from the wagon and turned in time to see Mrs. Yates exiting the church. Mavis's daddy followed next, his head lowered in discussion with Sheriff Thorpe. The two men glanced her way. Had someone tattled already? Their eyes moved past her to where a group of young men gathered, Jimmy among them. In the centre stood Danny Thorpe, telling a story that set the whole crowd laughing. They were loud boys, all of them, who talked too much, especially when they had nothing to say.

Mrs. Yates was almost to the wagon now. The blacksmith jumped down and helped her into her seat. Then he climbed into his spot and took up the reins.

The horse trotted forward, and Mavis imagined her note burning a hole in the blacksmith's pocket. *Please let it reach Ellie,* she said to herself. *And please let her write back.*

CHAPTER 17

Monday was laundry day at the Yates's too. Every week, like clockwork, two of Old Lady Yates's dresses danced in the wind on the line behind her house. Sometimes, when the wind was calm, they moved in a slow dance, and other times when the wind gusted, they danced at a pace that would exhaust. There wasn't much to distinguish between the dresses other than a slight change in hue. Why the old woman didn't have more dresses was beyond Ellie. She had enough money to wear a new dress every day of the year. Denying herself that luxury indicated Old Lady Yates had an impoverished character. She was too responsible to have fun.

Ellie sometimes walked through the clothes and sheets, hidden from view, and imagined she was in a maze in England, lost in the expansive greenery. She had to close her eyes for that image because the laundry lines provided a reduced landscape.

There was a space between hanging the wash and taking it down that lasted anywhere from one hour to three, depending on the weather. The sheets gave the best privacy as they hung almost to the ground and reminded her of a child's hastily constructed fort.

One day, Ellie examined a pair of Old Lady Yates's underwear and saw stains on the cotton that proved she was human and fraying at the seams that proved she was cheap. Two of her dresses were pinned by the shoulders and hung side by side like they were friends. Ellie imagined they'd argued and had yet to make up. She felt the fabric and determined the dark brown dress was of better quality than the tan one. Still, brown and tan were dull. Old Lady Yates could use some colour in her wardrobe. In Washington, DC, Willis had bought Ellie a turquoise blue dress that accentuated her eyes. It was the finest dress she'd ever owned. She said thank you because it was expected, and she'd admired her body in the mirror without looking at her face. The dress hung in her closet, but she didn't plan to dress up for Willis. Putting finery on a scarred body made a mockery of beauty.

Life was even more boring at the Yates's than it had been at home, mostly because she didn't have Mavis as a distraction. Even Gertie and George had occasionally entertained. From her bedroom, Ellie could see Mrs. Yates's house across the way. One morning Ellie had parted the curtain to look out and seen the curtain part across the way at exactly the same time. Were they *both* spying on one another? She had hastily dropped the curtain and wished Willis had built the new house out of sight of his mama's.

Boredom took Ellie outside, and she soon got her bearings. She discovered the new house sat almost directly in the centre of the property, like a hub, and there were four spokes that jutted out, and at the end of each was a cluster of shacks where the workers lived. Ellie learned the areas were called quadrants; each had its own large garden and ten to twelve dwellings of various sizes like a series of tiny towns. A path ran in a circle on the outer limits and linked them all together. Ellie had walked from the south quadrant to the east and enjoyed the curiosity of the children who'd stared at her but were too shy to ask about her veil.

Her meanderings eventually always brought her back to where she'd started, and she stood outside her house and felt pleased that the one Willis had built for her was so much nicer than his mama's. How did Old Lady Yates like looking out at Ellie's nicer house every day? Maybe it was a good thing after all that the houses were close.

A light breeze tickled the back of her neck where her hair had grown enough to hang down a bit. She fetched her cigarettes from inside the house, asked the cook for some lemonade, and sat on the porch swing.

Mona appeared out of nowhere. "Charlie gave me this," she held out a piece of paper that had been folded into a small square. "He said to tell you it's from your sister."

The sun immediately got brighter. The birds sang with greater intent. Ellie took the note. Mavis hadn't forgotten her! She quickly unfolded it.

Dear Ellie,

I'm so glad you're back. I waited for you at church, but you didn't come. I've missed you more than the bees miss their flowers; more than the barn cat misses her litter when they're taken away. More than you love new dresses. More than ... you get my point.

I was trying to figure out how to follow you to wherever you went. I even had a bag packed, but then Mamie told me you were back. What happened? You said you'd rather die than marry Willis. I don't even want any of your things; I just want to see you. I'm not allowed to talk about you at home. No one is. It's like you never existed. Since you can't come home, then maybe you could ask Willis if I can come and live with you. I don't care if daddy gets mad. He's mad all the time anyway since you left.

If you're reading this, then I sent it with Mrs. Yates's driver who brings her to church. I'd give it to Mamie to send along to Sliver, but I'm not sure she'd approve. I hope it reaches you. Please figure out a way to reply and tell me when I can visit.

Love,
Mavis (XOXO)— "Gullie"—your bird in the sky

Ellie held the note to her heart. Then she folded and tucked it into her bodice. She'd been reduced to living as Willis's wife. Did she want Mavis to see her like this?

⌐ On the next laundry day, Ellie stood beside the laundry line, took Old Lady Yates's dark brown dress in her hand, and cut a slit in the bodice.

The maid who did laundry lost her job for being careless.

Mona delivered another note from Mavis.

Ellie let a couple of wash days pass before cutting a hole in Old Lady Yates's other dress. Who would she fire this time? Willis mentioned at dinner that his mother believed someone was intentionally destroying her wardrobe. They both agreed perhaps the old woman was becoming paranoid. Who would do that?

Shortly thereafter, Ellie noticed that the cloth napkin on her breakfast tray was the same fabric and colour as the dress Willis had bought for her in Washington. Sure enough, when she looked, the dress had disappeared from her closet. Ellie couldn't help but smile to herself. The old lady caught on fast, but she had met her match. What Mrs. Yates didn't understand was that Ellie had nothing more to lose. But Mrs. Yates did.

The best way for Ellie to get back at her was to hurt her son.

CHAPTER 18

October turned to November. Hunting was in full swing and gunshots frequently punctured the quiet dawns and dusks as birds fell from the sky.

Mavis collected stumps of wood and made a little seating area at the intersection where her daddy's and Willis's land met. From there, she looked for signs of Ellie in the distance.

Every Sunday morning, she pressed a note into Charlie's calloused grip, inviting Ellie to meet her there, and every Sunday afternoon, she waited.

> *I saw you on the porch, Ellie. Why didn't you come?*
> *I know you know I'm here. Didn't you see me waving*
> *my handkerchief?*

Christmas came and went, but the normal festivities weren't normal at all because of the empty chair at the supper table and the knowledge that Ellie was one farm over, sitting at her holiday meal.

The Jones's held their annual party to welcome the New Year and their new son-in-law, Silas Grove, who delivered goods to their family store. Posey had caught his eye from the start, Mrs. Jones boasted. She hoped to be a grandmother within the year and refused to listen to any gossip that circulated about Silas. She simply adored the tales he told about life in other places.

Danny Thorpe sat beside Mavis at the party and bragged about himself as if that would make him interesting. Why was he suddenly talking to her? She tried to appear interested, but she found herself staring at his jaw and wondering if it hurt from overuse. At one point she looked across the room and found her parents watching her. That was two odd things: Danny paying attention to her, and her parents watching him paying attention.

The calendar year changed.

Mavis had just about given up hope of ever hearing from Ellie, but the following week at church when she pressed her note into Charlie's palm it wasn't empty. She took the note that was still warm from his hand, replaced it with her own, and hurried to the side of the church to read it.

> *Dear Mavis,*
>
> *Willis will be away from the house for most of the day on Tuesday. Come any time after 10:00. I'll be waiting for you.*
> *Bring my comb with the ivory handle, the one with the wide teeth.*
>
> *Love,*
> *Ellie*

Monday was a season in itself and lasted twice as long as usual. On Tuesday, Mavis took the well-worn path that ran past the negro shacks. A door in one opened and banged shut. Cadence, who often helped Mamie, shook a small woven rug in the air, revealing her belly swollen with child. Mavis waved and smiled. Cadence nodded.

Flower buds decorated the tree branches in the grove. Soon they would bloom their white blossoms and garnish the trees like ribbons in a girl's hair.

A scrub jay sang in the branches. Mavis looked around, watchful in case her brother or daddy were nearby, but the bird only commented on the lushness. She passed the spot where she'd set up stumps for the visit with Ellie that had never happened. Willis would be gone until suppertime. It was already after lunch. Mavis hadn't been able to get away sooner without drawing attention to her departure.

She walked faster. The house was closer now and got bigger as she approached. Ellie was on the swing! Mavis hadn't seen her since August. She counted on her fingers. Almost six months ago.

She ran when the ground got smoother. Something moved in her peripheral vision and she turned, afraid Willis had come home early, but it was only Charlie out by the barn.

Then she was on the porch and in her sister's arms, burying her nose in her neck and squeezing her tight. "Oh, Ellie. I've missed you so much!"

Ellie didn't smell like home anymore, and her hair was scrappy like a boy's. It stuck up at odd angles because it wasn't long enough to hang down straight yet or to curl. It would be years before Mavis could braid their hair together again. Most of Ellie's face was hidden behind a veil that was the same colour as her dress. Only the top half of her face showed, but Mavis could tell by how Ellie's eyes crinkled that she was smiling. Mavis reached up to remove the veil.

"Leave it."

"You don't have to be shy with me, Ellie. I don't care what you look like."

"Well, I do."

Mavis took Ellie's hand and sat beside her on the swing. Ellie's free hand rested on her stomach. Something was different. Her belly was rounder than usual. "Ellie?"

Her sister followed her gaze. "I'm due in June."

"You're going to have a baby?"

"What else would I be having?"

Mavis hadn't missed that tone, but still, her heart lifted. "You must be so happy."

Ellie looked at her as if she had tracked dog dirt onto the porch. "Happy? I'll never be happy again. But Willis is over the moon about me being pregnant. It's not fair. Why does he get to be happy? He's the one who ruined my life."

Mavis had imagined a more joyful reunion.

"Anyway," Ellie said, looking away, "I don't want to talk about it. Tell me how things are at home. Does Daddy ask after me? I had half-hoped Mama might come visit once all the dust settled."

"We're still not allowed to talk about you. Daddy's still mad all the time, and Mama's in her room a lot."

Ellie stared into the yard. "Did you bring the comb I asked for?"

Mavis reached into her pocket and handed it to her.

Ellie pushed it back. "Maybe my hair will grow faster if someone else combs it for me."

And just like that, they fell into their old roles with Ellie telling Mavis what to do and her doing it. Mavis stood behind Ellie and dragged the comb gently over her scalp and through her short hair. "I've been talking to you in my head so much, Ellie, that I don't know where to start. Tell me about your trip. You actually got on the train? Where did you go?"

"Oh Mavis, I had quite the adventure. When I got to Fort Lauderdale, I bought a ticket to Washington, DC. You know how Daddy always rants about the government? Well, I thought it would be fun to be near the folks who make him so angry, the ones who make all the laws."

"You always wanted to get on that train."

"Yes, but I had hoped under different circumstances. Union Station was both thrilling and terrifying. There were more people there on the night I arrived than the entire population of Neelan Junction put together. I'd never seen so many people in one place in my life. The main streets are lit by electric lights, so even when it's dark you can still see. I passed a hotel that was fourteen stories tall. I didn't know buildings could be that tall."

"Where did you stay?"

"I stayed in the most *beautiful* place. I wish you could have seen it. The carpet was so thick I couldn't see my feet. There was a chandelier in my room, and in the daytime, when the sunlight hit the crystals, pink and blue and green lights danced on the walls. And there were silk sheets on the bed and fat feather pillows. It was divine."

Mavis imagined it all, everything gold-dipped and shining. "You always end up with nice things. What was the name of the hotel? Maybe I'll go there one day. It must have been expensive."

"The Excelsior, and it *was* expensive. I wouldn't have been able to stay there for long." She picked at a thread on her skirt. "I was trying to figure out where to go next, but in the end, I didn't have to worry because Willis showed up. My *husband*."

Mavis heard the disdain. "He wasn't your husband then. Why did you marry him? You said you'd rather die first."

"Well, I guess I chose living over dying. To be honest, I'm not sure I made the right choice. You must have figured things out by now, and surely folks are talking."

"Not to me they're not." Except at church when Missy Richardson said her daddy called Ellie a 'whore.' And at school when Betsy Hargraves asked if Mavis preferred dark meat too. And when Mavis passed the barber shop after Ellie had left town, Mr. Wynn wondered if anyone in her family had any hair to donate. Was he laughing about Ellie's bald head? And how did he know?

"Well, I hope they're at least telling the right story," Ellie said. "I wouldn't want people to be making things up."

"What is the right story? I might have made things up too."

"Do you really want to know?"

"Is it that bad?"

She shrugged. "It depends who you ask."

Mavis thought of all the things Ellie had told her or done over the years that she wished she could forget, like lying that Desperate had grabbed her. And lying about losing her purple ribbon. And being with Samuel in the parlour and Jedediah in the work shed. Ellie taking what she wanted, because she could, without thinking of the consequences for others. What made Mavis think that Ellie would tell the truth about anything? "I want to know."

"Okay." Ellie took a deep breath. "As God is my witness, this is the honest truth." She made the mark of a cross over her heart. "On the day Willis showed up uninvited, I woke up early and went out walking. I remember it was a beautiful morning. The ground was covered in dew, and I walked barefoot to feel the moisture between my toes. As

I passed the tool shed, I was suddenly curious to know what was inside. Does that ever happen to you? You see something you've seen for your whole life, but you've never really *looked* at it? Well, that's what it felt like. You know the shed I'm talking about? The one with the door that hangs at an angle."

"I know it."

"Well, I had a powerful urge to see what was inside. So I went in. There was an old hand plow propped against the wall, covered in rust and cobwebs, and an axe balanced on a nail. Ordinary things. I was about to leave when Jedediah came inside. He must have been watching me. You know which one I mean?"

Mavis saw a basket of oranges balanced high in the air. "Of course, I do. I told you his name."

"He blocked the door when I tried to leave, and he ... he did things to me." Ellie stared at her hands folded in her lap. "I couldn't get away. And when I finally *did* get away, Willis was standing on the hill, and I guess he thought I'd been in the shed because I *wanted* to be, not because I was forced to be, and even Daddy didn't believe me. Ouch!"

Mavis had stirred up a small knot with the comb. "Sorry." She couldn't remember anyone forcing Ellie to do anything, but she had missed her sister and wanted to believe her. *Needed* to believe her. "You know what they did to him, don't you?" Her voice cracked. "And to his wife?"

"They shouldn't have done that."

But they did. Because of you.

Why couldn't Ellie just admit it was her fault? Had she ever said she was sorry for anything? But no apology would bring back the lost lives.

Mavis didn't tell Ellie that she'd gone to the bridge after hearing Mamie tell Sliver what had happened. Mavis didn't want to believe her daddy and brother had done what Mamie said. She needed to see for herself, so she'd taken a shortcut through the grove and walked until she saw the bridge's old wooden beams casting a sturdy shadow in the creek. She paused at the bank and kept her eyes cast down, noting how low the water was. Rocks that normally were covered with water stood exposed and dry. When had it last rained?

She scanned the edge of the creek, each time drawing her gaze closer to the bridge.

Look.

Don't look.

Back and forth.

Then higher and higher. Until …

Two pairs of feet were suspended in the air, toes pointing like dancers. One pair had trousers above the ankles. The other pair jutted from beneath a long skirt.

Mavis's eyes crept higher.

Their knees.

Their torsos.

Their frozen expressions.

Their eyes feasted on by birds.

She turned and ran, but some images, once let into the mind, could never be outrun. She saw them again now.

"So now you know, " Ellie said. "You were there for Willis dragging me back to the house. Goodness he was angry, wasn't he?" She laughed, turned around, and took the comb.

"It's not funny."

"*It's not funny,*" Ellie mimicked. Her veil was off. The skin on both cheeks had overlapped and bunched along the cut lines. The scars were thick blood-filled veins. Ellie caught her looking and pulled the veil up again.

"They're not so bad," Mavis said.

"Lying doesn't suit you."

It doesn't suit you either. Mavis sat beside her on the swing again, thinking, what good is beauty on the outside if a person is ugly on the inside? Maybe Ellie's outside matched her inside now.

"When I was in Washington, I put a towel over the mirrors, so I didn't have to see myself. Every morning I washed my face and put some of Mamie's ointment on, hoping that it would help with the scarring. It was a week before I had the courage to take the towel down."

"What happened when you looked?"

"I saw the damage and thought: *Who will have me now?*"

"So you married Willis."

She shrugged. "What would you have done?"

"I'd have contacted my sister and asked for her help."

Ellie laughed. "How would you have helped? By robbing a bank and jumping on a train?"

"You're the one who said I should never throw myself away. You're the one who always talked about love. And look!" She swept her arm out to include everything at the Yates's.

"Circumstances change sometimes. A person has to adapt or die." She pulled a gold cigarette case from her pocket and opened it. "Want one?"

"No!"

Ellie lit a match. "Don't look so shocked, Mavis. I can do whatever I want now. Who do I have to impress?" She drew deeply on the cigarette and exhaled.

Mavis watched the smoke disappear on the breeze. A curtain ruffled in the upstairs window of the house across the way. "Is that where Mrs. Yates lives?"

"Yes. That's the old house. Doesn't it look terrible next to this one? I should ask Willis to build a big fence, so I won't have to look at that eyesore and so she won't be able to spy on me. She hates me. Did you know she stole one of my dresses? I pretended I didn't notice."

"Why would she steal your dress?"

"Who knows? She is of an age where her mind is deteriorating."

Mavis didn't mention seeing the curtain move. "Will you be in trouble for me visiting?"

Ellie shrugged. "I guess I'll find out. There's not much else Willis can do to me now though, is there?"

"No. I guess not." She rested her head on Ellie's shoulder and sighed. "I've missed you. I can't believe you're going to have a baby."

CHAPTER 19

After that first visit, Mavis came around as often as she could and watched Ellie's belly expand like a gourd on the vine. June approached and the rainy season coaxed out blossoms on the Southern Magnolia trees. Inhaling the fragrant scent, Mavis couldn't help but be giddy. She, Mavis Marie Turner, was going to be an Aunt. She wanted to share the good news, but no one at home was allowed to talk about Ellie. But Mamie listened. She had to.

Mavis found Mamie in the kitchen, her sleeves were rolled up to her elbows. Flour covered the part of her apron that had leaned against the counter. She had just finished working four mounds of dough and placed damp towels over each of them for the second rising.

Mavis started talking as soon as she saw Mamie, saying what a wonder that Ellie was having a baby. Could Mamie believe it? Did she guess it would be a boy or a girl? Mavis hoped for a girl. She hadn't thought to ask Ellie what she wanted.

"Enough about that baby," Mamie finally said. "Does Master Willis know you visit?"

"I don't know. He's never there when I go."

"And how do you know he won't be there?"

"Charlie gives me notes. At church. From Ellie. She lets me know when Willis will be away."

"Charlie? The blacksmith?"

Mavis nodded.

"The midwife's boy?"

Mavis had no idea whose boy he was.

"Are you trying to get him killed?"

"I only get notes from him."

"What do you think would happen if Master Willis knew?"

"About the notes?"

"Yes. Think on it. A note, carried by a black man, and written in his wife's hand. We're talking Miss Ellie, who already has a history ..."

"They're only to let me know when he'll be gone!" She hadn't done anything wrong! Why was Mamie angry?

"How old are you now?"

"You know the answer to that. I'm almost sixteen."

"Old enough to know better." Mamie put her face close to Mavis's and spoke real slowly, leaving gaps between each word. "You. Leave. Charlie. Alone. Do you understand me? If you've got notes for your sister, you give them to me. I'll make sure she gets them."

"But how will I get notes from Ellie?"

"I'll figure that out. Maybe from Sliver. Or Mona. Or Beanie even. Doesn't she help out in the kitchen there? But from now on, you give your notes to me. Understand?"

Mavis nodded. She couldn't shake the feeling she'd been accused of something she hadn't done. "Besides," Mamie continued, "I got something for Ellie. For her baby." She rummaged through a cupboard and removed a small patchwork quilt. "It's not much, but it's something. I'll be getting it to her soon."

"That's so nice." Mamie had something for Ellie's baby while her own mama didn't. "Why can't my parents just forgive Ellie? She said what happened with Jedediah wasn't her fault. She just went into the shed to look around."

Mamie stared at her with another hard look. "And you believe her." She said it as a statement.

Did she believe Ellie? She sure wanted to.

"I thought you was clever, but now I have my doubts. Have you got eyes in your head?"

"Where else would they be?"

Mamie didn't laugh. She gestured for Mavis to sit down then sat across from her, putting her elbows on the table and leaning in. "I'm going to say this once, and then I'm not going to speak of it again. Understand?"

Mavis nodded.

"Ellie got caught having relations with Jedediah."

"I know that, but she said Jedediah forced her to."

"She lied."

Mamie was a trusted source; even so, it was hard for Mavis to have her suspicions confirmed. She had assumed she was the only one who knew about Ellie's lying, but if Mamie knew then lots of other folks might too.

Something on the stove started to boil over and Mamie jumped up. She took the lid off the pot and steam rose into the air.

"What about when Ellie met Samuel in the parlour those times? Did she ..."

Mamie was beside her again in an instant, her face twisted into a funny shape. "What did you say?"

"Nothing." She stood up to leave but Mamie grabbed her forearm.

"Ellie took Samuel into the parlour?"

"I thought you knew."

"How would I know?" Mamie made a sweeping gesture with her arm. "You think I have time to watch what's going on around here when I'm working all the time? Why didn't you tell me?"

Why was it so clear now that she should have told Mamie? "I didn't know that I should, I guess. I thought maybe Ellie was just playing a game."

Mamie had stopped listening. She untied her apron and hurried out of the kitchen.

"I'm sorry," Mavis called after her. What would Mamie have done if she'd known sooner?

She climbed the stairs to her room and lay on her bed. She had a sinking feeling in her stomach. Why had she covered for Ellie instead of thinking Samuel might need protecting?

She was of an age that no longer allowed her to use childhood as an excuse. Gertie and George were children. Had she not told Mamie simply because she'd enjoyed having a secret to lord over Ellie? In truth, she hadn't given Samuel much thought at all. But now, knowing what had happened to Jedediah because of Ellie, she understood what Mamie had known from the start: what happened to Jedediah could have happened to her Samuel too.

If Ellie wasn't her sister, she wouldn't like her at all. Nothing was ever her fault, and that meant Ellie was never sorry for anything.

But a baby would offer her a fresh start. Even if she didn't love Willis, having a child to love would focus her attention on something positive. It would give her something to do. It would alleviate the boredom she so hated.

Mavis rolled off the bed and went to apologize to Mamie for not telling her sooner. It crossed her mind that she should apologize to Samuel too, because maybe if she'd said something right away, he wouldn't have had to spend as much time with Ellie. Unless, of course, he'd been there by choice? No. The consequences were too great for him. Plus, she'd seen his shoulders, slouched in defeat. There hadn't been any joy in that room for him, of that she was certain.

Mamie was nowhere to be found, and Mavis quickly gave up looking.

CHAPTER 20

Storm clouds gathered on the western horizon. That's how Sliver knew Master Willis's baby would introduce itself by the end of the day. Everything Miss Ellie did required some kind of fanfare, and there were fireworks threatening the June sky. Thunder. Lightning. And soon, horizontal rain. Nature was gearing up for a show, and Miss Ellie was stepping up to see if she could overshadow it.

In the garden, Sliver worked her fingers around the stems to the base of the weeds to bring the roots out too. She threw them to the side where a small pile grew into a larger pile. As she worked, the tips of her fingers dried out and grew raw. But there was something else, perhaps the quality of the day's light, that released the grief in her bones. It was a flat light that levelled all surfaces like it had on the day Gideon disappeared. He'd walked away, and she'd almost called out to tell him to be careful where he was walking. To watch out for snakes. To not trip over the pocket gophers' mounds and twist an ankle. It was that same kind of light. But he was her man not her child, so she stopped herself from giving counsel. And she never saw him again.

She stood and stretched. Sometimes a thunderstorm came with only one large cloud; other times, thunderstorms brought a family of clouds —cousins, nephews, grandparents, the entire gamut, to join in a family feud. Those were the storms that went on the longest, and as the sky darkened she imagined it was filled with kin. Whose, she didn't know, but already she felt the lift, the updraft so necessary to unleash the storm. How bad would it be? She was grateful not to know what each day would bring because the knowledge might be too much to bear.

Imagine if she'd known about Gideon. *You have four days left together.*
Three days left ... Imagine if she'd known about the coming deaths.

Eight years after Gideon disappeared, influenza arrived like its
own season and killed so many, including two of her children. Willow
was fifteen and Jonah only eleven. Would it have helped to know in
advance? *You have one week left to hug two of your children. You have*
five days left ... *two days left* ...

The sickness had started in the big house with Mrs. Yates and her
son Willis, who was just four years old. They burned with fever and
lost liquid from both ends. Aunt Harriet and Sliver cared for them. It
was a messy business. Then they cared for the many negroes holed up
in their shacks and dying when that fever spread. And then the sickness
came for Sliver's children.

Willow got sick first. Then Jonah. Sliver had never nursed people
so hard in her life, wringing the sickness out of the damp cloth well
away from her shack so it wouldn't find its way back by crawling up
the dry soil to her doorstep. She washed their weakened bodies and
washed them some more to get the germs off, but the sickness had
managed to get inside where she couldn't reach. And she had briefly
reacquainted herself with God, having lost touch after Giddy disappeared, and prayed hard to have her children spared. They were
visible reminders of Gideon; she didn't want to lose any more of him.

So what did she do?

What did she do?

This part pained her.

She offered God Charlie. *Take him instead, but please leave me*
Gideon's babies.

Maybe Charlie knew what she'd prayed for, because she found
him inside the sick room, lying between Willow and Jonah, holding
their hands and calling the sickness out of them.

Willow died first.

"Maybe God only needs one, Mama," Charlie told her.

Jonah died two days later.

By the end of the week, Aunt Harriet was gone too.

Seth, Becky and Charlie survived, and Mrs. Yates and her son too, but a dozen negroes died on the grove and almost every family in town lost people.

She added Willow and Jonah to her list of people who were missing. She didn't forgive God for taking them, but she accepted they were gone. *For you, Gideon. Now you have two and I have two.* Maybe he needed comforting in the afterlife.

For weeks afterwards, every time she looked at Charlie she was ashamed to have offered him up. Hadn't life taught her she didn't get to choose what happened? Didn't she know that by now?

⌐ Raindrops started to fall, thick and heavy. Sliver lifted her face to receive them then heard someone yelling her name.

Mona appeared, saying Miss Ellie's water had broke. "You'd better come. She thinks she's dying."

Sliver knew that first babies took their time, so there was no rush, but the skies were opening up faster, and her work in the garden was done. Miss Ellie had been coddled her whole life, and she was coddled even more here. Sliver knew from Mamie that the Turners hadn't hired full-time help for some time, but Master Yates wanted Miss Ellie to be waited on, so he made Mona his wife's full-time maid. According to Mona, Miss Ellie was impossible to please, which was saying something since Old Lady Yates didn't have much sugar in her.

The clouds dropped even lower in the sky bringing night down early. Electricity danced in the air. Sliver went to get her bag.

"Is it time?" Beanie asked when Sliver came in the kitchen door.

"That's what I came to see. You might as well put some water on to be ready."

"Like I need something else to do."

"How's your mama?"

"Still alive. Barely. Her lungs has just about given out."

Sliver remembered how her eyes and nostrils had burned the first time she'd visited Slew Town, and that was without going near the turpentine vats. Beanie's mama had been stirring those vats for years.

"You tell her I asked about her, okay? And don't forget to put that water on."

Sliver took the stairs from the back kitchen to the second storey. At the top of the stairs she paused and listened. It was eerily quiet. The heavy air, thick with humidity, had gathered in the hallway and muffled all sound. She knocked at Miss Ellie's door. "It's me, Sliver."

There was no reply.

She waited a moment and knocked again. Still no answer. She opened the door slowly, in case Miss Ellie was sleeping, and stepped inside.

It was unnaturally dark, even for a stormy day. The curtains were closed. The still air indicated the window was closed, too. Sliver opened it a crack to let in the rain-soaked air.

"Close it."

She jumped and turned. Miss Ellie's eyes stared dully from her face. It was clear she was scared and exhausted. That didn't bode well. It was too soon for her to be tired. "It's hot in here."

"I like it like that."

"You're going to get hotter in time, and so is this room. If you don't need the fresh air, I do." Sliver the maid couldn't speak her mind, but Sliver the midwife had greater liberty. She walked to the bed and felt for a pulse at Ellie's wrist.

"Where's the doctor?"

"In town."

"Why isn't he here? Willis said he'd get the doctor."

"He can't make it because of the storm," Sliver said, lying. "So I'm here." Somehow Old Lady Yates had talked her son into letting the midwife deliver the baby. *It was tradition*, she said. *It was women's work. Why pay extra when we have a perfectly good midwife on hand?* Sliver had heard those words before but hadn't expected Mrs. Yates to repeat them.

Sliver rested her palm on Miss Ellie's forehead to check her temperature, and her touch set a contraction in motion. Miss Ellie arched her back and grit her teeth as the first wave of pain began. Sliver knew the body started out slowly, to prepare the mother-to-be for the much greater pain coming.

Her stomach growled, and she thought about tomatoes, plump

and juicy inside their impossibly thin skin. The juice of oranges was held in tight by a much thicker skin. A peel. But a tomato? So fragile in its casing. As her hunger grew, she imagined cutting thick slices, laying them out on bread, and watching the salt disappear as it melted into the juices.

Hours passed.

If the sun set, they couldn't tell. It had been dark most of the day.

Beanie brought her a dinner tray and Sliver was grateful.

As Miss Ellie's pain increased, her eyes showed more of their whites like an animal trapped in a barn fire.

Sliver called Beanie to bring the water up. The contractions came faster now. Miss Ellie had less time between them to curse Willis, so she turned her attention on Sliver.

Why can't you make the pain stop?

You're enjoying this, aren't you?

DO something! What are you good for if you can't help?

Sliver squeezed Miss Ellie's hand and told her to keep going. She was doing just fine. Sliver closed her ears to the insults hurled her way. A woman in her darkest pain often said things she didn't mean. Or said things she meant and claimed pain as an excuse afterwards.

At five in the morning, the baby's head crowned.

"Push," Sliver said.

The scars on Miss Ellie's cheeks throbbed like a hose with something stuck inside. Sliver wondered if they'd hold.

Miss Ellie's screams intensified.

"You're almost there," Sliver encouraged. "Push. Push."

The baby slipped out and Miss Ellie fell back onto the pillows in the joyous absence of pain.

Sliver held the newborn, slick from delivery, and marvelled. This was the best part of all, the part she never tired of — holding that new gift in her hands. She cut the cord and began her examination to ensure the baby had all its parts. A little flap of flesh dangled between its legs. Master Willis had wanted a son. At least his wife had done him that kindness.

A moment later, Miss Ellie started moaning again and got all scared, thinking she was having twins. Sliver hid her disbelief. White women didn't tell their daughters nothing. All babies arrived with luggage; delivering the spongy afterbirth didn't hurt near as much or take as long. She gave a light pull on the cord and out it came.

She finished cleaning Miss Ellie and the baby as Mona tidied the room. Then she handed the infant to its mama. "Congratulations. You have a son. I'll let Master Willis know."

Sliver took the pot of pink-tinged water that remained and let herself out.

The temperature in the hall was at least five degrees cooler and a relief. She'd been in Ellie's room since the previous afternoon. Dawn was breaking. Already it was lighter. She'd go to the kitchen first, and then she'd find Master Willis and tell him the good news. Then maybe she'd ask Beanie to make her some breakfast.

CHAPTER 21

Ellie cried fresh tears when the door latched behind the midwife. The indignity of it all! Pushing a baby out like an animal in a field was bad enough, but doing it in front of the midwife? Had Mona been in the room too? And Beanie? It all felt like a blur. Willis said he'd bring the doctor; she didn't believe the storm had stopped him, and that meant it had to be Old Lady Yates's doing. If that proved to be true, Ellie had to admit that Willis's mama might have won this round.

Fatigue didn't allow her anger to fully ignite. There was a baby in her arms. A boy, Sliver had said. He was light as air. His tiny mouth puckered and sucked as if something was stuck on the roof of his mouth.

That had come out of her? No wonder it had hurt. She was both intrigued and repulsed. Delighted and horrified. She wanted her own mama. Or Mavis, someone who loved her fully, who would give an indication of how she was to behave. What she was to do next. She was so alone here. Who loved her? Willis? It didn't count if she didn't love him back.

When she was a child, she had spent many afternoons in Mamie's kitchen. She had felt loved then, or at least she hadn't stopped to question if she *was* loved. She closed her eyes and conjured up the scent of one of Mamie's fruit cobblers coming out of the oven. The golden crust. The soft chewy bits resting in the thick, buttery peach juice. Even when Mavis tried to spoil her pleasure by saying cooked peaches smelled like sweaty feet or dirty socks, Ellie couldn't contain her anticipation. Mavis and Samuel had usually been with her. They'd have finished playing some kind of game and identified their hunger. Those had been good days. The *best* days. What had she wanted then? More. Always more. She always took the largest serving of cobbler with the most cream. She always ate fast to make sure she could have seconds before it ran out.

She hadn't been searching then for a door that would take her to the outside world, to a place where she could live fully and quell the restlessness that burned inside her. Such a fury it was, that restlessness, like dust devils whipped up inside her. Samuel had opened the first door, and Jedediah had opened the second. And she'd walked through both doors and found what? She wiped her nose with the back of her hand and dried it on the bedsheet. Pleasure? Yes, but not the physical pleasure she had hoped for. No, the pleasure had come in having the power to make someone do what she told them to do. She finally understood it was the only power she had.

She was Ellie Louise—her daddy said she could have whatever she wanted. But it wasn't true at all, for apparently she had wanted too much.

The baby's warmth seeped through his blanket and onto her skin. She stared at the newborn and felt a mild amazement. His tiny mouth opened as if to cry. How small his lips were. How very delicate.

Ellie had started out in life just like the baby she held in her arms right now. Tiny and helpless. A daughter to a mother who at that time only had one son. What had her mother felt, holding baby Ellie? Love? If so, where had it gone?

The curtains were still drawn but a soft light illuminated the edges. The sun was making its rise. What day was it? Monday. Yes. *Monday's child is fair of face.* That was true. Her baby was beautiful to look upon.

But this was Willis's son. The child he'd so desperately hoped for and would now celebrate. Willis would dote on the boy. He had gotten what he wanted.

Meanwhile, she had lost everything. Her scars pulsed in time with her heart.

What future did she have but to watch Willis's happiness bloom?

Oh, but the child fit so perfectly in the crook of her arm. He had lovely dark lashes, thick as her own, and tiny, tiny fingernails on impossibly small nail beds. She pushed against her instincts to protect him, to see if they would yield. How long before Willis came into the room, his fat fingers splayed and reaching? His moist lips stretched into a smile?

Ellie undid the quilt that Mamie had stitched with her own hands, the one Mavis had delivered saying it was proof that Mamie still loved her.

The baby's eyes were open but unfocussed. His tiny hands were curled into fists as if he already knew he had a fight ahead.

Ellie wiped at her own tears. Nobody cared about her.

She pulled the baby close to her chest. His soft hair tickled her nose.

Then she thought of Sliver on her way to tell Willis the good news, and a door slammed shut in her mind. The baby would fulfill Willis's ridiculous happily-ever-after narrative — marry Ellie Turner and have a son.

There was no way she'd let Willis win when she had lost so much.

No, not *lost*. When so much had been taken from her.

The baby's skull felt fragile as an eggshell. His black hair was silk beneath her fingertips. His head a melon in her palm. The roundness of bone ... She ran her fingers over his crown until ... There. Yes. There. The soft spot. She pressed down gently. It felt mushy, like the bruised flesh on an apple. She continued to circle the spot and imagined a whirlpool effect, like the eddies in the small channels on Sugar Creek after the rains. How sweet that water, and oh the bruised and malleable flesh.

Ellie lifted the baby and kissed him gently on the cheek. Such a sweet, innocent boy. "I'm sorry," she whispered.

She held his skull in her left hand and covered his soft spot with her right thumb. She watched her thumb sink, like bare feet in mud. Her thumb belonged to someone else, just like the baby belonged to someone else. How curious to watch her thumbnail disappear.

She kept the pressure firm until Willis's son's eyes no longer saw, until his fists stopped moving.

How quickly the breath left his body.

How quickly he became dead weight.

CHAPTER 22

The June sun kept the worst of its heat to itself the afternoon following the baby's death when Master Willis's son was lowered into the ground in his tiny coffin in the cemetery beside the south grove in a plot not far from Willis's father's grave.

The solemnity of the occasion gave Miss Ellie valid reason to dress in black and to wear a dark veil. Only her eyes, wet with tears, or, Sliver thought, shining with satisfaction, were visible.

They were a small crowd at the graveside — the preacher, Master Willis, Miss Ellie, Mrs. Yates, Miss Ellie's sister Mavis, Beanie, and Mona — but the mosquitoes and sand flies found them nonetheless and had them swatting in irritation, willing the preacher to hurry his words.

Sliver saw how tenderly Master Willis put an arm around his wife's shoulder and noted how Miss Ellie tolerated the gesture because of the people who had gathered for the burial. And she recalled Master Willis's words when he'd held his dead son in his arms: *Now I know that the devil is patient.*

Mrs. Yates stood beside the grave and nodded to herself as if she'd predicted her grandson's death and had already been through it. Sliver had stood beside her on the day Miss Ellie arrived. She'd seen the bride dressed in black but hadn't known then that the wedding outfit foreshadowed this grieving. She didn't think like that.

Miss Ellie's sister Mavis was crying as if the baby had been her own, but Sliver knew how easily white women turned on the tears. Typical. The cycle would continue with that one. She was the one who'd put Charlie in danger, passing him notes and not thinking of the trouble that could come his way. Thank God Mamie had told Sliver and made it stop. Did Miss Mavis think Charlie could turn down her request? *No thank you, Miss. I'd rather not deliver the note.* Selfish, selfish, selfish. It made her blood boil. Negroes got killed for less, but Miss Mavis, like her sister, probably wouldn't care.

Right now, Miss Mavis had a handkerchief to her face and was drenching it with tears. It meant nothing. That was just a skill they learned like how to wipe their backsides. When they got caught doing something they shouldn't be doing, they cried and lied and cried and lied. Miss Ellie had cried about her baby, too, but that didn't change the initial impulse to do him harm or the outcome.

Sliver regretted leaving her alone with her baby but knowing that now wasn't worth much. Master Willis had gone out for some air when she went looking for him, likely to keep himself awake after a long night of waiting. It didn't take her long to find him and tell him the good news. Maybe fifteen minutes? They heard Miss Ellie screaming on their way back to the house. When they burst into her room, she held a blue baby towards them and turned on the waterworks.

"Do something!" Master Willis yelled.

Sliver tried. Oh yes, she tried. For the baby. For Master Willis. But a baby that blue wasn't about to turn white again. Even so, she scooped him up, pushed air into his lungs, massaged his chest, and did everything she could short of substituting another white baby in its place. Finally, she shook her head and said she was sorry.

She carried the infant into the room next door to leave the grieving parents to their pain. Now that she was alone, she put the baby on the bed and lifted each limb, looking for signs that would explain the situation. He'd been fine when she left him. She was certain he'd been perfectly healthy. Her investigation showed nothing until she looked at his skull.

Sliver's eyes locked with Ellie's at the graveside. A current of information passed between them in seconds, and Sliver saw the recognition dawn in Miss Ellie's eyes before she turned away.

Behind the preacher, Mrs. Yates continued to look spiteful. For a minute, Sliver considered the thumb print might be hers.

The year was 1936. The preacher threw some dirt down, and the family members followed suit.

The sound of dirt hitting a coffin never changed. It was one of the saddest sounds Sliver knew. She hadn't been able to do that for Gideon because there'd been no body. And because there'd been no body, there'd been no ceremony to mark the event. Which meant Sliver didn't have a gravesite to visit to pay her respects. But she'd thrown dirt down on Willow and Jonah and been happy, then, that Gideon had been spared that grief.

Twenty-six years she'd been without him. Master Willis had been a baby himself. Miss Ellie hadn't even been born yet, and Charlie was still a half-formed thing inside her.

She looked at the cemetery and thought it was like a garden.

Only in this case, as the coffin was lowered and covered with dirt, a seed was being planted to grow a child.

And that seed, if watered and cared for, would grow into a boy.

That's how Sliver knew more boys were coming — because the soil was so rich here, and because the world was full of gardeners.

CHAPTER 23

The tropical storm that made landfall before Ellie's baby's birth and death brought high winds that took down many branches in the Turners' orchards and flooded low lying fields. June was always a rainy month, and the high humidity and heat made time move as if it was making its way through molasses.

Mavis visited her sister daily after the funeral because Willis hoped company would help his wife move through her grieving. Ellie mostly sat in the rocking chair she had planned to nurse her baby in, as if rocking were a form of transportation that would take her away from her current situation. But the chair stayed in the room and didn't take her anywhere, and her arms were empty save for Mamie's quilt that she held in her lap.

"The preacher wanted to visit," Ellie said, "but I wouldn't receive him. His God is a punishing God that keeps track of people's wrongdoings. I don't want to hear him trot mine out as if he knows me."

"You're not being punished."

"How do you know? Maybe I am."

"God doesn't sacrifice babies to teach adults lessons."

"He sacrificed his own son."

"But he wasn't a baby."

"Do you think it's better to let him grow up and *then* kill him?"

"God didn't kill his own son."

"He let it happen. What's the difference?"

Mavis wanted to argue but wasn't sure God's watching his son be killed was any better.

Mona knocked at the door and brought in a tray of lemonade. A turquoise cloth runner lined the tray.

"Where did that come from?" Ellie asked, pointing at the cloth.

"Mrs. Yates gave me and Beanie some material a while ago to make napkins, runners, and rags." She handed Ellie a glass as if she was an invalid.

Ellie took a sip and made a face. "It needs more sugar. How many times do I have to tell you I like my lemonade sweet?"

"I'll go get some," Mona said.

"Never mind, just go." Ellie waved her off. When she was gone, Ellie pointed at the runner on the tray. "Remember how I said one of my dresses went missing? That's the material. You heard Mona. The old lady gave it to her. That's proof she stole my dress. She does it to get under my skin. I told you she hates me. Why would she do this now? After I've lost a child?" She started to cry.

"Oh, Ellie. I'm sorry. I'd be upset too, but Mona said it was from a while ago. I don't think she'd do it now, given what you've been through. I can't imagine why she'd be so mean. Do you want me to talk to Willis?"

"No! I won't give her the satisfaction of thinking I'm upset. I'll just have to find a way to get back at her, that's all."

Mavis recognized the look of determination that crossed Ellie's face. "You shouldn't be thinking about revenge right now. You need to be resting up."

She snorted. "For what? I hate this place. The only time I get to escape is when I'm sleeping. The trouble is, I always wake up. Has Daddy asked about me yet? Or Mama?"

Mavis thought about lying but didn't. "No."

"Do they know my baby died?"

"I can't say for certain, but I suspect they've heard from someone in town. Do you want me to bring you anything on my next visit?"

Ellie shook her head. "There's nothing to bring."

"You look pale. Maybe you should nap. I'll come back tomorrow or the next day, okay?" Mavis stayed until her sister lay down and turned her back to the room.

Her mama was waiting for her when she returned home.

"There you are. Why is it I can never find you when I want you? Where have you been anyway?"

"Out walking, Mama."

"In this heat? Where?" She tucked a loose strand of hair back into her bun.

"Down by Sugar Creek."

"As long as you're not over at the Yates's."

It was as close as she came to saying Ellie's name. Mavis decided to risk asking. "Have you heard any news about what's going on over there?"

Mrs. Turner pretended she hadn't heard and plumped the flowers in a vase. "You'll be running your own home soon, and I don't believe you're ready for it yet."

Mavis thought of Mona bringing Ellie lemonade and Ellie reaching out her hand to take it. That didn't take much preparation. "I'm sure I'll be fine when the time comes. *If* the time comes."

"It'll come all right, and maybe sooner than you think."

It was the way her mama said it that gave Mavis pause.

"You're not some rogue beast, Mavis, available to roam wherever and whenever you want. You need to start acting your age."

Mavis exaggerated her age when she wanted to be older and minimized it when she didn't. "I'm only fifteen."

"Not for much longer. You heard about Amy Everett?"

Amy was the same age as Ellie. The girls in town made fun of the undertaker's daughter, saying she held séances in her bedroom, conjuring up the souls of the dead bodies chilling in her basement.

"Last year, Amy told her mama she'd rather be tarred and feathered than marry. Imagine, a girl not wanting to marry. What other prospects would she have? She can't live at home her whole life, preparing dead bodies for burial. It makes me squirm just thinking about it. In any case, she's finally come to her senses. She's to marry the druggist's son next week."

"Bobby Alexander?" He had tied frogs to the train tracks when he was younger. "Why on earth would she do that? He's an awful human being."

"Perhaps your standards are too high, Mavis. Time will take care of that. I'm having some of the ladies over for tea this afternoon, and I'd like you to serve us."

"Oh Mama, please. I would prefer not to. Can't Mamie to do it? Or Cadence?"

"I did not ask if you wanted to, Mavis. It's a skill you need to learn. Now go and freshen up. And put that green dress on. It's such a lovely colour with your eyes. Be ready for 2:30."

There was no escape. And the green dress had been lovely with Ellie's eyes.

"Mrs. Thorpe is coming," her mama said.

Mavis froze. The sheriff's wife?

"She's looking forward to talking with you."

Mavis spun around. "To me?"

Her mama had one hand raised in the air, her palm facing Mavis. "I don't want to hear it. It's time to face your responsibilities. Your daddy and I ..."

"Mama, if this has anything to do with Danny Thorpe, I don't like him. I *more* than dislike him, I ..."

"I said Mrs. Thorpe is coming to tea. I never said she was bringing her son."

Because you didn't have to.

"I regret not guiding Ellie more," she said, surprising Mavis by saying her sister's name, "and I will not make that mistake again."

"The mistake was Daddy making Ellie marry Willis against her will!"

"A girl needs to know she has security ahead, Mavis. That comes from marriage."

Security? How could her mama talk about security when her own husband had been selling off land for years to make ends meet and, if what Ellie said was true, selling off a daughter, too? Was *that* security? It looked more like it was *children* who bought security, daughters to marry men with money and sons to attract women with money. The last time her mama bought a new dress was after Ellie was married off to Willis.

"I don't need security, Mama." *I can always go live with Ellie.*

"This is not just about you, Mavis. Your father and I make decisions for the good of the family. The Turner name and reputation had been built up over generations. *Generations.* And your sister damaged it in a single day. I will *not* have people whispering behind my back or thinking Gertie and George deserve less all because of Ellie's inability to curb her base instincts. She is making us all do more work because of her selfishness, and that's not anybody's fault but hers. So I suggest you direct your anger at your sister and not at me. In the meantime, those of us left in the wreckage will do what we must to set things right." She brushed her palms together as if she'd just completed a job that pleased her.

Mavis glimpsed the map in her mama's mind. Ellie's marriage to Willis had brought them money, but Mavis's marriage to the sheriff's son would restore the Turner name in the community. The sheriff would never allow anyone to speak ill of the Turners if his own son was married to one. What Ellie had taken from them, Mavis would return.

"Mama. Please. Don't make me..."

"You will serve tea today in the parlour at 2:30, and you will not disgrace me. Do you understand?"

She nodded.

"Good. Now go and get ready. And for goodness' sake, run a comb through your hair."

Mavis left.

Nothing good ever went on in the parlour.

CHAPTER 24

Danny Thorpe had been born with an extra set of hands; Mavis could only keep her eyes on one pair at a time. She'd never done so much swatting in her life as she'd done since Danny started coming around. Chiggers and mosquitoes were one thing; Danny was another kind of pest all together. Her parents had come to some agreement with the Thorpes that found Mavis in Danny's company far too often in the months after she served tea. When forced to be with him, Mavis spent much of her time pointing out the attributes of other young women in Neelan Junction. Didn't Betsy Hargraves cook a beautiful cake? And poor Posey, her husband so recently killed in a train wreck. She must be lonely. Was it true she was with child? A wife, a widow, and a mama all in the same year. She certainly could use a man to help her.

But Danny paid Posey no mind and talked as if she was somehow responsible for her misfortunes.

"How was Posey supposed to know that train was going to crash?" Mavis asked. "Are you saying it's her fault that her husband died?"

"I'm saying didn't she ever wonder why he was on the train so much?"

"What do you know that you're not saying?"

"Only that Silas Grove was not an honest man." Danny had her arm tucked into his and gripped it tight. They walked down Main Street, nearing Alexander's Drug Store where some of his friends loitered outside. He lowered his voice. "My daddy did some investigating. Turns out Silas Grove had another wife in Fort Lauderdale."

"No! I wouldn't believe everything I heard if I was you. How could he marry Posey if he was already married? That's illegal."

"He could if nobody knew. He liked to gamble, and he was in debt. That's a bad combination. After the marriage, Mr. Jones noticed his store was going into the red. Apparently Silas was helping himself to the money."

Mavis sniffed the air to see if Danny had been drinking.

"He had poker debts with some of the boys here, too, and the son-of-a-bitch died before paying up."

Mavis bristled at his language. If Danny wasn't trying to impress her now, in the early stages of their courtship, then he likely wouldn't try to impress her later.

Danny steered her towards his friends, young men like him, who smelled of cigars and whiskey and who took up more space than their bodies required. "When you're living in town, you'll know more about what's going on."

"I don't want to live in town. I'm fine where I am."

"Well your daddy's not fine with it."

"What's that supposed to mean?"

"You'll soon be too old to be living with your parents."

"I disagree."

"Your daddy's probably afraid you'll head to the shacks like Ellie. Didn't she start going when she was your age?"

Mavis tried to pull her arm away, but he had a firm grip.

"That's why I'm going to marry you — to put a stop to that kind of talk."

"Ellie's baby died, Danny. Show some respect."

He snorted. "She can't even do that right."

Mavis ripped her arm out of his. "What did you say?"

"Nothing. Plus, that happened a while ago."

"There's no time limit on grief, Danny. People should just mind their own business, keep their opinions to themselves, and worry about their own petty little lives. I've already told you I don't want to marry you."

Danny laughed. He had a beautiful smile; she'd give him that, even with that chip in his right front tooth. "It's not up to you, Mavis. It's up to me."

⌐ In the days that followed, Danny continued to insert himself into her days. Sheriff Thorpe came by one afternoon and met with her daddy behind closed doors. That made Mavis nervous, but even suspecting she was the topic of conversation, she was surprised at breakfast a few days later to see a headline in the paper announcing her engagement to Danny Thorpe. Nobody had even spoken to her about it! Her hands shook as she skimmed the article to see if a date had been set. Mavis hadn't wanted to believe Ellie when she said they were Daddy's property, to do with as he saw fit, but the evidence was obvious now.

She left the house before her mama came downstairs and made her way to the Yates's.

Mona let her in. Ellie was in the living room. It was filled with cigarette smoke. The curtains were half drawn; the sunbeams illuminated the smoke and dust, making them appear inseparable. Ellie was seated on the couch. She put a fresh cigarette to her lips and lit it from the butt of the previous one. She was still dressed head to toe in black, and for a moment Mavis's problems seemed small. She stood in the doorway and waited. "Ellie?"

Her sister gestured for her to come in.

"I'm glad to see you out of your room. Are you feeling any better?" Such a stupid question. What did *better* mean in this circumstance?

"Not really, no." Ellie exhaled a thick cloud.

"Did you hear the news?"

"If by news you mean your engagement, of course I heard. I read the paper. I suppose congratulations are in order, although I never would have pictured you with Danny Thorpe."

"That's not funny. Congratulations are *not* in order. You, of all people, should know that. I don't know what to do, Ellie."

"I don't think you have any options."

"There has to be. Aren't there always? What if you told Willis you needed money for something, and we ran away?"

"You and your running away. Is that your only solution to things?

There is no running away, Mavis. I should know. Willis already brought me back once. Plus, do you think the sheriff would allow Danny to be embarrassed that way? The wedding has already been announced. That means it will happen."

Rage bubbled inside her. Was she to be helpless? "I hate this! Can't you at least *pretend* for a minute that I might get out of it? It's not fair. I've never done anything wrong."

"Never done anything wrong?" Ellie snorted. "Is that the measure you're using, whether you've done something wrong or not? Because that suggests you think I deserved to be married off to Willis."

"Of course not, but you did give Daddy some cause to be angry. That doesn't mean I'm saying he was right, but you shouldn't have been sneaking around."

"Sneaking around? On my own property?"

"It's his property, not yours, and what would you call being in the shed with Jedediah? Or the parlour with Samuel? If it wasn't sneaking around, then why was the door locked?"

"Well, maybe it *was* a bit sneaky." The corner of her mouth turned up and she laughed. "Oh come on," she said when Mavis didn't join her. "We are both leading lives we never wanted. What is there to do but laugh? Crying hurts the head after a while. You think because you never gave Daddy cause to be angry that you'll somehow be treated differently? What I've been trying to tell you for years is that Daddy can do whatever he wants with you. Just like he did to me. Remember how he used to own two hundred and fifty acres? Willis told me he's down to thirty now. He's lost two hundred and twenty acres! Daddy borrowed too much from the bank and couldn't repay it. So if he can't make money off his harvest, he'll have to make money off of us. We are his human harvest, Mavis. Or his human livestock if you will."

Mavis let that sink in. She wished someone would open a window. Her eyes watered from the smoky air. "What am I going to do?"

"You'll do what I do and what most women do: make the most of it."

"How are you making the most of it? You never even leave your property. Have you been to town since you married?"

Ellie pulled her gold cigarette case from her skirt pocket and tossed it into Mavis's lap. "I make the most of it by finding things I want and getting them. Plus, there's this." She gestured to her face. "I won't give people the satisfaction of pitying me."

"But what if I don't want anything?"

"Everybody wants something, Mavis. Even if it's only to make someone else miserable. Do you know Willis asked me the other day if I was happier now that you can visit. He told me he just wants me to be happy. Can you believe it? Happy!"

"What did you say?"

"I told him it's a bit late for that."

Ellie's comment, in a strange way, helped Mavis. Why fight if there was no way out? Ellie had taken a train to get away from marrying Willis, and that hadn't worked.

Mavis strolled through the field and kept her eyes on the ground to watch for snakes. She kicked at a rock that was heavier than she thought and hurt her toe. If marrying Danny Thorpe made her parents happy, or in some way contributed to Gertie and George having a better life, then maybe it was her duty. She would accept her lot. She would become one of the town women who volunteered at the library and at church socials. She would add her name to a list and deliver food to families who'd welcomed newborns or suffered misfortunes.

It didn't matter whether she looked forward to something or dreaded it because it would all come and go. The sun rose. The sun set. The moon waxed. The moon waned. The mares foaled. The birds migrated. The orange trees flowered, and the blossoms turned into fruit that ripened and fell. The wedding would come and go too. Her *life* would come and go. Mavis Turner or Mavis Thorpe. At least her initials wouldn't change. Did it matter what her corpse was called as it was lowered into the ground? She would carve some purpose out of a life she would never have chosen for herself. She would work hard to find some happiness in her lot.

CHAPTER 25

Ellie had used the occasion of her baby's death to move Willis out of her bedroom. She would make her grief last as long as possible if it meant keeping Willis out of her bed.

And she did grieve. Her heart was not made of stone. She had buried her child and entered another season since throwing dirt down on his impossibly small coffin. Looking at her hands folded in her lap, she marvelled at what they'd done. The image of a thumb disappearing surfaced often in her mind. That thumb hadn't been hers, had it? It was the trauma of childbirth that had distorted her thinking. Maybe if Sliver had given her something to eat before leaving her alone with the baby, she would have had a clearer mind. Because she would never do that to a helpless little baby.

The midwife knew. When their eyes had locked at the funeral, Sliver hadn't dropped her gaze like she used to.

Initially, Ellie had worried she'd tell Willis, but nobody would take a negro's word over a white person's. Sliver could be killed for accusing her of such a heinous crime. For lying. For even *insinuating*. Still, Ellie had prepared her story, to be ready, just in case, but Willis had never questioned her.

The rocking chair sat before her bedroom window and offered a view of activities that occurred at the front of the house. She rocked in it now and blew smoke towards the open window. Joseph Mark Yates. That's the name she'd requested for her baby's tombstone. June 15, 1936 – June 15, 1936. A perfect repetition, the month and numbers centred so neatly beneath his name. And fifteen letters in his name, to match the numbered day.

The poor boy. It wasn't his fault. That's what was hard, and in navigating the emotions around mourning for her baby, Ellie built an even greater case against Willis. It was *his* fault she had done what she'd done, and it pained her that he didn't even know what he was responsible for.

The first anniversary of her baby's death came and went. Ellie hadn't let Willis return to her bedroom yet even as more months passed.

She could see the barn door from her bedroom window, just behind the old house. It opened and Willis led his prize stallion out, its flanks muscular and defined. Was he going riding? Enjoying himself so soon? He was free from the guilt of killing his child. Who was he talking to? His mother crossed the courtyard and stood near him.

Ellie's resentment sparked and flared. Mrs. Yates hadn't even acknowledged her at the funeral. Their silent war continued. If losing a baby didn't elicit any kindness from her, then nothing would. If she had only said she was sorry for her loss, Ellie would have melted into her arms.

She wiped angrily at her tears. Was she that hungry for kindness that she'd accept it from Willis's mother? Yes. She would have. But that moment had passed.

My mama says you think you're too good for me.

Your mama's right.

The blacksmith came out of the barn carrying Willis's saddle. Some discussion followed as he put the saddle on, cinched the girth snuggly, and held the horse's bridle as Willis mounted. What was his name again? She searched her mind. Mona had extended her hand with the note. *Charlie gave me this, from your sister.*

Charlie — the midwife's bright-skinned boy.

Ellie's isolation continued. She wasn't invited to Mavis's wedding. She had hoped for the opportunity to turn down the invitation, but instead, she read about the event in the paper: who was in attendance, what food was served, and what the bride wore. The only thing that choked her up was reading how cute Gertie and George had looked in their little outfits. She missed them, even if they had been annoying, but she wouldn't want them to see her now. She was glad that, in whatever memory they had of her, she was still beautiful.

When Mavis was finally free to visit, she arrived not by foot through the path that joined the orchards but by carriage from town, sitting stiffly on the front bench, the reins clutched in fists as if she expected the horse to bolt at any moment. Ellie watched from the window as the blacksmith took Mavis's horse. She put out her cigarette and went down to the porch.

"Well, if it isn't Mrs. Danny Thorpe." Ellie hugged her. "Mavis was so much easier to say. Only two syllables instead of five. I'm sorry I missed your wedding. I might have come if I'd been invited."

"And I might have invited you if I'd been allowed," Mavis said with a hint of a smile.

It was close to eighty degrees. The sun was directly overhead, but there was a light breeze. "Let's sit outside. I read about the wedding in the paper. It sounded lavish."

Mavis laughed. "You and your vocabulary. Washington, DC was 'divine.' My wedding was 'lavish.' If that means fancy, then yes, it was as fancy as anything can be in this town. Danny and his friends were loud and unmannered. The sheriff gave a long-winded speech about the need to exert vigilance. He kept referring to the riot in Rosewood, as if Neelan Junction was under threat. I had to get Danny to explain it to me later. Did you know about Rosewood?"

"Only that two people were murdered."

"More than that. Danny said lots of negroes were killed."

"I wasn't counting them."

"It happened in 1923. Rosewood's in Levy County. Danny said it started because some negroes complained about a lynching. Did you know that?"

"No. I was six in 1923. I wasn't reading the paper then."

"We wouldn't know much about much if we had to read the paper to know things. Ellie. Anyway, the sheriff went on so long I started to think the wedding was just an opportunity for him to make a campaign speech."

"Poor you. The sheriff always has to be the centre of attention, no matter where he is or what the occasion."

"It takes one to know one." Mavis laughed.

"What's that supposed to mean?"

"Nothing, Ellie. Don't be so touchy."

"Who says I'm touchy?" She tried to ignore the comment. "Well I hope the food was at least good."

"To be honest, I don't remember much. Did you hear that Amy Everett married Bobby Alexander?"

"Yes. Why on earth would she do that?"

"As if you have to ask, *Mrs. Yates.*"

"Don't call me that. I am not Willis's mother, *Mrs. Thorpe.*"

"It's awful, isn't it, to be called by the name of your husband's mother?"

"It is, but never mind. Tell me, what's it like with Danny, anyway? The being married part?"

Mavis blushed.

Ellie laughed. "The dogs and cats do it in the barn, the horses and cows do it in the field ..."

"I get it."

"And the men and women ...

"Stop!"

"Oh my!" Ellie put a hand to her heart in mock exaggeration. "You are worse than Mama. At least she has age as an excuse for her modesty."

"*Modesty is a sign of refinement,*" Mavis said, mimicking her mama.

"*Repeat after me, girls,*" Ellie added. "*Above all—virtue, restraint, prudence, and modesty!*" She shook her head. "All that talk of virtue over accomplishments was enough to drive me mad." She ran her hands through her hair and let some strands fall to the porch for the wind or for someone else to clean up. "Does Danny at least treat you with respect?"

Mavis stared at her hands.

"You can tell me," Ellie said and waited. "No? Okay, did he ever tell you the story of how his front tooth got chipped?"

"He said from wrestling."

"Well, that's one word for it I guess." Ellie pushed the cuticles back on her fingernails.

"What's that supposed to mean?"

"Speaking of Amy reminded me of it. At a dance a few years back, she wound up and smacked him one."

"Amy Everett? Hit Danny?"

"Do you know another Amy?"

"I can't picture her doing that. Why?"

"Because he was trying to take liberties," Ellie said.

"With her?"

"With her maid."

"Amy's maid was at the dance?"

Ellie rolled her eyes. "Of course not. I think the dance was the first time Amy had seen Danny since he'd tried to take liberties with her maid."

Mavis still looked confused.

"Don't play stupid, Mavis. You really are gullible. Do I have to spell it out for you?"

"No."

"Good. Amy really wound up. It's a wonder she didn't break her hand. She's such a meek creature. I think I've only heard her speak a few times."

"I bet she's even quieter since marrying Bobby, trying to get a word in edgewise," Mavis said. The sisters made their "eating a lemon" face.

The clouds moved in. October would be rainy. It wasn't until mid-November that hurricane season officially ended. They sat quietly in the swing, enjoying the breeze.

Mavis finally broke the silence. "What are you thinking?"

"I'm thinking about you and me being married and the different set of rules that gives men the freedom to pursue pleasure but punishes women. What are you thinking?"

"That I'd like some lemonade."

"You're so easily pleased." Ellie called Mona to bring some.

"And what you said isn't entirely right," Mavis added. "The different set of rules gives white men freedom, not all men." She had never told her sister about seeing their daddy emerge from Mamie's shack. "Don't forget what happened to Jedediah."

"That doesn't count."

"Why not?"

"Daddy always said negroes aren't to be trusted."

"Daddy says a lot of things that aren't true, but that doesn't mean we have to believe them, does it? One of the good things about growing up is having the ability to make up your own mind about things instead of believing what other people tell you."

"I've always made up my own mind," Ellie said. "You're a little slow to the gate."

"Well, not everything you say is true either. Remember how you said our lives would be more interesting if we lived in town? Well, I'm living in town now, and my life's not interesting at all."

"It's your own fault if you aren't having an interesting life. You'll never be as pretty as me, but at least you can go out in the world and not have people gawk at you."

"Is that supposed to make me feel better? Look at us. You don't like Willis and I don't like Danny. And I'm quite sure poor Amy never wanted to marry Bobby. Is there no love in the world?"

"Maybe that's why people read books," Ellie said, "to find a world in which love *does* exist."

"Well if it's only in books, then I guess you won't be finding it, will you?"

"Laugh if you will. I know how to read; I just choose not to." She patted her pockets and looked beneath the swing. "Have you seen my cigarette case? I can't seem to find it."

"Did you ask Mona?"

"Mona probably stole it. All I can say is life is what you make it, Mavis. You have to make your own opportunities."

"Maybe I don't know how."

Ellie shrugged. "Maybe you could learn."

CHAPTER 26

Mavis took the reins from Charlie's hands and remembered the notes she'd once tucked inside them. Mamie had called him the midwife's boy and accused her of trying to get him killed. "Thank you."

He nodded and turned back to the barn. She flicked the reins and set the horse in motion. Being around Ellie made her doubt the things she thought she knew or have questions about things she didn't know. Why had she never heard about Amy punching Danny? Or Danny taking liberties with Amy's maid? And how sad that she wasn't surprised. Did all the men she know take such liberties?

On her wedding night, Mavis had worn the white lace nightgown her mama had given her and wondered why, if men were animals, she was wearing lace. A suit of armor might have been more appropriate. As she waited for Danny, she remembered Ellie saying that one day a man would arrive to put out her fire. She wished she'd asked what a woman was to do if there wasn't any fire to put out.

Danny had delivered her home and gone out with some friends after their wedding reception. Mavis waited up for him but finally fell asleep. It was almost dawn when she heard something being dragged across the porch just outside her window. That something turned out to be a drunken Danny. His friends stripped him and put him into bed before leaving as quietly as liquored men can leave. Mavis had neighbours to be embarrassed about now. Had everyone been wakened by the commotion?

She sat in the chair in the corner of her bedroom and stared at the man her parents had made her marry who lay snoring in bed. He smelled of alcohol, cigarettes, underarm sweat, and the faintest hint of urine. The sheets would have to be washed. She hoped he wouldn't vomit. At some point she fell asleep again, sitting propped in the chair.

Too soon, kitchen noises woke her. Danny's childhood maid, Carlina, had arrived. She'd been one of their wedding presents. Mavis didn't know how that worked, giving a person as a gift. Did the sheriff pay her wages? Was that the gift part? Did she even *get* wages? Mavis dressed quietly in the bathroom and went into the kitchen.

"Good morning."

Carlina nodded.

"I'm Mavis."

"I know."

Mamie would already have a pot of water boiling on the stove, ready to drop an egg into it. "Could I have some breakfast? Toast and a poached egg?" She wasn't used to asking and felt like an intruder in her own home. Her mama hadn't prepared her for how to handle help.

Carlina delivered her breakfast to the dining room; the toast was overdone, and the egg yolk was cooked hard. Mavis salted it liberally and tried not to feel sorry for herself. She could forgive a lot of things in life, but a hard yolk was not one of them.

When she finished eating, she walked from one room to another. Thankfully, all the rooms spilled into a hallway, so she could move from one into another in a circular route without having to retrace her steps. When she got dizzy, she could change directions. What was a new wife to do? She wished Lucky had come with her. Danny had forbidden it. He said town people didn't have pets in the house. He said the cat was better off having a barn to catch mice in. He was probably right, but that didn't stop her from missing Lucky's engine in her lap.

It was noisier in town than at home. Voices travelled, as well as the sound of carriages and the occasional car. She looked out the window. Here, it wasn't workers making the noise, but townspeople walking about and doing their errands. How odd to be so close to the shops and not have to arrange to make the trip. She could go out right now and visit the bakery, the butcher shop, the general store, and the post office and be back within the hour. Or she could make individual trips to each place and spread out her errands.

Carlina crashed about in the kitchen as she worked. If it was Mamie, Mavis would have someone to talk to. Perhaps she would visit the library and ask Danuta Duncan if she required any help or if she knew where she might volunteer her services. Not keeping an eye on Gertie and George would add hours to her day, let alone not being at her mama's beck and call.

Her breakfast had long since digested by the time Danny made groaning noises from the bedroom. Was that a summons? How was she to know? Anxiety grew in her stomach as she waited, but he remained quiet. When he finally did get up, he looked bloated and sick. There was a slight yellow tinge to his complexion. Carlina fussed over him like he was a little boy, swearing that the strong coffee, greasy eggs, and burnt toast she was about to make would soak up his sick like sawdust and help him to feel better.

The house felt too small with Danny in it. When he stood in a doorway, he stood in the middle of it, so nobody could get by. When he sat on a couch, he took the centre space and sprawled. She felt him watching her. Did he regret their marriage too?

Carlina called him to the table. Mavis sat with him while he ate and made small talk. What were his plans for the day? Did he have any work to do? What did he want Carlina to make for supper?

He ate quickly, washed each forkful down with coffee, and slowly began to look better. When he finished, Carlina topped his coffee once more and took his dishes to the kitchen. Mavis got up to go to the bathroom. Danny was waiting for her when she came out, blocking the hallway. Before she knew what he was doing, he spun her around and pinned her against the wall. Carlina was doing dishes on the other side, so Mavis didn't cry out as Danny lifted her skirt and thrust into her.

It happened too fast for her to react. She hadn't imagined it this way at all.

He finished quickly. "There. Now it's official."

Tears burned her eyes. She returned to the bathroom to clean herself. The humiliation was greater than she'd imagined. *Men are animals, that's all you need to know.* Her mama's words made more sense now. Was that how Danny intended to win her affection? She stayed in the bathroom for over an hour, playing a series of scenarios out in her mind, from engaging in violent acts of bloodshed to complete avoidance. In the end, she decided to do what she'd seen her own mama do her whole life, pretend nothing had happened and find ways to endure.

Danny didn't touch her again for weeks.

⤙ Her days in Neelan Junction passed slowly. Slew Town provided a constant drama. When the stories were particularly violent, Mavis looked to the back page obituary section in *The Neelan News* where negroes were allowed to list their dead. From there, she'd turn to the auctions, to see whose property or equipment was up for sale. Then she might read the editorial, to see what Eddie Dumfrey had to say. He had inherited the paper and the editorial role from his father. The *old* Mr. Dumfrey lacked imagination. His headlines had been staid and matter-of-fact. But Eddie, who was not much older than Danny, enjoyed seeing people fight. His headlines read like small explosions.

Mavis always got to the paper first in the mornings as she was out of bed earlier than Danny, stepping over the clothes he'd dropped on the floor. Often they were blood-stained.

Negro Rape Fiend Meets Justice
As long as white women are the target of rape by coloured men, then lynching will remain a necessary pastime.

What had happened this time? The story didn't provide enough details. And what did the reporter mean by a necessary pastime? Perhaps *popular* was a better word. When was lynching necessary?

Large Crowd Expected in Fort Lauderdale. Nathan Jones to be Lynched ...

For what? Again, the story didn't give an explanation. It only listed train departure times and advertised group rates. The school was to be closed for the day in order for children to make the trip with their parents.

Mavis turned to the editorial page and was pleased to find a letter from Mrs. Booth, who had moved to Neelan Junction the previous year from Orlando. Her husband, Edwin Booth, was the new banker. He had replaced Mr. Brantford, whose wife had run off with the schoolteacher, Mr. Mays, and disgraced the family. Sad as it was for the Brantford children, Mavis couldn't help but admit the letter section had become more interesting since the Booths' arrival.

> *Dear Editors,*
>
> *I am appalled by your obvious desire to create tensions between the races. A person reading your paper would think he lived in the Dark Ages. As far as I can tell,* The Neelan News *simply makes up stories to promote racial violence and further Klan propaganda. That is not the mark of strong reporting but rather the mark of inadequate fabricating. A newspaper in this day and age should not celebrate that Florida led the nation in lynchings per capita from 1900–1930. You are in the business of reporting news, not conjuring fantasies. If I wanted to read fictional tales, I would subscribe to a literary publication. I shall cancel my subscription immediately if the paper does not begin to* report *rather than to* make up *its news.*
>
> *Sincerely,*
> *Mrs. Edwin Booth*

Florida had led the nation in lynchings? Mavis read the letter again and marvelled at the woman's bravery. Where did she get her courage?

Danny came into the dining room and dropped heavily into his chair. He reached for the paper. "Anything interesting?"

"Just the usual."

He turned to the letter page. "Mrs. Booth. What's the windbag saying today?" He read for a bit then snorted. "Why doesn't she celebrate that we lead the country in orange production?"

"I kind of enjoy her letters."

"*Inadequate fabricating.* She must take her dictionary out to write like that. Just because she's from the big city doesn't mean she gets to rub our noses in things. She's no better than any of us."

Carlina brought his meal in. Danny filled his mouth and barely chewed before swallowing and filling it up again. Mavis turned away.

"What's your problem?"

Sparrows chirped loudly in the tree outside the window. *You're my problem.* "I think Mrs. Booth is right. The paper has gotten much worse since Eddie took it over these past months. Why doesn't he write about the coincidence of black sharecroppers disappearing while still being owed wages? Why isn't he the least bit critical of the recent lynchings?"

"It's called keeping the peace, Mavis, but you wouldn't understand."

"Why wouldn't I understand? And whose peace?"

Danny looked at her with irritation. "*Our* peace. Do you have any idea how hard it is to protect what's ours?"

What did he see that she didn't? She thought of Mamie and Samuel and Sliver and Faith and Cadence and Mona and Beanie and Charlie and the many, many negroes she'd seen working over her lifetime who hadn't been any trouble at all. "I just can't see how it's that much work, Danny. The ones I know just do what's asked of them and then go home." *If they're not interfered with.*

He stared at her as if she hadn't bathed in months. "Some days I don't think it's worth it."

"Don't think what's worth it? Keeping them in check?"

"No. Taking that allowance."

"What are you talking about?"

Carlina came in to take the dishes.

"Why do you think I married you?"

Mavis waited until Carlina left to respond. "I have no idea why you married me. I tried my best to change your mind."

"Yeah, well, it wasn't my idea either. I did it for the money, that's all."

"What money?"

He wiped the grease from his mouth with a napkin and stared at her as if she was intentionally being difficult.

"I honestly have no idea what you're talking about."

"Every month, your daddy gives me money. In return, I take care of any business that might come up."

Now she was even more confused. "What business might come up?"

"Reputation business. If Daddy hears that anyone is talking about Ellie in a negative light, he gets me and the boys to pay them a visit."

None of this made any sense. "But my family doesn't have any money."

"It's no wonder women aren't in business. I'll make this as simple for you as possible. Willis bought a large part of your daddy's grove when he married Ellie."

"To pay you?"

"No, to pay for Ellie. That was enough for your daddy to put a down payment on this house, pay me an allowance, pay off his other debts, and have some leftover. He's got Gertie and George to think of."

It was too incredulous. Her daddy was too cheap to pay anyone an allowance, let alone buy a house. "I don't believe you."

"Go ahead and ask him."

"How much does he pay you?"

"That's none of your business." He called out for more coffee. A young black woman Mavis had never seen before came in from the kitchen and filled his cup. She didn't make eye contact and left quickly.

"Who was that?"

"That's Rosetta." Danny returned to the newspaper. "She sometimes helps Carlina."

"Since when?"

"Since I decided it."

Mavis snorted. "And is your allowance paying for that too? Am I to have no say in running the house?"

"Running the house?" he scoffed. "Carlina says you don't do a damn thing."

"That's because she won't let me! She talks to you, does she? Because she certainly doesn't talk to me."

"This conversation is finished." Danny drained his cup and stood up. "Don't forget the train leaves early tomorrow, so make sure you're ready."

She didn't want to go to Fort Lauderdale to see a lynching. "You can go without me."

"Everybody's going, Mavis. What'll I say when people ask where you are?"

"Tell them I'm sick." That was true. She was sick to death of Neelan Junction and the people in it. She couldn't be the only one staying home, could she?

"Jimmy and Sandra are going. Your folks are taking Gertie and George. There'll be no one to visit and nothing to do. Everything's shutting down for the day."

Ellie wouldn't be going, but only because of her face. Would Willis go without her? The Booths certainly wouldn't be going. In fact, Mavis expected a good letter to the editor: *Why on earth, on a regular day of commerce, were the businesses in Neelan Junction, save for the bank and the post office, closed for the day?*

"I'll be fine," she said, relieved to hear him considering her request. "If I'm bored I could always visit Ellie."

"If you're healthy enough to want to visit, then you're healthy enough to come with me."

It would be hot in Fort Lauderdale. Hotter because of all the people pressed together, anxious to get a better view. Danny would have more fun without her.

"What did he do, anyway?"

"Who?"

She looked at the paper for the name. "Nathan Jones."

"He tried to rape a white woman."

"So he tried but didn't?"

"Even *thinking* about it is enough."

"If I was feeling up to it I'd go," she said, lying. "So you're right; I'll just stay home."

She looked at the train schedule. It was leaving at 8:30 a.m.

She'd have an entire day without Danny.

CHAPTER 27

Sliver had nothing to do with Miss Ellie after her baby's funeral, and the months and seasons passed. Sometimes Sliver saw her out walking and remembered Mamie's warning that she could appear and disappear without sound. She'd almost forget Miss Ellie lived at the Yates's at all and then there she'd be, walking up the drive—a black cloud with legs. One morning she saw her come out of the barn and thought she ought to remind Charlie to watch out.

Her days were full; she took care of Mrs. Yates and worked both the gardens for the main house and her own. She was also the only midwife around and still caught babies. Gardening was just another kind of birthing because nature, like a woman's body, always welcomed new life, and Sliver enjoyed the harvest.

Sometimes, when she worked too hard, her right leg throbbed as if her heart was located in her ankle instead of her chest, and that throbbing turned her mind to those boys in the wagon, and she'd wonder what damage they'd done to others since driving their carriage into her when she was just a girl. Punishment for her daddy's business doing too well. Customers came to the front door of the store to buy fresh produce and dried goods, and customers came to the back door to summon Sliver's mother to deliver babies.

The white merchants in Georgia hadn't liked their black customers paying cheaper prices and doing their business elsewhere. That smelled too much like independence. And if the black man became independent, well, didn't that scare the hell out of them? They were right to be scared, but not for the reason they claimed. Black men worked hard, *much* harder than any white man Sliver had ever seen. They worked harder and loved harder and played harder because they knew nothing came from nothing. Put side by side, the black man out-performed the white man by a country mile, and the white man's paper-thin ego couldn't stand to be showed up. So what did he do? The white man destroyed the competition by any means possible, and he made up lies and imposed laws to ensure his own victory. They lied in Georgia, and they lied in Florida too. How their tongues didn't turn black and fall from their mouths from all the lying, she'd never know. And she'd also never forgive those boys for running her down or those men for killing her mama, but by now she had accepted it had happened. There was a big difference between accepting and forgiving. What else could she do?

Sliver rested the hoe in the dirt, leaned on it, and looked about. The tree where she'd first seen Gideon up on a ladder was almost three decades bigger now; its branches reached higher and farther. It had happened before that an orange had rolled to her feet while walking past the grove. Always, she'd look around expecting it was Gideon who'd coaxed it her way before remembering it couldn't be. He'd done that before, rolled an orange her way like he was bowling her off her feet. How he'd laughed. He was the one who taught her that the oranges on the outside of the grove ripened first because they got more sun. *Look,* he said. *Do you see? Now that you know you'll see it everywhere.* He was right. How had she never noticed that herself?

She was twenty-five when Gideon disappeared but felt like a baby herself even with babies needing her. At first, Sliver trained her mind to think Gideon's physical absence would make their reunion that much sweeter. All she had to do was be patient. The reward would come. But as the days and months and years passed, conjuring his image became harder, even though she tended the memories in her mind as carefully as she'd nurture a plant that didn't thrive — hoping, always hoping, and not yet ready to give up. When her firstborn Seth turned twenty and left to work in the shipyards in Fort Lauderdale, following in her uncle's footsteps, Sliver felt like she'd lost Gideon a second time, because sometimes when she'd come upon Seth from a certain angle her heart would flood with joy thinking Gideon had come back for her. That's how much he resembled his daddy. Then the joy became grief that surprised her each and every time.

The curtain in Mrs. Yates's upstairs window fluttered. Was it the wind or Mrs. Yates spying on Miss Ellie? Sliver wiped her brow and looked to the new house. Miss Ellie was sitting on the porch, swinging in that damned swing. The Turner sisters had wasted many good hours of the day on the swing at their house, thinking they was doing something. Sliver saw no use in that leisure. Mrs. Yates had it, and what was she doing? Tormenting herself by hating her son's wife and stealing her dresses and belongings for spite. Mona and Beanie told Sliver everything. They'd been the ones to cut the dress up into bits to make new cloth napkins. And recently, Ellie had accused Mona of stealing or misplacing her gold cigarette case.

Showing Miss Ellie some kindness would go a long way, Sliver thought. The girl had to be lonely; Mrs. Yates ought to recognize lonely. Every time Sliver stepped into her room, the woman started talking as if she was starved for company. She'd quit going to church when Master Willis's son died. Sliver could only speculate that Mrs. Yates didn't want anybody feeling sorry for her. What would it be like to be so alone with one's thoughts? Master Willis didn't invite anyone to visit either. Sliver didn't know if he was ashamed of Miss Ellie or if she refused to be social. In any case, the house that he had built to impress received no visitors.

Sliver looked about the garden and decided to call it a day. She couldn't work in the heat for as long as she used to. She gathered her tools just as Miss Ellie stepped off the swing and stretched her arms over her head. Then she turned sideways so Sliver saw her profile. Was it intentional? Miss Ellie's belly was rounding out like she had a pea in her pod. A child had definitely rooted there. Sliver did a quick calculation and determined a spring baby.

Her suspicion was confirmed when Ellie got so sensitive to smell that she told the cook to stop preparing meals even before she'd made her menu. Mona and Beanie, and even Willis, started tiptoeing even lighter months before that baby was actually born.

In February, Sliver planted sweet potatoes, eggplant, and squash.

In March, the weather got warmer and invited Miss Ellie outside more. Her sister visited more frequently, and Sliver got used to seeing the two women on the porch together, Miss Mavis's hand resting on her sister's ripe belly.

In April, the Azaleas and Rhododendrons upstaged the orange trees with their beauty. Sliver planted bush beans and helped her daughter Becky give birth to her fifth child.

In May, Sliver put okra in the ground and checked for pests on her tomatoes. Master Willis's baby was coming soon. She slept with one ear listening, waiting for the knock she knew was coming.

She was in the garden, bending into one of those winds that blows in hard from the coast, when Mona came running saying Master Willis was hurting Miss Ellie.

Sliver ran for the house in time to see him rush blindly out the front door and head for the stables. She went around the back, hurried up the stairs, and knocked on Miss Ellie's door. "It's Sliver, Ma'am, can I come in?"

Someone was shouting outside. She ran to the window at the end of the hall in time to see Master Willis charge out of the barn on his favourite horse, pulling hard on the reins. He loved that horse. What had happened to make him treat it so?

She didn't knock when she got back to the room and instead burst in. Miss Ellie was lying on the floor. There was blood on the bed sheets. The distinct odor of birth and shock lingered in the air. A white bundle lay on the bed. A baby mewled from inside. Sliver processed it all, adding the pieces together bit by bit and arrived at a startling conclusion: Miss Ellie had birthed her own child alone in the night.

She knelt down, cradled Miss Ellie's head in her lap, and felt for a pulse. A viscous line of blood and saliva ran from her mouth down to the floor. Sliver gently wiped the moisture away and looked for the source of blood. A tooth was missing. Master Willis must have hit her. She was knocked out cold.

Sliver stood and scanned the room. A pair of blood-crusted scissors were on the bedside table, likely used to cut the umbilical cord. A basin was half-filled with bloody water. The placenta, already drying out, sat in a bowl next to the bed. Sliver checked it quickly to make sure it was intact and guessed the birth had happened eight to ten hours earlier. Miss Ellie had been prepared for when her time came.

Sliver picked up the bundle on the bed and pulled back the blanket. She almost lost her grip from the shock. The baby's skin was dark. Curly hair hugged its scalp. Sliver peered inside the diaper to confirm its sex. He was a perfect little mulatto boy. His bud of a nose looked like Miss Ellie's. And his eyes were light just like ...

Her heart tipped in her ribcage.

Charlie.

She recalled that day seeing Miss Ellie leave the barn, but it hadn't occurred to her ... How had she missed this?

Fear rendered her senseless for a moment. Her mind was blank. *Gideon help me. What do I do?*

Time was ticking.

She rocked back and forth, trying to formulate a plan.

The baby started to cry.

Miss Ellie still lay unconscious on the floor.

Where had Master Willis gone? To get Sheriff Thorpe? How long before he returned? And what would he do to the baby?

Terror finally got her moving. She wrapped the baby up again and tucked him into the crook of her arm. Just because Ellie hadn't harmed him yet didn't mean she wasn't about to. She had used the baby to hurt Willis. Now that she'd accomplished that, the child would be useless to her. And if Willis came back and found the baby alive, Sliver couldn't predict where his rage might take him.

The baby had stopped crying when she clutched him to her heart; he was God's little offering, a miracle of life. She stepped out the back door and ran.

Becky's shack was in the north grove. Her daughter was already nursing a child. Sliver arrived with the newborn and told her a woman in Slew Town had died giving birth. Nobody would claim it, so Becky had to nurse this one too. *Don't ask so many questions!*

The baby started to cry again.

It's hungry. Help him.

Becky had a big heart. She couldn't say no to a baby. She lifted the newborn to her breast.

Sliver ran back to the house, piecing together what was now obvious. Miss Ellie had wanted to hurt her husband, and if he found out who the daddy was, then Charlie was a dead man. What if he already knew? What if Miss Ellie had offered up his name with glee?

Sliver returned to the house, hoping Charlie would still be alive by the time she could get to him. She told Mona to change the sheets and tidy the room while she half-carried, half-dragged Miss Ellie down the hall to the toilet. Then she cleaned her up and helped her back to bed.

Miss Ellie's mouth was swollen. A bit of dried blood that Sliver had missed was crusted on her chin. Seeing her injured and bruised reminded Sliver of her initial arrival and how she'd almost felt sorry for her then. She didn't feel sorry for her now.

She wet the corner of a towel with warm water and dabbed at the remaining blood on Miss Ellie's face.

"Where is he?"

"Master Willis rode off. He hasn't come back yet."

"Not him. Where is my baby?"

"The baby?" Sliver shook her head and repeated the story she'd fabricated. "The baby didn't make it. I'm so sorry." She kept her eyes on her task to avoid Miss Ellie's gaze.

"You're lying. There was nothing wrong with that baby. What did you do with him?"

"I'm sorry ..."

"Give him back."

If Miss Ellie had issued an invitation or a plea, instead of a command, Sliver might have responded differently, but now her resolve strengthened. Charlie's life was in the balance.

"Give him back or I'll tell Willis whose baby it is."

Moisture gathered in Sliver's armpits. Miss Ellie didn't want that baby for any reason but to hurt her husband, and she'd already done that. She didn't need Charlie anymore either. He had served his purpose and was easily sacrificed. *Help me, Giddy. What do I do? What do I do?*

She smoothed the bedcovers to give her hands something to do and to buy more time while she calculated her next move. Would Miss Ellie really tell Master Willis who the father was? A multitude of scenarios played themselves out in Sliver's mind, each with their own consequences, until only one remained: she had to keep the baby away. That might be the only way to save Charlie.

"Do you hear me?" Miss Ellie was shouting now. "I want my baby back!"

"Your babies have a history of dying," Sliver said in a low, calm voice.

"Only my first baby died!"

"And this one's no exception."

They might have continued their standoff indefinitely if Master Willis hadn't stormed into the house with workmen at his heels.

The men walked past the bedroom and soon could be heard overhead, dragging things and banging hammers. What now? A man could only be hurt so much before he did worse in return.

"I'm sorry for your loss," Sliver said and left the room.

She'd called Miss Ellie's bluff. Master Willis wouldn't care about the baby; he'd be happy to know it had died. And if there was no baby to re-ignite Master Willis's anger, maybe Miss Ellie wouldn't feel the need to tell him who the father was.

If Sliver's risk paid off, both Charlie and his son would live.

If it didn't …

She felt her skin tingling and thought the body was nothing but a vessel for grief. If something happened to Charlie …

She waited for Master Willis to come back downstairs. When he finally did, she told him the baby had died. He looked relieved even though he didn't meet her gaze.

She told a lot of lies that day. And she found out firsthand that a person's tongue didn't turn black and fall out.

Some lies, she now knew, simply needed the telling.

CHAPTER 28

Ellie dozed in and out of sleep and woke to the sound of hammering.

Her tongue found the spot where her tooth had recently been and explored the tender gap. Her breasts were two fists punching out of her chest. She hadn't slept much, having laboured through the night. She ached all over. Where was her baby? Sliver said he was dead, but that couldn't be true. Ellie had nursed him. He had been fine.

She touched her breasts and recoiled. Two large cabbage leaves cupped them. She remembered now. Sliver had placed them there, saying they would help draw her milk down and ease her discomfort. Why would Sliver do that? Cause her pain and then try to ease it?

Oh but the look on Willis's face.

Ellie had called him into the room and told him he had a son. His surprise had been genuine. Nobody had told him she was in labour. The baby was wrapped tightly in a blanket and cradled in her arms. She handed him over. Willis's expression moved from excitement to shock to rage in swift succession.

She was grinning widely when he dropped the baby on the bed and swung his fist. If she'd been ready, she'd have blocked the blow with her arm or at least ducked.

She raised her hand to her mouth again and felt the bruising. It had been worth it.

Her breasts tingled as her milk let down. She was leaking from every part of her body, including her eyes. Maybe if she talked nicely to Sliver, she would bring the baby back. Maybe if she promised not to tell Willis Charlie was the father. Maybe Sliver didn't know the baby was Charlie's. How would she? Charlie wouldn't have told her, would he? All that mattered was Ellie wanted to nurse him. Was he crying somewhere while her own breasts were full to bursting?

But nobody came. Already her victory began to pale in light of her own loss. After he'd hit her, Willis had shaken her so hard she'd thought her neck was going to snap. She hadn't mentioned Charlie, had she?

She pulled a cigarette from the crumpled pack on her bedside table. The match sparked and fizzled before she blew it out. She placed the cigarette gingerly between her swollen lips and inhaled.

The hammering continued throughout the day and into the evening. Sliver didn't return. Mona brought some food on a tray and Ellie begged her to tell Sliver to come, but Mona backed out of the room saying Master Yates had forbidden anyone to visit.

Willis came for her at bedtime.

He grabbed her by the elbow with one hand and picked up her rocking chair with the other. Neither of them spoke as he guided her out of the bedroom and towards the narrow stairway that led upstairs. Willis pushed her ahead of him and followed only to put the rocking chair down on the bare floor beneath the pitched roof. Then he closed the door without saying a word, slid a deadbolt into place, and retreated down the stairs.

Everything made sense now. Willis had moved her to the only room in the house with no access to any doors that would take her downstairs or outside. To a room with a window too small for a body to pass through.

Ellie surveyed the room. A single bed was pushed against a bare wall that met the sloped roof. Beside the bed was a round table. On it was a small lamp and an ashtray. An oval shaped woven rug in earth tones covered the plywood floor. Opposite the bed, Ellie's dresser had found a new home. On the end wall, a small window looked down on the front of the property. At least she'd be able to see who was coming and going from here. Maybe she'd even be able to catch a glimpse of the sunrise.

The silence was welcome after the constant day of noise.

She dragged the rocking chair next to the window with its four small panes of glass. There was nothing for her to do but pretend her new situation was to her liking and was her idea. *Dear Mavis*, she'd write if she had pen and paper. *You'll never guess what's happened now.*

She put a pillow on the rocking chair. A rush of blood escaped when she sat down, soaking the thick pad Sliver had made for her. What had they done with her baby?

It's yours, Charlie. Yes. It's yours.

She'd first come across Charlie by accident. Walking around the property, she'd wandered into the barn and seen the blacksmith. He had his back to her and was hunched over. A horse's front leg was upturned between his knees, and he was busy trimming its hoof with a tool that was part pliers and part scissors. She walked up close to him without his knowing because of the noise from the forge. The horse was only six feet away. She had always been partial to the smell of horses.

Ellie stood behind Charlie and quelled the desire to reach out and touch him. Her loneliness had just about swallowed her up. It was a physical ache powerful enough to curve her spine and almost double her over.

She didn't stay long that first day because she'd learned. Oh yes, she'd learned. Jedediah was dead because of her, and Samuel was lucky to be alive. She left without uttering a word.

But still, it had been a comfort to be near him, and once her feet had taken her to the barn, they wanted to repeat those steps, and Ellie found herself watching Charlie more frequently from her hiding place near or in one of the horse's stalls.

He often talked to the horses as he worked. One day, she noted his voice had a different tone, and Ellie realized he wasn't speaking to the horse anymore.

"I know you're there, Miss."

She froze.

"I can smell the soap you use. It's house soap."

She lifted her hand to her nose and took in the lavender.

He stood outside the stall door. "I don't want no trouble, Miss."

Samuel had said those same words in the parlour. And Jedediah in the shed, back when she'd still been beautiful. Back when she hadn't known her most valuable possession could be taken from her.

What had Charlie heard about her? "Neither do I."

"You best go now before anyone knows you're here."

Ellie left, but she'd never been good at doing what she was told. Who would Charlie complain to? His mama? What could the midwife do?

A few days later, she found herself staring at Charlie again. Sometimes she'd leave without him even knowing she was there. Other times she'd stand in his sight, so he'd be sure to see her. That went on for months, her visiting and him pretending not to know she was there.

One day, he wished her a good morning and asked how she was. She almost cried. No one, besides Mavis, ever asked how she was. Charlie's conversation was sunlight after a long rainy season, but he was skittish, listening as hard as he could for anyone approaching.

"I shouldn't be talking to you," he said.

"Well, then, I'll do the talking and you can listen. How's that?"

And that's how it went for a while, Ellie talking and Charlie listening. And Ellie talking even when she suspected he'd stopped listening. She'd worn him down by her visits, or by his knowledge that he couldn't stop her from visiting.

At some point he started talking too. "Why do you wear that scarf?"

"It's a veil. I wear it because what's underneath isn't pretty."

"I heard you got cut."

She nodded. "What else did you hear?"

"I heard that some people died."

"That part's true too, but I didn't want it to happen."

Charlie was grooming a horse and had it tied with two ropes at the halter. He used a hard rubber brush, and when he made circles on the horse's belly, the horse threw his head in the air and swished his tail.

"He likes that," Ellie said, laughing.

"He does." Charlie patted the horse's flank and looked at Ellie. "Can I see?"

She knew he meant her face. It was the way he asked that moved her. Softly. Compassionately. Not scornfully like Willis's mama, wanting to gloat, but with a kind curiosity.

Ellie unhooked the loops around her ears and removed her veil. She watched him take in the damage.

He took a moment before he spoke. "Somebody did that to you?"

It was the tenderness in his voice that made her eyes fill, the incredulity. She nodded, reached for his hand, and put it on her cheek. He traced each scar softly with his fingertip and wiped her tears away with his thumb.

The sloped ceiling trapped the heat in the upstairs room so it was stifling. Oh to go to the watering hole and float on her back in the cool water. How excruciating to be denied that pleasure.

The rocking chair rocked by itself when Ellie stood up and lay down on the bed.

Once again, her world had shrunk.

If Willis had hurt Charlie, it would be all her fault.

Had it been worth it?

CHAPTER 29

Mona thrust a piece of paper into Sliver's hand. "You said if Ellie wrote any notes to give them to you. She said this was for Charlie."

Sliver took the folded note. "You did good."

"He won't be mad, will he?" Mona asked.

"No. He's not expecting anything from Ellie."

"Okay, because I don't want Charlie to be mad."

Everybody loved Charlie. He'd always been a help. "You did good, Mona," Sliver repeated. "He won't be mad. I'll talk to him."

Mona walked off, shaking her head like she doubted her good deed.

Sliver tucked the note into her dress and went to the shack she shared with no one because a midwife's hours are random and necessary. She closed the door and listened hard to make sure no one had followed her. Then she opened the note. It had only one word on it: *Yes!*

The exclamation mark provided the necessary clue. Charlie had known it might be his.

Sliver struck a match and held it to the edge. The paper quickly turned to ash and dropped to the floor like the dust had dropped from the sky when Miss Ellie had first arrived.

Sliver's anger ran hot. Did Charlie for one minute think Miss Ellie actually *cared* for him? Couldn't he see she had only used him for her own means?

Sliver had been five months pregnant when Gideon disappeared. Mixed in with her profound grief was the dread that the baby feeding off her and pushing out her belly might not be his. Her other children were eight, seven, five, and three when Charlie was born, and her heart was so broken it barely pumped enough oxygen through her veins. How tired she'd been. How discouraged. She and Gideon were to raise a family *together*. That was the deal he made when his body covered hers and they enjoyed their loving. She had never wanted to do it on her own. She needed him. She wasn't strong enough alone.

⌐ The first time Old Man Yates caught her, Sliver was climbing the stairs to put clean laundry away in Mrs. Yates's bedroom. She'd let her guard down because he hadn't once tried to touch her all the time she'd been there. She'd married Gideon by then and had four children.

She didn't know a big man could move so quietly. He came up behind her on the stairs. Some things she'd never forget. His breath, quick against her ear. The way he shuddered when he released himself. And him saying, *You keep that to yourself,* when he'd finished, as if she had something to crow about.

Afterwards, Sliver had cleaned herself up and vowed to be more vigilant. She hadn't told Gideon. What was done was done.

But in the following months, Old Man Yates caught her more than once. He even came into her home. One afternoon, Gideon returned from work early and found him leaving their shack and Sliver pulling her dress down over her hips. Her expression told him everything.

She grabbed his arm when he tried to storm out. "Leave it, baby. Just let it alone. I'm fine. It's okay." What else could she say?

But she could see his wheels turning. She could see him thinking that all his life he'd done everything he'd been told. He'd gone where they told him to go and worked until they told him to stop. And he'd believed minding his own business and doing his best was like armour that would protect him and his family. But it wasn't true. She saw the light dawn in his eyes: He was controlled. He would always be controlled.

The Gideon she had known from her early days, the one who set the sun free when he smiled, disappeared. She didn't like to remember the Gideon who'd cried in her arms. For letting her down. *No, Giddy, you never let me down.* For standing by and letting it happen. *It only started a few months ago. And you didn't know it was happening.* For not being able to stop it. *It's not your fault! Please. Pretend you didn't see.* For being weak. *You're the strongest man I know! I need you. I lost too much already in my life. I can't lose you too.* For not being a man. *Oh, Giddy.*

She waited until she was almost four months pregnant to tell him she was with child. For the first time, he didn't rejoice. He just turned things over in his mind. He'd never been a man to hate, but he changed. And the thing was, Sliver knew it wasn't his hate from that single incident that burned him, but the accumulation of hate over his lifetime and from ancestors and friends that finally wore him down.

Two days later, Old Man Yates fell from his carriage and hit his head when his heart gave out. That's what Doc Wilson said when he examined the body. Sliver might have believed that story if Gideon hadn't disappeared at the same time. When he didn't come home that night, she knew. How no one put two and two together was baffling. Gideon had run, thinking he'd hang for murder. He didn't stick around to find out that nobody cared the old man was dead.

When Charlie was born and placed in her arms, she knew it would have killed Gideon, for Charlie's skin was brighter than the rest of their children's. She remembered looking down at her baby and thinking, *Gideon killed because of you, and Gideon likely died because of you too.* That's when she fully acknowledged he wasn't coming back. It was like she'd been holding her breath until the baby came, not willing to focus on anything else but keeping steady for her other children, but finally her heart could speak its truth. Giddy was dead. He'd have gotten word to her otherwise.

She had two choices: she could love the child, or she could hate the child. Accept him or blame him. She knew it wasn't his fault, directly. But could she forget all the circumstances that had brought about his arrival? As she was trying to decide what path to take, Seth, Willow, Becky, and Jonah all gathered around the bed and cooed and smiled and grabbed at the baby, not noticing or caring about his shade, not picking up on the grief in the air, just celebrating his arrival and asking if he could sleep with them in their beds. It was the first spot of joy they'd shared since Gideon had disappeared. And they needed some joy.

Sliver had arrived in Neelan Junction with hate bounding like a rabbit through her veins. It was a poison she drank hoping it might kill others. Gideon had lifted that hate by the scruff and slowed her pulse so she could breathe deeply instead of gasping for air.

Tired from labour, she had closed her eyes and let her heart govern her emotions. She stood at a crossroads. She had a decision to make that would govern her future. Would she turn towards hate or towards love? Her children had their hands on the baby. They were tickling his tiny fingers, touching his nub of a nose, and laughing as his face changed shapes. The laughter was rays of sunshine, the best medicine of all. She lifted the baby to her breast and allowed him to latch on.

Sliver looked at the ash on the floor from Ellie's note and thought, *That's how quickly dreams go up in flames.*

Ever since Charlie was a boy, she'd told him white folks were only afraid of two things: not getting what they wanted and losing what they already had. So they were scared all the time, she said, and a scared animal is dangerous. Did he understand that? They were always groping and wanting and lying and stealing and killing.

When her children were old enough, she'd told them about her own daddy. He was never a slave himself but grew up with family who had known nothing but. He told Sliver that freedom was a state of mind. A person didn't just stop being a slave on a Monday when he'd been a slave every day of his life leading up to that day. So even though her daddy was born free, he was surrounded by people who had never known freedom. Many of the slaves starved to death or got sick and died directly after the war because they were turned off plantations and left to fend for themselves. *You want freedom? Take it. Off you go.* There hadn't been any transition for most. Hundreds of thousands of men and women and children who'd only known slavery died from disease and starvation after being liberated. The number was likely bigger. All that hope! It wasn't supposed to work like that. There was a great tragedy attached to that freedom.

Her family's story was a long one, so she told it to her children in parts, like it was a meal with many courses to be enjoyed and not rushed in one sitting.

Her daddy didn't get the chance to know her children, but he met Seth and knew he was third generation free.

⌐ It turned out nobody went looking for Miss Ellie's mulatto baby. Even so, Sliver remained on alert. She brought more food to Becky's and asked her to keep nursing the baby while she figured things out. *Please. Do it for me.*

A few days passed before she had calmed enough to summon Charlie to her shack.

"Sit," she told him when he arrived.

Charlie pulled out a chair, lowered himself into it, and picked at a gouge in the wooden tabletop to keep his eyes averted. Then he looked towards the pots of basil and rosemary Sliver had brought in from the rain. He put his big hands flat on the table and made it rock. "I can fix that for you," he said, "and make it even."

"That's not what I called you for."

Sliver stared at him until he finally lifted his eyes. "Were you kicked in the head by a horse, son? Cause I don't see no other reason for why you're here." Fear brought out the meanness in her.

"This is about Ellie, isn't it?"

"Ellie? Is that what you call her? She's *Miss Ellie* to you!" Sliver's hands were shaking. "I *told* you to watch out for her, didn't I? What didn't you understand?" Last summer, she'd walked into the barn unexpectedly and Charlie had swung around from the forge; she'd known right away he had wanted her to be someone else because he'd tried to hide his disappointment. But she hadn't thought it was Ellie he was waiting for. "You have no idea what I've lost in my life."

Charlie's bare feet shuffled against the wood floor; he would get splinters if he didn't stop, but he wasn't a child anymore. She didn't need to tell him that. He looked down at his hands resting on the table. She waited him out.

"How was the baby?"

"It's not yours, if that's what you're asking. That baby was so white

I thought I'd go blind." She watched his face. Was that relief or disappointment? "And it was sickly and not likely to live long," she added for good measure. "If you had your hopes up that it was yours, then I *know* you been kicked in the head."

He kept his eyes down.

"Let me guess. She said she'd tell Master Willis if you didn't cooperate."

He didn't respond.

"I know news travels, and I know you heard about Jedediah and Delia unless you've gone deaf too. A white woman making a black man do what she wants doesn't make you special one bit. It just makes you convenient."

Charlie's shoulders sagged. "I know."

Sliver wanted to take him into her arms, like she'd done when he was a boy and she'd found him plucking a chicken that someone had left at her door as a gift for her services. He was always helping, people and animals. Bringing home wounded birds and healing wings that had been broken, holding his siblings' hands as they lay dying. His heart was born good. He'd have understood that Miss Ellie was broken inside, wounded beyond belief, and he'd have wanted to help. "If she cared about you one bit, she wouldn't put you in a position to be killed. Cause you wouldn't be the first!"

Charlie slowly nodded.

She sat back, crossed her arms, and breathed more freely. "I asked you here because I got a message from Mr. Irwin in town. He needs another blacksmith. He said you could live above the shop, in the empty room. He'd treat you good. I made sure to ask, and your wage will be more than what you get here."

Charlie didn't answer.

"I think you should go. Do you hear me, Charlie?"

"Why should I leave home? What's the hurry, Mama?"

"The hurry is he'll find someone else. And leaving home isn't always a bad thing. Last I heard, your brother Seth is doing fine, and he left home. Plus, I told Mr. Irwin you'd take it and would be by tomorrow."

"What about Master Willis?"

"I told him you're leaving. He said he'd be sorry to see you go, but he understands."

In truth, Sliver had no idea what she'd tell Master Willis. She had to believe telling him the baby had died would help him to overlook Charlie's leaving so soon afterwards. It was risky, but she had to do something.

"Go now," she said. "I'd say please but I'm not asking."

Charlie nodded. He recognized she was moving him away from Ellie, but he was smart enough to know she was trying to keep him safe.

Becky continued to nurse Charlie's boy and absorbed him into her family. Another baby so soon after her own made little difference. Nobody questioned that a mulatto baby from Slew Town would need a home. They named him Jerome, and the name suited him fine.

CHAPTER 30

It was almost lunchtime and still Danny lay snoring in bed. Mavis had already gone to the post office, visited the library, mended two shirts, and read the newspaper. It didn't feel right, a man sleeping in the daytime, but Danny's work kept him out late at night. If it could be called work. Sheriff Thorpe had appointed him a deputy. Danny had special shirts made for himself and the six other deputies he personally chose. He wanted them to look official, he said, and Carlina ironed his shirt so the creases were crisp even if they only lasted a short time in the humidity.

Now that he was a deputy, Danny carried a gun with him everywhere he went. When he'd been drinking, which was often, he pulled it from its holster to admire it. Mavis felt a drunken Danny with a gun was more dangerous than anything else she'd experience in daily life. All he talked about was how much trouble was going on. There had been a recent rash of fires. Some of the negroes had lost everything. Just the previous week, Mavis had passed a family walking on the road out of town — two parents and six children — carrying their belongings. When she told Danny how sad it was, he said they needed to learn how to tend their fires properly, but Mamie told her it was the men throwing torches into their homes that needed to learn how to tend fires. Was it a coincidence, Mamie asked, that every family that got burned out had also been owed wages?

Some days walking around town, Mavis felt people looked at her differently. They either held her gaze for a fraction too long or avoided it entirely. Had she become paranoid? The previous day, Mavis had looked across the street and seen Mamie talking to a black woman by the grocery store. They both turned to look at her. Mamie had shaken her head "no," and Mavis wondered if she was being condemned or defended.

And then there was Carlina.

The previous month, Mavis had come home unexpectedly because she'd forgotten something. She entered by the front door as quietly as possible to retrieve what she'd forgotten without notice. She heard women's voices in the kitchen. Curiosity got the better of her. She pushed the door open and saw Carlina arguing with Rosetta, the young black woman who'd brought Danny coffee. Rosetta's eyes were swollen from crying. Sliver was there, too, holding a light-skinned baby so new it barely filled the blanket it was wrapped in.

"Is everything okay?" Mavis asked.

Carlina's face registered surprise and then instantly transformed into a blank mask. There was nothing to worry about, she said. Her cousin was just tired.

"Can I help with anything?"

Rosetta wiped her tears and turned towards Carlina and the midwife.

"It's her first baby," Sliver explained, handing the baby back to Rosetta. "She's just needing some help with the nursing. She'll get the hang of it in no time."

The baby began to cry its newborn wail. Sliver put her arm around Rosetta and led her and her baby out the back door.

Mavis had collected what she'd forgotten and gone about her day. Something hadn't felt right about the exchange in the kitchen, but she'd shrugged it off just like she'd shrugged off other odd moments in her married life. She asked Mamie about it later.

"Who knows why she was there. Likely she just wanted her mama."

"Who did?"

"Rosetta."

Mavis was more confused than ever. "Is Sliver Rosetta's mama?"

"No, Carlina is."

"Carlina said Rosetta was her cousin. I distinctly recall her saying her cousin was tired."

Mamie shrugged. "Maybe I got it wrong."

Danny finally emerged from the bedroom just as Carlina was ready to serve lunch. His eyes were bloodshot, and his right hand was bandaged. Even so, Mavis could see his fingers were swollen. He smelled of cigarettes, alcohol, and sweat. He needed a bath.

Danny asked Carlina for a cold press and held it to his forehead when he sat down.

"You were out late."

"There was trouble at Slew Town, and then there was trouble with Willis."

"Willis?"

"He drowned his sorrow at the bar. Drinks were on him."

"What sorrow?"

"Didn't you hear?"

Mavis shook her head. "Hear what?"

"His baby died."

"What?" She jumped to her feet. "The new one?"

Danny nodded.

"I don't believe you. Ellie would have sent word." She had been happy about a May baby. *A spring flower.*

"I don't think she's allowed. I couldn't make out half of what Willis was saying he was that drunk, but it sounds like he's got her locked up."

Mavis restrained herself. Danny enjoyed getting her upset and then saying he was only joking. This could be one of those times. "When did she have the baby?"

He shrugged. "A couple of days ago maybe. I didn't ask."

No. It couldn't be true. She'd have heard. Somebody would have told her. She changed the subject. "What happened to your hand?"

"Just a little misunderstanding that needed fixing."

Danny went out again as soon as he finished eating and Mavis raced over to the Yates's.

Someone new came out of the barn to take her horse and carriage. She was too concerned about Ellie to ask what had happened to Charlie.

She knocked at the front door and waited. *Hurry. Hurry.* Would no one come?

Mona finally answered but didn't stand aside like she usually did. "I'm sorry, but Miss Ellie's not receiving visitors."

"I'm not a visitor, I'm her sister."

"Master Willis's orders."

"He told me before that I could see her! You know that."

"He gave new instructions."

"Please, let me see her."

"No Ma'am. I'm sorry."

Mavis knew it would do little to take her frustration out on Mona. "Is it true Ellie's baby died?"

Mona nodded.

"When?"

"A few days ago."

"Has the doctor been to see her? Is she alright?" Her own sister was right upstairs, and she couldn't see her?

"The midwife's taking care of her."

"Where's Willis. I'm sure he'll let me see Ellie."

"He's not feeling well."

"Can you at least tell Ellie I was here? And tell Willis I'll be back again tomorrow. It's not right for him to keep me from her. Especially now. Tell him that."

The door closed. Mavis heard the deadbolt slide into place. She repressed a violent urge to kick the door down.

She returned the next day.

"Your sister says to go away," Mona said. "She says to leave her alone."

"Are you sure she knows it's me? Try again."

Mona disappeared inside. When she returned, she shook her head and closed the door.

Mavis stood on the porch, unsure what to do next. A curtain flut-tered in Old Lady Yates's window across the way. Would she know anything? Mavis looked around. It was so hot the air rose from the ground like a genie from a bottle. Someone was working in the garden in the full sun. Was it the midwife?

Mavis walked over and watched. Finally she cleared her throat. "Sliver?" How strange to have known of her for so long but never spoken to her before. "I'm Ellie's sister, Mavis."

"I know." She continued to weed between the rows.

"I came to visit, but no one will let me in. Did her baby die?" Mavis hoped if she kept asking, the answer might change.

"I'm afraid so."

"Is Ellie in the house?"

The midwife nodded.

"And she's okay?"

"Master Willis doesn't want her to have visitors."

"Why?"

"I can't say."

"You can't say because you're not allowed, or you can't say because you don't know?"

"Because I don't know."

"Did Ellie's baby die the same way her first one did?"

"I can't say."

Mavis sighed in frustration.

"Your sister's going to live, if that's what you want to know."

"Thank you. That helps. Can you tell her I've been stopping by and want to see her? That I'll come whenever she asks for me?"

"I'll do that." Sliver stood up and then seemed to lose her balance. She staggered a step or two.

Mavis rushed forward and grabbed her elbow. "Are you okay?" She guided the midwife to the bench beside the garden. "You shouldn't work in this heat without a hat. I'll get you some water."

There was a barrel beside the garden with cups hanging from the side. Mavis filled one and gave it to her.

"Thank you. I got a bit light-headed for a minute."

"The sun will do that." She sat with Sliver until her dizziness passed.

When Mavis left, the curtain was still drawn in Ellie's bedroom window.

⚞ She returned the next day and the day after that and continued to be turned away. Each time she asked if Ellie had been told it was her, and each time Mona nodded.

"Can you give her this note? Remind her I'll come whenever she wants me to. Okay? Or tell her she can write to me."

On one of her visits, Willis answered the door when she knocked. He stepped out as if he'd been waiting for her, grabbed her arm, and pulled her towards the barn. "Ellie's not receiving visitors. Didn't Mona tell you that?"

"Yes, but I'm not a visitor ..."

He had her by the carriage now. He leaned in close; she felt his breath on her cheek. "If I see you around here again, I'll get my knife out and carve more initials into your sister's face. Do you understand me?"

Mavis nodded, too afraid to speak.

"Good." Willis turned his back to her and walked away.

Her hands were shaking as she took up the reins. She turned the carriage towards her childhood home. Mamie would know what she should do.

⚞ "Do you want your sister getting hurt?" Mamie asked.

"Of course not."

"And do you believe Willis will hurt her if you visit again?"

Mavis nodded. He'd hurt her before.

"Then there's your answer. Stay away."

"But Ellie doesn't have anyone else!"

"You don't know that."

"Okay then, she doesn't have me!"

"That part's true." Mamie took her hand. "I've known you and

Ellie all of your lives, and here's what I know: people around Ellie often find themselves in trouble. And when Ellie makes trouble, you try to smooth it out."

"I'm not sure that's true."

"Then explain why you didn't come to me when you knew she had Samuel in the parlour."

Mavis had no explanation. "I don't know."

"I gave up on Ellie when I found out she put my Samuel's life at risk. And if you were smart, you'd give up on her too. Let her fix her own mess for a change. Now I've got work to do."

Before leaving the house, Mavis visited with Gertie and George. They were happy to see her, and she thought about all the energy she directed towards Ellie at her younger siblings' expense.

Maybe Mamie was right. Maybe it was time for her to focus on something other than fixing her sister's life.

CHAPTER 31

Sometimes Ellie heard footsteps on the stairs and her heart quickened as she imagined Mavis bounding up to see her. Mostly, though, the footsteps belonged to Mona, who brought her food, but sometimes footsteps stopped at the top of the stairs and she heard breathing on the other side of the door. It had to be Willis, but he never came into her room.

To pass the time, she rocked in her chair and stared out the window. Or she lay on her back in bed, stared at the corner where the wall and ceiling met, and watched the progress of a spider spinning its web. She told stories to herself and hummed songs. She played word games, picking a letter from the alphabet and naming as many words that started with that letter as she could.

The letter U. *Untimely. Uterus. Unhappy. Ugly. Upheaval. Unbearable. Umbrella. Udder.*

In the first few days of her confinement, Sliver brought more cabbage leaves to relieve the pressure in Ellie's breasts. There was no escaping that her body had recently birthed a child. Mona brought fresh rags for her bleeding and water so she could keep herself clean. Ellie had given up asking about her baby, but she hadn't stopped mourning him.

A week passed.

S. *Seven. Sex. Siamese. Surrender. Safety. Salacious. South. Sabbath. Salt.*

And another week.

She stewed in self-pity. Then resentment honed its blade, and she re-felt all the wrongs people had done to her, starting with her daddy for letting her think she could have whatever she wanted then moving to Willis for disfiguring her, robbing her of options, and locking her up. When he'd had the house built, had he imagined the upstairs for this use? Had it been his mother's idea to lock her up? Ellie wouldn't be surprised, but if that were the case, then she'd have to know about Ellie's crime. Willis wouldn't want her to. He'd have told her that the baby died and left out the details.

It turns out I'm not the only liar.

She pulled the inside of her left cheek into her mouth between her molars and held it there, biting down gently so she could feel the edge of the scar tissue.

Why hadn't Mavis come? Maybe Danny wouldn't let her visit. Or maybe Willis or Sliver had told her the truth. Perhaps Mavis was disgusted by her. Or maybe Willis had lied and told Mavis she was dead. That would explain her sister's absence. And what about Charlie? Had something happened to him? Someone else took care of the horses now.

Questions. All she had was questions. Her tears didn't fall straight down her cheeks but followed along the ridge of scar tissues. On her right cheek, they stalled in the bottom of the W before spilling over and falling down. On her left cheek, they followed a path to the bridge of her nose and then down the jagged cut towards the corner of her mouth. She could catch those with her tongue, and she did so now at the thought of Charlie being hurt. He'd been good to her. He'd been kind. And it was different than with Samuel and Jedediah, who hadn't had a choice. She hadn't pressed herself on Charlie. At least not in the same way. He'd *wanted* to be with her. Hadn't he?

A. *Absence. Alabama. Apple. Airplane. Adventure. Arson. Alligator.*

If only she had something to read. Or a journal of some kind to write in. Anything.

Sliver didn't come anymore. Was Mona to be her only visitor? Bringing food and removing the chamber pot?

Sometime into her fourth week, the footsteps on the stairs didn't stall at the top. The deadbolt slid open and Willis appeared, looking as if he'd chewed hard on something and finally worked it out in his mind. She swung her legs over the side of the bed, wishing for a second that her hair at least looked nice. Ellie had grown accustomed to the smell of herself. Was that a look of disgust in Willis's eyes?

"I have a proposition for you."

Look what you have reduced me to.

"I am prepared to give you your freedom and enough money to go away from here and start a new life. I give my word that I will not follow you or try to make you change your mind."

I don't want a new life. I want my old life back. The one before Willis's knife had cut her — when she could still entertain the prospect of joining a travelling show. Or climbing into the cockpit of an airplane and flying over the seas. Or selling clothing at a fancy boutique in New York. Or maybe even becoming a movie star or model. Didn't Willis understand that after what he'd done to her, she couldn't *have* a new life?

"Are you interested in my offer?"

He hadn't even told her what she'd have to do. She shrugged noncommittally.

"I want a son. That's all I ask. Give me a son, and you can have enough money to go and make your own life somewhere else."

Ellie hid her surprise. He could kill her, make it look like an accident, and marry someone else; that's one of the scenarios she'd imagined. Willis had enough money that Sheriff Thorpe would overlook her death. Nobody would miss or mourn her, not even Mavis who hadn't bothered to visit.

"Why would you want a child by me, knowing what you know?"

He was slow to answer, even though he must have asked himself that question countless times. He looked at her with pity in his eyes. Pity!

"Because I need a proper ending."

A proper ending? How incredulous. He wanted to make something right out of all that had gone wrong? It was too late for that. This story would never have a happy ending.

"How much money?"

"One generous, agreed upon, sum. I'll pay it when the baby's born, and we will have no more communication after that."

She saw a flicker of hope in his eyes.

I am prepared to give you your freedom. Was freedom even possible, given her disfigurement? And did she want it? Being alone in Washington had been terrifying, but she'd been nearly penniless then. It would be different if she had money. She wouldn't be running. She'd have the means to live comfortably somewhere. And maybe Mavis could leave Danny and come live with her. They could be alone together, like they'd once imagined.

"Has Mavis been by to see me?"

"No. She wants nothing more to do with you."

"I don't believe you. Mavis has always forgiven me."

"I asked her to come, but she refused. She knows what you did, and she knows it was no accident."

Willis wouldn't want it known his wife had given birth to a mulatto baby. Had Sliver said something? That was doubtful because she'd be worried about Charlie. Unless she'd told Mamie. Her mind raced. Yes. Mavis was still close to Mamie.

"Well?"

Did he expect her to decide on the spot?

"I need to think about it. And while I'm thinking, I want a book."

"A book?"

A book. You know, pages of words housed between two covers. "Yes. To pass the time."

A shadow crossed his face. Clearly he'd expected an immediate *yes.* He crossed the room to the door and bolted it loudly behind him.

That night, she dreamt of Willis sitting at the table with a cup of tea and a big pot of honey. Only it wasn't a spoon he used to scoop the sweet liquid into his cup. When he finished, he licked the excess honey off the razor's edge.

Willis let a week pass before he returned and threw a package on her bed. "Have you given my offer any thought?"

She'd been unable to think of anything else. "Yes."

"And?"

"I have a few conditions of my own."

They bartered back and forth until finally they reached an agreement. Ellie would be released from the room when she was definitely with child and no sooner. Willis needed to know the child was his. She would return to her room downstairs when the midwife confirmed her pregnancy. At that point, she would be allowed to walk outside again. If the child were a daughter, the entire process would begin again, including returning her upstairs until she was pregnant once more. If she gave birth to a son, she would be free to leave as soon as she felt strong enough to do so. Willis would have his lawyer open a bank account in her name, into which he would deposit a lump sum of money. No more money would come after that payment, and there would be no contact between them after she left. In addition, she would sign a legal document that waived her right to see her son. If Willis ever spotted her in the vicinity of Neelan Junction, he would have her arrested.

The conversation took over an hour. Finally, they finished, and Willis stood awkwardly before her. "I brought you a book, like you asked." He gestured to the package on the bed.

Did he want her to thank him?

He stood there, dumbly.

"We might as well get this over with," she said and lifted her skirt.

⌒ Ellie opened the package after Willis left. She hoisted the book up and down as if it were a newborn to be weighed. Almost one thousand pages. She had to admit, he had done a good job.

The book's title was written in black capital letters on a yellowy-brown cover—a shout not a whisper—*Gone with the Wind*. In the foreground, a young Scarlett O'Hara (what a delightful name!) with an impossibly small waist bound in a hoop skirt stood before two white men who clearly admired her. A white-pillared mansion filled the background. The novel had come out in June 1936, the year after she'd married, the month her first child had died, and even Ellie, confined and grieving as she was, had read about its popularity in *The Neelan News*.

She cracked the spine.

Ellie lifted her skirt for two months until a baby firmly rooted. Sliver confirmed the pregnancy and, as promised, Willis moved her back into her bedroom on the second floor. The greatest luxury was in having access to the bathroom once again and being able to resume her spot on the porch swing. She wondered if Mrs. Yates enjoyed having her in her view again.

Her belly grew, much faster this time than in the previous pregnancies. Ellie hoped for Mavis's carriage to pull up, but her sister never came. What had she been told?

Her belly grew, and Ellie dreamed of freedom. Of dead children. Of kittens in a sack. Of two sisters, soaring high above the ground on outstretched wings. *Hey Gullie, Gullie, Gullie!* Except Mavis had flown in a different direction without her.

Her belly grew, and she imagined her final parting from this place. Willis would drive her to the station, to be sure she got on the train. He'd be relieved to see her go. She had hurt him. He would never be the same. But she would leave a son behind to carry on his name. And that son would never know his mother. Was that the happy ending he wanted?

She imagined all of this as the child grew inside her, and she thought if she were an animal, she'd be a cow, placid and fecund, tethered by her head in a stall.

CHAPTER 32

Every labour had its risks, but Sliver was confident Miss Ellie's would go smoothly. After all, it was her third child; her body had a memory to mimic. Still, Sliver knew that a woman's fear increased with each pregnancy because she knew the magnitude of the pain that was coming. First time mamas could only *imagine* how badly it might hurt, but repeat mamas knew. Sliver had experienced that fear herself.

She checked in on Miss Ellie three times a day as her time approached, placing her palm on her stomach to feel the thunder inside. Finally, the day came when Miss Ellie's water broke and contractions contorted her face with pain. Sliver called Mona and told her to get supplies. She would not leave Ellie unsupervised this time.

As the labour progressed, Miss Ellie set her mind to the task and bore down to complete it as if it were a chore to be dispensed with. For six hours Miss Ellie pushed through her pain, and when the baby finally slipped into Sliver's hands, she cleaned it, saw it was another boy, wrapped him in a blanket, and left Mona to care for his mama. She had strict instructions to follow.

She carried the newborn out of the room without letting Miss Ellie hold him, took him downstairs, and handed him to Master Willis.

"Is it a boy?"

She nodded.

"And he's fine?"

She nodded again. "He's healthy and has all his parts."

"And you've arranged for a wet nurse?"

"Yes." She had moved a girl named Tessa from Slew Town into an empty shack. Sliver was saving her, too.

He smiled down at his son and kissed his cheek. Years of worry left his brow. Then he handed the baby back. "My wife is forbidden from seeing the child, do you understand?"

Sliver nodded.

"Not to nurse him or anything. She will be leaving as soon as she's ready to travel."

Leaving? Had Sliver known, she might have allowed Ellie to hold her son for a minute. Supervised. "Where?" Sliver needed to know so Charlie would stay safe.

"That is for her to decide, but away from Neelan Junction. For good."

The baby started to cry that specific thin wail of a newborn wanting to nurse. Sliver rocked him in her arms.

"Take him to the wet nurse," he said. "And remember, Ellie is not to see him for any reason."

Again, Sliver nodded. He didn't need to spell it out for her.

She had set the wet nurse up in the shack beside hers. It was even smaller than her own, with one room that had a bed, a stove, and a sink in it. The outhouse was close enough to the shed to not make the travel a chore but far enough to keep the smell and bugs away. Sliver had promised Tessa she'd have her privacy and that no men would bother her. She hoped that would be true.

Tessa's baby was sleeping when Sliver arrived. She stayed long enough to make sure Master Willis's baby latched on okay and drew some milk down.

"I'll be back soon. Don't let anybody in. At least for the next few days. No one."

Sliver had seen a lot of things in her day, but as she pieced together the circumstances of this birth, she knew it would remain unusual. If she understood correctly, Miss Ellie had just bought herself a way out of Neelan Junction, and she'd used her own flesh as currency.

It was a twist on a story Sliver knew too well. Her people had lived through generations of having their children taken from them against their will, but Miss Ellie seemed to have agreed to this exchange and was profiting from it.

Knowing she was leaving was both a relief and a worry. What was she getting from leaving, and where would she go? She'd written to Charlie before. Would she do so again?

CHAPTER 33

Three days after giving birth, Ellie's belongings were loaded into the car. Mona opened the back passenger door for her, and she slipped inside. Willis was nowhere to be seen. Someone she didn't know was at the wheel. Nobody waved to her as the car pulled away. She could have been a piano tuner leaving as quietly as she'd come.

At the station, Ellie boarded the train and had a porter store her belongings. This time, she wasn't running away. She had permission to leave and money to do so. Her heart beat calmly in her chest. It had no need to fluctuate.

The veil covering the lower half of her face fluttered gently, her breath a constant breeze. She found a seat by the window and dropped into it. A few minutes later, the train pulled out of the station and gradually picked up speed. Just a few miles away was the place where she'd been born — the two-storey white house with the wrap-around porch; the well-worn path to the shade tree with the curved and naked branch that held the weight of a man and more; the broken-down barn with the door that squealed, the hayloft that hid treasures, and the bridge over Sugar Creek where Jedediah and his wife had taken their final breaths.

Men are animals. That's all you need to know.

She smelled the dirt floor in the tool shed, the acrid scent of male sweat, and recalled the giddy feeling of trespass, of doing something she shouldn't be doing but going ahead anyway. She smelled the hay in the barn and the comforting aroma of horses. If she closed her eyes, she could be riding a stallion, or a great winged beast that would carry her high above the ground as she soared in her own body. A shiver ran through her.

Once again, she was leaving her entire life behind her, but this time, with the money she had, she wouldn't need to impress or please anyone. She was still young, just twenty-three, but no man would have her now. She wasn't sure if she should celebrate or cry.

Her face was reflected back to her in the window. Her hair had come back full and shiny, just like Mavis had predicted it would. She reached up and unhooked the veil. Her scars stared back, ridged and ragged. She fought against a horrible realization: she had lost.

And if she had lost, that meant Willis had won.

All the money in the world wasn't worth Willis thinking he'd won. She put her veil back on.

A burst of laughter erupted in the back of the train car and drew closer as a group of men walked up the aisle. They didn't linger when they saw she was alone. It was a death of sorts, to be young and unnoticed, but she was getting used to deaths.

She had left three babies behind. Two in the ground and one with the man she hated most in the world.

Who was nursing her baby? No. That was the wrong question. Who was nursing Willis's son?

It was 1940. Union Station hadn't changed in the almost six years since Ellie had been there, but she certainly had. This time she didn't cower in the waiting room but stepped right into the crowd. This time she found a porter to take her luggage directly to the taxi stand. This time she told the driver to take her to the fanciest hotel in the city.

The Mayflower had chandeliers in the lobby that hung from the ceiling like clusters of diamonds freshly released from a vault. Dark panels of polished wood offset the shiny brass fixtures at the front desk. If only the clerk hadn't scrutinized her veil-covered face, she'd have felt truly rich.

She took the most expensive room available, then she penned a quick note to Willis's solicitor so he would know where to send information about her bank account. She left it with the desk clerk to post.

The bellhop carried her bags to her room. She tipped him, closed the door, and scanned her surroundings. The bed had a large burgundy canopy overhead. There were sitting chairs and a couch with ornately carved wooden legs, and a dressing table polished to a great shine with a large mirror in a wooden frame. She draped a plush bath towel over the mirror. The carpet was so thick she felt as if she was floating. It was better even than the place she'd lied to Mavis about when she'd first left home. Ellie put her arms out beside her and spun around and around in the large room until she fell onto the bed and had to lie still until her dizziness passed. Such opulence!

Her stomach growled. She picked up the phone and ordered the dinner special from room service. A different bellhop delivered it on a cart and set it up for her on the table. He pulled off the metal lid covering to reveal a roast chicken with baby potatoes and vegetables. Then he uncorked the bottle of white wine and poured a little into a glass for her to sample. It was both wet and dry and made her nose itch, but she nodded to show it would do. An entire bottle to herself.

After satisfying her hunger, she soaked in the claw foot bathtub and tried not to notice her swollen breasts and stretch marks and the loose skin around her waist that would take some time to return to normal.

She dried herself off outside of the bathroom because she couldn't cover the mirror over the sink. When it was time for bed, she climbed between the sheets. The bed felt enormous for one person. She turned out the lamp and stretched an arm to the empty space beside her, feeling the silkiness of the sheets against her palm. Once, she'd imagined being with John Worthington. Or Ledger Jones. Once, she'd imagined leaving Neelan Junction and finding a big city man with money. Instead, she'd taken her restlessness and ambition and tried to satisfy her desires. Had she been drawn to Samuel, Jedediah, and Charlie because she could tell them what to do? Or was it that she was engaged in an illicit activity and enjoyed the thrill of getting away with something?

Charlie had felt compassion for her. She would always remember that. He had loved her, hadn't he?

She adjusted the pillow that was fluffy as a cloud and made a nest to cradle her head. She fell asleep remembering how gently Charlie's fingertips had traced her scars. If only he could have erased them.

In the morning, she opened the heavy curtains and was surprised to find the sun already halfway up in the sky.

She hadn't slept so soundly in years.

Her new life had begun.

PART THREE

1940 — 1963

CHAPTER 34

If the women in Neelan Junction kept track of special events, then the fall of 1940 was memorable. After almost a four-year absence, Mrs. Yates and her son Willis returned to church and re-claimed their family pew, fourth from the front. Mr. Calder, the stationmaster, had told everybody by then that Willis's wife had boarded the train and abandoned him or been sent away, depending on what mood he was in when he told the story. Everybody secretly relishes when a rich man is taken down a peg.

The great surprise was that Willis returned to church carrying a newborn in the crook of his arm. That made tongues wag fast. The baby's name was Eugene.

How could Ellie abandon her baby?

It wasn't natural.

Did you hear that Willis's mama called Ellie a devil? Well, no wonder!

Suddenly, everybody had a story that could be linked to another story that predicted Ellie's abhorrent behaviour from the time she was but a girl. Everywhere Mavis went, a conversation either halted or began as people fished for information to add to the gossip. It turned out that most people had never liked Ellie at all. Or so they said.

Mavis settled into her church pew second from the front since marrying Danny. She had just taken her gloves off when Willis entered the church carrying his son with his mama following right behind. It appeared having a son gave Willis the boost of confidence he'd lacked his whole life. He looked taller. He held people's gaze until they looked away. He didn't nod too readily, and he didn't explain why he and his mother had been absent from church. He didn't explain a thing. His new confidence meant people didn't ask him to.

Because there was now a pew between them, Mavis couldn't just turn around and talk to Willis even if she wanted to, so she approached him as soon as the service ended.

"Where's Ellie?"

"She's gone."

"I know that. *Everybody* knows that. Do you have an address for her?"

"She didn't tell me where she was going, and I didn't ask."

"But she's your wife. How can you not know?"

Willis didn't appear to have the patience to give an explanation. "None of this is any of your business. I would ask you to mind your own."

"Ellie wouldn't leave her baby behind unless you did something to her."

Willis's smile was more of a grimace than a grin. "You don't know your sister at all."

"Well that's partly your fault. I would have visited if you'd let me. I could have been a help with her pregnancy and with the baby!" She leaned forward. "Can I see him?"

Willis stepped backwards and hugged his son closer. His mama came up then and whisked the baby away. "My son will have nothing to do with his mother or with her family. Ellie is lucky I let her go, after what she did. Rest assured you'll hear from her if she needs something. That's the only time she thinks about others, when they can do something for her. But I guess you know that." He strode off and joined his mama, who was showing off the baby to a circle of women.

There was a finality to their conversation that troubled Mavis.

Danny came up and took her arm. "He acts like he's the first man to have had a son."

The bitterness in his voice made her realize Danny was jealous. He wanted a son and didn't understand how Mavis hadn't gotten pregnant yet. In their marriage bed, on the rare instances when he reached for her, Danny treated her body as if it required a regular servicing. Neither one of them appeared to take any pleasure in the act.

On the one occasion when Mavis's breasts grew tender to the touch and she suspected she might be with child, she remembered the conversation about Mamie's potions and decided ants in her belly was a better option than Danny's baby. The world didn't need another Danny in it. She feared his son would grow into a man who took what he wanted and left wreckage in his wake, and she didn't believe her guidance as a mother to help her son behave otherwise could offset the powerful traditions in the area. So she had put the small bottle filled with brown liquid to her lips, closed her eyes, and chugged it down while trying not to think she was swallowing ant juice. When the bottle was empty, she wiped her mouth and waited for the tickling inside that she suspected would soon follow. She bled two days later. It wasn't the first time her dates had been off, so she couldn't definitively link the two events.

The fall of 1940 was also memorable because it marked an increase in nighttime violence.

Danny turned nocturnal. He came home in the pre-dawn hours, waking her when the screen door slammed, his discarded boots hit the floor, or when the mattress bounced as he fell into bed. Within two minutes, his snoring reached every corner of the room. What kept him out so late? His answers never satisfied.

Sometimes she woke before the birds started their song to find the bed still empty beside her, the smell of smoke on the breeze, and the sounds of dogs baying. Were those gunshots? They sounded to be coming from the direction of Slew Town. She'd ask Danny about it the following day, but he never seemed to know what she was talking about.

But people talked. Or boasted. Mavis heard rumours of mutilations. Of black skin sizzling as it was branded. Of castrations and electrocutions. Of lynchings and drownings and disappearances. Carlina didn't talk to her, Ellie was gone, and Mamie was always busy, so Mavis read *The Neelan News* and ruminated on things, wondering what was missing in life if people found fulfillment in their days by causing harm to others. Danny said he had a job to do, keeping the coloureds in line, but Mavis couldn't help but wonder if he and the deputies weren't the ones starting the problems they believed needed fixing. It was like being in the fire brigade and lighting fires to have something to do.

Was it easier for her to recognize that Danny stirred up trouble because Ellie had done the same thing? Even as a child, Ellie had lied to test reality. It was as if she was stuck on how to end a story so made things up to see how they'd work. What would happen if she said Desperate grabbed her when he came begging for food? How much could her words change the course of a day? Had Ellie been satisfied when the sheriff doled out his justice? Was that how she'd imagined the story would end?

The bedroom was dark, but Mavis was wide awake. The room smelled of alcohol and cigarettes. It might have been birdsong that released her from sleep, or it might have been Danny's snoring. Whatever the case, the early hours between deep night and morning felt the longest. Lying beside a husband she didn't love and imagining all the mornings ahead where she'd have to wake beside him, she began to cry. Five years had passed in a flash. Ellie disappearing. Ellie returning. Ellie's baby dying. Mavis marrying. Ellie's second baby dying. Eugene being born, and Ellie disappearing again. Mavis was only twenty years old but already the future seemed like a punishment.

She remembered Danny as a boy, cutting into the front of the line to get another turn hitting Desperate with a stick. Even then he'd been cruel. But her brother Jimmy had been right behind him in line, and her daddy had helped throw the noose over the shade tree branch. And while it might seem that Ellie had started it all, Mavis could see now that she'd simply added to a narrative that already existed, one in which lynchings and picnics went hand in hand.

Ellie was gone, and she hadn't even said goodbye. So where did that leave Mavis? More alone than she'd ever been. Ellie had ruined the Turner name and Mavis had been put into service to restore it.

She'd been duped. Used. But did that require a lifetime of submission to Danny?

She brushed the tears from her face with a rough hand. She was pathetic. Every morning after Ellie left, she'd gone to the post office, but a letter never arrived.

As the days and weeks passed, Mavis knew Willis was right: Ellie didn't need her, which meant she might never hear from her sister again.

CHAPTER 35

The house at the corner of the heavily treed lot was old and showed obvious signs of neglect. The blue paint that had once been fresh had long since faded and was pulling away in curled strips like skin from a sunburn pulls from its host. The porch stairs needed fixing. A board on the second step was nearly rotted through. But what surprised Ellie most when the taxi pulled up was the brand-new white picket fence that stood out from the general decay of its surroundings, as if the owners had started from the outside first with the care of a woman who selects her dress carefully to accentuate her best features but then who forgets to bathe.

Ellie loved the fence with the paint so fresh it still looked wet. And she loved that it would mark what was hers. The blades of grass on the inside of the fence would be hers. The birds that landed in the trees on her property would be hers, for however long they chose to stay. And the seven cherry trees in the side yard lined in a perfect row would also be hers. Whoever had neglected the house had continued to pay attention to the yard. In springtime, Ellie knew, the trees would be beautiful and fragrant. And every blossom would be hers. Not her daddy's. Not Willis's. Hers.

Ellie felt an immediate comfort when she stepped inside the house. The staircase was on the same side of the entranceway as the house in which she'd grown up. The upstairs bedrooms were situated in a similar fashion to those in her youth. Even the kitchen was set up in much the same manner. If Mamie had been standing at the counter rolling out biscuits, Ellie would not have been surprised.

She was far from home, yet it felt as if she'd returned for a visit to her childhood.

The living room had a large front window, and, because the house was on a corner, the sightlines stretched down the block and into the distance. She welcomed that long view because in parts of her life she'd been deprived of a vista, and she well knew the mental damage it produced.

The man showing her the house was named Mr. Crawford. He wore a fine cut suit and attempted to look engaged as he made small talk even though he kept looking towards the door. "Will your husband be joining us soon? I'm sure he'll see that, although there is much work needed, the house is very sound."

Ellie didn't fill the silence. She felt his curiosity to see behind her veil. It was the same look everyone gave her, a hunger to know what the fabric was hiding. She had put makeup on her eyes and knew they were beautiful. She also knew Mr. Crawford imagined the rest of her would be beautiful to, and Ellie curbed the desire to pull the veil down to see the shock it would elicit. Yes, things could be worse than people imagined.

"And there are many bedrooms for your children. Do you have children?"

"Three," she replied. "I had three."

He didn't appear to note the past tense and looked at his watch.

"How much?" she asked.

"I beg your pardon?"

"What is the asking price for the house?" Ellie spoke slowly, as if he needed help to understand her.

Mr. Crawford stuttered something about never speaking money matters with women.

"You can discuss them with me or not at all."

He mentioned a figure.

She nodded and continued her tour. When she was finished, she told him her solicitor, Mr. Dunedin, would be in touch. She let herself out and walked back to the taxi that she'd asked to wait at the curb. Settling herself in the backseat, she surveyed the house again. It was perfect. She would make an offer on the house. *Her* house. Yes. It was just right.

The street sign said Michigan Avenue. She'd left Florida, gone to Washington DC, and would live on an avenue named after Michigan. What a world.

⌇ After buying the house, Ellie, for the first time in her life, felt in charge of something. She issued instructions to contractors. She chose colours and picked light fixtures and tiles and fabric. She would make sure all the decay and rot had been addressed before she moved in.

And while she enjoyed being in charge, she missed being able to share her ideas with Mavis, and she revisited all the reasons she'd come up with for why her sister hadn't visited: Danny wouldn't let her; Willis wouldn't let her; she knew about the mulatto baby and was disgusted that Ellie had crossed the colour line; she was a sheep, always following the herd. Well, too bad for her. Ellie wasn't going to beg for attention. If Mavis thought she was better than Ellie, then she'd have to live with the consequences. Mavis had benefitted more from having a big sister than Ellie had benefitted from having a little one. So Mavis's was a greater loss.

Ellie made one decision after another with little hesitation, and when the house was finally ready, she moved from the Mayflower to her Michigan Avenue address. This would be her home. This would be where her new life began.

In the mornings, *The Washington Post* was on her doorstep when she woke up. She made herself a pot of tea and read the newspaper cover to cover. She no longer had room service and had to fend for herself. She needed a maid. It would be nice to have another human presence in the house and to have her meals taken care of. When the first maid stopped showing up after two weeks, she hired another one, but a maid wasn't a friend, and the maids here didn't take orders as naturally as the maids back home. They appeared to have more options.

The days passed and Ellie waited for something to happen or to catch her interest. Now that her house project was complete, she had nothing to occupy her. She rocked in her new rocking chair and stared out the slope of lawn towards the street. She didn't wear the veil at home, so she could breathe freely. She rocked and stared. Stared and rocked. Large oak trees flanked both sides of the road, their branches gnarled and twisted like arthritic fingers. Squirrels moved swiftly and nimbly upon them.

There was no Mrs. Yates across the way to torment.

She had no husband to actively despise.

There was no barn to visit or lover to secretly meet.

She didn't like cooking when the maid didn't show, and shopping was out of the question because she hated being stared at and preferred not to leave her house.

She needed something to do. A hobby. Anything.

The lunch hour was nearing. Meals were the only thing that marked her day. She felt like a tiger at the zoo, pacing back and forth at the fence, remembering a past freedom. Only she didn't have any spectators, and her fence was of her own making. She had enough rooms in her home to wander in and out of, but was this house to be her new prison?

Gone with the Wind sat on the coffee table, its cover tattered from use. She'd brought it with her when she left Neelan Junction in case she was bored during her trip. How hungrily she'd read it when Willis had first brought it to her. It had transformed her tiny upstairs room into an entire world to be lost in. Out of boredom, she picked it up again and began to read. Scarlett, for all her fiery ambition, had been, in the end, a colossal let down. Flipping through it again, Ellie understood she could never recover her initial enthusiasm because she already knew how the story ended.

Scarlett hadn't won either.

Scarlett, admired. Scarlett, defending a way of life. Scarlett, determined to make a life for herself. And the philandering Rhett turning the knife. The story ran too true to Ellie's own life. She didn't want to re-live that time in her life or Willis's nocturnal visits.

She closed the book and stared at the cover. The narrative was far too predictable. Anybody could write a book like that. Even *she* could write a book like that.

The shock of the idea caused her heart to stutter.

The sudden hope scared and enticed her.

In a matter of seconds, the thought grew from a seed to a stem with leaves on it.

Then it became a sapling, rooted more firmly in the ground.

And just as quickly, it became a full-grown tree.

Yes!

Hadn't Mamie always claimed she had a fanciful imagination? And hadn't Ellie told stories as a child, to make Mavis laugh and to pass the time? Writing was something she could do from home. No one would have to see her. And once she completed a manuscript, she could send her work out by post. It was a job of the utmost privacy. It *required* solitude.

She waited for an obvious flaw in her logic that would destroy her enthusiasm, but none came. Writing would give some structure to her days. A reason to get up in the mornings.

She paced the living room and began a list of things she'd need. A typewriter. Paper. One of the upstairs bedrooms could become a study. She'd need a desk and a proper chair with casters. One that would spin. And a dictionary to look up words and to expand her vocabulary.

She clapped her hands. Thank God! She would have gone mad from boredom.

She went out front and sat on the porch swing she'd had installed. Her house was set back far enough from the road to not have to speak to passers-by. The cherry trees in the side yard blocked any view from the neighbour's house next door, so her privacy was secure. The air had cooled, but there was still some warmth in the early afternoon sun.

Her mind continued to race. She would buy a stained glass lamp for her desk. It would send coloured shafts of light onto the white walls. And in that light, she would create characters—women, young and old, married and single, who would find ways to enjoy their bodies and live out their dreams fully; she would put those dreams on paper. She would defy conventions and let her imagination run wild. She was truly free in that she had nothing to lose and no one to impress. She didn't even need to make money from her writing. Willis had been more generous than she'd expected.

The wind eddied around her. It shook a large spider web that had secured itself in the top corner of the porch.

A woman walked by pushing a pram. Ellie observed her as if she was a character in a book she was writing. The woman wore a grey skirt and white short sleeved blouse. She had a sensible heel on her shoes that gave her a slight lift but was also comfortable for walking. A scarf covered her hair, and a pair of sunglasses kept the sun out of her eyes. A small purse hung in the crook of one arm. How efficient she looked. How committed to her task.

But maybe the pram was simply a prop that gave the woman something to do. Maybe it was even empty. Ellie laughed out loud. One subtle adjustment changed everything. A woman walking with a pram was normal but walking with an empty pram? What was she then? Deranged? Plotting? Women in the city might be as lost as women in the country. Ellie recognized an edge of panic in the woman's gait. In fact, the more she watched her, the more she imagined that the woman *needed* the pram to stay grounded, as if it was the only thing that kept her from breaking into a run. Ellie continued to watch her until she was out of sight.

Having money made Ellie realize how little freedom she'd ever had in life.

She had been disowned and discarded.

But now her financial independence meant she wouldn't have to censor herself at all in her writing. Nevertheless, she decided a pseudonym would be in order, to ensure her anonymity, and she already knew which one to use.

She pushed gently with her feet and set the swing and her imagination in motion.

Women lusted after sex and money and power just like men did; she was proof of that. Only, they went about it differently because they had to. Because they were denied independence.

Ellie would set her book in the Old South, like Margaret Mitchell had done, but Ellie's rivers and creeks would flow with orange juice and turpentine, and they'd be sopped up by cotton and tobacco and legal tender in the form of bills. In her world, muscular slaves would walk about with a sheen of sweat on their skin and white women would sit on porches, their eyes shaded by their bonnets, and peek out above their fans, watching, always watching while trying to be invisible.

Ellie remembered the mulatto children on her daddy's land and all over Neelan Junction. If she was any indication, not all of them came from black mothers. And wasn't that a story that needed telling? Mixed race babies born out of revolt from white women's wombs?

A dog barked down the block.

The mailman appeared and delivered letters to the neighbour's mailbox.

She needed a name for her protagonist. Something as memorable as Scarlett O'Hara. She played with a few and said them out loud, to gauge how they felt on her tongue, until finally deciding on one. Then she began to craft the opening sentence.

Isabelle Montgomery was the most beautiful girl in …

Where? Not Neelan Junction. She needed the freedom of a place entirely imagined. She scrunched her eyes tight and coaxed her brain to work. She imagined a nameless southern state—Alassippi or Mississbama—in the antebellum years. A place where the plantation owners made more money from breeding and selling slaves than they did from raising cotton or tobacco. Where greed and lust and hatred were doled out with serving spoons at every meal. Or maybe it was simply a memorable place name she needed; she could leave readers to determine the state.

Isabelle Montgomery was the Mistress of Magnolia Hall, and she was the most beautiful girl in the entire country.

Yes. Why not? In the entire United States of America.

At seventeen, her blonde hair …

Excitement fluttered in her belly.

She heard Mamie's voice asking, *Are you telling tales again, Miss Ellie?*

"Why yes I am," she said out loud. "Tall tales."

The desk couldn't arrive soon enough.

CHAPTER 36

The post office was the unofficial meeting place for all the residents of Neelan Junction. Mavis found sitting outside the post office to be a substitute to the porch swing she and Ellie had once used to escape from their boredom. When the weather was fine, which was often, people sat on the benches outside and exchanged pleasantries beside the planters filled with flowers that Postmaster Skinner's wife tended with great care.

Watching people was its own form of entertainment. On Thursdays, Mamie would stop by before lunch to share news. Sometimes Samuel came on days when Mamie was too busy, and Mavis was able to exchange a few words with him. From time to time, she caught a glimpse of Ellie's son Eugene with his grandma or with Willis. Seeing how much that boy had grown astonished her. Sometimes months would pass between sightings, and when she saw him again she understood why people said children grew like weeds. Eugene was also a physical reminder of Ellie's departure. How old was he now? Almost seven? Yes. Ellie had been gone that long.

The sun felt good on her arms as she sat on the bench. She enjoyed letting her body gather the heat and store it for later when she took shelter inside. Rosetta, Carlina's daughter or cousin, Mavis still didn't know which, came out of the post office with a letter. Three young boys waited for her off to the side; the eldest held the younger boy's hand. Mavis hadn't seen Rosetta since that day she'd been crying with the baby in her kitchen. That was the eldest, was it? And now he had two brothers. How big he looked next to them. There was no mistaking they were related. Rosetta said something that made the older boy smile and a half dimple appeared in his cheek.

Just then, Mrs. Booth exited the post office with a clutch of letters in her hand. Mavis screwed up her courage to greet her. "Good morning."

"Oh, hello. I didn't see you there. My eyes must be adjusting to the light after being inside. I'm Mrs. Booth," she extended a hand. "But please, call me Margaret."

Mavis nodded, knowing she never would, and took her hand. "I'm Mrs. Thorpe. You can call me Mavis. We haven't been formally introduced."

"Well it's good to make it official." She gave Mavis an appraisal. "Thorpe did you say?"

Mavis nodded.

"Danny Thorpe's wife?"

Again, Mavis nodded.

Mrs. Booth gestured to the letters in her other hand. "Well I guess you know these aren't likely fan mail."

"I don't know why it's taken me so long to introduce myself. Your letters are the only thing I enjoy reading in the paper." Mavis felt her cheeks colour under the woman's scrutiny.

"Thank you. I must say I'm surprised. I'm confident it's not an opinion shared by your husband."

"That's true." Again, she felt embarrassed by the woman's close scrutiny.

"May I sit for a moment?"

"Please." Mavis moved to the side to make room.

"People often unfairly assume that wives share their husband's views, but unfortunately that is so often the case. I'm pleased to know you think independently. More women ought to try it." She held the letters up in the air. "I can also now safely assume you're not the author of any of these. People who write and hide behind anonymity are cowards. They describe in great detail and with apparent delight the methods by which they are going to do me harm."

"That must be awful to read."

Mrs. Booth shrugged. "Sadly, one gets used to it after a while. It's the price I pay for speaking my mind. People don't take kindly to having their character called into question."

"No, I suppose not."

"Outspoken women are easily criticized; it's good to know I have at least one admirer in town, besides my husband, of course. From now on, I will think of you reading my letters to the editor as I write. By the way, does your husband work for Reggie Richardson?"

"No, why?"

"He is so often in Slew Town that I wondered."

How would she know that? "Danny is one of the deputies."

"Deputies?" Mrs. Booth snorted. "Is that what Klan members call themselves now? Lord help you if you believe that. The Klan has been gaining in strength since the Depression. Everybody wants to blame someone for their hardships. The negro is an easy target."

Mavis must have looked dumbfounded because Mrs. Booth reached out and patted her knee. "No offence, Mrs. Thorpe."

"Mavis."

"No offense, Mavis, but I have told my husband repeatedly that this town could use a good eye doctor. People here don't seem able to see what's going on farther than a few inches from their face. It might be the greatest case of near-sightedness I've ever witnessed."

Danny a member of the Klan? "I've had my suspicions," Mavis replied, as if that would separate her from the others, "but Danny never really answers my questions."

Mrs. Booth recognized her embarrassment. "You're not the only one who has difficulty seeing the truth, my dear. My dear husband believes me to be too charitable in my assessment of others. Where I see near-sightedness, he sees willful ignorance. He thinks people here are fine with how things are and see nothing wrong with it, but I prefer to believe otherwise. There *are* good people about. Sadly, they're often not outspoken. Which begs the question if they are good at all." She waved a hand through the air beside her head to discourage a bee's attention. "The problem with people who are good is that it is difficult for them to imagine doing things to others that they would not do themselves. So their very goodness becomes a defect. Again, forgive my directness, but I have learned it's beneficial not to ignore one's instincts." She stood and stretched, her letters still bundled in her hand. "If I were you, I wouldn't speak about our little conversation to your husband. I can predict the outcome: he will dismiss me as an outside agitator, and then he will find a way to make you feel crazy for any suspicions you might have about his behaviour. The great fault of Klansmen is they believe themselves to be individuals when in fact they are an assemblage of clichés."

An assemblage of clichés? What did that mean?

Mrs. Booth held out her hand again. "Now, I shall leave you to enjoy the sun again. Thank you for the conversation. We must do it again. Please, stop by for tea sometime. I so rarely have visitors."

"Thank you. Maybe I will."

Mrs. Booth walked away. None of the women nearby acknowledged her as she passed.

⤙ Danny was seated at the dining room table reading the newspaper when Mavis returned, an empty plate sat to his side.

"Where were you?" he asked.

"At the post office." The knuckles on his right hand were scabbed over. What did he do in Slew Town? If Mrs. Booth knew he spent time there then people must be talking.

"Anything come?"

"Just a seed catalogue." She dropped it on the table and it sounded like a gun going off.

Danny jumped and put a hand to his chest. "Jesus Christ! Be careful."

Did he have a guilty conscience?

He turned back to the paper and began to rail against unions and the rise in communist activity. In his mind, the two were obviously linked. He flipped the page and must have read something funny because he suddenly laughed, and a half dimple appeared in his cheek as if an invisible finger had poked an indent.

It was a déjà vu moment. Hadn't she just seen a cheek with that same marking? Where had she been? The post office. Her mind continued its search. Rosetta and her boys. The eldest.

Oh.

Her knees buckled and she sat down. Was that part of the nearsightedness Mrs. Booth had pointed out? It had been right in front of her face all along.

Danny saying he'd called in Rosetta to help Carlina around the house.

Rosetta crying in the kitchen.

The midwife holding a mulatto baby.

The boy with a half dimple when he smiled.

The siblings that looked just like him.

Words spilled from her mouth. "I saw Rosetta at the post office today with her boys."

"So?"

"How many does she have now? Three?"

"How would I know?"

How smug he looked, staring at the paper, not even glancing her way. "Yes. How would you know? I looked at them and thought how much they remind me of someone I know."

He looked up from the paper and held her gaze; his eyes issued a warning.

Mavis was too angry to be scared. It was the middle of the day. If he tried to hurt her, she would scream her head off. Surely a neighbour would hear her. "Guess who they reminded me of?"

Danny stood up and walked behind her chair. His hands came down on her shoulders and squeezed at the space on either side of her collar bone, which made her wince. He leaned down and spoke into her ear. "I don't know who they remind you of, but you wouldn't want to get Rosetta into any trouble, would you? It would be a pity if something happened to her and the boys ended up in Slew Town."

How she hated him, the 'deputy' who took what he wanted because he could and thought that made him somehow strong. Did any of her 'allowance' pay for Rosetta? If so, Mavis hoped Rosetta found a way to save some to one day get away from Danny too.

Danny released her and returned to his chair. He flipped open the paper again. "Just remember that your stock fell because of Ellie, so before you entertain the idea that running off would make you happy, just ask Ellie how that worked for her. She got away from Neelan Junction, but she's probably just as miserable somewhere else, living off the money Willis paid to be rid of her."

"How would I ask when I don't know where she is?"

"Write her a letter."

"Oh, and just put her name on an envelope without an address? That's not how the postal system works, Danny." The conversation was taking her away from the one about Rosetta. She didn't want her anger to lose its arc.

"According to Postmaster Skinner, Willis once sent something to Ellie through a solicitor. At least that's what he told my daddy."

It was either a trap or a conciliatory gesture. She remained wary. "If that's true, then why didn't you tell me before?"

He shrugged. "You never asked. Plus, everybody was happy to see Ellie go — your parents, Willis. I figured you were too."

Mavis chewed her lower lip for a moment and played through some scenarios. "So if I gave you a letter, you might be able to get it to her?"

"Probably, yes."

She inspected him closely. If he was the father of Rosetta's boys, he could certainly be the father of other children too. Her anger didn't stem from his being unfaithful — if she loved him that might be true — she didn't like that she provided an alibi for him and gave him some legitimacy. He couldn't be an awful man because look at his respectable wife. Until today, Mrs. Booth had assumed Mavis shared her husband's beliefs. Other people would think the same.

Danny grabbed a toothpick and began picking between his molars. She turned away before he flicked a chunk of food out.

Danny was trying to be helpful, and that just proved that people could be complicated, both in the giving and in the taking.

⟜ Mavis felt certain Danny would rescind his offer or make it known that his daddy had no way of getting a letter to Ellie, but the next day he confirmed he could get it to Ellie's solicitor.

"So she'll get it?"

"I can't promise that. She might be dead. Daddy says if someone's been missing for seven years or more, they can be pronounced dead. And that would mean Willis could marry again."

"Marry again?"

"He's been courting Pearl Wilson. How do I know that and you don't?"

Doc Wilson's daughter? Mavis had gone to school with Pearl. She used to sing everywhere she went—in church, in school, on the street. Everyone said, *Pearl Wilson sings like a bird.* And then one day at school, Ellie and her friends said, "Why don't you sing us a song, Pearl?" As if her gift was a birthmark shading her face. Pearl never did sing after that. Mavis always wished she'd said something to Pearl. Anything. Like, *Your voice is beautiful.* But she hadn't said a thing.

"Do you think Ellie's dead?"

Danny shrugged. "I don't think about her at all."

She couldn't be sure a letter would get to Ellie, but at least now she had a possible address. Mavis left the kitchen and went to find some stationery. She'd give the letter to Danny right away while he still seemed willing to help.

CHAPTER 37

Ellie's first book, *The Magnolia Tree,* came out in 1944 under the pseudonym Randall Hunter. Sales were brisk. The book went into a second printing. And a third. Isabelle Montgomery was either loved or hated; whatever the case, readers wanted more, and Ellie was amazed. All her life she'd been praised for her beauty and not for her cleverness. And now look! With her first royalty cheque, she bought herself a gold cigarette case with the initials RH inscribed on it. She bought it with *her* money, not Willis's.

Southern Justice was published in 1946 and continued Isabelle's story. Once again, sales were brisk. But not all reviewers praised Randall Hunter's work. Some were less than kind. *Randall Hunter outdoes himself this time. An outhouse is likely cleaner than that man's mind.* Another wrote, *The book is a senseless depiction of human degradation. It is sexual exploitation dressed up as cheap circus.* Ellie had laughed out loud at that review.

Maybe it was the anonymity of writing under a pseudonym, or maybe it was that by the time reviews came out for a book, she was already well into the next one, but whatever the case, Ellie found bad reviews to be more entertaining than the good ones. They didn't at all impede her ability to write. Now, for example, she was well into her third book, *The Cathedral,* that was scheduled for a 1948 publication. Reading a review that *Southern Justice* was nothing better than a *lurid potboiler of forced breeding* only encouraged her to add more to the discussion. Her books continued to sell; bad reviews sometimes did more for sales than good reviews.

She was startled by the sound of something breaking in the kitchen. It sounded like a glass had shattered. Not only was the new maid clumsy, but she also talked too much. Ellie suspected she snooped through her belongings, too. She'd taken to counting the exact amount of money she had in her purse because she was certain that some had gone missing. She also made sure to keep her cigarette case with her. No, she didn't like this maid, but she also didn't welcome the headache of finding a new one. She was already on the fourth one since buying her house. Or was it the fifth? Good help was hard to find. All she wanted was someone to clean, shop, cook, and take care of her mail. How hard could that be?

She lit a cigarette and looked at the clock. Lunch was late. Again. She turned to the mail stacked on the edge of the desk. An envelope from her solicitor sat on top. What did he want?

She opened it and found another envelope inside, addressed to Mrs. Ellie Yates, c/o the solicitor. The cigarette that was part way to her mouth stalled mid-flight. She'd recognize that handwriting anywhere.

March 1947

Dear Ellie,

I hope this letter finds you. Danny said the sheriff might be able to get it to you, and I hope that's true. I would have written sooner if I'd known where to write, and this letter would have been longer if I'd known you would receive it. However, as I'm not sure you will, I will keep it short.

I kept waiting for you to send for me, like you said you would, but you never did. Why haven't you written?

Danny said as it's been almost seven years since you left, and as no one's heard from you, Willis will be able to tell people you are dead, and they'll all believe it. He's gotten close to Pearl Wilson. Danny said Willis plans to marry her.

Did you know Willis named your son Eugene? He grows

like a weed. I see him in town sometimes but am not allowed to speak to him.

What happened that you went away, Ellie? Willis wouldn't tell me what you did, but I'll forgive you. I always did. I know where you come from and what you've been through. And I know you wouldn't have left without your baby if something bad hadn't happened.

Please write if you get this.

Love,
Mavis

Ellie's hands shook as she put the letter down. It was almost a month old. Why had it taken so long to reach her?

She stood up and paced the room. Mavis would *forgive* her? For what? *She* was the one who'd abandoned Ellie! Where had she been after her second baby died? And where had she been when Ellie was pregnant and waiting for her third? Mavis should be the one asking for forgiveness. *What did you do ...?* How typical. Mavis blamed her for everything, yet she'd been there that day Willis cut her. She'd seen what Willis did to her.

Ellie sat down again at her typewriter and tried to focus, but it was no use. The letter had thrown her. Now her whole day would be off schedule. She picked up her typewritten pages and stacked them into a neat pile.

Willis couldn't marry again—he was still married to her. And Pearl Wilson? That homely little songbird? He should have married her in the first place. It was a much better match. Ellie could have kept her beauty. Jedediah and his wife might still be alive. And her babies ... But instead Willis had wanted other men to envy him. Did they envy him now?

She hated the name Eugene. Willis couldn't even do that right.

It wasn't fair that he be happy.

She had agreed to never contact Willis and their son again, but nobody had said anything about not contacting Old Lady Yates. Such delight she had taken in spurning Ellie. Had she won, too, by getting rid of Ellie? What good had it been hurting Willis if his mama didn't even know the full extent of her actions?

She put a fresh sheet of paper into the typewriter and began a letter.

CHAPTER 38

Mornings were usually the time Mrs. Yates got talking, as if keeping her mouth shut for all those sleeping hours gave her the need to exercise her jaw. And Sliver's was the ear she talked into.

"Morning, Sliver."

The old woman's breath smelled rank first thing. "Morning, Ma'am." Sliver put the tea tray down next to the bed and poured a cup.

"I was just thinking that I haven't cried in years." She launched into a conversation as if they'd been in the middle of one. "I used to cry so easily when I first married Thomas, but he soon put a stop to that." She reached for the cup Sliver passed her. "*Stop crying*, Esther, he'd say, pushing his face into mine. *Don't be such a blubbering baby.* After a while, I didn't like to give him the satisfaction. He used being a baby as such an insult, but he wanted children. I always found that strange. Don't you?"

"Yes Ma'am, I do." Sliver opened the curtains and let the light in. Eugene was on his porch across the way, pushing the swing hard so it banged into the house on the upswing. *Bang. Bang. Bang.*

"I was also thinking that you've been my most constant companion over the years. Did you know that?"

Sliver turned and focused on the hollow in Mrs. Yates's throat, the round gap between the collar bones at the base of her neck. It was as close to making eye contact as she came. "You've got Master Willis, Ma'am. And you've got Eugene too."

"Yes, but it's not the same. I've always felt in some way that you and I are connected."

Sliver kept her face impassive even as anxiety crept in.

"We both lost our husbands on the same day. Did you ever think about that?"

Did she ever think about that? Almost every day. But not about Old Man Yates, about Gideon. And he was *hers* to talk about, not Mrs. Yates's.

"The coincidence of us both becoming widows on the same day?"

Sliver wanted to sit down to stop the dizziness that had suddenly come upon her.

"Only in my case, I was glad Thomas wasn't coming home. I'll admit I'd prayed for it sometimes, but I don't think you shared that joy, did you? Of your husband not coming home?"

Was she enjoying Sliver's discomfort? Mrs. Yates had at least buried her husband to know she was a widow. Without Gideon's body, Sliver could never be fully sure. She turned to the dresser and opened the top drawer, to make sure the contents were neat and to keep her hands busy. She picked up a scarf to refold it. Ellie's gold cigarette case fell out and back into the drawer. She held it up in the air.

"Now what's that doing there?" Mrs. Yates said. "Where did you find it?"

"It was tucked into your scarf. Miss Ellie looked everywhere for this." Sliver still remembered how upset Miss Ellie had been, not wanting to leave without it, accusing Mona and Beanie of theft. What if something had happened to one of them?

"Well I don't know how it got there." Mrs. Yates waved it away as if it was nothing. "As I was saying, I've always suspected I had your husband to thank for my Thomas's disappearing, but I never had the chance."

"No Ma'am." Sliver drifted back to the day when Doc Wilson had pronounced Old Man Yates dead. His body had been laid out in the parlour. Sliver had washed it and seen how his skull had turned to pulp in the back. All she'd been able to think was, *What has he done?* And, *Where is he?* But she couldn't ask because wasn't it obvious that the dead white man on the table would be tied to the black man she suspected was now missing?

"What was his name?"

She remembered making supper for her kids that night and looking out the window, knowing, as each minute passed, that Gideon wasn't coming home.

"Sliver?"

"Yes?"

"I said, what was his name?"

She cleared the blockage from her throat. "Gideon." She said it louder. "His name was Gideon."

"That's right. I remember now. And you never heard from him again?"

Sliver shook her head.

"I'm sorry to hear that. Do you think he ran off?"

Why was she asking? "I don't know."

"It's an awful thing negroes do, running off. How many children do you have?"

She was asking now? After knowing Sliver for more than thirty years?

Bang.

Mrs. Yates looked with annoyance at the window. "What on earth is that racket?"

"It's Eugene hitting the swing against the house."

"Well I wish he'd stop. What was I saying?" She reached for a letter that lay on her bed. "Oh yes. How many children do you have?"

Her question was in the present tense. "Three."

"Only three? I thought you had more."

I did. Don't you remember? I took the sickness from your house into my own.

"And the youngest? What's his name again?"

"Charlie. But he's not here anymore."

"Right. He used to drive my carriage."

"Like I said, he's not here anymore. He's been gone for years."

"Was he born after Gideon left?"

Sliver sensed a trap being set but couldn't figure out how it was unfolding. What did she know? "Pardon?"

"I asked if Charlie was born after Gideon disappeared."

Sliver nodded. A drop of sweat trickled down between her shoulder blades and inched into the small of her back.

"Doc Wilson thought Thomas might have died from head trauma. The back of his head had slivers embedded as if he'd been hit with a piece of wood, but I told him Thomas had probably hit it hard when he fell out of the wagon. I said he'd been complaining of chest pains for some time. Why have an autopsy? There was nothing to be done about it, was there? Thomas wasn't coming back to life."

Now Sliver understood why nobody had gone looking for Gideon. Mrs. Yates must have wanted her husband gone so badly that she didn't care how his death happened.

"He wasn't a good man, was he? My husband?"

Sliver looked at the woman lying in bed with a teacup in her lap. White folks had a habit of asking for the truth but then punishing the truth teller. "I guess it depends on who you ask." It was clear that Mrs. Yates was circling something else.

"One more question before you go. What happened to Ellie's second baby? Did he really die?"

Sliver's hand was on the doorknob. Her heart was in her mouth. "It's God's honest truth when I say I didn't birth that child. He came in the middle of the night so fast that Miss Ellie didn't call me in time. But yes, Master Willis's baby died." How easily truth could be twisted. What she'd said was true; the baby Mrs. Yates was referring to wasn't Willis's.

"But if he *had* lived, he'd be just a year older than Eugene, wouldn't he? About the same age as that mulatto boy with the light eyes. What's his name?"

Bang.

Sliver turned the handle, pretending she hadn't heard the question. "I'm going to tell Eugene to stop making that racket."

She closed the door before Mrs. Yates could object and put her hand on the wall to balance herself as she went downstairs. What had changed that Mrs. Yates was asking so many questions? Why her sudden interest in Jerome after all these years?

Sliver was familiar with paranoia. All her life she'd known fluctuating conditions of security and threat. It took its toll knowing how quickly her well-being could be threatened.

She crossed the courtyard, climbed the stairs to the porch, and grabbed one of the chains on the swing to keep it from hitting the house. "That's enough," she told Eugene.

He pushed it hard again, and she almost lost her balance trying to hang on. "I said that's enough."

"I don't have to listen to you." He was only eight, yet he looked at her as if she was dirt. She curbed the instinct to cuff the boy hard on the ears. That's what she'd do to Jerome if he talked to her in that tone, which he never would.

He kicked out with his feet. "*Let go.*"

"I will. And then I'm going back to tell your grandma that I tried to get you to stop making such a racket like she asked. And if I hear the swing hitting the house, I'll say you don't care that she wants you to stop." Her voice was shaking. She turned to go and heard him pull phlegm into his throat. "I wouldn't do that if I were you."

"Or what?" He spat, but she didn't feel anything hit her as she walked away. The cycle was continuing. Eugene was growing up to be trouble just like those boys that had knocked her down fifty years earlier and just like the sheriff and his son and all his friends who took what they wanted and thought it was their right. For a while, Sliver had harboured the belief that Master Yates, being a better man than his daddy, would raise a better son, but that didn't appear to be true.

She went back to Mrs. Yates's house and listened. Eugene had moved on, but the disquiet in her midsection continued. Gideon hadn't needed to run at all. She would have preferred not knowing that information.

She sat at the kitchen table and put her head in her hands. What a muddle her life had become. Here she was protecting the son of the son of the man who had caused her husband to disappear. Jerome, who was Charlie's son, sired by Old Man Yates. Ellie hadn't known that Charlie was her own husband's half-brother. That almost counted as incest.

Oh, Giddy, what a mess. What am I going to do?

He'd been a handsome young man at the top of a ladder, pulling stars from the sky. Then his eyes met hers and something transferred between them.

What's wrong?

I have suffered immeasurable grief.

And the image she would forever recall. Gideon descended the rungs, pulled some oranges from a pail, and set them in motion. Her brothers had laughed for the first time in a week. The sides of her own mouth had turned up.

He had done that. Gideon had altered their world. He had plucked stars from the sky and showed her with careful attention, they could be rearranged. And always, she imagined the one hovering at the top of the rotation as the North Star, and Gideon kept placing it there, again and again, to show her she could be free.

CHAPTER 39

In the summer of 1947, after almost nine years of marriage, Mavis was wakened in the small hours of night by the sound of footsteps on the porch and a loud knocking at the door.

She pulled on her robe and ran to open it. Jimmy stood there, his hat in his hand and anguish in his expression, three deputies at his side.

"What's wrong?"

Her brother stood mute.

"Jimmy? Did something happen to Mama? What?"

"It's Danny. He's dead."

She felt herself sway. *Dead?* Jimmy grabbed her elbow to steady her.

"Not just dead," one of the deputies said. "Murdered."

Jimmy explained as he helped her to the couch. The deputies had been called in to follow up on a complaint. Rudy and Bo, two cousins from Slew Town, were standing outside Alexander's Drug Store when Jimmy's wife came by. One of them saw Sandra was pregnant and said something to her about the identity of the baby's father. The other boy laughed. Glen Skinner, the postmaster's son, had heard it all. He reported the incident to the sheriff, who sent the deputies to pick them up. The boys resisted arrest, so the deputies were teaching them a lesson in how to be mannered when one of the boys wrestled the knife out of Danny's hand and slid it between his ribs.

"We tried to save him," Jimmy said. "But he'd lost too much blood."

The shock of the news made it difficult for Mavis to follow the story. Danny was dead? Slew Town boys making fun of Sandra's pregnancy? In front of the drug store and in full view? She tried to picture a knife slicing between his ribs but saw a coin dropped into a vending machine instead. She imagined Mrs. Booth hearing that story and shaking her head. It didn't sound right at all. Was this story an incident of near-sightedness? She looked at the men gathered in her living room, itching to get back outside and find someone to hurt. Outraged that one of their own had fallen. Klansmen with blood on their hands; their uniform shirts couldn't add any decency to what she saw in their eyes. Hatred made a face unrecognizable.

"I wanted you to hear it from me," Jimmy said. "Lock the door as soon as we leave and stay inside. Don't open it for anyone."

"Why? What's happening?"

"Do you want me to send for someone? For Carlina?"

Mavis shook her head. She'd rather be alone. "Where are you going?"

"The sheriff has us all out tonight. Someone's going to pay for this. Don't you worry. Just stay inside."

"But didn't you say you already caught the boys who did it? Hurting more people isn't going to bring Danny back."

"Just lock the door behind me."

The clock in the hallway showed it was just after four in the morning. Mavis stayed awake, listening hard for sounds of trouble. Was that the wind or an animal howling? Someone knocking nearby or a shutter banging?

By six-thirty, she knew Carlina wasn't coming. Mavis made her own coffee and poached an egg so the yolk was soft and made toast just like she liked it, evenly buttered to all four corners.

She peeked out the front door and saw *The Neelan News* on her doorstep. The headline screamed in larger letters than normal: ***Danny Thorpe Murdered***. They must have just had time to get the headline printed before deadline. Women and children were advised to stay home until order was restored. Below the headlines was a photograph of two lifeless and torched bodies, identified as the killers: Rudy and Bo. Sheriff Thorpe wasn't satisfied. *Where there is smoke, there is fire*, he said. A posse was rounding up troublemakers.

Eddie Dumfrey's editorial demanded justice.

Mavis did as she was told and kept the door locked and curtains drawn. Later in the afternoon, her daddy arrived and told her to gather her belongings. "I'm taking you home. It's not safe to be alone right now."

Her mind felt cloudy. She couldn't see her own thoughts. It dawned on her she was a widow, just like poor Posey whose husband had died in a train crash. At least Mavis wasn't pregnant. That was a blessing, but should she be thinking of blessings already?

Gertie was waiting on the front porch of the house and fell into her arms in tears. She was sixteen already and swept up in grand ideas about love. How tragic that her older sister's love story had prematurely ended. Mavis let her believe in the drama and allowed George to carry her bag to her childhood bedroom. She unpacked and then went to the kitchen to be consoled by Mamie but found Mamie needed comforting too. Samuel hadn't come home. He'd gone to visit his wife Tessa's family in Slew Town the day before. He'd never stayed out overnight before.

"Samuel's a good boy. He probably just got stuck there because he knew it was dangerous to be out on his own," Mavis said. "I'll ask Daddy to watch out for him."

Mamie didn't look convinced. "Your husband got killed. The sheriff's son. How many of us will have to die to make up for it?"

As the hours passed, news from town began to trickle in. The posse had burned down the black church. A few members of the congregation who tried to stop them were dead.

"Was one of them Samuel?" Mamie asked.

Nobody knew, and it wasn't safe yet to go looking.

Samuel was still missing two days later when Danny's funeral took place.

The church filled to capacity and beyond. Preacher Heath talked about Danny as if he was a man Mavis would have admired, and she listened to the kind words everyone said and wondered if they knew her husband in a different way or if lying was in their blood. In the procession line after the funeral, Mavis shook hand after hand and responded in rote. *Thank you. It was a shock, yes. Tragic.*

She was surprised to see Mrs. Booth in the line. She took Mavis's hands in hers and leaned forward to speak quietly.

"I'm truly sorry for your loss, dear. If there's anything I can do to help, anything at all, please call on me." She held Mavis's gaze and Mavis felt a tiny bit of the woman's courage transfer when she pressed her hand.

Afterwards, the procession moved to the cemetery behind the church. It had rained earlier in the day, and the dirt piled beside the freshly dug grave glistened as if it had been sprinkled with crushed diamonds. Mavis imagined Danny reaching out from his coffin to pluck those tiny jewels as if they were free to claim. In life, he'd excelled at getting something for nothing or in profiting from his belongings. In death he might too.

Around her, all the faces that had gathered to watch Danny's coffin lowered into the ground had a uniformity about them, as if the same thoughts were passing through their minds at the same time. But Mavis didn't have access to those thoughts. She stood on the outside of their circle and felt her own isolation. Nobody had questioned the incredulity of Rudy and Bo making a disparaging remark to a white woman. It was an obvious death sentence, which was why it was so improbable. Why had the deputies taken those boys out into the woods to begin with? She was so tired of the same old story.

Sheriff Thorpe threw the first handful of dirt. He'd aged twenty years overnight.

Danny's mother threw the second handful of dirt. She rarely spoke because the sheriff did most of the talking, but she hadn't spoken a word since her son's murder.

Mavis threw the third handful of dirt and remembered putting dirt down on Ellie's firstborn's coffin. How much smaller the grave had been to receive his body.

The reception took place at Sheriff Thorpe's house. So many people gathered that the yard had to be used. A table was set outside and covered in food. Punch was available for the children who soon forgot about the solemnity of the occasion and ran around playing games. Mavis looked for Mrs. Booth but didn't see her. Gertie stood with a group of young women her own age, eyeing some boys who stood on the periphery. Seeing Gertie poised on the cusp of her own transition into womanhood, Mavis couldn't help but wonder how her daddy would profit from her. It was crushing to think her little sister would suffer the same indignities of being in a loveless marriage or to imagine she was property still.

A bee buzzed around the edge of her glass, drawn to the sweetness on the rim. It landed with its impossibly thin legs and proceeded to walk down the inside of the glass.

So many questions ran through her mind. How long would she be able to live alone in her house? Who would take care of the credit at the store? Being the sheriff's son had given Danny access to many things, such as credit, but Mavis wouldn't have that same status. How would she make money? It was doubtful her daddy would give her the allowance.

At one point, she went into the kitchen to escape the same conversation that she'd been having over and over again with people sharing their condolences. Sheriff Thorpe appeared at her side and tucked a loose strand of hair behind her ear. She was too surprised at the feel of his hand brushing against her cheek to know how to respond, so she did nothing and pretended she hadn't noticed.

In the days that followed, *The Neelan News* continued to run stories detailing the murder and the aftermath. Only two people were charged with Danny's death. Both had been killed resisting arrest. At least a dozen additional negroes had been killed for not cooperating with the investigation or for allegedly inciting further violence. Half of Reggie Richardson's shacks in Slew Town had been burned to the ground. The occupants who weren't prisoners and therefore able to leave asked Reggie for their pay, but he said he'd already paid them, and it wasn't his fault if their money had burned inside their homes. Those families were escorted to the county line.

Mavis returned to her house in town. She walked from room to room, touching the walls and feeling guilty for thinking how much bigger the house felt without Danny in it and how much more at ease she felt when she was alone. Carlina wouldn't come back, even if Mavis wanted her to, which she didn't. But the sheriff stopped by. He said being in Danny's house kept the memory of his son alive for him. Was there any possibility she might be with child? Mavis shook her head and turned away from his great disappointment.

Samuel was still missing. Mamie said his wife's family was one that had been sent off from Slew Town, so there was a possibility Samuel had gone with them to help them get settled. But he would have sent word to Tessa if he was okay. He'd know Tessa would be worried, and his children. Tessa already had a child when they married, and they'd had two more together. Mamie's eyes were puffy from crying.

"Maybe he's just waiting until it's safe to come back," Mavis said, hoping if she said it out loud it would be true. Mamie's daughter Faith came into the kitchen and rubbed her mama's arm to comfort her. "Everybody's looking for him, Mama. We'll find out something soon."

"Maybe if you make a cobbler, he'll come." Mavis meant it to be a comfort, because Samuel was known for his cobbler leg, the hollow one where cobbler disappeared because he ate so much, but the word cobbler sent Mamie into a crying fit, and Mavis wished she'd kept her mouth shut.

The sheriff knocked before coming into Mavis's house at the start, but it didn't take long for him to dispense with that courtesy. One morning she was sitting at the breakfast table when he suddenly appeared, having let himself in. She hid her surprise and offered him some coffee before asking about Danny's will, but he said everything was taken care of, that she had nothing to worry about. But she did worry. Would she be allowed to stay in the house? And was she imagining it, or did the sheriff's increasing attention merit concern?

That night, the sheriff stopped by after dinner and sat in her living room when she went to bed, saying she must be scared to be on her own and not to worry because he was there. She said she was fine, and he could go on home, but he stayed.

Mavis closed her bedroom door and propped a straight-backed

chair against the doorknob in case he tried to come into her room. In the morning, he was gone.

She had no desire to return and live at her parents' house, but she didn't want to stay in a house that the sheriff visited at whim.

What was she to do?

Whose property was she now?

CHAPTER 40

Sliver had been particularly jumpy since Danny Thorpe's murder. How many dead negroes made up for the death of one white man? She had never figured out that equation. It was never a question of justice. Where was the justice in the congregation losing their church? Even though she hadn't gone in decades, she knew gathering together to pray and sing mattered to many. Sliver was glad her son Seth had moved away, and she told Becky and Charlie to keep their eyes on the ground and their mouths shut. *Whatever you do, don't sass back.* Now was not the time to be funny or cute. A black man was always a boy. And a boy was always more vulnerable to abuse than a man.

But she didn't share all her opinions with her children. She had never told them, for instance, that they shouldn't be surprised when a black man murdered; they should be surprised it didn't happen more often.

But being extra vigilant was exhausting. Sliver didn't sleep well at night because she had both ears cocked for footsteps or knocks. For whispers and the sound of feet running. It took her back to the days when Gideon hadn't come home and she called out at every noise: *Giddy? Is that you?*

Some boys playing by the swamp found a body floating and tangled in the weeds. In warm, shallow water, decomposition worked quickly. Even so, they could tell by the clothing that it was a man. The boys were too scared to fish him out or turn him over, so they ran back to the Yates's and got their families. Word spread fast. Who could it be? Samuel? He'd been missing for a week. Everybody held their breath.

Sliver arrived as the body was dragged out of the water, heavy with bloat, the gases inflating the corpse. They moved him gingerly to keep the body as intact as possible. There was a bullet hole in the back of his head. When they turned him over, the breath Sliver had been holding for days slowly released. He was dressed in the clothes Mamie and Tessa had described. It had to be Samuel. There was another bullet hole in his stomach. Whoever did this would have shot him in the stomach first, knowing he would suffer. They would have taken their time, maybe asking him to beg for his life before telling him to turn around and shooting him in the back of the head. Maybe they'd even made him kneel and told him to pray.

Sliver had the men fashion the blanket into a makeshift sling to carry the body. She would walk with them to deliver Samuel's remains to his mama and wife. Sliver had brought him into the world, cleaning him up and putting him into Mamie's arms. She would do the same thing now in reverse.

She limped behind the sad procession and had her own private cry. Samuel had been a gentle boy all his life. A good son to Mamie, a good and caring husband to Tessa, the wet nurse who'd arrived broken from Slew Town with a baby to nurse and a job to nurse Master Willis's new son Eugene. Samuel had made her happy and given her more children to love. He'd been a good daddy too. He didn't deserve this end. No sirree. Mamie and Tessa and the kids didn't either.

She looked with fresh eyes at the place she'd called home for the greater part of her life and thought about all the death she'd witnessed or heard about here and in Slew Town. Maybe there was no justice anywhere. Maybe the *idea* of justice only made people unhappy.

The ground beneath her feet was rough, pitted with divots and hollows. She found it hard to keep from stumbling.

Trouble kept coming.

It had never really stopped. It was just spaced out enough for her to believe it might not come again. But it always did.

She saw herself now as a vessel worn smooth from use. A vessel for children, wanted and unwanted. A vessel for love. For pain. For suffering. She carried it all, and she would try to carry some of Mamie's pain too, because seeing what had happened to Samuel was just too much for a mother to bear.

⌐ Sliver sought time in the garden to ease her pain. Hands in the dirt encouraged her to believe in a greater design. When there was a death, she transplanted something to mark it. She had started that tradition when Giddy disappeared, planting Lantana at the edge of her garden because it flowered year-round and was drought resistant. Nothing could kill it, and it had a citrus sage scent that reminded her of the times she'd buried her face into Giddy's skin and drawn in his citrus smell. In the full sun, the plants grew strong and flowered continuously, reminding her that Gideon was always with her.

For Samuel, she chose Blue Daze. It flowered year long and was beautiful in its delicacy. It also had that double meaning, for it was blue days indeed with Samuel's absence and the simultaneous absence of others. Murder. Not absence. Murder. And they were all in a daze just thinking about things.

She soaked the roots for an hour to make sure they would stay moist even when the hot winds blew. It wouldn't do to have something that was planted in memorial die. That hadn't happened yet.

She watered and weeded and planted and repeated. All year long. One day after another. That's where Jerome found her when he came running full speed one afternoon and doubled over beside her.

"Eugene made me," he gasped. "And Mrs. Yates is mad."

Sliver grabbed him by the upper arm and gave him a firm shake to set his thoughts straight. "What happened? Tell me."

"Eugene told me to take a basket of oranges to Old Lady Yates. He told me to go to the front door."

"You know you're not allowed at the front door! Who's doing your thinking for you?"

"Eugene said his grandma said so. He said to do it, or he'd cut my pecker off. I don't want my pecker cut off. How would I pee? What would I hold on to in the night?"

"*Eugene said. Eugene said.* You're older and smarter than that boy. What happened?"

"I did as he said and knocked, and Old Lady Yates opened the door. She told me to look her in the eyes, so I did. But right away I could tell she was mad, so I ran. Then she went after Eugene and I heard him screaming because she beat on him. And now he'll blame me!"

"Come." She grabbed Jerome's hand and dragged him to Becky's.

She had always suspected she might have to take Jerome away one day, and with Danny Thorpe's murder still on everybody's mind, and Mamie mourning her son hard, and with everything in such a state, she felt that maybe the time had come.

She put his things in a bag and told Becky not to tell anybody that he'd gone, not even her own kids. Not yet anyway. Then she tied her shoes and took him to Charlie's at the blacksmith shop in town.

Trying to keep a young boy quiet in a small room was like asking a wasp to bypass a picnic. She told him to stay inside. She'd be back. She said if Charlie came, say she'd explain everything. Then she ran home again.

She had been careful to keep Jerome away from the main house, but now she imagined the worst: Mrs. Yates had figured out he was Ellie's second baby and hadn't died after all. Why else had she been asking those questions that day? She'd tell Willis the boy was alive. Maybe they'd call Sheriff Thorpe to dole out punishment. Maybe they'd come for Sliver, too, for lying about everything.

She'd been gone for over an hour. Her body pitched from side to side as she hurried up the dirt road to the Yates's. Her daddy always told her to look to the stars to navigate when she was lost, but what good was that advice in the daytime when no stars were visible in the sky? *How do I run, Gideon? Teach me how.*

She formed a plan. First thing, she'd stop in and say a quick hello to Mrs. Yates and get a feel for how severe the trouble might be, or if there was any trouble at all. Sliver approached the house and saw the bare feet of a child swinging back and forth beneath the branches on the rope swing fastened to the willow tree. Eugene. Lurking. Always lurking. He had too much of his mother in him.

Sliver entered by the kitchen door. She'd surprise Mrs. Yates with a cold drink. She made a glass of lemonade, added extra sugar, and gathered her nerve. Footsteps pounded up the porch stairs. Was it the sheriff already? The lemonade sloshed over the rim when she turned, but it was Eugene who pushed through the screen door.

"Grandma?" He stopped short when he saw Sliver.

She extended the lemonade. "Here. Take this and go on outside."

"Where's Grandma?"

"She asked me to help with her bath."

Eugene reached for the lemonade and exited as noisily as he'd entered. Sliver went upstairs. The silence and heat grew as she climbed. "Mrs. Yates?"

She knocked and put her ear to the bedroom door but heard nothing. She stepped inside.

White curtains flapped at the window. The double bed was made and empty. Something moved in the corner of the room and Sliver's legs gave way as images of her own mama came flooding back. *At least they left her clothes on,* someone had said, as if that would console. A note had been fixed to her mama's body. *Your children are next.* Sliver remembered thinking, *I'm ready right now.*

But the body hanging in front of her now was Mrs. Yates's. Her eyes bulged from their sockets, exaggerated in size. Her mouth hung open, as if she'd just remembered what she'd forgotten.

The noose was attached to the wooden beam in the ceiling. Mrs. Yates was wearing lace up shoes with a blunt heel, as if she was ready to go out walking. Normally she took her shoes off when she was in the house, but she must have known that she'd be travelling, and travelling great distances. Mrs. Yates had been waited on her entire life. She never had to lift a finger if she didn't want to. No one would have helped her throw a rope over the beam. How many tries had it taken before she got it? And how on earth did she know how to fasten a noose? Did they teach that at their schools?

She said a quick prayer and scanned the room. A letter lay open on the dresser.

June 1947

Dear Mrs. Yates,

I'm sure you never expected to hear from me again. I never expected to write.

It's been over seven years since I left Neelan Junction, and I can't say I miss it. I'm writing because I hear Willis plans to remarry. As I am still alive, and as we never officially ended our union, in the eyes of the law that would be illegal. How embarrassing for you if everyone found out. Willis forbade me to ever contact him or our son, but he never said I couldn't write to you. I suggest you inform him that the label bigamist is not one he desires.

What lie did Willis tell you about the child from my second pregnancy? Ask him. Or ask the midwife. She told me the baby died, but if there's a bright-eyed mulatto a year older than your white grandson, he is your grandson too, in a manner of speaking, as legally I am still your daughter-in-law. If you had been nicer to me, maybe I wouldn't have felt the need to hurt Willis so much.

I know it's hard to keep track of children in the south. I know, too, that your husband, like most of the men in Neelan Junction, preferred to visit the shacks than his wife's bedroom. I wonder how many siblings Willis really has?

Yours truly,
Ellie Turner ("Yates")

Sliver's hand went to her chest to keep her heart from bolting. Master Willis could not see the letter. Or his mama hanging. She had to move fast before somebody came. She stuffed the letter back in the envelope, tucked it into her dress, righted the overturned chair, stood on it, gripped Mrs. Yates's body around her thighs, and lifted. The rope went slack, but when Sliver removed one hand from the body to access that slack, the body dipped, and the slack disappeared. She was sweating hard in her hurry to do what needed to be done, but she didn't have the strength to do it alone.

A piece of paper stuck out from Mrs. Yates's dress pocket. Sliver pulled at the edge and saw it was a note.

Dear Willis,

Didn't I tell you that Ellie Turner would bring nothing but trouble? And didn't you ignore me when I begged you not to marry her? This is what throwing the devil against the wall looks like.

Sliver pocketed the note. Master Willis didn't need to see that, either. She closed the bedroom door and ran out of the house. Eugene was nowhere to be seen, but that didn't mean he wasn't waiting and watching. Panic sent adrenalin through her system. She ran to Becky's. A new thought plagued her: if Ellie had written Mrs. Yates, then maybe she'd written Charlie too.

Becky dropped everything when she saw Sliver's distress and followed. She grabbed Mrs. Yates around the knees and lifted with all her strength while Sliver stood on the chair and loosened the noose at Mrs. Yates's neck. After some struggle, she was successful.

The old woman had already started to stiffen. Sliver stepped down from the chair and helped Becky lower the body.

"Grandma?"

Sliver spun around. Eugene stood at the door, his mouth hanging open.

"Tend to the boy," Sliver told Becky in as calm a voice as possible, but Eugene had already started to run. Had he seen the noose?

"Quick! Untie the rope."

Becky unlooped it from the rafters.

"And help me get her into bed."

They worked as fast as their panic allowed. Sliver untied Mrs. Yates's shoes. It wasn't normal that she'd be in bed with her dress on, but Sliver didn't have time to change her. Eugene had probably gone to get his father.

Sliver massaged Mrs. Yates's eyes until she felt a loosening and the muscles became malleable. Her mama had taught her this trick because not all women survived childbirth, and it was a kindness to the family to not see the suffering in a dead woman's eyes. Sliver closed the lids and kept firm pressure on until she thought they would hold.

"Get a scarf from her top drawer!"

Becky found a yellow scarf, and Sliver tied it around Mrs. Yates's neck to hide the noose marks. It was the best she could do. Mrs. Yates was a God-fearing woman and suicide was the devil's hand. Her son didn't need to know that Miss Ellie had paid a visit.

Mrs. Yates almost looked peaceful when they were done. The covers were pulled up to her neck. Her mouth drooped down in one corner, but the agony of her death had been erased.

They heard footsteps on the front porch. Becky still had the noose in her hands and looked wide-eyed at Sliver.

"Under the mattress!"

They stuffed the rope in as far as they could.

A heart attack, Sliver said when she consoled Master Willis. A painless death. She must have felt weak and taken a nap, that's why she was in her dress. Or taken a slight chill, see the scarf at her neck? A good way to go. In her sleep.

Willis knelt beside his mama's bed and nodded his head in grief.

"I'm sorry for your loss, sir."

Willis bent his head. "Me too."

Eugene stared at Sliver from behind his father's back. His eyes were swollen. She could tell he wanted to accuse her of something, say she'd given him lemonade so Sliver could kill his granny, but he just stared. For now. What would later bring?

Sliver's mind had already turned to Jerome, thinking what her next step would be. There was trouble here now. It had been a long time coming, and she'd had enough of it. She had some money tucked inside an old tin on her shelf in her kitchen, an emergency fund for a situation like this. Not enough but a good start.

Miss Ellie's letter was tucked into her bodice, and Mrs. Yates's note was in her pocket.

Later, when she undressed, she'd see that the ink from Ellie's envelope had bled onto her flesh like a tattoo with the house address on Michigan Avenue. Washington, DC.

God couldn't have made it any clearer.

She put Ellie's letter and Mrs. Yates's note on a plate on her table and lit a match. She watched the paper blaze for a moment and then turn to ash. This was the second of Ellie's letters she had burned. Hopefully, it would be the last.

CHAPTER 41

Mavis was almost asleep when she heard a knock at the door. She sat up, wondering what bad news had arrived. Then she thought maybe it wasn't a knock she'd heard but the sheriff letting himself in. She leaned into the darkness and listened hard. The knock repeated itself. It came from the back door. She felt herself relax. Front door news was worse. She dressed, moved the chair she'd wedged under the doorknob, and went to the kitchen door.

A solitary figure stood in the darkness. She squinted. "Sliver? Is that you? Come in." She guided the older woman to a kitchen chair.

"I'm sorry to bother you and to show up just like that." She sat heavily in the chair and clasped her hands between her knees to steady them. "I never asked for help in my life, but I don't see any way around it."

"What's wrong? Has something happened?"

"My Becky's boy might have got himself into trouble with Eugene. There's been some kind of misunderstanding. It might be nothing, but it might be something, and you know what happens when there's any trouble with a white boy, especially now."

"Does this have anything to do with Mrs. Yates's death?" News travelled quickly in Neelan Junction.

"Yes and no," Sliver replied. "The boys got tangled up on the same day, but Jerome had nothing to do with her dying, if that's what you're wondering."

"No, I wasn't thinking that."

"I couldn't bear anything happening to him."

"I know."

"I lost too much in my day. I don't expect you to understand, but I need help and I didn't know who else to ask."

"Do you want me to have Jerome here?"

Sliver shook her head. "No. I'm worried Eugene's cooking something up. I got Jerome staying at my boy Charlie's for the night, but I feel like something terrible is going to happen to him if he stays, and I can't sit around and wait for it." Tears rolled down her cheeks. "Samuel was a good boy too, but that didn't help him."

"I know." His death had hit Mavis hard. Harder even than Danny's. She hated that the men who had killed him likely went to her church and would never be punished for their crime. As soon as she heard the news, she'd visited Mamie's shack. It was smaller inside than she'd imagined but clean and well-organized. Faith had let her in. Mamie was in bed, staring at the low ceiling. Mavis had sat on the edge of the bed and rested a hand on Mamie's leg. "I'm so sorry, Mamie. I'll miss him too. I'm so, so sorry." And even though Mavis had nothing to do with his death, she couldn't help but feel guilty because the timing around Danny's death and Samuel's was related.

"How can I help?" she asked Sliver.

"I need to borrow a little money. I'm taking Jerome away from here. I have enough for two train tickets but need a little extra to get us started wherever we go." Sliver would send the money back as soon as she got work, which wouldn't be long, she said, because she wasn't one to sit around. She'd worked her entire life.

Sliver's arrival was a coincidence too obvious for Mavis to overlook. She had been wondering what her next step would be, asking for signs, and Sliver had showed up looking for help. Was this her way to leave Neelan Junction?

Mavis gave the idea room to run. She wasn't one to strike out on her own. But if she took the train with Sliver and Jerome, maybe that would be the momentum she needed to start a new life too.

But could she?

Her mind began listing all the lies she would have to tell or secrets to keep in order to get on the train, and she realized how tired she was. Everyone in town and at church sided with the sheriff's belief that a woman wasn't supposed to live on her own. Her own parents thought she should move back home; she didn't want to live under her father's roof again, but she didn't like living under the roof that felt more like the sheriff's than her own.

Just yesterday, Mavis had looked out the window and seen Sheriff Thorpe coming up the walk. Without thinking, she had rushed down the hall and slipped into her bedroom closet. The front door opened, and he called out her name. She heard his boots in the kitchen and then in the hallway. Then he was in the bedroom; the bedsprings creaked as he sat down, as if he was familiar with being in her bed. She knew it was only a matter of time until he acted on that familiarity. Her heart beat so loudly she was sure it would give her away and he'd find her crouched and hiding in the closet, her dress soaking up the sudden sweat beneath her arms. How would she explain herself?

She listened as he opened a few of her dresser drawers and looked through her things. After a while, he left the bedroom. Was that the front door closing? Mavis stayed in the closet for an extra ten minutes in case he had pretended to leave and was instead standing in the front room, waiting for her to come out. Was this to be her new reality?

"I'll loan you the money," Mavis said, "but on one condition: I'm coming with you."

Sliver shook her head. "No. We'll be okay on our own. I promise to pay you back. You don't need to come to be sure that'll happen."

"I know you'll pay me back. It's not that. It's just, now that Danny's dead, I don't have to stay here anymore, but I don't know how to leave. Going with you feels like the perfect opportunity." Mavis would find out how much money she had in the bank. Her daddy had paid Danny's allowance, so wasn't that money really hers, since it came from her family? "We can take the night train. Tomorrow. I need a day to get some money. And we'll figure it out as we go. But for now, we won't tell anyone. Okay? Not anyone."

"I only need a little money," Sliver repeated. "I planned on just me and Jerome going on our own."

Mavis squeezed Sliver's hand, remembering how Mrs. Booth had transferred some courage. "It'll be easier with me along. Meet me at the train station tomorrow night. I'll be there ten minutes before it's set to leave." Already she had started making a list. At the top of the list was money.

Sliver left and Mavis went back to bed, but she was too excited to sleep. First thing in the morning, she sent a note to Mrs. Booth saying she would pay a visit at 10:30. When she arrived, she apologized for inviting herself on such short notice and then, with little lead up, confessed her situation. "I am leaving town, and I need money from Danny's bank account. I have the right to it, but I can't have the sheriff knowing. As your husband is the manager, is there any way he might allow me to take some out?" She paused to catch her breath and then continued. "I can explain —"

"The less I know, the better," Mrs. Booth interrupted. "It will come as no surprise that I am not a fan of Sheriff Thorpe, so if you don't want him knowing why you need the money, then it's likely for a good cause. Do you know how much money is in the account?"

"No." Danny never discussed finances with her. What if the account was empty?

"That's fine. Don't worry. How much do you need? I'll speak to my husband at lunch. The manager can sometimes make special allowances. I've always believed a woman should have full access to her husband's banking situation. My husband agrees. So we'll just hope there's some money in the account."

"I am taking two negroes with me," Mavis added.

"Even better. They will do well to get away from here, presuming you are going north, of course. And don't worry: my husband and I know how to craft a good story when we need to." She rubbed her hands together and looked pleased. "This town needs some excitement of a different variety." She left the room for a moment and returned with a sheet of paper and a pen. "Write that you'd like to withdraw the bulk of the money from your husband's account and then add your signature. That will give some legitimacy to the transaction, for my husband's sake."

Mavis did as she was told, relieved to have someone taking charge. "We are hoping to leave tonight."

"Good. There's no sense waiting around, is there? I will send a basket of flowers to your house this afternoon. Inside the basket you will find an envelope with money. I can only hope the sum will be enough for your needs. If there is no money, then I will pay you a personal visit to let you know. But for now, let's hope for the best." She hugged Mavis, then held her at arm's length. "Good luck, my dear. I am glad you decided to trust me. Your instincts are good."

Were they? Mavis hoped so. On the way back to her house, she nodded at the people she passed on main street and experienced a sudden love for Neelan Junction that she could only attribute to her decision to leave it. Right now, she only knew what she was losing. She had no idea yet what she might gain.

She spent the afternoon carefully choosing what to pack. She wanted to travel light, believing if she carried too much from this part of her life she'd merely replicate it in the next. The flowers arrived as planned. The envelope of money was thinner than she'd hoped, but it was better than nothing at all.

How slowly the time passed as she waited for darkness to descend. She made herself a light meal with the food on hand. It was never good to start an adventure on an empty stomach. What if the sheriff stopped by? She stashed her suitcase in the closet, just in case.

The hours passed and the shadows grew in the front room. Soon, she required lamplight to see. She walked from room to room and surveyed the contents. Was there anything she'd regret not taking? Her wedding picture hung on the wall in the living room. The photograph had been taken on the church steps. She smiled bravely into the camera. Danny's right eyebrow was lifted a little higher than the left as if he, too, couldn't figure out how he'd gotten there. Not even a decade later, death had wiped the mischief clean off his face.

She would travel light. The picture would stay on the wall.

She didn't bother to lock the front door when it was finally time to go and left the key on the inside table. It was a short walk to the station, yet her courage waned with each step. Who did she think she was, pretending to be brave? Planning was one thing, but taking action was another. Where was she going? And to do what? It wasn't too late to go back home and return the money to the bank in the morning before the sheriff or her daddy found out. But Sliver and Jerome were waiting at the station. Mavis had promised to be there, and she recalled the spark in Mrs. Booth's eye when she had learned of Mavis's plan. This might be her only opportunity to do something out of the ordinary, and if she didn't take it now, another one might never present itself.

The streets were deserted. She was happy not to have to make up a story for why she was out with a suitcase.

Sliver and Jerome emerged from the shadows when she arrived on the platform. Mavis hadn't allowed herself to think they might not show up.

"This is Jerome," Sliver said.

A young boy with light eyes stared up at her.

"Nice to meet you, Jerome. Sliver, do you need me to get your tickets?"

"No. I got ours."

"To Fort Lauderdale?"

She nodded.

"Okay. I'll be right back."

She left her suitcase and approached the ticket window with her heart pounding. "Good evening, Mr. Calder."

"Mrs. Thorpe. I'm surprised to see you here. I don't recall the sheriff mentioning you going anywhere."

"That's because he doesn't know. I'm making a quick shopping trip to surprise him with a gift. He's been so down since Danny's death. We've both been, so please keep this to yourself."

Such a sad time, he acknowledged. How good that she was trying to brighten the sheriff's spirits.

She slipped her money across the counter and marvelled that her hand kept steady. "Just one way for now, in case I need extra money for the gift. If so, I'll wire for more."

The train whistle carried on the breeze, announcing the train's imminent arrival. Sound carried great distances in the night. She took her ticket and stepped outside again. The cars were segregated, so Mavis arranged to meet Sliver on the platform in Fort Lauderdale and decide where to go from there.

"I already know we're going to Washington, DC," Sliver said.

"That's where Ellie went the first time she left home!" How perfect. Mavis remembered her sister's descriptions of tall buildings, luxurious rooms, and crowded sidewalks.

"You don't need to come with us," Sliver said, taking Jerome's hand in hers. "Like I said, I only need a little extra money to get us started."

"I know. But there's strength in numbers. Don't forget that. See you soon."

They boarded their respective cars. Mavis walked quietly down the aisle, past some passengers who rested their heads on the window and appeared to be sleeping, and settled into a seat. Her heart matched the rhythm of the train as it picked up speed. She stared at her reflection in the window. It felt fitting, somehow, because it was her own self, her *old* self, that she was looking at for hopefully the last time.

She imagined the rhythm of the train was an eraser on a chalk board, and the writing on the board that had been her life story was quickly disappearing. Still, she experienced a brief pang. Leaving meant severing ties with her family. She was another daughter to be disowned.

The farther the train travelled from Neelan Junction, the more Mavis began to relax. And the more she began to relax, the more she understood how living a life written by others was a sentence of sorts. For too long, she had allowed someone else to wield the pen. With Danny gone, maybe she could finally live her own life.

CHAPTER 42

The Fort Lauderdale station was quiet in the not yet dawn light. Mavis spotted Sliver and Jerome on the platform and followed them to the counter where they purchased tickets for the next part of their journey, which would be much longer, at least twenty-four hours on the tracks.

Mavis had worried that she'd be in charge of their journey; she had never been in charge of anything in her life, not even running her own home, so she was pleased that Sliver had a plan.

They had a three-hour wait before boarding their next train for Washington, DC. Sliver pulled some food from her bag and shared it: biscuits spread with homemade jam. Oranges. Avocadoes. A bag of pecans and some other odds and ends. There wasn't much, but Mavis ate gratefully and guiltily; she hadn't thought about food and realized some of the things she'd left in her cupboard would have been easy to pack. She had been too focused on getting on the train.

The station grew busier as the morning passed. Mavis looked frequently at the main entrance, imagining the sheriff barging in and bellowing her name. Had Mr. Calder kept his word to not speak of her trip? Mavis felt certain he would tell his wife, who would tell the postmistress, who would tell … The hands on the large clock over the doorway weren't moving quickly enough, but as with any interminable waiting, it did finally come to an end.

This time when they parted to get on their separate cars, Mavis gave Sliver some money in case she needed to buy any snacks. Once again, they agreed to meet on the platform at Union Station, and once again Mavis boarded the coach and found a vacant seat by the window. Only when the train began to pick up speed did she finally relax.

She had always imagined getting on a train one day and having an adventure, but she'd assumed it would be with Ellie; what a turn of events to be with Sliver and Jerome instead. It was the bravest or stupidest thing she'd ever done. She was both elated and terrified.

The train passed through rural and urban areas. Mavis slept fitfully, waking to look out at stations in Georgia, South Carolina, North Carolina, and Virginia. They passed the backs of people's homes and wide open fields. They travelled through rain and broke through to sunshine before finally reaching their destination.

Mavis clutched her bag tightly to her chest and stepped into Union Station, wishing with all her heart that Ellie was there to meet her. The sisters would hug and laugh and talk over one another, joyful in their reunion. Instead, Mavis entered a world already in motion and moving at a dizzying pace. There were people everywhere. She smelled grease and underarm sweat. Garbage rotting in a bin. She smelled her own body, leaching anxiety. What if Sliver and Jerome had left without her? That fear flared but dissipated when she saw Sliver standing against a wall, holding Jerome's hand.

She hurried toward them with relief. "What now?"

"Jerome's hungry. First thing we need is something to eat and then a place to sleep," Sliver said.

"Didn't you eat on the train?"

"It was too expensive."

Mavis spotted an information booth across the busy concourse. "I'll go ask a few questions. I'll be right back."

She tried to look unafraid. Ellie had come to DC on her own once, and somehow she had managed. *With* a scarred face.

A heavyset and balding man at the desk asked her budget and how long she planned to stay. He saw her glance over her shoulder and followed her gaze.

"Are they with you?"

"Yes."

"Your maid and child will need their own lodging. Most places don't let the coloureds mix."

Sliver wasn't her maid, but what did he care? Mavis took down the names of a few places within walking distance and tried to memorize the directions. In Neelan Junction, she only had to know where Main Street was, but here ...

"Is the Excelsior Hotel nearby?" She'd often imagined it over the years—Ellie's feet sinking into carpet thick as quicksand. *If I'd stood in one spot long enough, I'd have disappeared right down into it!*

"The Excelsior? Never heard of it."

"You must know it. My sister stayed there. She said it's one of the fanciest hotels in Washington."

"Look, lady. I've been working here for more than thirty years. I know every fancy hotel in the area. She must have given you the wrong name, or the wrong city. Now I've got to help the next person."

Mavis hadn't noticed a line starting behind her.

She retraced her steps. "The man said there's a place nearby. Come on." She took Jerome's hand and had a flashback to holding Samuel's when they were children. That was a lifetime ago. Now he was dead. Grief washed over her. She still couldn't believe it.

Sliver picked up their bags, and they left the station.

The first two places didn't take "friends."

"Miss Mavis, it doesn't matter if we're together or not. We can split up. I'm about to fall asleep standing."

It mattered to Mavis that they stay together. She'd never been alone before. She didn't know if she could be.

They stopped in front of a narrow, unpainted wooden boarding house with a vacancy sign outside. Mavis worried the screen door would come off in her hand if she gave it enough of a pull. A young black woman looked up from the desk in surprise when she entered. Her hair was braided tight to her scalp in perfect rows.

"Are you lost?" she asked as they filled the entranceway.

"No. Well, sort of. We're looking for a room."

"Here?"

"Yes," Mavis said. "We've been travelling and need a place to sleep."

"And you want to stay here?"

Sliver took over. "Or we could stay here, and my friend could find a room somewhere else if need be. The boy is hungry, and we're exhausted."

"We'd rather stay together," Mavis said.

"Or separate," Sliver said.

The woman stared at them for a moment. "I only have one room. You'd have to share."

"That's okay." Mavis held her breath.

The clerk, whom they would come to know as Lydia, reached behind her for a key.

Both Mavis and Sliver let out sighs of relief.

They climbed a steep staircase to the second floor. Lydia handed Mavis a key and pointed to a door.

The room had two single beds with an aisle between them just wide enough for a person to shimmy through. Next to the window was a four-drawer stand-up dresser, an end table, and a lamp. A small sink was bolted to the wall beside the dresser, and on a shelf to the right was a hotplate. Lydia was kind enough to bring a cot for Jerome. When the cot was open, they would have to climb over it to get to the bathroom in the hall, but they were just happy to have found a place to stay.

They closed the door, locked it behind them, and felt all the tension they'd been carrying for the past two days slip away.

"Are you sure you're okay with this?" Sliver asked.

Mavis nodded. She had never shared a room with a negro before. "Are you?"

"It'll do until we get something of our own. Which bed do you want?"

Mavis put her bag on the one closest to the window.

Someone knocked at the door.

The two women froze. Sliver gestured for Mavis to answer it.

Lydia stood in the hall with a tray of sandwiches in her hands. "I thought you might like these. It's not much, but it's all I've got."

Sliver came to the door and reached for the tray. "Bless you, child. I don't know where I'd have found the energy to go find food." She handed a sandwich to Jerome, who ate hungrily.

Watching how quickly his food disappeared, Mavis handed him half her sandwich. She felt a sudden protectiveness for him. What had happened with Eugene that they felt the need to run? She didn't know the full story, but Jerome was just a boy, plucked from his life like a ripe berry and dropped into an entirely new existence. What if she couldn't help him?

She'd never been so exhausted in her life. The bed was small, but the sheets looked clean. She washed in the bathroom and changed. Then she returned to the room and crawled into bed even though it wasn't even dark. "I'm sorry, Sliver, but I've just got to sleep."

"I know. We're all tired. Don't you worry about us. I'll take care of Jerome."

Mavis put her head down on the pillow and turned towards the wall. It wasn't long before her eyelids dropped heavily and sealed shut.

CHAPTER 43

Sliver stared with envy as Miss Mavis climbed into bed and closed her eyes. It was like getting them into the boarding house had sapped all her energy. She didn't even think twice about going to bed. Or claiming the bed by the window. So how did she think she was helping again?

All Sliver had wanted was to borrow a little bit of money; she hadn't anticipated the woman would latch on like a barnacle. Worse still, she acted like she was doing them a favour, like her being with them would be a help, but so far it had only made things more difficult. Sliver would have found a room for her and Jerome right away if she hadn't had a white woman in tow. She'd expected to be in charge of Jerome; he was still a boy. But Miss Mavis? Would she never get free from caring for white people?

It was quieter in the room than she'd expected. The street noise that might have once seemed unbearable paled by comparison to the riotous commotion at Union Station. She'd been terrified by all the ruckus but pretended to be calm, for Jerome's sake. She'd expected trains on a single track, but the size of the station had been a shock to her senses. Cigarette smoke and diesel was thick in the air, and motors and whistles and voices rang out. She'd repressed the urge to lie down to see if it was any quieter on the floor. Outside, car horns blared and sirens wailed as if they'd arrived at a crime scene. And people moved so fast they might as well have been running. It had been quite a day. She was glad it was over.

Sliver was the first one up in the morning. She went down the hall to wash herself then waited a while longer before waking Jerome. She wanted to have a look around and see what there was for food. Did Mavis want to come?

Mavis rolled over and turned towards the wall. She said she just needed a bit more sleep. They could go on without her. Sliver wouldn't have minded going to bed and not having to get up except she never in her life had had that option.

She asked Lydia for the house address to get word to her kids back home, and Lydia told her where the post office was and how much a stamp cost.

Dear Becky,

We arrived safe. Please let Charlie know. You can write to me at this post box if there's any news. I'm sending this by Mamie just in case. Kiss your babies for me. I miss you all.

Love,
Mama

She added a note for Mamie, saying how easy the train had been and planting the seed that she, too, could pull up stakes and transplant herself. She'd be welcome anytime. Sliver didn't expect Mamie would ever take her up on that offer, but it was a way to let her know where to find help if she needed it. The streets here were filled with coloured people. Sliver didn't stand out at all, aside from not knowing her way around.

That first day, she and Jerome walked until their feet hurt. They sat on a bench across the street from the White House and watched people coming and going. "Do you see that building there?"

Jerome nodded.

"That's called the White House."

"Because it's white or because only white people can go inside?"

Sliver had never thought about it like that before. "I don't know. Maybe both. That's where the president of the United States of America lives."

"Who's that?"

"Right now it's Harry Truman."

"Hairy?" Jerome laughed and scratched himself in an ape-like fashion. "Cause he's covered in hair?"

Sliver had forgotten what it was like to be with a young boy. She gave in to the silliness. "Yes, because he's covered in hair."

She and Gideon used to talk about bringing their kids north. Those conversations felt like they'd happened yesterday. She paused to reflect on how old her children were. If her numbers were right, Seth was forty-six, Becky forty-three, and Charlie thirty-eight. How old did that make her? Sixty-three? She counted again to be sure. Yes, sixty-three. *Gideon. I'm sixty-three! How did that happen?*

She imagined him laughing. *You didn't die.*

"That's right, Giddy," she said softly. "I didn't die."

There was a lot to see in the capital. She and Jerome walked great distances. At night, he fell asleep on his cot, his mouth falling open almost right away. Sliver's heart broke looking at him. He'd be ten in the coming months, growing into his ideas and forming an image of the man he'd like to become. Had she done the right thing by bringing him here? How was this a better life?

The next day Miss Mavis stayed in bed too. And the day after that.

Sliver and Jerome settled into a routine. In the mornings, they went out and explored their new home. They walked because walking was free, and they marvelled at the things they saw around them. The crowds. The buildings. The way people dressed and spoke. Such funny accents they had. And look at all the churches!

They walked until Sliver's limp became pronounced, then they turned around. When they got back to their room, Jerome told Miss Mavis about all the sights he'd seen that day and about the things that had surprised him while Sliver got some food together. If anything could get Miss Mavis up, it would be Jerome telling his stories. He could sure talk, that boy.

Miss Mavis told Sliver to take money to buy things as if her purse was magical and would keep filling up. She didn't seem to understand that money didn't grow on trees. Sliver paid Lydia for the room; she bought food for the three of them; she did what she could, but she knew by what was left and the rate she was spending, even though she was careful, that she could not wait for Miss Mavis to get up and contribute. A person didn't wait for the hurricane to hit before boarding up the windows.

Somebody had to make sure they could keep a roof over their heads and food in their bellies. And that somebody was named Sliver. S-l-i-v-e-r. She found her way to a pawn shop and sold the gold cigarette case she'd taken from Mrs. Yates's dresser. Was it stealing if she helped herself to something that had been stolen?

Every place she went, she looked to see who was working where. Nobody here had Whites Only signs in their windows, but they didn't have to.

It took her a few days to work up the courage, but one morning she got up before the others and found her way to Michigan Avenue. Lydia had explained the bus numbers and route times. When the first bus pulled up, Sliver pretended it was an ordinary thing she was doing, even though she'd never ridden a bus in her life and felt too old to learn new things. She climbed the stairs and stood with coins in her hand, not knowing where to put them. Thankfully, the driver was kind, otherwise she might have given up straight away; he took her fare and explained how she'd make her connection and how she could get back, and some of Sliver's fear went away.

The morning sky had an orangey-pink tinge to it. Sliver felt the stirrings of hopeful possibilities, but she curbed her optimism because she'd learned that getting excited about things meant she had expectations, and that only caused her grief. She could have asked Lydia to help find her a job, but Lydia had done enough for them already. And Sliver didn't know her place here or understand her options, and she didn't have time to find out.

Michigan Avenue was a block off the bus route. Sliver looked for the address and soon found herself standing outside a two-storey house on a corner lot with cherry trees in the side yard behind a white picket fence.

The curtains in the front window were closed. Nothing appeared to stir in the house. Miss Ellie had never looked after herself back home, and despite the passage of time, Sliver didn't expect she had learned new skills. She was likely sleeping, but if she had help, then the downstairs curtains would at least be open. A plan took shape in her mind. It was born out of desperation but was familiar at the same time. She had left home to give Jerome a better life. Living in a boarding house with an old woman and a white woman who stayed in bed all day, and sleeping on a cot not knowing what his days would be filled with, that was not a better life.

The night before last, after she'd turned out the light, she'd heard Jerome crying quietly to himself and knew that homesickness had set in like an itch he couldn't scratch. She invited him into her bed and asked him to tell her all the things that he was missing: Becky, her kids, home-cooking, and even Eugene. He missed the open skies. Salt in the air. Oranges fresh from the branch. Catching snakes. Swimming at the water hole. Swinging in the rope swing beneath the willow tree. Running barefoot. He missed singing in church and how he felt when everyone sang in tune together. Sliver added her own misses: gardening, the herb pots in her shack, catching babies, knowing everyone. They made a long list of all the things they missed until he finally drifted off, but Sliver lay awake for a long time afterwards, thinking of all that she'd taken from the boy; she had to give him something better to make it worth what he'd lost. His skin radiated heat beside her. She recalled the shock of first laying eyes on him, swaddled in that white blanket, and Miss Ellie using her Charlie for revenge. But something good had come out of that situation: Jerome.

Birds chirped and whistled in the cherry trees. She saw a flash of red in the branches. A Cardinal? Sliver could knock on the door right now and see if her services might be required, but that would require having a conversation, and she hadn't told Jerome she'd be gone when he woke up.

She took the bus back to the boarding house and found Jerome sitting up in bed waiting for her. Mavis still had her back turned to the room. She wasn't getting up today, either.

"Take some money from my purse," she said. "I'll be alright. I just need a bit more sleep."

Sliver took Jerome's hand and gave it a squeeze. Waiting on someone else to get things done had never been an option for her back home. It wasn't an option for her here either.

Two days later, she arranged for Lydia to watch Jerome in the afternoon, and she retraced her steps to Miss Ellie's. This time, she opened the gate, walked around to the back, and knocked on the door.

CHAPTER 44

Ellie was deeply immersed in recreating the sounds and smells of the South for her next book when she heard a knock at the kitchen door. How she hated interruptions. The knock came again a minute later, and Ellie remembered she'd recently fired another maid.

She stood from her desk and went downstairs. Maybe the maid had returned to apologize. She opened the door and the birds momentarily stopped singing.

"Sliver?" She felt momentarily confused. Out of place even. Had writing about her days at the Yates's somehow summoned the midwife? "Is that you?" What a silly question. Of course it was her. She looked exactly the same save for the added white in her hair. "What on earth are you doing here?" *How did you know where to find me?*

"I'm looking for work."

Not a *hello* or a *how are you?* Just straight to business. "You've come a long way for that. Is there no work in Florida?"

"None that I want."

"Well, come in. There's no sense talking on the back porch."

Ellie tried to see the kitchen through the midwife's eyes: a stainless steel sink tucked into the middle of a counter that was bare save for a loaf of store-bought bread sitting in a basket. Tall wooden cupboards that ran straight up the walls on either side of the sink and joined to the high ceiling. It looked bereft. Was that the right word? Neglected. Nothing was baking in the oven or cooking on the stove.

"Have a seat."

"I'm looking for work."

"Yes. You said that, but I can't help thinking you're here for some other reason. Did Willis send you? Or Mrs. Yates? What do they want to know?"

"Master Willis never talks about you, and Mrs. Yates is dead."

"Dead?" What a disappointment. "How?"

"Her heart stopped."

Ellie sucked her cheek and nodded. "I'm sure Willis would have kept you on."

"I can start right away if you need me."

What was she hiding? Was Charlie with her? "Did you come by yourself?"

"I'm alone, yes."

Ellie's stomach rumbled. She hadn't eaten since breakfast. Maybe Sliver was an answer to a prayer she'd never learned the words for. "I'd need you to shop, clean, and take care of my mail. You can read, can't you?"

"Yes, I can read."

"Good, because I'm a writer now. Come, let me show you my books."

⌇ Ellie gave Sliver a tour of the house. She'd already seen the kitchen. It could use the smell of onions simmering in butter or bread cooking in the oven. The living room and dining room were also on the main floor. Upstairs, she showed Sliver the bedroom, guest room, study, and bathroom. Ellie's room looked out on the front yard. "It's nothing special," she said, leading her to the room at the end of the hall. "This is my study." The large window looked out on the cherry trees and let in a lot of light. Was Sliver impressed by the black typewriter sitting on the centre of the wooden desk with a half-typed sheet of paper in it? A sheaf of papers was stacked beside it; that was the only bit of neatness. Her ashtray needed emptying. The garbage can was also full. A half-filled old mug of tea had a thin layer of skin coating the surface.

"It looks like I need a maid, doesn't it?" A pile of books on the floor leaned against one side of the desk. Bookshelves lined the other walls and were overflowing with books. Some boxes were piled in the corner. For the first time, she noticed the dust.

Ellie put her hand on one of the shelves where the spines were neatly lined. "These are my books."

Sliver nodded but didn't seem to understand what Ellie had said.

"The books I wrote," she added.

"You wrote those?"

"Yes, I did. Every word and every punctuation mark."

Sliver glanced at the spines, many of which were duplicate copies of the same book. "But it says they're by Randall Hunter."

"That's my pseudonym. The name I write under," she explained. Where would Sliver have heard the word before? "I wanted readers to think the author was a man. I thought I'd get published easier, which was likely true. Plus, my subject matter isn't exactly ladylike. The books are part of my Magnolia Tree Series. The first one is called *The Magnolia Tree*. Then came *Southern Justice*. *The Cathedral* will be out next year. It's with the publisher now. I'm working on the one after that, *The Rope and the Gun*."

Sliver didn't look as impressed as she should. Ellie was disappointed, but what would the midwife know about writing?

"It's hard work, writing," Ellie added. *Much harder than doing chores and keeping a house.* "It takes discipline."

"I imagine it does," Sliver said.

"But I guess you wouldn't know much about that. Come." Ellie walked downstairs and returned to the kitchen. "That's the end of the tour."

"You're the only one who lives here?"

"Yes. There are no hidden rooms or anything." Did Sliver understand the reference? Surely she remembered the room where Ellie had been kept. The room where Sliver had climbed the stairs to confirm her pregnancy.

Again, the midwife's face didn't change expression. Ellie had no idea what she was thinking. What a turn the day had taken. She wanted to hug Sliver and hit her at the same time. Mrs. Yates was dead? She'd never answered the letter Ellie had sent. Had she even read it?

"When can I start?"

Sliver's voice surprised her. "What?"

"I said, when can I start?"

"Oh. Right away. Tomorrow would be just fine."

"The day after would be better."

Ellie nodded. "Okay. I'll see you then. First thing. By the way, what is your last name?"

Ellie stood at the front window and watched Sliver round the side of the house, let herself out the gate, and hurry down the street. What a liar. If she was here alone, she wouldn't be rushing. *You can't fool your own,* Ellie thought. A smile lifted her scars. A liar could spot a liar from a great distance.

She picked up the phone and dialled her solicitor's office. Mr. Dunedin helped her with everything. He'd know what to do or who to hire. Hadn't Willis used a detective to find her when she'd disappeared? Her heart sped up and slowed down at the same time so that her pulse ran with a skipping gait. She put her hand to her chest to calm it.

"Her name is Sliver Lanier. She'll be starting work at my house on Wednesday. Apparently she's just arrived from Neelan Junction, and I want to know if she's here by herself or if she brought someone with her."

She sorted out the details and was satisfied when she hung up. Wonders never ceased. Sliver in Washington, DC? Ellie never would have imagined that. She buttered a piece of bread, sprinkled a little sugar on top, and put it on a plate. Even with the excitement of the day, she still had a deadline to meet. She returned to her study and sat at her typewriter, her mind alive with ideas. Sliver's unexpected visit had unleashed images and memories, scents and sounds, and her fingers raced to keep up with the story that was now telling itself.

CHAPTER 45

Sliver left Miss Ellie's irritated and relieved. *Not know discipline?* She could have slapped her silly for that one. And why did she need a house that big all to herself? Greed, that's what it was. Greed like marrow in the bone. She could only fill one room at a time, and that left more rooms empty than filled.

Nevertheless, Sliver's relief outweighed her irritation, and she returned to the boarding house with a lighter step.

"Guess what? I got a job!"

Jerome jumped up and down on the bed and hooted.

Mavis actually rolled over and smiled. "You did? Doing what?"

"Taking care of a woman and cleaning her house."

If Mavis had asked who the woman was, Sliver might have told her. But she didn't, and until she asked the right question, Sliver would keep that information to herself.

"What am I supposed to do when you're at work?" Jerome asked.

"You're going to go to school."

"Really?" Excitement and fear filled his eyes.

Sliver nodded. "I always said you was smarter than most. Now you can show me if I'm right."

"But I've only ever gone to that one-room school back home."

"School is school," Sliver said, not knowing if it was true. "We'll go over today and sign you up. Lydia told me what school to go to. You'll have to work hard."

"The school by the park?"

They had passed the brick school with the playground and the grassy field and seen all the white kids playing. "No. That one's full." Schools were segregated here too. He'd find that out on his own.

"Does that mean for sure we're not going home?" His voice was soft, like he was holding something in.

"No, we're not going home. What did I say we was looking for?"

"A better life."

"And where did I say we'd find it?"

"Here."

"That's right." She patted his head and then lectured him about paying attention in school and working hard. Did he understand? Because a person had to work hard to get a better life. It didn't just fall from the sky like a duck in hunting season.

She looked around the room they shared. Mavis had been in bed since they'd arrived. As soon as she got herself up and could take care of herself again, Sliver would thank her for helping them and tell her they were moving on. It was time they got their own place. It was time Mavis got her own place too.

On Wednesday, Sliver got up early, caught the bus, let herself in the kitchen door at Miss Ellie's, and left it open wide to let out the stench of loneliness that had sheltered inside.

The kitchen had all the basics: pots and pans, utensils, sharp knives, and a hodgepodge of spices cobbled together without any plan in mind. Looking in the cupboard, Sliver found dried herbs in bottles and knew she could do better. She'd plant fresh ones. The back yard got enough sunlight for her to grow some in pots. Maybe Miss Ellie would let her dig up some of the grass and plant a garden. She rolled up her sleeves. If this was going to be her kitchen, she was going to clean and organize it to her own standards. Glasses on the left. Plates on the right. Forks, spoons, and knives, left to right and in that order.

She was still organizing and scrubbing two hours later when the doorbell rang. The mailman handed her a sack of mail.

The bag was heavy. Sliver brought it to her chest and held it with both hands like a busy toddler. There must have been at least a hundred letters inside. Maybe two hundred. All addressed to Randall

Hunter. People actually had time in their days to write letters to an author? This was big city if she'd ever heard it.

Sliver had never spent much time at school herself, but her mama had made sure she'd learned how to read. *There may be times when it's best to pretend you can't, but knowing how to means you'll always know what you're putting your name to.*

Sliver sat at the kitchen table and pulled a few envelopes out. Miss Ellie told her to pick out a half dozen by readers who praised her work.

> *Dear Mr. Hunter,*
>
> *I could not put* The Magnolia Tree *down and stayed up all night to finish it. Poor Isabelle. My neighbour got herself into similar trouble. When she disappeared, I always wondered what happened to her, but I never did find out. I am going out this afternoon to buy* Southern Justice.
>
> *Yours sincerely,*
> *Stella Smith*

Well that didn't hardly seem worth taking the time to write.

> *Dear Mr. Hunter,*
>
> *You have written the unspoken history of the south: white women who feel neglected by their husbands find their satisfaction where they can. Or white women who get so tired of seeing their husbands' mulatto offspring that they seek their own revenge (and enjoy it). Or white women who have been told their entire lives that the negro is sex mad end up looking at the negro like he is sex mad. Of course, the great irony is that the perverted lens of forbidden desire is created by the very men who want to forbid white women from having sexual relations with black men.*
>
> *As you write about this so well, I can't help but wonder*

*if you're writing from personal experience. Did your wife
follow a similar path as Isabelle? If so, I guess sales from the
books are your reward.*

*Sincerely,
Jill Hansen*

Reading the letters, Sliver felt like she was eavesdropping on a group of white women having tea. She hadn't read Miss Ellie's books but gleaned a good deal from the mail. None of the letter writers noted the danger black men faced when white women lusted after them. Were they simply disposable props for pleasure? And what about the anxiety for the black men's loved ones? She'd been terrified for Charlie. And Mamie for Samuel. And Jedediah didn't get a second chance.

After reading dozens of letters, Sliver's curiosity was piqued. She pulled a copy of *The Magnolia Tree* from a shelf in Miss Ellie's study and opened to the first page.

> *Isabelle Montgomery was the Mistress of Magnolia Hall, and she was the most beautiful girl in the entire country.*
>
> *At seventeen, her blonde hair hung in perfect ringlets as if God had portioned it into equal sections and wrapped his finger around each one so that when he let go, a coiled spring was released. And each spring was its own energy source that allowed Isabelle to fit much into her days. But it was her eyes that halted people in their tracks—they were an emerald green and framed by thick dark lashes. They were like cat's eyes, and they sent a strong message: Isabelle Montgomery could take chances; Isabelle Montgomery had nine lives.*

Sliver rolled her eyes and started to skip; Isabelle was selfish, beautiful, lustful, and spoiled. Her sweat glistened like little diamonds on her upper lip in the heavy Florida heat. Diamonds. Ha! Sweat was sweat like swamp was swamp. White people's sweat stank too.

Sliver skimmed a few chapters before having enough. She put the book down and shook her head. The only thing white folks seemed to think about was sex, sex, sex. The more lurid the better. Was sex only about power for them? Where was the love? Did Miss Ellie think she could turn rape, lynching, and poverty into something of interest? Something to profit from? Did she never look in the mirror to see where her own warped cravings had landed her—alone, stuck in a house she never left, with a face marked by her own sins? A mother without any children living in a house without mirrors?

Any negro living anywhere in the country knew that rape was a word that gave white folks an excuse for killing; the trouble was, it didn't recognize the white rapists.

Sliver returned the book to the shelf, finished dusting the study, and put half a dozen letters from the day's mail on Miss Ellie's desk. The typewriter had a sheet of paper in it, half-filled. She always ended her writing day by stopping in the middle of a sentence. That way, she told Sliver, she'd pick up where she'd left off and not stare into space wondering what to do next. Sliver leaned in to read what was there:

> *Esther tried the bedroom door and found it locked. She began a steady rocking in her chair that set her mind in motion. What next? What next? What next? She ran her tongue around her mouth, over the missing space where her tooth had once been before her husband had beaten her. Raymond wasn't supposed to come back so early. How was she to know he'd return and find her in bed with Jedediah? Oh but the look on Raymond's face. She'd shocked him speechless.*
>
> *She put a hand down to her belly and felt the gentle swell where new life had sprouted. She had no idea*

Sliver's anger ignited. How dare she write Jedediah's name so easily, as if he was a mere character? Esther had no idea all right, and neither did Miss Ellie. And using Mrs. Yates's first name, Esther, for a main character would have her former employer turning over in her grave. Sliver couldn't help but feel sad for the woman she'd helped free from the noose.

She emptied the wastebasket and looked around the study. Miss Ellie had exchanged the upstairs room in Neelan Junction for the house on Michigan Avenue—one imprisonment for another. But at least her self-imposed imprisonment here meant Sliver could rest easy; Miss Ellie wouldn't follow her home and find out Jerome was with her, getting ready to go to school and to work hard to earn good grades.

Sliver sorted the mail daily, always keeping an eye out for anything unusual. There was no underestimating a woman who could kill her own baby. Ellie had re-invented herself as Randall Hunter. She could re-invent herself again.

As Sliver moved about the house doing her duties, she had ample time to reflect. The anxiety that had been in the pit of her stomach for the past couple of weeks was gone. For the first time in a long time, she had woken without feeling guilty for leaving her family in Neelan Junction and taking Jerome away with her. She had landed on her feet after all. Still, she couldn't help but be disappointed. All her life, the North had been dangled in front of her as a place of freedom and possibility. As a place of hope, but here she was, in the land of freedom, once again serving a white woman and barely getting by.

CHAPTER 46

Mavis **slowly woke** from a dream in which the train she was on had left the tracks at the bend and continued on into the sky, upwards, like a bracelet flung from a wrist. The coach was completely empty. Sunshine streamed in all the windows. She stood in the middle of the aisle, a hand on a seat on each side to keep her balance. Why she was on the train and where it was going didn't matter at all. It was the sudden freedom that was exhilarating, knowing the train had uncoupled from the tracks and no longer had to follow a prescribed route.

She opened her eyes. Jerome's face was inches from her own; she almost screamed.

"Sliver said for me to watch out over you. Are you okay, Miss Mavis? Do you need something?" His concern was genuine.

"I'm just tired, Jerome. I'll be okay. Where's Sliver?"

"It's Saturday. She's at work."

Right. And it wasn't a school day. Sliver had no choice but to leave him. Mavis closed her eyes but could feel him looking at her still. She'd known from the start that Sliver hadn't wanted her along, but she'd convinced herself she'd be useful. She'd grown up with her daddy lecturing that white people carried the heavy burden of caring for the negro. It was their obligation to do so and to keep them in line and deferential. But who was the burden now? If not for Sliver and Lydia bringing her food, she might have wasted away.

Jerome continued his staring.

"Is there something else you wanted to ask me?"

He nodded.

"Okay. I'm listening even if I close my eyes. It feels nice to have them closed. What do you want to know?"

"Eugene said your sister was his mama."

"That's right."

"He said her face got cut up by a negro and they lynched him, and she ran away because she couldn't stand being ugly."

The conversation was a surprise. "I didn't know Eugene talked about his mama."

"His grandma told him about her."

Mavis didn't like to think of the stories. "Well, her face was cut, that part's true, but not by a negro, although he was blamed."

"Eugene said he might kill me one day, too."

She opened her eyes.

Jerome's lower lip trembled as he spoke. He blinked fast to control the watering in his eyes. "He said he wouldn't get into any trouble because nobody cared when negroes was killed or disappeared. He said he could do whatever he wanted to me, any time. Is that true?"

Yes. She took Jerome's hand. "Lots of what went on in Neelan Junction wasn't right." No one had been charged with Samuel's murder. "That's one of the reasons Sliver took you away: to give you a better chance in life."

"I know. That's what she keeps telling me, especially when I miss home. But what I can't understand is why she didn't take anybody else with her. Why not Becky and some of her kids too? And what about Charlie?"

"Have you asked her?"

He shook his head. "I don't want to make her sadder than she already is."

Sliver was sad? "I wish I had more answers for you, Jerome. There are some things I miss about home too. Like feeling familiar in my place. Or recognizing people on the sidewalk." She looked around the room. "And I had a nicer room back home."

He smiled.

"And I didn't have to share it."

"I shared a room with four other kids."

"Becky's?"

He nodded. "But I'm not hers. That's why my skin's lighter. My mama died in Slew Town when I was born."

Mavis saw how he tried to make it seem okay. "I didn't know that. I'm sorry you didn't get a chance to know your mama."

He nodded and looked away. "I stayed with Charlie before leaving, and he said a person's colour doesn't matter because black and white aren't even colours, they're shades."

"Really?"

Jerome nodded. "He said it has to do with physics. Something about colours having wavelengths, and black and white don't. I didn't really understand."

"I don't know anything about physics," Mavis said.

"Me neither. Charlie had a book on it. I just nodded when he talked."

Mavis smiled. "I know this is a strange situation," she said, gesturing at the room. "But we'll figure things out as we go. Okay? I hope you know you're safe with me."

"I know. Sliver told me that too. She said you brought her water one day when she was in her garden and feeling sick. She said you might be the first white person to offer her any care in her life."

Really? "Well, it seems all we've got right now is each other." Was that even true? Sliver and Jerome had each other; Mavis was the one who only had them. "I'll get up soon and help. I just need a bit more sleep."

He propped himself up on his elbows beside her and rested his head in his hands. Samuel used to lie on his stomach on the kitchen floor like that, his knees bent and feet in the air. A pang of grief nudged her heart. Mamie had identified his body. She said there hadn't been much left of his face. A sob escaped.

"Are you okay?"

"Just a hiccup, I'm fine. When is Sliver back?"

"After supper. Lydia said she'll give us food. If you're okay, I'll go see if she needs any help."

"I'm okay."

But she wasn't. Something had taken root in her, grief perhaps, and she didn't know how to shake it. Most of her life, she'd thought herself blameless because she had never initiated any harm. But since when was doing nothing a virtue? Lying in bed, she'd had lots of time to review her life. She had known Danny was up to no good on his night patrols but thought ignoring it was the better thing to do. She'd agreed with Mrs. Booth's letters printed in *The Neelan News* but kept that agreement to herself. She remembered how nobody talked to Mrs. Booth that day at the post office. Why hadn't Mavis spoken about Mrs. Booth's letters to the editor with other women? The only time she had stepped outside of her observer role was when she boarded the train with Sliver and Jerome. But she couldn't even claim to be brave because she'd latched on to Sliver's coattails and tried to make it seem like she was doing them a good deed by tagging along. Where was the courage in that?

In truth, she was pathetic.

It was quiet in the room. She rolled over. The wall was a foot from her face. Dents and scratches had accumulated there over time, and she stared until they took different forms—a bear's snout, table legs, a curved umbrella handle—nonsense items that nevertheless held her fascination. She closed her eyes and hoped for sleep.

The days bled into one another. And then, inexplicably, after ten days in bed, Mavis woke to find the darkness had shifted. Her gaze yearned to go farther than the wall at her face. She rolled over. Shafts of sunlight streamed through the window, and she wanted to feel the heat on her skin. And what was that bird song? She had never heard it before.

She swung her legs over the side of the bed and sat up. The bathroom was free, so she ran a hot bath. When Jerome came home from school, he was excited to see her upright. Was it her imagination, or had he grown since leaving Neelan Junction?

"What happened to you?" She pointed to the gap between his pants and the tops of his shoes. He needed some pants. She checked her purse; there was no money left.

When Sliver came back after work, Mavis asked where it had gone.

"Where did it go? How did it last is more like it. I used it to pay for food. And for the room. And a few school supplies for Jerome. It's all gone because there wasn't much to start with. I asked my boss if I could get paid for the days I already worked, and she said she'd give me an advance tomorrow. If she remembers, we should have enough to keep us going until I get my full pay. Any more questions?"

Mavis hadn't meant to interrogate. She wanted to say she was sorry. Instead, she said, "Thank you."

The next day Mavis felt good enough to go outside. It was time to get moving. She asked Lydia for directions to Jerome's school, and then she washed and dressed. She'd surprise him by picking him up.

She'd forgotten how busy the sidewalks were and how quickly people moved here. Perhaps because she longed to see a familiar face, she imagined she saw Ellie standing at the corner. The woman's back was turned towards her, but the hair colour was the same, as was the height and build. Mavis rushed up and touched the woman's shoulder. She turned around; her cheeks were unblemished, her eyes the wrong colour. "I'm so sorry," Mavis said. "I thought you were someone else."

The woman walked away.

A decade had passed since she'd seen Ellie. How ridiculous to think she'd simply bump into her on the street. Ellie had left Neelan Junction and never said goodbye, and she'd never replied to the letter Mavis had sent via her solicitor. Flustered and preoccupied, Mavis got lost on the way to Jerome's school. She wandered down a side street and then turned back when she realized her mistake, but not before seeing a Help Wanted sign in the window of a business. By the time she arrived at the school, Jerome had already left. She retraced her steps to the Help Wanted sign. This time she read the name of the business: Malone Oil. It was located on a small industrial street, two blocks off a busier thoroughfare and sandwiched between a mechanic's shop and a welding shop. Mavis didn't know what skills she had besides waiting for others to tell her what to do, but poverty was a great motivator. Plus, she had been Sliver's burden long enough.

She entered. The floor to ceiling window looking onto the street hadn't been cleaned for some time. The sun could barely get through. Dust coated the magazines that lined the table in the waiting area. The carpet in front of the reception desk, where it had been trampled the most, was threadbare. No one was at the desk.

"Hello?"

"I'll be right there," a voice called from the back.

Two minutes later, a middle-aged man with greying hair and dark-rimmed glasses emerged from the back, wiping his hands on an oily rag. "Can I help you?"

"I've come about the job," she said, gesturing towards the sign.

"What qualifications have you got?"

"What do I need?" Perhaps the sign was a posting for an actual mechanic!

The man put the rag in his back pocket. "Can you type?"

"I can learn. I'm a fast learner."

"Can you do books?"

"I've been reading my whole life."

He laughed. "Not that kind of books. What I mean is, can you balance accounts? Do payroll, that kind of thing?"

Mavis blinked back tears with the realization she had no skills. "As I said, I catch on to things quickly. You won't need to show me things more than once."

He studied her.

She had dressed neatly. Her hair was clean and upswept. She knew she would add a touch of class to the dingy office.

"Have you ever had a job before?"

Was marriage considered a job? It should be. "No. But I can tell you what I would do first thing if you hired me."

"What?"

She nodded towards the front window. "I'd scrub that window so people could see that work goes on inside, and I'd dust off the table and tidy the sitting area so someone might actually want to use it. And in time, I'd replace the carpet."

"The name's Robbie," he said. "Robbie Malone."

"I'm Mavis Thorpe."

"Well, Miss Thorpe, I can't promise I'll have the money to replace the carpet, but you're right that this place needs a good cleaning. Can you start next week?"

She nodded, not trusting her voice. She'd never been so grateful for anything in her life. Hope stirred the sediment in her belly.

Finally, she had some news of her own to share with Sliver and Jerome.

CHAPTER 47

The boarding house had been too small for them from the start. Now that Miss Mavis was working, Sliver could finally get a place with Jerome and not feel guilty. She wanted to find an apartment close enough to his school so he could keep walking, and one on a bus route so she could still get to work. All she had to do was break the news to the barnacle. She chuckled to herself. Miss Mavis wasn't so bad, but she needed to be on her own too. Be pushed out of the nest, so to speak. Find her own wings instead of thinking she was helping them with her pitiful flight.

Sunday was Sliver's only day off. She and Jerome had seen a church nearby with its black congregation streaming out when they were walking by one day, and Jerome had asked if they could go. She hadn't stepped foot inside a church since her mama's death, but she couldn't deny she felt a pull. Maybe it was to lessen Jerome's loneliness. Maybe it was to lessen her own, but she took to going, knowing her daddy wouldn't spite her if going made her feel good.

On this Sunday after church, Sliver sent Jerome on an errand and returned to their room by herself. She didn't want him there for the conversation. He had a soft spot for Miss Mavis and would likely beg Sliver to let her keep living with them.

Sliver climbed the stairs and went into the room. The barnacle was sitting on her bed reading a book. "It's time for us to find our own place," Sliver said, jumping right in.

"I've been thinking about that too. Maybe we could find a house to rent. Or a three-bedroom apartment."

Sliver hadn't anticipated Miss Mavis would interpret the "us" to include her. "I meant me and Jerome."

Mavis looked up, her face innocent as a baby's. "What about me?"

What about you? I've been taking care of you since we left. "I figured you could find your own place now that you're working."

"But I thought we would stay together!"

You thought wrong.

"Why wouldn't we stay together?" she persisted.

"Don't take this as a slight, but I've worked for white folks my whole life; I don't want to live with them too." Sliver braced herself for what she knew would come.

"But Sliver, this is different! I'm not like them. We're *friends*. Isn't that why you came to me? Friends often live together. Plus, I can help out with Jerome. And we can save money living together. He can have a better life. That's what you want for him, isn't it? Doesn't that make more sense?"

Friends? Sliver worked hard to keep her face neutral. Miss Mavis thought they were friends? "I appreciate what you did for us, and I said I'd pay you back, but I don't want to keep living with you."

"But why?"

"Because I wouldn't be able to stop myself from serving you, and you wouldn't be able to stop yourself from being served."

"That's not true! You haven't had to serve me."

Sliver bit her tongue. What did she think had happened the whole time she'd stayed in bed? She'd been taken care of. By who? By Sliver, Jerome, and Lydia. Who borrowed a pot from Lydia to make food in? Who brought her the cooked food? Who made sure they had money to pay for the room? People didn't just live; a whole structure was needed around them. Miss Mavis was too used to that structure magically being there to know how much work went into supporting it. That she was blind to the truth only confirmed what Sliver knew. "As I said, I'm grateful for all you've done for us. I only wanted to borrow a little bit of money. That's why I came to you. That was all."

"But without my money—"

"We'd have got by," Sliver interrupted. "I had enough to get us started. I just wanted a little extra just in case." She didn't mention pawning Miss Ellie's cigarette case. "Jerome and I aren't abandoning you. We just want our own place."

"But ..."

"And we'll help you to find one too, if you need help."

By this point, Sliver was ready to offer anything to have the conversation end. She didn't want Miss Mavis to start crying and have to be the one to do the consoling. She got to her feet.

"Jerome will be back any time now with some groceries. I'll get some food started."

Sliver found a place first. The apartment only had one bedroom, but it was all Sliver could afford.

"Jerome can have the bedroom," she told Miss Mavis, who'd pointed out it was too small. "I get up first anyway, so I'll take the couch."

"Do you have any furniture?"

Sliver nodded. Through Lydia, she'd lined up a used couch, a single bed, and a small table and chairs for the space beside the kitchen. She took Jerome's hand. "We're starting out slow, but I have a helper."

"And one day we'll get you a garden, right Sliver?" Jerome said. "Just like the one you used to have back home."

Sliver smiled. "That's right."

"If we lived together," Mavis said, "we could get a bigger place and maybe it would have a garden."

Jerome got excited by that idea and reached for Miss Mavis's hand. "And Sliver, maybe you could have your own room and wouldn't have to sleep on the couch."

"We've already had that discussion," Sliver said, looking pointedly at Miss Mavis to make it clear she was annoyed that she'd brought it up in front of Jerome. "Me and Jerome will just have to make do until we can get our own plot of dirt someday. And you're welcome to visit us often, right Jerome?"

"But if she lived with us, she wouldn't have to —"

"Right, Jerome?"

"Right."

"I told Lydia we'd be out at the end of the month," she told Miss Mavis, "so you'd better find something soon."

There was no official sign that marked the colour line in Washington, DC; it was more a feeling, or a sense of prosperity. The buildings got closer together on the black side. The yards were smaller, and the sidewalks were chipped, and there were fewer flowers and trees. Sliver knew white people could be poor too, but they had more areas in the city that allowed them to be poor in; their skin colour didn't determine their address as much. A white person could live on the wrong side of the tracks, but there was another spot beyond the tracks that always had room for the coloureds. Miss Mavis found an apartment as close as she could to Sliver and Jerome's, and even though it was just on the other side of that line, her building was quieter, and the streets were better lit and less crowded. But the real kicker was that her rent was cheaper.

On their first day in their new place, Sliver listened to all the noises in the building so she could know what was regular and what might be cause for alarm. People talked in the hallways as they passed her door. The first few times, she thought someone was coming into her apartment. Somewhere nearby, a baby cried and Sliver's palms itched. She hadn't caught a baby in some time. A siren wailed as it raced past the building. She looked at Jerome. "I expect we'll get used to the noises here in time. It's better than the rooming house." She missed her one room shack at the Yates's. It hadn't been much, but she hadn't had to share any walls.

"I wish Miss Mavis was still with us," Jerome said when they ate their supper. "Do you think we'll still see her?

"For a while, I expect." *Until she gets busy with her own life.*

"She was nice to me."

Sliver thought that over. It was true. Even without her knowing

Jerome was her nephew, Miss Mavis had treated him kindly. Maybe she would tell her about the connection one day. But if she told Miss Mavis, then she'd have to tell Jerome, and then she'd have to tell Charlie, and that would lead to a whole big can of worms.

"So was Lydia. And don't forget, we were nice to Miss Mavis too."

CHAPTER 48

The more Mavis learned about business at Malone Oil, the more she discovered ways to improve it. And the more ways it improved, the better business became. By 1953, almost six years after she'd started, Robbie Malone had purchased two more trucks and hired four new drivers. Payroll was on track. The books were up to date. Mavis had replaced the carpet in the waiting area and had a fresh coat of white paint applied to brighten the walls. She placed planters filled with flowers outside the front entrance and made sure to have fresh cut flowers inside. Even the men grew to expect the extra spots of colour.

And as Robbie got to know her, he told her of the Malone family's journey from Ireland in the 1850s. He spoke of their poverty and disease and the filth in which they had lived, and how they took any jobs available and were called all manner of derogatory names. "But look at me now!" His pride was evident. Each generation had more opportunities. "I'm my own boss."

Robbie taught her how to drive, and on weekends he often let her take the delivery car home. Her co-workers were all male and married, so she stayed mainly to herself. She had never had to make new friends before; she'd simply followed Ellie and eventually been included.

After a few years at Malone Oil, Robbie told her she should buy her own house instead of living in an apartment. He said her money should go to paying off her own mortgage instead of somebody else's. Owning a house meant no one could tell her to leave. Why have money sitting in the bank doing nothing? Mavis thought he was joking. She didn't know that women could buy houses. It had never occurred to her, and it was some time before she agreed.

One day she'd taken a wrong turn and found herself on a side street she'd never noticed before. A for sale sign was on the front lawn of a yellow stucco bungalow that looked like it had been well maintained. She passed the house a few more times in the following week to see if the sign was still up and was relieved each time to see it hadn't sold. She mentioned it to Robbie, and he set up an appointment with the realtor that afternoon. He said it would be a great investment. Men looked at things that way—as investments. Women wanted homes and men wanted investments. Could she really afford it?

The house itself was nothing special—800 square feet, with three small bedrooms, a bathroom, a kitchen, and a living and dining area. The wood floors in the living room had been lovingly cared for, and the linoleum in the kitchen had been replaced in the last five years, but it was the south-facing back yard that sold her. The owners were an elderly couple who loved to garden. Besides a small patch of grass near the back door, the remainder of the yard was staked and ordered with trestles and all manner of devices to allow plants to grow straight and strong. Mavis couldn't help but see Sliver there, keeping things in order.

Mavis brought her to see the house. "I'm thinking of buying it," she announced. "But I have never worked a garden in my life. I'll only make an offer if you agree to take care of it for me."

Sliver remained silent, but her hands had twitched at her side.

"You can plant whatever you want and come by to work it anytime. What do you think? Should I make an offer?"

Sliver nodded and turned away, and Mavis pretended she didn't see the desire Sliver had turned to hide. Knowing Sliver would garden helped Mavis to get over the guilt of having a house to herself while Sliver and Jerome still shared a one-bedroom apartment.

When she had the car on the weekends, she often visited Sliver and Jerome. Did they need anything? Some extra groceries they could throw in the trunk so they wouldn't have to lug them? Was there any way she could help?

During the week, Mavis got in the habit of stopping by after work at least once. She'd find Jerome reading the paper or watching the news on Sliver's hand-me-down black-and-white television set that she'd saved for and finally been able to purchase. Jerome seemed old for his age. At fifteen, he towered over Mavis. He worked hard in school and earned good grades. He planned to be a lawyer or a politician. He said maybe one day a black man would be president. Mavis tried not to laugh at his enthusiasm. What did she know? Stranger things had happened.

The few times Mavis had asked Sliver about her job, the midwife had shrugged and said there wasn't much to tell. The money paid the bills. Mavis knew what part of town Sliver worked in, what bus route she took to get there, and even what her schedule was. Things might have gone on like that forever, except one day Jerome let something slip about Miss Ellie.

Mavis's neck snapped up. "What did you say?"

The air emptied out of the room.

Jerome looked apologetic and afraid at the same time as he sent a silent apology to Sliver.

"Take your books to your room," Sliver said.

Mavis looked from Jerome to Sliver and back again. "What's going on?"

"Nothing's going on," Sliver said.

"Did he just say Miss Ellie?"

Sliver sat at the kitchen table and pushed back the cuticles on her left hand.

Mavis's mind landed on a startling conclusion. Suddenly it was clear why Sliver kept so much to herself. "Are you working for Ellie?"

She didn't respond.

"Sliver?"

"Yes."

"Are you working for Ellie?"

"I said 'yes'."

Mavis felt like she'd been punched in the stomach. Ellie was alive, here, and Sliver *worked* for her? "Why didn't you tell me?"

"You were going through a bad patch when I first got the job, and then time moved on."

A bad patch? "Wait. You've been working for Ellie since we got here?"

Sliver nodded.

"Are you telling me you've worked for my sister since we got here and never once thought of telling me?" She stood up and began to pace. "Do you have any idea how many times I've wondered what happened to her? If she was dead or alive? Sometimes I even conjure her into being and have random sightings of her in the grocery store, at the bank, or on the street corner."

"Don't you dare talk to me about wondering where a loved one has gone."

Sliver's voice was low and without inflection. It succeeded in deflating Mavis's righteous indignation and reminding her she was in Sliver's home. She sat back down and tried to calm herself. "How did you find her?"

"She sent a letter to Mrs. Yates just before I left. It had her return address on it." Sliver stood up and cleared the supper dishes as if nothing out of the ordinary had just occurred. Then she filled the sink and immersed her hands in the hot, soapy water. "You know what that means, don't you?"

"What?"

"That she could have written to you too, but she didn't."

That truth hit hard, but Mavis pushed it aside. Ellie was alive! And in the same city, not far away at all. Mavis experienced a physical ache in her stomach, a *need* to rush over to her sister. "Where is she? Can we go there now? Has she ever asked about me?"

"Miss Ellie only ever talks about herself."

"Poor Ellie. She must be so lonely. I have to go see her!"

A plate slipped from Sliver's hand and dropped into the sink as she spun around. "Poor Ellie? Is that what I just heard? *Poor Ellie?*"

"Yes. I feel sad for her. I'd have visited straight away if I'd known she was here."

"Well you can thank me, then, for keeping you away!"

Mavis had only seen Sliver angry once, when Mavis had asked where all her money had gone. But something else was wrong now. "What's going on, Sliver?"

Sliver's lips were pursed tight. She turned back to the sink and rubbed furiously at the plate. "I don't know if I want to have this conversation with you or not."

Mavis didn't say a word. She grabbed a dishtowel and joined Sliver at the sink.

"Mamie told me things about your sister before she first arrived at the Yates's, so I didn't expect to like her much. But then I learned more things while she was there, enough that I don't feel sorry for her one bit. I saved my sorrow for Jedediah and Delia who left three children behind because of your sister's selfishness. And for poor Samuel and his family. Maybe he got shot because of your sister, too."

"Ellie never told anyone about Samuel."

"She told you. How else would you have known to tell Mamie?"

"Ellie didn't tell me; I found out. I saw her leaving the parlour and Samuel was inside. I don't think he even knew that I knew."

"Oh, you 'found out' but you never said nothing, did you?"

"No."

"Why?"

"I didn't think it was any of my business."

"Well maybe if you had, Samuel would still be alive."

Mavis had never considered that. "How?"

"I don't know. I don't have a crystal ball. Maybe Mamie would have sent him off somewhere. If you change one thing, you change everything, that's what my mama always said. But I had other reasons for not telling you Miss Ellie was here. As far as I'm concerned, you're better off not seeing her." Sliver submerged her hands into the soapy water, and Mavis imagined her pulling an infant out from the suds.

"What other reasons?"

"I don't want to say."

"You have to now."

"No I don't. Not if I don't want to. You're in my home. I get to do as I like here."

"Please Sliver?"

She considered a bit longer before agreeing. "Just remember you were the one who asked. Here goes: your sister killed her first baby."

Mavis laughed. There were many things wrong with Ellie, but she wasn't a murderer. "That's ridiculous."

"You think I'm joking? I was there. Your sister killed her baby."

Mavis put the plates away and sat at the table again. "I don't believe you. Why would she do that?" She sifted through childhood memories to try to make sense of what was going on. Ellie lying about the sack full of kittens. Ellie lying about Desperate. Ellie stepping on spiders and smearing her gut-mucked shoes on the floor. Ellie arranging to meet with Samuel in the parlour. Ellie threatening, *I'll kill your cat.* Ellie hiding in the closet so Mavis had to do more work. Mavis had to admit her memories about Ellie weren't always great. "And the second baby? I suppose you're going to tell me she killed it too?"

Sliver hesitated again. "I don't know that I can say."

"You've started something now, Sliver. Let's finish it."

Sliver dried her hands on her apron and sat across from Mavis. "Okay then. Are you ready?"

"Yes."

"And you promise not to talk to Jerome about it?"

"I promise."

"I mean never."

Mavis crossed her heart. "I promise."

"Okay." Sliver took a deep breath as if drawing in courage. "That second baby didn't die."

"What happened to it?"

"That second baby is Jerome."

Mavis's vision turned inwards. She travelled back to her childhood kitchen and heard Mamie's voice, *Are you really as thick in the head as all that?* And Mavis, claiming she had eyes all right, yes she did. Eyes in her head. Where else would they be? But now she understood Mamie's frustration. Clearly, Mavis only saw what she wanted to see. What she *hoped* to see. What she was *supposed* to see, not what was right in front of her eyes.

Jerome was Ellie's son?

She continued to put the pieces together. Ellie with Samuel, Ellie with Jedediah, and Ellie with ... who? If Sliver had taken Jerome, that had to mean she was connected to his daddy in some way. Her mind darted about and then landed. The blacksmith. Her messenger. How easily her notes had nested in his large palms. Sliver had left not just to protect Jerome, but to protect Charlie too.

"He's Charlie's boy, isn't he?"

Sliver nodded. "Jerome doesn't know yet, and I'd like to keep it that way. And Miss Ellie thinks her baby died. So you can't tell her either."

If I see you around here again, I'll get my knife out and carve more initials into your sister's face. "Willis knew about Jerome?"

"He sure did, but not who his daddy was."

His threat to keep her away from Ellie made sense now. She had been punished, yet again, for her indiscretions.

"It wasn't Jedediah who cut Ellie, was it?" Sliver asked.

"No. Willis did. I was there."

Sliver nodded. "Mamie said Miss Ellie's face hadn't been cut when Master Willis caught her and brought her back to the house. If Jedediah had done it, Mamie would have seen it. So there's your answer right there about why your sister killed her first baby: revenge. But that wasn't enough, so she used my Charlie to get back at Master Willis even more."

It was too sick to believe. Could it really be true?

"Tell me why you let people think it was Jedediah who cut your sister."

"Because that's the story my daddy and Willis told; I didn't think anyone would believe me." Mavis put her arms on the table and dropped her head onto them. Suddenly, her neck wasn't strong enough to hold up the weight of knowing.

"But you didn't even try."

"No. I didn't try."

They sat quietly for some time.

Mavis finally broke the silence. "I always wondered what happened to Jedediah and Delia's children. Do you know?"

"They went to Delia's sister's in Slew Town."

"I'm glad they had somewhere to go."

"You've never been there, have you?"

"No."

"Because if you had, you wouldn't be glad. Last I heard, they were burned out and never got the money they were owed. That's the real story. I don't know what your people are saying."

Her people? "I'm sorry, Sliver. It's just hard for me to believe my sister could do something so terrible."

"And it's hard for me to believe you can't believe it." She stood from the table. "Look at the time."

Mavis understood she was being asked to leave. "Can I have her address?"

Sliver wrote it on a piece of paper. "Go on a Sunday, when I'm not there. And don't tell me when you're going. I don't want to know."

"Is there a particular time of day when I know she'll be home?"

Sliver snorted. "She never leaves the house."

Mavis called Jerome in from the bedroom to thank him for supper. She looked at him with fresh eyes. How had she seen Danny in Rosetta's boys and not seen Ellie in Jerome? It was a new narrative she'd never thought to investigate.

She gave him a hug and smiled. He was a good boy. A smart boy. He was her nephew.

CHAPTER 49

On Sunday, Mavis drove slowly down Michigan Avenue. The houses on both sides were large and situated on double-sized lots. The trees on the avenue formed an arch, and she imagined that when the leaves changed colour, they would look like millions of stained glass cathedral windows reflecting the sun's light.

Was she in the right place? It felt too tranquil here.

She confirmed the address and pulled to the curb outside of a two-storey blue and white house with a large porch. There was even a porch swing hanging to the right of the door. The side yard was filled with cherry trees. How fragrant they must be in their spring bloom.

She cut the engine and sat for a minute. Suddenly, this didn't feel like a good idea anymore. Sliver was right: if Ellie could write to Mrs. Yates, she could have written to Mavis too. It couldn't be any more obvious that Ellie didn't want to see her, but for some reason, Mavis wanted to make Ellie say that herself.

The front gate stuck a bit on the walkway then swung shut behind her. Mavis walked to the front door and knocked before she lost her courage. As she was deciding whether to run or stay, the door opened and Ellie stood before her. A burgundy veil covered the bottom half of her face. Her dark hair was full and wavy.

The sisters stared at each other for a moment.

"Well, this is a surprise," Ellie finally said.

"To me, too."

"I'd say moreso to me, as you're the one who drove here."

She kept her hand on the door and didn't move. It occurred to Mavis that she might be sent away.

"Well, there's no sense gawking at one another," Ellie finally said. "You might as well come in."

That was as good an invitation as any.

"You can put your hat there, if you like." Ellie gestured to a table by the door. "I was just making myself some tea. Would you like some?"

"That would be nice. Please."

"Make yourself at home."

Ellie disappeared and Mavis walked into the living room. Every flat surface had stacks of paper piled neatly. Bookcases bulged with books. A rocking chair sat facing the living room window. Mavis remembered the disarray of Ellie's childhood bedroom and could see Sliver's hand at keeping things ordered.

A few minutes later, Ellie returned with a teapot and a tin of store-bought cookies and placed them on the coffee table. "Have a seat." She gestured at the couch. "What brings you to Washington, DC? Are you visiting?"

"No, I live here now."

Ellie raised an eyebrow and poured tea with a steady hand. "Sugar? Milk?"

"No, thank you." How formal they were with one another. She was taking her cues from Ellie, as she always had, and it was clear a tearful reunion wasn't in the cards.

"I'd have had someone fetch the tea for us," Ellie said, "but I'm alone on Sundays."

"Yes, I know. Sliver told me."

Ellie's calm demeanour cracked. "You've seen Sliver? Is she working for you, too?"

"No. She doesn't work for me. How would she have time? We left Neelan Junction together. She's my friend." *Don't mention Jerome.*

"Your *friend*?"

"Yes. You know, a friend is someone you care about. We lived together when we first arrived, before she got her own apartment."

Ellie stirred her tea. *Clink. Clink. Clink.* She undid her veil to drink and exposed her scars. "What about Danny?"

"He died in 1946." Had Sliver really told Ellie nothing? Had Ellie not asked?

"I didn't know. I'm sorry. And is that why you left?"

"No, it just felt like the right time."

"Because you'd always planned to leave." The way Ellie said it highlighted the absurdity of the statement. "I'm confused though. If you came with Sliver, why are you only visiting me now? She's been working for me for years already."

Don't mention Jerome. Don't mention Jerome. "Because I only just learned she worked for you last week."

Ellie stared at her with a superior look that Mavis wished she could wipe from her face. "I'm having a hard time following your story. Isn't that something a *friend* would tell you? And I guess if you are her *friend* you would know things about her, too. Like how old she is. And if she has siblings. And what happened to her husband. And how many children she has and where she was born and if her parents are still alive. Yes?"

Mavis could see where Ellie was heading and didn't want to go there, so she didn't respond.

"My guess is I know more about her than you do, and I don't call her my friend."

Mavis hated that Ellie still knew how to get the upper hand.

"Well, I must admit your visit is a surprise. You look so much older than I remember. I imagine I do too. How long has it been since we last saw one another? Thirteen years?"

"Longer, actually. You left Neelan Junction thirteen years ago, but I haven't seen you since right before your second baby was born."

"That's right." She took another sip of tea. "Time flies, doesn't it? Tell me, why are you really here?"

Mavis had rehearsed a speech on her way over in the car. "I came to find out why you abandoned me. You left without saying goodbye and you never contacted me. I kept waiting to hear from you." She heard the whine in her voice. *Do not cry!*

"It's not that complicated. I'm surprised you didn't figure it out on your own. How does a mother justify leaving a baby behind? How could I possibly explain myself? I know people thought I was a monster. Plus, you were the one who abandoned me. You never came, even when you knew my second baby had died too."

"What? I visited every day! *You* sent me away. Mona said you didn't want to see me, and then Willis threatened to hurt you if I kept coming."

Ellie's eyebrow arched. "Mona told me you didn't come. And Sliver never mentioned you'd been there either."

"Sliver was there?"

"You didn't think I'd deliver my own baby, did you?"

"Because I specifically asked Sliver to tell you I'd visited."

"Well your *friend* never did. And Willis said you wanted nothing more to do with me."

"And you believed him?"

Ellie shrugged. "Let's just say I wasn't at my best. It's water under the bridge now. Plus, it was all Willis's fault."

"What was? Your leaving?"

Ellie pointed to her face. "This. Do you know he actually tried to *apologize* once for scarring my face? What did he expect me to say? *It's okay. I forgive you?*" She sucked the inside of one cheek, and then switched to the other side, as if she could pull the scar tissue through her flesh and swallow it down. But the scars didn't budge. Ellie gestured towards one of her bookshelves. "I bet you never thought I'd become a writer, did you? I've published five books now, and I'm working on another."

"What books?"

Ellie rolled her eyes in exasperation. "Right. I forgot. Sliver didn't tell you I'm a writer, either. I thought *friends* talked to one another."

"They do. We do. And stop saying it like that, as if we couldn't be friends. I hate that."

"Well, if Mavis hates it ..."

"Stop."

Ellie's face was flushed. She fanned at herself with her hand. "I'm sitting here thinking that maybe Sliver doesn't tell you anything for the same reason I don't: because you're too fragile."

Mavis stared into her cup and blinked hard to keep her eyes from tearing up.

"Or maybe there's another reason."

"What?"

"That you're not in the habit of asking darkies questions."

"Don't call her that. And we talk all the time."

"If that were true then you'd know she worked for me and that I'm a published author. I've made more money from my writing than I ever received from Willis."

Mavis saw Ellie's pride inflate her like a balloon. She thought of Sliver coming to Ellie's house six days a week, cooking her food, doing her laundry, washing her dishes. She thought of Sliver raising Ellie's son, and of Jerome applying himself at school, knowing he had to work three times as hard as the white boys to ever get ahead. She thought of Sliver accumulating furniture for her new apartment, one piece at a time, slowly rebuilding her life and making a new one for Jerome. Filling him full of hope. Cautiously fanning his ambition. And here Ellie sat, with her tea and fancy biscuits, thinking she should be admired for writing books?

Ellie crossed the room and pulled a book from her bookshelf. "This is the latest." She handed it to Mavis. "It has sold more than all the others."

The Attic Dweller. It was a shiny paperback with a colourful and lurid cover. "But it's by Randall Hunter."

"Don't you remember?"

A memory surfaced like a catfish in a pond. Ellie wishing she could be a boy and have adventures. *I'd pick the name Randall.* And Mavis adding the surname Hunter. Boy-Ellie. Super-Ellie with her bow and arrows. She flipped the book open randomly and began to read.

> *Esther woke up.*
> *Her head was groggy; her body ached.*
> *Where was she?*

Her eyes scanned the room. The ceiling was sloped, like an umbrella half-closed.

"I draw on personal experience for that one," Ellie said returning to the bookshelves. "From the time Willis had me locked up."

"You were locked up?" Was this another one of Ellie's stories?

"Yes. Why do you think I wasn't free to answer the door? He locked me up until I was pregnant with my third. *Eugene.* How I despise that name. And when he was born, I left. That was our agreement. I'd like to let Willis know how much money I've made from my writing, but I agreed never to contact him or our son. I named the main character in *The Attic Dweller* after his mama. My readers can't get enough of Esther. What an awful human being she was. When Sliver told me she was dead, I can't say I was upset." Ellie gestured towards the book again. "Some of the reviews I got for it were scathing." She stared into the corner of the room, as if reading from a script: "'*The Attic Dweller* has the power to ruin the sexual purity of an entire generation of women.' An entire generation!" She laughed. "As if I have that power. But the best one was the reviewer who speculated that Randall Hunter was a black man writing about his sexual exploits with white women. My sales really got going then."

"I guess you'd know about sexual exploits."

Ellie's face hardened. It happened in stages right in front of Mavis, her features moving from putty and setting into stone. "How dare you come into my house and think you are better than me? Huh? I draw on experience from my upbringing. The same one that you had. Where we were the ones being *served* not doing the serving. That attitude is inherited — like a blood type or a talent."

"Or a disease," Mavis said. "Don't try to pretend you had a special set of circumstances."

"And don't try to pretend you didn't. Or have you gone colour blind *Miss Mavis.* Does Sliver still call you that? I'm guessing she does. And like I said, if she's really your friend, then you'd know things about her, but I bet you only know Sliver as she relates to you and your life."

Mavis stood up and grabbed her purse.

"Oh, wait. I get it," Ellie continued. "You're one of those white people who think having a black friend erases your own past. You probably petition for desegregation and act as if the colour of your skin is meaningless or think you're innocent just because you want to be. Well you're wrong, Mavis. Dead wrong. I know where you come from. You can't just leave it behind by deciding it was wrong or wishing it had been different. You spent time at the shade tree too. You let Mamie serve you throughout your childhood, and then Carlina did your dirty laundry and cleaned up your mess, and if you lived in Neelan Junction today, a set of black hands would be serving you still, and you wouldn't see anything wrong with that because that's the way it's always been. And if you were mad about me being in the parlour with Samuel, it was probably because I got there first."

"Stop it!"

The sisters stared at one another, the colour up in their cheeks.

"Don't you DARE use Samuel's name as some kind of ammunition. He's dead! Okay? Someone shot him and left him to rot in the swamp. And maybe if I'd told Mamie that you had taken him into the parlour, then maybe she'd have sent him away and he'd still be alive. So maybe you killed him, too."

"Too? What are you talking about?"

"I know you killed your first baby. Sliver told me."

Ellie snorted. "Sliver said that? And you believed her? I might have wanted to get back at Willis, but I'm not a murderer."

"She also said your second baby died, and that you sold your third baby so you could leave."

"Maybe I should give Sliver a turn at my typewriter." Ellie twisted a piece of hair into a ringlet around her finger. "I don't know why she's feeding you lies, but what does it say about you that you believe them? She should mind her own business is what she should do."

"You're saying Sliver lied?"

"I'm saying Sliver took my second baby and said he died. You'll have to ask her why she did that. As for the third baby, there's some truth there. Willis wanted a son, and I wanted my freedom. We both got what we wanted."

A dog barked outside.

Ellie's stomach growled audibly in the quiet room. She looked down at it, surprised. "And I did write to you. I wrote to you almost every day for a while."

"Why would I believe you? I never got any letters."

"That's because I never sent them. Wait here." She went upstairs, returned with four hardcover notebooks, and handed one to Mavis. "I wrote to you here."

Mavis opened it.

August 1940

Dear Mavis,

You'll never imagine where I am right now. An unusual set of circumstances has brought about a great change in my situation. I am on the train for the second time, leaving Neelan Junction and travelling to Washington, DC, but this time I have chosen to go.

I can feel my pulse in the tender flesh between my legs — the parts we are never allowed to speak about. Childbirth is such an ordeal. I had another son. Apparently my body is good for reproducing male heirs.

I am happy to be leaving this place where I am supposed to sit with my ankles crossed in the parlour and look amused when I am hopelessly bored and where my mind has no intellectual outlet, and my body withers in its prime.

This time I leave with enough money to last me my lifetime.

The countryside speeds by. I am both afraid and exhilarated. What lies ahead? If I had my beauty still, I would have no fear. If I had you with me, I would have no fear.

I just realized only one letter separates scared from scarred.

I am alone, and I am so afraid.

Mavis closed the notebook. "Why didn't you send them to me?"

"Because I lost everything, Mavis, and when you stopped visiting me, I thought I had lost you too."

They had both been robbed of the comfort of being together. And in that moment of feeling close to Ellie, Mavis wanted to tell her that her second baby hadn't died at all, that Jerome was alive and well and smart and funny, but she didn't because Ellie had never wanted Jerome except to get back at Willis. He'd served his purpose. "I should be going."

"And I should get back to work." Ellie went into the kitchen and returned with a paper bag into which she placed her published books. "If you get a chance, send me a note and tell me what you think of them." She handed Mavis the bag and remained standing. The visit was over.

"Can I take the notebooks?"

"No. Not yet."

"When?"

"I don't know."

They looked at each other warily. Mavis waited for Ellie to hug her and Ellie waited for Mavis to make the first move. And then the wait made them both awkward, so they did nothing.

Ellie delivered her parting blow. "Just remember, you're not as good as you think you are *Miss Mavis.*"

"I'll do that. And the same goes for you. Maybe I'll see you soon."

"You never know."

Mavis let herself out. Ellie locked the door behind her.

She stood on the porch, the bag of books in her arms, and watched the swing sway gently by itself in the soft breeze. For a second she saw two girls there, joined by a thick braid between them. Then the image of the Turner girls vanished and she was Mavis Thorpe, alone again.

CHAPTER 50

Mavis drove away sick with disappointment. Never, in all her reunion imaginings, had it ended with a cool goodbye at her sister's door. It was hard to believe no one had told Ellie of Mavis's visits. Or was that just another one of Ellie's convenient lies? And somehow Ellie had skipped over whether or not she'd killed her baby.

Mavis pulled into the alley behind her house, parked behind her garage, and checked her watch. Sunday mornings Sliver went to church with Jerome. Then she came by to garden. She'd be here soon.

Mavis hung her coat on the hook inside the back door then put Ellie's books on the kitchen table stacked so the spines faced her and arranged them according to publication date. Ellie a writer? She shook her head at the wonder of it. There were five books in all: *The Magnolia Tree* (1944), *Southern Justice* (1946), *The Cathedral* (1948), *The Rope and the Gun* (1951), and *The Attic Dweller* (1953).

Mavis did the math. Ellie's first book had been published four years after she'd left Neelan Junction for good. Danny was still alive then, and Mrs. Booth still wrote letters to *The Neelan News*. It felt like another lifetime ago.

Mavis sat at the table, opened *The Magnolia Tree*, and began to read.

> *Isabelle Montgomery was the Mistress of Magnolia Hall, and she was the most beautiful girl in the entire country.*

The lush humidity and swamp scents returned Mavis to her past. It was as if someone had delivered a box of her childhood belongings and dumped them into her lap. She handled each memory carefully. Was it real or made up? Did it really belong to her? And if so, did she want to keep it, or was it safe now to discard?

Isabelle stood beside Mamie's stove and watched the cook strip the skin from the chicken that only hours earlier had pecked through the slops spilled from the kitchen bucket. Mamie sliced the meat from the bone and cut it into small bits. She was in a good mood, so she sang as she worked.

Mamie's son Samuel jumped around on the balls of his feet and made his mama laugh. Isabelle felt a dark jealousy stab into her midsection. She wanted to be the one to make Mamie laugh. Isabelle picked up some oranges that lay on the table and began to juggle. "Look, Mamie! Look!" And even though Mamie's response lacked a genuine enthusiasm, Isabelle felt a sudden rush of affection for the cook and buried her face in Mamie's skirts, wrapping her small arms as far around Mamie's waist as possible.

The moment was interrupted by a knock at the door. Isabelle ran and opened it. A dishevelled negro stood on the steps; he looked surprised to see a little white girl answering the kitchen door. "Excuse me Miss, can you spare some food for a starvin' man?" He looked her right in the eyes. Isabelle clutched at her face. Oh, her eyes were burning. Everybody knew that if a darky looked you in the eye, you'd drown before your next birthday. She didn't want to drown. And then he grabbed her arm with his filthy hands and started to drag her out onto the porch. Mamie screamed. Samuel ran up and began to hit him.

Mavis put the book down, sick to her stomach. That wasn't how the day had gone at all! And to write that Mamie and Samuel had helped bring about the beggar's death?

She swatted the air beside her head as if flies had flown out from the book into her own kitchen. How hot that day had been. Even now, she could smell the awful mud pie of blood and dirt that had mixed into a thick paste.

Had they simply been bored?

Was that why they'd done what they'd done that afternoon?

Sliver's knock at the door pulled Mavis from the past into the present. Sliver insisted on knocking even though Mavis told her she didn't have to. "Come in!"

She waited until Sliver had taken off her coat before speaking. "I went to see Ellie this morning."

"You didn't waste any time."

"She was surprised to see me."

"I expect so."

"Lots of what she said didn't make sense to me. She said you never told her I'd visited after Jerome was born, but that can't be true because I distinctly remember asking you in the garden to tell her I'd visited, and if I remember correctly, you said you would."

"Did I say that? It's been a long time. Maybe I remembered it wrong."

"Ellie said Mona didn't tell her either. Nobody did, even though I visited every day. Willis told her I'd abandoned her, and I guess she believed it because everyone else was lying to her too."

Sliver stared at her hands.

"But the biggest lie of all was telling her that Jerome died."

Sliver made eye contact and held her gaze. "I'd tell that lie again."

"I know." Mavis had thought it through and didn't see any good alternatives. "Still, why didn't you tell her I'd been to see her? I thought we were friends, Sliver."

"We weren't then."

"And now?"

"As much as we can be."

"What does that mean?"

"It's nothing. Let it be."

"No. I want to know what you mean. Ellie seemed shocked by the idea we were friends. She kept saying if we were friends that I'd know things about you."

"What do you know about me?"

"I know you're a midwife, you work for Ellie, you lived at the Yates's for most of your life, and you're raising Jerome."

"That's all true. How many children do I have?"

Mavis felt Ellie staring over her shoulder, ready to rub her nose in her own ignorance. Mavis knew of Charlie and Becky. There were others, weren't there? "Four?"

Sliver shook her head. "I had five, and I could tell you were guessing. Ellie's right that a friend would know that. And a friend would know two of them died from influenza when they were young. And while we're on the topic, didn't you ever wonder what my husband's name was and what happened to him? I can tell you pretty much everything about your life, and I didn't even grow up with you. I asked questions. Mamie gave me answers. And maybe I asked because I needed to, because my survival depended on it in a way that yours never has. Now, if it's alright with you, I'm going to do my gardening."

Mavis felt her face colour with embarrassment. She said nothing as Sliver went out the back door. How she hated to admit Ellie was right: the only things Mavis knew about Sliver were the things directly related to her. A friend would know personal things because she'd ask and take an interest. She sat with her shame, not liking the feeling one bit.

She picked *The Magnolia Tree* up again and skipped through the part about Isabelle attending the lynching.

She read through the afternoon, stopping only to say goodbye when Sliver left. She read through supper, having lost her appetite. Before she knew it, she needed a lamp to read by. She yawned. Just one more chapter. She'd turn the light out then.

⚞ By the following weekend, Mavis had finished the first four books in the series and was reading *The Attic Dweller*. In it, Esther discovers her husband is spreading his seed liberally amongst the dark women. Her pride is wounded. Does she not excite? Is she not enough? She seeks revenge and invites a slave into her bed when her husband is away.

Then Esther becomes pregnant. Who is the father? Is she carrying a slave's child or her husband's? She bites her nails to the quick. Her mother arrives unexpectedly to be there for the baby's birth. That only increases Esther's anxiety, and she asks the doctor for opium to help with her headaches. The baby is born with dark skin, and her mother packs her belongings and leaves without saying a word to her daughter. Esther consumes her stockpile of opium, and when her husband arrives, he is denied the satisfaction of applying his anger because his wife is unconscious, but she does not die, and when she finally wakes, her baby is gone, and she is in the attic.

As in the previous books, the female protagonist blames others and behaves without remorse, and Ellie's white male characters, while fixated on preserving the purity of southern women, head to the negro shacks after dark. Yet it is the white women who are punished for crossing the colour line, not the men.

Ellie's skill, and Mavis had to admit she had some, was in describing the emotional world of her female protagonists and the motives for their actions. They were hung like paintings on walls to be admired. They craved some form of power because they were so powerless themselves. Mavis found the plot to be outlandish, and Ellie's blind spot was transferred to her characters: in wanting the freedom the men had, the women never stopped to question if what the men did was right to begin with.

All her life Mavis had been trying to understand or excuse her sister's actions, but she had overlooked what had been staring her right in her face all along: Ellie had always done what she wanted. Ellie had never asked to be saved.

Mavis finished the book and placed it next to the others on her bookshelf. Then she took a bath to cleanse her flesh and to forget that, at times, she'd been caught up in Ellie's plots and forgotten to be outraged.

After she'd dried herself off and put on her nightgown, she took some stationery from her desk.

July 1953

Dear Ellie,

You asked that I write and let you know my thoughts on your books. Here they are: Clearly you have some skills. I found myself swept away at times with the imagery of place. What I don't understand is why you don't put those skills to better use. You could write a good book, Ellie. Why don't you?

She wasn't sure how to sign the letter. Love? Sincerely? Best wishes? In the end, she just signed *Mavis*.

PART FOUR

1963

CHAPTER 51

The blast from high-pressure fire hoses hurtled the black bodies down sidewalks like rag dolls. Those who were unharmed scrambled to their feet and ran. The others lay crumpled in puddles on the ground, waterlogged and wounded.

There it was before Sliver on the evening news: Birmingham at its finest. Bull Connor gone mad.

She closed her eyes to the violence.

At seventy-eight, she didn't move or think as fast as she used to. It was harder to be invisible or to blend into her surroundings when she was a step behind everybody else. The world seemed to have sped up; she didn't know where her eyes were supposed to land anymore, and when she closed them, she lost her balance and had to reach out a hand to find a wall or something solid to keep herself from tipping over.

Such a gradual decline ageing was. She was grateful it didn't happen overnight. Too often now, her mind slipped into the past because the past was a far greater landscape than the future. In so doing, Gideon was more often by her side, his hand a warm shell in hers. She liked that. And sometimes, their babies were in bed with them in that sweet holding space between waking and dreaming. She was glad she hadn't known when they were all crowded together in their bed, her man and her babies, that those moments would be the best of her life. She'd assumed better moments would overshadow them, one good moment strung to another like a beaded necklace. That hadn't been the case.

And now look.

She opened her eyes and scanned the crowd for Jerome. He'd come by one night to tell her he was going.

"I'm not here to ask permission," he said. "Birmingham is the best thing that has happened for civil rights in a long time. Television crews and reporters are practically *living* there. We couldn't get better press if we paid for it. No one could script such blatant hatred and abuse."

"You *have* paid for it. We both have. Every single black body in this country has paid for it. Don't for a second think otherwise! Do I need to buy you a compass? Cause you are heading in the wrong direction!" She'd brought him North to save him, and here he was going back to help save others. He was a lot like his daddy. Charlie would do the same thing.

"A compass." Jerome laughed and laughed. "I'm going to tell Trudy that." He wiped his eyes. "To get me a compass next Christmas."

Trudy Ashton was his wife. He'd met her at a civil rights protest. He'd gotten involved with a group he called Snick. Sliver never could remember what it stood for: Student Non-Violent something or other. He and Trudy shared a passion for justice. She was good to Jerome, and Sliver liked her, but when he announced he wanted to get married, she argued he was too young. He was smart though and asked what her life had been like when she was his age. She admitted she was already pregnant with her third child. After that, she could hardly counsel patience. And now Sliver was the impatient one: Jerome had been married almost four years already, and Trudy's belly still hadn't swelled. She should have at least one baby straddling her hipbone by now.

Policemen swung their batons as if they were hitting pop flies on a Sunday afternoon and someone on the corner was selling popcorn and crackerjacks, only it was people the batons were hitting, not baseballs, but still the crowd roared.

The camera spanned wide to show how many people had gathered. White people of all ages stood on the fringe, their faces contorted and ugly. A violent energy ran like a current through them to the police and back again. *Hit him! Kill him!*

Jerome had told her about a college lecture in which one of his professors said racism was a form of infantilism that took root before children could defend themselves against their parents' hatred.

Infantilism? "What does that mean?" she asked.

"Children don't have a developed intelligence yet," Jerome said, "so they're vulnerable. Doesn't that make sense? Children wouldn't be racist if their parents didn't fill their heads with racist views."

"Children are vulnerable," she agreed. "Your professor is right about that. Their little eyes and ears soak everything up like bread in milk."

Strong leadership was the answer, Jerome said. Martin Luther King Jr. was the man to watch. He was smart. He was compassionate. He preached non-violence, and his following was growing. Yes, he would lead black Americans to freedom. Thank God Nixon hadn't won the election because Kennedy was sympathetic to their cause. King and Kennedy, together, would bring about great change. What a time to be alive!

A German shepherd police dog lunged for the pant leg of a black man. Two white women, their hair perfectly coiffed as if fresh from the beauty parlour, screamed obscenities. On the sidewalk, some white women held picket signs: *Keep Alabama White,* one read. *Close mixed schools,* read another.

Jerome had been sixteen years old in 1954 when the Supreme Court ruled it was unconstitutional to separate children in public schools on the basis of race. He came home from school carrying the newspaper and danced Sliver around the kitchen as he explained what the Brown vs Board of Education decision meant. He was so excited. *I can go to school wherever I want!* That's when he announced he wanted to be a lawyer. A lawyer!? How would they ever have the money for him to go to college? *Don't worry,* he said. *My grades are good. I'm sure I'll qualify for a scholarship.* Sliver had worked hard to keep her mouth from hanging open. *Schools gave money to educate black men?*

And he'd been right. He got a scholarship to attend Howard University and Sliver's heart almost burst out of her chest with pride. She made sure his wardrobe was respectable and that he had what he needed and cried when he left on the day his classes started.

In his first year at university, he and Sliver watched black students in Little Rock be blocked from entering school by the state's national guard. *Where's the law now?* she'd asked.

And here he was, nine years later, in the most segregated city in the United States, where nobody seemed interested in following *the law.*

That's what makes Birmingham the best place to protest, Jerome said.

Dr. King called on the federal government to not invest one more penny into the city until it faced the realities of desegregation. *If we can win there,* King said, *we can win anywhere.*

The camera moved again and focused on a black woman. Waterlogged and dazed from her journey down the asphalt, she stood up and rested her hand on the brick building beside her. A police officer came up behind her, lifted his arm above his head, and brought his baton down on her shoulders. She fell to the ground.

Bodies rolled down the street in the hurricane unleashed from the hose.

The camera shifted again and focused on Bull Connor's face. His receding hairline made his forehead bigger, making his whiteness even more on display. Flanked by his supporters, he pulled the cigar from his mouth and parroted Governor George Wallace: "Segregation today, segregation tomorrow, segregation forever!"

The crowd cheered.

Sliver nearly jumped from her skin when her phone rang. She put her hand to her heart and walked to the kitchen. *Please, don't be bad news. Don't be bad news.* "Hello?"

"Sliver, it's me," Miss Mavis said. "Have you got the news on?"

"Yes."

"I can barely watch. I didn't see Jerome. Did you?"

"No."

"It's way worse than I thought, Sliver."

It took television for you to know?

"I can't just sit around and watch what's going on. Do you think Jerome and Trudy would let me help with that group they work with?"

Sliver's eyes were still on the television screen. Some of the protestors being hauled into police paddy wagons were children. Children!

"Sliver?"

"I heard you." *I can't be in charge of your helping.* "Ask them. They said they're always needing volunteers."

"Okay. I will. I'm going to phone Trudy right now to see if she's heard from Jerome. I'll call you right back if I hear anything, okay?"

She nodded.

"Sliver? Do you want me to come over? Are you okay?"

"I'm fine. I'll be better once I know Jerome's okay. Be sure to tell Trudy to call if she hears anything."

"I will. And Sliver?"

She hung up before Miss Mavis could say she was sorry about something. Lately, all she did was apologize. The scales had finally fallen from her eyes, and she saw racial injustice everywhere. *Sorry. Sorry. Sorry.* Sliver never said it was okay because it wasn't. Plus, what would accepting her apology do? If she wanted change, that was *her* work to do. Loving black people didn't mean her job was done, and it didn't make her innocent.

Still, she had to admit she was surprised that Miss Mavis had stayed connected to her and Jerome. It was fifteen years since that night they'd met on the platform in Neelan Junction and boarded the train. She hadn't expected that.

She chuckled to herself remembering her conversation with Miss Ellie the day after her sister's unexpected visit.

Why didn't you mention my sister came with you?

You didn't ask.

She returned her attention to the television and her fear returned. There was Bull Connor again, Birmingham's Commissioner of Public Safety. How was it in the interest of public safety to call out the dogs and turn on the fire hoses? If that didn't make people shake their heads then nothing would.

The news from Birmingham only reminded her that every time Jerome left her apartment, she might never see him again. She put the images of violence and disaster she'd just seen on the news in the vault she carried in her mind and closed the door tight. She kept Jerome outside of that vault. He was too special. He always had been. She'd asked herself many times over the years why she had left Charlie and

Becky and her grandchildren behind to save Jerome's life, especially since Charlie was Jerome's daddy, and Charlie hadn't been conceived in love. Then Ellie had used Charlie to get back at Willis, so likely Jerome wasn't conceived in love either.

So why had Sliver run with Charlie and Ellie's boy?

She'd only come up with one answer: Charlie's being born right after Gideon's disappearance had likely saved her life and, in turn, the lives of her other children. In her deepest grief, she'd told herself Gideon had died for this baby, and it was true, even if the story benefitted from a selective honesty. But if Gideon had sacrificed his life because of Charlie, well, Sliver would sacrifice her life for his baby, too. Saving Jerome was just an extension of her earlier decision to honour Gideon by caring for Charlie. Not that it was simple. No. Only that it was right.

"Why'd I bring you here?" Sliver asked Jerome.

"For a better life."

"Say it again."

"For a better life."

"And you think you'll find it by going to Birmingham?"

"I think I already found it for myself, but I need to help others find it too."

She kissed his cheek and pulled him close.

"And I have one more thing to share," Jerome said. "Some good news. Do you want to hear?"

"Your definition of good news might not be the same as mine but go ahead."

"Trudy's pregnant."

Sliver smacked his shoulder. "You waited until you were leaving to tell me!" That was the best news she'd heard in years.

The station went to a commercial and Sliver got up to change the channel. Maybe a different station would have additional footage.

She got comfortable on the couch to watch out for Jerome.

Today wasn't any different from the days she'd already lived. She'd continue the pattern and put one foot in front of the other, like she always did. She'd do the next indicated thing.

If there was wash in the washer, she'd hang it on the line.

CHAPTER 52

Mavis stared at the crowd of white people cheering on the police. It was mostly young men on the television screen, but there were women there, too, dressed as nicely as if they were going to church, but their mouths were twisted and pulled wide, their foreheads were scrunched, and their nostrils were flared. Hatred made their faces uglier than any scars. And the gestures! It was painful to watch the ugliness, so she turned away.

She imagined her father in the Birmingham crowd and Jimmy and the sheriff and the deputies and the preacher too. And her mama and Gertie and George and any children her siblings had by now. Then she imagined Ellie, a fire hose in her hands, her legs spread wide to keep her balance for the surge that would come when the water was turned on. Only it wasn't water that shot out but books. Hard cover. Soft cover. The spines broken and pages flapping. Missiles of hatred launched like grenades.

Was this the crowd Sliver imagined when she referred to *her people*? Surely Sliver didn't think Mavis fit in with them, did she? And was that the only choice for her? To hate or be hated? What about the white people who stood in solidarity and were beaten by protestors? Didn't that mean something?

Jerome had asked her once how long slavery had lasted, and she hadn't known.

"That's part of the problem," he said. "Being comfortable in not knowing."

She swallowed her pride and asked. "How long?"

317

"The first African slave ship arrived in Virginia in 1619."

What was the appropriate response to that knowledge? To say she was sorry? The injustice was staggering. The harm unforgivable. But there'd been abolitionists, many of whom had been raised in slaveholding families. What about them? Could *they* be her people?

Still, Birmingham begged the question: Had nothing changed?

Mavis had inherited the same set of beliefs as her sister. Why had she been able to renounce them and Ellie hadn't?

Her sister had published three more books since Mavis's visit a decade earlier. She'd written all those words but hadn't taken the time to respond to Mavis's note.

She turned the television off and said a prayer for Jerome. He was right: Kennedy couldn't ignore what was happening in Birmingham. How could anyone watch that footage and ask for patience?

Mavis had read somewhere that babies were born with all their parts except for kneecaps, which grew outside of the womb. When Jerome had told her about his professor who believed racism was learned behaviour, she'd told him about the kneecaps. *Maybe we can think of hatred like kneecaps. It's not part of the body at birth but only grows outside the womb.*

But Jerome didn't like that analogy because it assumed it had to happen; kneecaps grew. Did that make hatred inevitable?

Bone can be broken, she argued. *And bone can be re-set.* She was proof of that, wasn't she?

⌁ The violence in Birmingham was fresh in her mind on Saturday when Mavis parked outside the SNCC office near Fourteenth and U Street. Trudy greeted her and gave her the tour of the small space. She swept her arm wide, as if she could make the office larger by exaggerating the gesture. It contained six filing cabinets, a large table, and half a dozen or more straight-backed chairs. Papers were scattered over every flat surface, and mail overflowed from two large bins on the floor. "As you can see, I'm a bit behind sorting through the mail. I'm not here as much as I'd like to be." Trudy's paying job was at a bank.

She showed Mavis where to put her purse and sat at the table. "Let's get started."

Trudy put a stack of letters in front of her. "I usually sort them into three categories: one that requires a response, one that's just for our files, and one that goes directly into the garbage."

"Which ones go into the garbage?"

"You'll see." She ripped into an envelope. "Oh. Here's one. *Thanks for bringing all the troublemakers to one spot. One bomb will wipe them out at the same time. Don't think the police are on your side.*" She lifted the letter by its edge with her index finger and thumb, as if it was something rank she'd found behind a dumpster, and dropped it into the garbage.

Mavis was shaken. "That's awful."

Trudy shrugged. "You get used to it. There are far worse. You'll see. To be honest, sometimes it's easier to deal with hatred when it's up front and not hidden. It's the people who smile with their mouths but send bullets with their eyes that I worry about." She moved efficiently through the mail, reading each letter to herself. The quiet was punctuated by the occasional thud of a letter dropping into the metal garbage can.

The first letter Mavis opened asked for information about registering voters, so she put it in the pile to be answered later. Another one contained an update. She opened another. *You are here for two purposes: to be raped and lynched.* Her hand shook as she slid the letter into the garbage. What unnerved Mavis was the numerous steps involved in sending such a letter: getting a piece of paper, putting vile thoughts to the page, addressing an envelope, finding a stamp, and posting it. There were many opportunities for a person to re-evaluate his behaviour along the way.

Trudy must have seen the look on her face because she told her to ignore the bad stuff. "As far as I'm concerned, any letter that starts with a derogatory greeting goes straight into the bin."

The next letter was an improvement. *I don't know what you do at your meetings, but my son comes home thinking his parents and grandparents are white supremacists. Not all white people are your enemy. Are you telling your recruits that?*

"Would a letter like this just go into the reply pile?" Mavis passed it to Trudy.

"Yes. We get a lot of letters from concerned white parents. Sometimes new recruits are overzealous, and suddenly sweet Tommy or Mary start asking difficult questions at Sunday dinner." Trudy paused, put her hand to her mouth, and looked suddenly ill.

"Are you okay?"

"I'm fine. I'm just a bit queasy lately is all."

Mavis raised an eyebrow. Did that mean what she suspected?

Trudy nodded. "I'm due in early February."

"Oh Trudy! That's the best news I've heard in a long time." Mavis jumped from her seat and hugged her hard. "Does Sliver know?"

"Yes. Jerome told her before he left."

Mavis looked around the office. "You're going to be tired. I could help out more often, if you'd like. During the evenings. I'm good at getting things organized."

"I'll try not to get too excited or I'll scare you away, but that would be amazing. I'll introduce you to everyone. Do you have the time?"

"I'll make the time."

A baby!

Maybe now Sliver would tell Charlie about his son. Charlie would want to know he was going to be a grandfather, wouldn't he?

⌐ Jerome returned home unharmed and with a renewed vigour for action. Being arrested hadn't dampened his spirits in the least. They couldn't sit on their laurels, he said. The City of Birmingham had agreed to desegregate lunch counters, restrooms, drinking fountains, and changing rooms within ninety days and to hire black people in front of house positions. But they had to keep pushing. Now was the time. Kennedy was sympathetic. The Birmingham Campaign had made the US look terrible on the world stage. They had to capitalize on the outpouring of sympathy both from fellow Americans and from world citizens. There was renewed commitment to organizing a march. He was all for it.

Mavis began a new routine where she went to the SNCC office every other day after work and also volunteered on Saturday afternoons. She was the only white woman there; not everyone made her feel welcome, but she vowed to earn people's trust. She wanted to help. She would stay for as long as they would have her. She swallowed her pride and asked questions about things she knew nothing about. What happened to the Freedom Riders who were beaten? When was that again? Didn't the police do anything? Sometimes her embarrassment at her own ignorance kept her quiet for a while and sometimes she waited for a private moment to ask Jerome or Trudy, but she made sure to not have to ask twice.

Why are Southern whites so afraid of blacks voting?

Jerome was patient and kind. *Because when the negroes were freed, they outnumbered the whites, who would have lost control of the social, political, and economic destiny of their area. It's about power. It's always about power.*

Bags of mail continued to arrive daily even as Mavis struggled to deal with the backlog. If everyone was busy or no one was there, Mavis answered the phone. And with each call and letter, she learned more and had a better understanding of why the March on Washington needed to happen in the first place. The acronyms no longer confused her. NAACP and SCLC and CORE and COFO and others became easy shorthand. When one of the volunteers found out Mavis was from Florida, she asked if Mavis had read Lillian Smith's work. Smith was a white woman from Florida too, who was a vocal critic of segregation. Mavis hadn't but left the office that day and went to a bookstore to order *Killers of the Dream*. It wasn't in stock, but the clerk placed an order and told Mavis that while she waited, she might like to read the book that was causing such a stir. Mavis left with a copy of *The Feminine Mystique* tucked beneath her arm and stayed up late two nights in a row reading about the problem that had no name. She wondered if it might be called boredom. Or panic. Mavis vividly remembered a restlessness bordering on panic that life would always be so dull. That she had so few options. Ellie had felt it too. They'd been like birds constantly flying into windows, thinking the clear glass was an open path to freedom.

When *Killers of the Dream* arrived, Mavis felt like the author had told her story.

> I learned that it is possible to be a Christian and a white southerner simultaneously; to be a gentlewoman and an arrogant callous creature in the same moment; to pray at night and ride a Jim Crow car the next morning and to feel comfortable in doing both. I learned to believe in freedom, to glow when the word *democracy* is used, and to practice slavery from morning to night. I learned it the way all of my southern people learn it: by closing door after door until one's mind and heart and conscience are blocked off from each other and from reality.

She underlined the passage and returned to it again and again with a mixture of relief and anger. How well Smith described the split. Mavis wasn't the only one who'd closed door after door. She wasn't alone. Most importantly, she wasn't crazy.

On June eleventh, President Kennedy delivered his civil rights speech. Mavis expected a celebration at the SNCC office the following day, but she arrived to find it empty. She let herself in and started to work. At the hour, the news announced Medgar Evers's murder. He'd been active with NAACP and was gunned down the previous night outside his house in Jackson, Mississippi, with his wife and children inside.

Mavis called Jerome to say she was sorry. Trudy answered and said she'd pass on the message. Sliver was there, too. They were mourning together.

Kennedy asked the civil rights groups to be patient, but Jerome scoffed. "Only someone who is already free would counsel patience."

Civil rights leaders told the president the March was going to happen anyway. He could set a date, or they would. So Kennedy did. For August twenty-eighth.

"August twenty-eighth?" Jerome said. "A Wednesday? Who's going to come in the middle of the week? Many of the people marching for jobs and freedom actually *have* jobs. They can't just take a day off mid-week. Plus, what about people outside the DC area who have to travel? How are they going to get back to work for Thursday? It feels like we're being set up to fail."

But having a concrete date released optimism into the air, as if the cherry trees had blossomed a second time and people tripped over themselves to see them.

"Change is happening," Jerome said when he stopped in the SNCC office. "It's finally happening. And it's happening now."

He hugged Trudy, put his head back, and whooped loudly at the ceiling.

Everybody laughed.

"And a baby on the way," Mavis added. "What a time to be born!"

CHAPTER 53

Ellie's fingers flew over the typewriter keys as the momentum of the narrative propelled her towards the end. Always by this point, the story was writing itself. The stage had been set, the characters all knew their lines, and the final scene was poised to flow like water released from a dam. A surge of energy pushed her through lunch and into the afternoon until, with relief, she typed the final sentence of her book. She hit the carriage return a few times to add some space and typed THE END.

She pulled the paper from the typewriter carriage and put it on the stack beside her. Another deadline met. Her publisher would be pleased. She lit a cigarette, filled her lungs with smoke, and exhaled with relief. Then she put a blank sheet of paper in the typewriter, typed *The Night Riders,* and placed it on top of the pile. She stared at the stack with wonder. She had done it again.

A book started with an idea. Then a blank page. One word after another led to a sentence. One sentence after another led to a paragraph. One paragraph after another led to a chapter. And one chapter after another led to a book. There really was no mystery to it, other than the delight of discovery along the way. *The Night Riders* was her sixth novel, and even though she'd been through the process five times before, she always lived with the doubt that she had another book in her.

Four hundred individual pages made for an impressive stack.

The Night Riders explored the history of Klansmen. Until doing research, Ellie hadn't known Florida was a Klan hotbed. Men in white robes, charging about on horses at night, setting houses on fire, burning crosses on yards, and attempting to curb black liberation. Mayhem and destruction. Vigilante justice. If it came out by year's end, it would be almost twenty years since the publication of *The Magnolia Tree*. Her sales weren't what they'd once been, but she'd certainly sold more books than she'd ever imagined and made more money too.

"Sliver!"

She exhaled a thick cloud of smoke and stubbed out her cigarette. The house was quiet.

"Sliver?!"

Ellie looked at the clock beside her desk and was surprised to see how late it was. Sliver had already gone home. How disappointing. She'd finished another book and had no one to share the good news with.

She went downstairs and found a pile of mail that Sliver had left on the kitchen table for her. She picked up a letter.

> *Dear Mr. Hunter,*
>
> *You make me ashamed to be an American. All you write about is fornication and lynching. While you may be satisfying your sick sexual appetite, you are also misrepresenting the good people who call themselves Christians. If one were to read your books as history, one would believe that thousands of black men and women were murdered by Christians. I do not believe they behave as you suggest. Hell will be too good a resting place for you.*
>
> *Eudora Wilkins*

Why had Sliver left that letter out? Her job was to find fan mail, not hate mail. She threw the letter back into the bag. She had never once claimed to write history. Why would anyone read her books as such? They were works of fiction.

Dear Mr. Hunter,

The Attic Dweller brought back memories for me. My sister
Jessie got pregnant by a coloured boy when she was seventeen.
She was sent away from our home in Illinois to stay with
relatives in Seattle. The baby was put up for adoption. It
broke my sister's heart. A few years later she took her own
life. I'm sure to this day that she missed her baby and the
man who fathered her child (she never told us who did). So
while she wasn't put in an attic and abused by her husband,
as your character Esther was, she certainly had more than
her fair share of grief. My sister's situation made me rethink
my ideas about interracial relationships. I loved her, and I'd
have learned to accept anyone in her life who made her
happy. I wish I'd told her that before she killed herself. So
I'm wondering if you might consider writing about an
interracial couple that loves each other. Anyway, it's just a
thought. Clearly you keep reworking the same material.
Perhaps there's a reason.

Yours truly,
Louise Milligan

Ellie took the letter into the living room, settled into her rocker, and re-read it. No one had ever suggested she write about love before. Sex between whites and blacks was forbidden by law where she came from. And elsewhere too. Not that that stopped anyone. Anti-miscegenation laws were just big words designed to regulate the primal act. Could sex that was *illegal* be loving? Maybe she should put the question to Louise Milligan. *Dear Louise, what next? Repeal murder laws?*

She chuckled to herself but had no one to laugh with her.

It was raining now, heavy drops. Ellie's stomach growled. She'd skipped lunch to finish her book. Maybe Sliver had left something for her in the kitchen.

Louise's comment nagged at her. *The Night Riders* had another woman who was punished for satisfying her physical desires. It might be a tired narrative, but it was a reliable one. Her readers liked to see the world view they were comfortable with reflected back at them. What was she supposed to do, write for black people? The idea was ludicrous. Her readers were bored white housewives, often trapped in loveless marriages, who enjoyed reading about illicit sexual liaisons. Maybe Louise Milligan should write her own books instead of trying to get Randall Hunter to write different ones. She continued to build a case against Louise as she walked to the kitchen. Why did *any* reader feel the impulse to ask a writer to change his style to suit her?

She found a casserole dish in the refrigerator. She lifted the lid: chicken and vegetables. Ellie slid the dish into the oven even though it hadn't preheated.

Back in the living room she poured herself a brandy and turned on a lamp to offset the grey. She held her glass up. "To *The Night Riders*."

The liquor burned a hot trail down her throat. She hated Louise Milligan for tamping down her euphoria. Was that the kind of reader she was losing? If so, maybe she didn't care.

You could write a good book, Ellie. Why don't you?

She took a second, larger sip of the brandy, and it burned an even hotter trail when she swallowed.

A good book was one that sold well, that's what she should have told Mavis. *The Attic Dweller* alone had sold over a million copies. Wasn't that success? So what if her sales had dropped some since then? So what indeed.

She filled her glass again.

She'd never been particularly drawn to happy endings.

She raised her glass in the air for an imaginary toast with Mavis. *To the past. It's what I know, and writers are supposed to write what they know.* She drank too fast and choked when some brandy went down the wrong pipe. She imagined Mavis challenging her. *You didn't live during slavery. That's not what you know.*

Go away, Mavis. Leave me alone.

By now, she could smell the chicken warming in the oven.

Loneliness sat like a heavy weight on her shoulders. Mavis visiting those years ago had made Ellie realize how lonely she truly was. She'd almost written to ask her sister to come back, but then she received Mavis's patronizing note and wouldn't give her the satisfaction of being needed. Her plan had been to wait Mavis out. What she hadn't anticipated was that Mavis had already gotten used to living without her.

Little Mavis. Gullie. Making it on her own.

Ellie didn't want the Mavis who'd showed up having learned how to drive a car; she wanted the *old* Mavis back, the one who'd shadowed her like a loyal dog. The one who'd thought Ellie could do no wrong.

Turns out they had both been lied to. She'd been told Mavis hadn't visited her after her second child was born, and Mavis had been told Ellie hadn't wanted her to. The lies had been different, but the results had been the same—they had been kept apart.

A vice tightened around her chest. The doctor had told her to take deep breaths when that happened, to calm the irregularity of her heart. If that didn't produce results, she was to put a pill under her tongue. They were on her bedside table. Nitroglycerin. Little Hiroshimas in a bottle. She breathed deeply but the vice didn't relent. She dropped into the rocking chair to wait for the pain to pass.

Something fluttered in her peripheral vision like a dragonfly, darting quickly in and out of sight, its eyelashes fanning the air like wings. *Joseph?* The alcohol had gone to her head. How perfect her little baby had been. Why hadn't she at least had a picture taken before ... before ...

She heard the whirring sound of a camera, but instead of it producing photos of her firstborn, it was churning out picture after picture under the shade tree.

Ellie had worn her white dress that day. How hot the afternoon had been. How ripe the smells. River mud. Fermenting fruit. Fried chicken. Lemon cheesecake. *Thank you, oh Lord, for this food that we are about to receive ...*

She dozed.

In her dream, her fingertips touched Desperate's pantleg, and the dark mole on her right arm began to spread. Blackness seeped out like ink and spread over her skin until her whole body had absorbed the colour. Suddenly she was Desperate's little girl, crying at what had been done to her daddy. Crying and crying as she grabbed his pant leg and tried to pull him down while someone else took her free hand and pulled her towards Slew Town.

Ellie jerked awake, disoriented. She stood up. Louise Milligan's letter fell from her lap to the ground. Her heart pounded an unfamiliar rhythm. She went to the kitchen for a glass of water then went upstairs to her study. She stuffed her manuscript into a large envelope and addressed it to her publisher. She licked the envelope flap and remembered the image of Willis licking honey from a razor's edge.

Returning to the kitchen, Ellie put the envelope on the table where Sliver would see it and make sure it was mailed. She spotted another letter she hadn't seen earlier, resting on her lunch tray. Sliver must have put it there to give to her on her lunch break, but she'd worked straight through. Ellie ran her fingertips over the creamy surface, the shiny black letterhead was raised like a birthmark. *Morgan House Publishing, New York.* A thrill went through her, reminding her of that initial letter, years ago, agreeing to publish her first book.

She opened it.

July 1963

> *Dear Mr. Hunter,* (The name was scratched out and "Randall" was written in by hand)
> *As you know, we plan to publish* The Night Riders *later this year and eagerly await the manuscript's arrival. However, it is with great sadness that I inform you our editorial board has decided to take a new direction. As such, we will no longer publish any more books that deal with the subject matter you've portrayed so well in your Magnolia Tree Series.*
> *Times are changing, and our readership is changing too. Whereas a new book by Randall Hunter once sold magnificently well, sales have declined considerably since you began publishing with us those many years ago (in 1944, if I'm not mistaken!).*

*We would love to continue working with you. Should
you have other book projects in mind, we'd certainly be open
to considering them. In the meantime, we look forward to
working with you on* The Night *Riders.*

*Thank you, in advance, for remaining loyal to our
publishing house. I regret that we never had the chance to
meet in person and share a brandy and a cigar. I do hope
your health offers you some reprieve now and in the coming
years.*

Sincerely yours,
Edward William Anderson
Morgan House Publishing
New York

The shock was slow to kick in. *It is with great sadness … no longer
publish … sales have declined considerably … open to considering them.*
It made no sense. Randall Hunter books had sold millions. Sales might
be declining, but they were still strong. Any idiot knew that times were
changing, but were *people* changing? There was a difference.

The elation she had felt at finishing *The Night Riders* was gone
now. "Edward William Anderson," she spat, wishing they could have
shared a cigar and a brandy. What a pompous fool. Nobody at the
publishing house had ever learned the truth about her. She'd claimed
an invalid status from the start to avoid having to be seen. Mr. Dunedin had handled the contracts.

The timer sounded to let her know her supper was ready.

What lie was she being fed? Publishing houses were businesses.
They existed to make money. Her books *still* made money.

If she didn't have her writing, what did she have?

How vividly she recalled crafting Isabelle Montgomery, the character who had started it all. What would Isabelle do if she received a
letter like that? She'd stamp her foot. Her ringlets would swing back
and forth like a pendulum in a grandfather clock, and the reverbera-
tions of her anger would be felt in the aftershock that rocked the house.

Isabelle Montgomery would not go down without a fight, and neither would Ellie Louise Turner.

She was her daddy's best girl.

She could have whatever she wanted.

CHAPTER 54

August 28th finally arrived. Sliver woke at the same time as usual. Out her window, the sky was clear and blue. No clouds promised a momentary shade. It looked to be a perfect day for the March She closed the curtains to the morning sun to keep the heat down and watched them dance in the slight breeze at the kitchen window.

Normally at this time, she'd be on her way to work, but Miss Ellie had told her to take the day off. She said she had an appointment that would have her gone all day, and she wanted the house to herself when she returned.

Sliver recognized a lie when she heard one. Miss Ellie couldn't do something nice for the sake of niceness. It wasn't her way, so Sliver didn't thank her but just said *that's fine.*

She had plans to meet Miss Mavis by the bus stop closest to the Washington Monument. The papers had announced so many road and bridge closures for the big event that it was silly to think about trying to get a car in there to park.

She ate her breakfast and took the morning slow. When it was time to leave, Sliver bent over to lace her shoes and was hit with a wave of dizziness that blurred her vision. She sat down to wait for it to pass, but the dizziness persisted. Maybe the heat had brought it on. Or maybe the stress of the day. She wanted things to go well for Jerome's sake. He'd worked so hard.

"What if nobody comes?" he had asked in the days leading up to today.

"They'll come."

"On a weekday?"

"On any day at all," Sliver said, not knowing if that was true but hoping it was. They'd had the same conversation every day for the past two weeks, and now maybe she'd be the one not going.

By the time she realized the dizziness was not going to pass, she phoned Miss Mavis to let her know, but she'd already left. Sliver made herself comfortable on the couch and hoped Miss Mavis wouldn't wait for her too long and miss any of the speeches. She should have her own friends to go with. Sliver sometimes felt sorry for her. She was trying so hard to atone for her past. She had no idea she'd only just put her toe in the water. Still, it was a start, and maybe it would keep her from drowning when she waded fully in.

If Sliver was honest, she'd admit she was relieved to be staying home. She moved too slowly to stay out of harm's way in a crowd. Plus, the media predicted there'd be violence. All liquor sales were banned for the day. The hospitals had even cancelled elective surgeries. That felt ominous, that the hospitals thought they needed to keep beds open.

She'd have a better view watching on television, she consoled herself, and she wouldn't have to press her damp flesh up against the dampness of other people's damp flesh.

Her eyes felt heavy, and she allowed them to close. Just for a minute, she told herself. A day off midweek was unheard of, and so, too, was a nap. She drifted in and out of sleep. Birds sang outside her window. Common birds. Wood Thrushes. Robins. Cardinals. Warblers. Their songs punctuated her dreams. When had she last taken the time to listen to birdsong? She once told Jerome that if she could be a bird, she'd be a hummingbird because they were the only bird that could fly backwards. She'd heard that somewhere. And she'd fly backwards to Gideon with hummingbird speed, lift him out of whatever trouble he'd encountered, and bring him safely back home.

She nodded off again and woke to a siren racing by.

The herb pots sitting on the high table in front of the living room window looked a bit droopy. Thinking they needed water made her thirsty. Sliver stood slowly and walked to the kitchen, moving her hand from the furniture to the wall and counter as she went. She filled a watering can and tended to the plants first; then she took ice cubes from the freezer and poured herself a glass of lemonade from the pitcher in the fridge. She placed the glass on the coffee table, turned on the television, and sat down. She remembered handing Eugene a glass of lemonade those many years ago so she could tend to Mrs. Yates. That had been a day. She took a sip and puckered at the tartness. How quickly the mind could travel through time and space.

But today was a day to be in the present not the past. Jerome had spent months helping to organize the March. Trudy, too. Even Mavis. Trudy had appreciated the help. She was tired in her first trimester. Sliver felt the familiar itch in her palms and rubbed her hands together. It had been a long time since she'd caught a baby. Every time she saw a pregnant woman, she had to stop herself from reaching out and touching the roundness while her mind automatically scanned the contents of her midwifery bag. Jerome was going to be a daddy! The first leaf was budding on his tree.

The television moved from an advertisement for dish soap to an aerial crowd shot of the Lincoln Memorial. The entire screen was filled with people. It was a sea of humanity. If she hadn't been sitting down already, she might have fallen over.

The camera switched to a close up of a man on stage. It was Sammy Davis Jr. She loved him. Who else was with him? Harry Belafonte. Sidney Poitier. If she'd gone in person, would she have seen them up close? No. But there they were, standing together. Was that Marlon Brando? And Paul Newman? Cameras always found the celebrities. She hadn't believed Jerome when he'd trotted out the names of people who might attend, mainly because by not believing it, she wouldn't be disappointed if it didn't happen. Wait — was that Jerome in the background? She leaned forward. Oh my. The wonder of it all. Her grandson. Helping to put on a show. *This* was what she'd left Neelan Junction for. This. Even then she'd known he would one day make a difference.

But with that pride came guilt, for she had denied Charlie the pride that a father feels watching his child do good in the world. Not letting Charlie know about Jerome had seemed like the right thing to do at the time, but it didn't feel right now.

The size of the crowd indicated a hunger and a great desire for change. She remembered the advice she'd passed on to her kids: *white folks is only afraid of two things — not getting what they want, and losing what they already have.* People didn't just give up things that benefitted them without some kind of struggle, even if what benefitted them caused others harm. Still, looking at the crowd, she felt a comfort to see how many white people were in attendance. She just hoped they wouldn't crow about it later and think themselves remarkable.

Someone was singing the gospel. Had she fallen asleep again? Mahalia Jackson's angelic face filled the television screen; her voice was calling down the Lord. Sliver raised her hands in the air to help bring him in for a soft landing.

Then Martin Luther King Jr. took his place behind the podium and acknowledged the crowd. Even in the heat, he managed to look comfortable in his dark suit and tie, his collar buttoned tight to his neck, the tip of a white handkerchief poking out from his breast pocket, and a hint of a smile beneath his moustache. It wasn't that long ago that he'd been in a Birmingham jail.

The crowd applauded for what felt like hours. All those hands coming together must have stirred up a welcome breeze. People shaded their eyes with their hands, or tucked the brim of their hats down low, or pushed their sunglasses further up the bridge of their noses to reduce the sun's glare. Everybody wanted some shade.

The reverend finally calmed the crowd and began to speak of the manacles of segregation and the chains of discrimination.

His descriptions were sharp and vivid.

He minced words but conjured murals.

He spoke of shameful conditions. Of urgency and justice.

Sliver felt a giddy pull of what life could be like if caught in his tide. No wonder Jerome loved the man so much. His words were a crystal ball that showed a better world in which people lived in harmony. Harmony. Such a beautiful word. If Jerome and Trudy had a baby girl, maybe they would name her Harmony. Sliver would try to remember to suggest it.

She listened to the preacher's dream and fit herself into it. She was a young girl, skipping in the fields. She was dancing close with Gideon, breathing in his citrus scent. She was a new mother, holding Seth at her breast, passing her love on through her milk. She was alone, shading her eyes and looking at the horizon, searching for Giddy's form.

She was broken.

She was partially mended.

She was never the same.

From her small apartment miles from the Lincoln Memorial, some kind of sound barrier was broken. Sliver heard the applause that erupted when the reverend thanked God that he was free at last, and for the smallest of moments, Sliver was there, with her people, and they were all entirely free too.

Too soon, the adrenalin of the moment passed and Sliver remembered she didn't trust dreams at all. She'd had them once too. Daydreams of Gideon in the orchard and nightdreams in which he had come home, like she knew he would, but then she'd wake, and his head wasn't on the pillow beside her.

When Jerome stopped by after the March, bursting with pride and relief and hope, Sliver saw Charlie in all his gestures, and she understood fully that she'd not only denied Charlie his son, but she'd also denied Jerome his father. That truth tempered her response to his enthusiasm even as she hugged him and told him he'd done good.

CHAPTER 55

Five days later, Sliver arrived at work and let herself in the kitchen door as usual. She sensed something was wrong as soon as she stepped inside. It was the same feeling as opening a jar of preserves and not hearing that *pop*.

It was Monday. Sliver hadn't been in since Saturday. The air was too still, as if nothing had disturbed it for a while. "Miss Ellie?"

A lonely teacup and saucer sat in the sink.

"Miss Ellie?"

Sliver listened at the bottom of the stairs but only heard the birds chirping in the cherry trees.

She lifted a foot.

Step. *Had she gone out? No, she rarely left the house.*

Step. *Was she sleeping? No, she was always awake this time of day.*

Step. *Maybe she was sick and hadn't heard her.*

Step: *Maybe she was so caught up in writing she didn't notice the time.*

Sliver called out again, louder this time. The third step from the top creaked like it always did, but this morning it sounded much louder.

Miss Ellie's bedroom door was closed. Sliver knocked before opening it, and in the opening, the air that had been trapped was suddenly released as if the room itself had been holding its breath because the air was so foul.

Sliver crossed the room, pulled the curtains back to let in the morning light, and opened the window wide. Miss Ellie was a mound under the blankets, tucked neatly into bed. Her mouth hung open.

Drool had dried into a white crust alongside the scar on her right cheek. There was an unnatural stiffness to her face. "Miss Ellie?"

Sliver pulled the covers back to feel for a pulse, but the body was already cool to the touch.

A prescription bottle filled with pills sat on the bedside table. The lid was off, and a glass of water sat beside it. Heart pills. Sliver remembered thinking to herself that the doctor had prescribed those pills so Miss Ellie would *have* a heart, but that wasn't funny now. If she had taken a pill, it hadn't been able to stop whatever had already started.

Sliver took it all in. The covers weren't in a tangle. There was no sign of disturbance. Somehow it didn't seem right that Miss Ellie should pass so peacefully after struggling against life for so long, maybe even since she was born.

The birds kept singing in the cherry trees. Sliver imagined a robin flying in the window and plucking the worms off Miss Ellie's cheeks. She reached her hand out and touched one of the scars. It was hard ridged, similar to some of the puckered caesarean scars she'd felt, bad home-jobs by inexperienced stitchers.

A numbness settled in Sliver's chest. She hadn't expected this sudden loss of life. What now? She'd have to call Mavis with the news. But there was no rush.

Jerome would go about his day, not knowing that his mama had just died. Did it matter that he'd never known her? No. It didn't. It really didn't. Did it?

At the grocery story Sliver frequented, Randall Hunter books were displayed in metal racks by the cashier next to the gum and magazines, with other glossy-covered books that were also trash, and whenever she saw someone pick one up, Sliver felt like saying Randall wasn't a Randall at all. He was a damaged white woman making money off other people's suffering and thinking she was making some contribution to life. Sliver had never once seen a black woman pick one up, so she kept her thoughts to herself and felt sorry for the readers interested in reading Miss Ellie's tired tales. Sliver didn't doubt that writing was a job that took effort; she'd seen Miss Ellie's determination and work ethic and would even admit that she had a little talent. Still, that she'd made so much money from those books felt like an insult. Sliver had opened a royalty statement from Morgan House Publishing once, and her eyes had almost popped out of her head. She'd never seen so many zeroes in one place.

The breeze had freshened the bedroom air a little, enough that Sliver could take a normal breath. She held it, exhaled slowly, and felt her shoulders drop.

Miss Ellie's face looked hard now, set in stone. She had taped the letter from her publisher to the wall beside her desk in her study and underlined the sentence, *Should you have any other book projects in mind, we'd certainly be open to considering them.* The blank sheet of paper she'd put in her typewriter in July was still there. To Sliver's knowledge, Miss Ellie hadn't typed a word in six weeks. Maybe it wasn't her heart that killed her. Maybe it was her failed imagination.

Miss Ellie Yates was dead.

That meant she couldn't hurt anybody anymore. Not Jerome. Not Charlie.

Sliver absorbed the new reality for a moment before realizing she had just lost her job. Who would hire an old woman whose pace had slowed? She had some money put aside but likely not enough to get her to her grave.

The weight of financial insecurity shifted the small bit of grief on her shoulders.

Sliver stood up. She'd deal with her own problems later.

For now, she had a body to take care of.

She went downstairs to the kitchen and called Mavis.

CHAPTER 56

Mavis left work and drove straight to Ellie's. She parked outside just like she'd done on the visit ten years earlier when she'd come looking for a friend and found Ellie instead.

Sliver met her at the door. Mavis walked into her arms like she used to walk into Mamie's and immediately started to cry. She took Sliver's comfort and didn't think, until later, that Sliver might have needed comforting too.

"What happened?"

"I don't know. She was dead when I got here."

Mavis followed Sliver upstairs and noted that she kept her hand on the wall to keep her balance as she climbed. When did she start doing that? Time wasn't slowing for any of them. *Please don't die, Sliver. I need you.*

"That's her study." Sliver nodded to the door on the left. "Ellie's down here."

Ellie lay on her back in bed. Her eyes were closed. The covers were pulled up to her neck.

"I don't think she suffered," Sliver said. "The bedding's not messed. There wasn't a fight."

Mavis stared at her sister, noting the soft weave of grey in her hair at her temples. They had all aged. Still, Ellie should have had more time. "She was only forty-six."

"Too young," Sliver said.

"When we were kids, Ellie told me she never wanted to get old because she didn't want to lose her beauty." In the end, the two were reversed and she lost her beauty first.

Sliver handed her a thin envelope. "This was on her shelf in the study. She told me once if anything ever happened to her to give it to you."

Mavis Thorpe was written on the front in Ellie's hand. Mavis put it in her purse to open in the privacy of her own home, where she would have time to recover, if need be, from whatever might be inside.

"After I visited, I thought she'd ask to see me sometime," Mavis said. "But she never did. I don't suppose she ever talked about me?"

"I'd be lying if I said she did."

Mavis nodded. "Was it her heart?"

Sliver pointed to the pill bottle next to the bed. "Most likely. That's what the pills were for. We can ask the doctor."

"I don't know that it matters. Knowing won't bring her back."

"No. It won't."

The doorbell rang. Mavis looked at Sliver. "Did you call someone?"

"Just you. That'll be the mailman. He always comes around this time."

"I'll get it." Mavis wanted to spare Sliver from having to rush down the stairs.

The mailman looked confused when she opened the door.

"I'm taking in the mail for Ellie today."

"Who's Ellie?"

"My sister. She lives here."

The mailman handed Mavis a large sack. "I didn't know Mr. Hunter lived with anyone."

It took Mavis a minute to understand his confusion. "They're relations," she said and took the heavy mailbag inside.

Sliver had made her way downstairs.

"Is this a normal mail day?" Ellie got as much mail as the SNCC office.

"Sometimes there's more."

"You're kidding. What is it, fan mail?"

Sliver nodded. "And some hate mail too."

"Did Ellie answer them?"

"Oh no. She didn't have time for that. I read through them—not all of them, I wouldn't have time either—and picked out some that praised her. She'd respond to those. Or Randall would. I guess no one will answer them now."

"Wow. I had no idea." Why hadn't Sliver mentioned how much mail her sister received? Ellie's comment rang in her head: *I thought friends talked to one another.*

Mavis well recalled her disappointment that Ellie hadn't asked any questions about her life when she'd visited. Not about where she worked or how she'd ended up here. Not even about how Danny died. Nothing. Selfish as always, she'd thought. Now Mavis wondered if she wasn't any different than Ellie. Maybe she didn't know things because she didn't ask any questions. Worse still, maybe she didn't ask Sliver any questions because she assumed she had nothing to say.

"When I visited Ellie that one time, I told her that you and I were friends, and she didn't think that was possible. I remember how mad that made me, but I'm not sure I've been a good friend to you, Sliver." She put the mail down in the living room then sat on the couch.

"I should call the doctor," Sliver said.

Mavis noted that Sliver had avoided her comment but let it go. Likely now wasn't the time for a heart to heart. Ellie's lifeless body waited for them upstairs. "Yes. Or an ambulance. One of the two. Or I could call if you'd rather."

Sliver sat in the rocking chair and stared out the window. "I'll do it. In a minute."

In big moments such as this, life didn't feel real. Yet Mavis knew this memory would remain, sitting with Sliver in Ellie's front room, with Ellie dead upstairs.

Mavis wanted to say something profound, something that would link her and Sliver together, but she didn't want to assume they felt the same way. "You know, for all the bad things Ellie did, she wasn't all bad. Having you and Jerome in my life is something I wouldn't trade for anything."

Sliver rocked a steady rhythm. "My mama always said *if you change one thing, you change everything*. I think that means you can't take only the good."

"And maybe you can't accept blame for the outcome, either. For a long time I blamed myself for what happened to Ellie. I told myself I should have lied to Willis when he came looking for her that day. It would have been so easy to say she was sick in bed. Then he wouldn't have found her with Jedediah." And if he hadn't found her with Jedediah, Jedediah and his wife wouldn't have been killed. And if Willis hadn't her cut face, Ellie wouldn't have married him or gone with Charlie. And if Ellie hadn't started everything and been caught, then Mavis wouldn't have married Danny. "But it's a long list of what ifs," she concluded. *And I wouldn't have you and Jerome.*

"You shouldn't have had to lie for her in the first place."

Mavis sat with that thought. "You're right."

"I'm going to call the doctor now if you're ready."

"I'm ready."

Within the hour an ambulance arrived and Ellie was lifted from her bed, put on a stretcher, and wheeled away. It was as dignified as it could be.

"Do you want a lift home, Sliver?"

"I guess there's not much for me to do here today, is there? Okay. I'll just lock up."

It was early afternoon by the time they left the house. Mavis drove slowly, amazed that people were going about their day not knowing that the planet had just gotten a little lighter because Ellie wouldn't walk on it anymore.

"What are you going to do now?" Mavis asked.

"I don't know. I'm too old to get another job."

"I mean, how will you spend your day? Can I come back and get you for supper?" It hadn't occurred to her that Sliver had just lost her job.

"Yes," Sliver said. "That would be nice."

Hanging between them, unsaid, was that Sliver was alone with this news. Jerome didn't know that his mother had just died. But neither did Eugene, and Mavis didn't feel the need to pass on that news.

"Sliver?"

"If you're about to say something about Jerome then please don't."

They'd had the conversation before. Mavis even understood why Sliver didn't want to tell Jerome about his mother. But now that Ellie was gone, would she at least tell him about Charlie?

They drove the rest of the way in silence. For now, losing Ellie was their grief to share. *Or maybe it's just mine*, she thought. *Maybe Sliver won't grieve Ellie at all. Why would she?*

CHAPTER 57

As soon as she got home, Mavis pulled Ellie's letter from her purse and sat at the kitchen table. She braced herself and tried to steady her hands as she opened it.

> *Dear Mavis,*
>
> *I have been feeling unwell for some time now. My heart, I believe, is truly broken, not in the love-sick way that term normally implies, but in the medical way to suggest there's something wrong with it. At times, it races unnaturally and then pauses for long stretches. When that happens, I have odd images of myself at various stages of my life. Perhaps it's true that one's life flashes before one's eyes when death is near. I feel like I'm watching a movie inside of my head, and the movie is about me, but it's not from my perspective. I am merely the actress, but someone else has made adjustments to my script. It's the strangest thing. Much of what I see doesn't align with my interpretation of the events, so I've been mulling things over. If I were an animal, Mavis, I'd be a cow chewing my cud.*
>
> *I have had a terrible summer for other reasons. My publisher sacked me because "times have changed." It rankles. Did you read* Mandingo? *It was published in 1957, thirteen years after* The Magnolia Tree. *The author makes Randall Hunter seem like a Puritan. Every other page has a negro*

baby getting its head bashed in or a slave being lowered into a vat of boiling oil! My books are so much better written, but Mandingo *is wildly popular and continues to sell, so what does my publisher know about sales and times changing? Maybe what he means is my books aren't awful enough.*

In any event, I have not written a "good book" like you wanted, but I've concluded I don't have it in me. Resentment runs too deep. Did you know that resentment means to "re-feel" things? I read that somewhere and it stuck. For years I have re-felt the wrongs inflicted upon me in my childhood. The injustices. They've infected every cell in my body. (Likely it is not a coincidence there are cells in our bodies. I have been locked inside of mine for too long.)

But as I mull over my life, I keep landing on the same thought: Daddy lied to me. From the time I was a little girl, he said I was Miss Ellie Louise. He said I could have whatever I wanted. He said I was his best girl. So I took what I wanted. And you know the outcome.

My heart is palpitating as I write this. My life agitates me still. If I'd been born a boy, none of this would have happened.

If you are reading this, then my heart has given way.

I leave you my notebooks on my shelf in the study. You can take them now. All of my wishes are outlined in my will, in a manila envelope in the top drawer of my desk. My solicitor, Mr. Dunedin, has the original. He is my executor and will assist with everything.

Also, I did receive the letter you sent me years ago. I didn't respond because I still believed that you'd never visited me after Jerome was born.

Jerome? Wait. Ellie knew about Jerome?

I watched that March on television. I couldn't have avoided it if I tried. I know that Jerome had something to do with the organizing. That's ironic, isn't it? That a child from my loins (do women have loins?) might help to unite the races? Wonders never cease. Maybe Jerome's the good book I've written. Did you ever think of that?

I've always loved you, Miss Mavis Marie. I've just been too proud to admit it. Pride was all I had left.

Love,
Ellie (aka Randall)

Mavis put the letter down on her chest and closed her eyes. This was too much. Ellie knew about Jerome?

The kitchen clock sounded like a bomb ticking in the quiet room as Mavis absorbed the truth that all this time, Ellie had known about Jerome. What would be in her will?

She couldn't wait to find out and jumped back in the car. At Ellie's, she let herself in with the extra key Sliver had given her and ran up the stairs. In the study, she opened the top desk drawer and found the manila envelope. *To be read on the occasion of my death.* She slid the contents onto the desk and began to read. When she finished, she read through the material again just to be sure. Then she ran down to the kitchen, picked up the phone, and dialled the solicitor.

She was still shaking her head at what she'd discovered when she returned to the study. She stacked the papers again and returned them to the envelope. Something fell from the pile onto the floor. She bent down and saw it was an old black and white picture, yellowed around the edges. Two girls in white dresses stood smiling next to the body of a shirtless negro hanging from a naked branch.

Desperate.

The sights and scents of that day at the shade tree returned: blood, dirt, sweat, flies on severed fingers. Everywhere flies. Buzzing. Buzzing. Cutlery clinking. Children laughing and running and playing. Cigarette and cigar smoke on the breeze.

In the photograph, a young Ellie stood closest to the body. Mavis stood right beside her. They were both smiling hard, cheeks bunched beneath their eyes, squinting into the light. Mavis remembered Mr. McCall telling them not to move and thinking she'd have to stand beside the dead man beneath the blazing sun for eternity.

She was wearing the white dress that had been a present for her tenth birthday. It was a practical dress her mama said, one that could be worn to church, parties, and picnics. It was the last new dress of her childhood.

She flipped the picture over. *Ellie and Mavis* was written in her mother's faded script. And in fresher ink, an arrow had been penned after the *and*. Ellie had written the word *Miss*.

Ellie and Miss Mavis.

It was a caress and a blow. An *I love you* and a *look at yourself.*

It wasn't hard to attach words to Ellie's action.

You're not as good as you think you are, Miss Mavis.

Remember where you come from.

She imagined Sliver or Jerome looking at the picture and asking, *who is that smiling girl* before turning it over to find out. Except Sliver would already know. It would be Jerome who was asking.

A pack of matches sat beside the ashtray on Ellie's desk. Mavis didn't hesitate. She struck one and held the flame to the edge of the photograph. Not because she wanted to hide anything but because that image no longer represented her. She watched her face turned black, then Ellie's. Then the flames found Desperate, and all three bodies blistered away.

Mavis dropped the disappearing image into the ashtray and stared until it turned to ash and completely fell apart.

When her nerves had steadied, she read Ellie's will.

Then she called Sliver.

CHAPTER 58

She hit every red light on the way to Sliver's apartment and was glad for the delay. Ellie's will would force Sliver's hand, and Mavis wasn't sure how she'd feel about it.

She rang Sliver's apartment buzzer and climbed the stairs when she was let in.

Sliver stood in her open door down the hallway, wiping her hands on her apron.

"It smells good." Mavis realized she had skipped lunch and was hungry. "I didn't mean for you to cook for me."

"I had nothing to do, so I started cooking. I needed to be busy."

"You're not going to believe what I found out."

"Uh-oh. I don't like the sound of that."

"It's not bad exactly, but you might want to sit down."

Sliver took off her apron and sat at her kitchen table.

Mavis sat beside her. "I read Ellie's letter as soon as I got home. She told me where her will was and asked me to read it, so I went back to her house."

"I know all that."

"Okay, I'll start with the good news then: Ellie left you some money."

"*What?*"

"And it's a sizeable amount."

Sliver fanned her face with her hand. "Are you sure you read it right?"

"I'm sure."

"What do you mean by a sizeable amount?"

"I mean a lot. Do you want to know how much?"

Sliver nodded but looked afraid.

"She left you one hundred thousand dollars."

"That's not funny. I'm too old for that."

"It's not a joke. Her solicitor will be in touch with you."

"You must not have read it right."

"Sliver, I'm sure."

"Well I'll believe it when I see it." She put her hand to her heart as if to slow its beating. "You said that was the good news. What's the bad news?"

"She left most of her estate to me. From what I can tell, she was worth a fair bit. More than I would have imagined. I thought Ellie was just bragging when she said her books sold well."

"I don't see how that's bad news."

"There's more. She left a quarter of her estate, plus her house, to her son."

Sliver's face moved from confusion to surprise. "She left money to Eugene?"

"She left money to her son Jerome Lanier."

Sliver stood up so fast her chair fell over. "That's not possible! She didn't know about Jerome."

Mavis picked up Sliver's chair and helped her back into it. "I was shocked too. In Ellie's letter she talked about the March and how her son had been involved. I called her solicitor to find out how she knew about Jerome. He told me she hired a private detective back in 1948. Right after you started working for her. He said she wanted to know if you'd come with a negro companion. She might have been thinking about Charlie, I don't know, but apparently, according to the files, the detective identified a young negro boy and got information from his school. Ellie put two and two together."

Sliver put her hand to her chest again. "I might have to take one of her pills. Does that mean she knew you were here all that time too?"

"I asked the same thing, but Mr. Dunedin couldn't say. But remember how I didn't leave the rooming house for a couple of weeks after we got here? Everybody there was black, so maybe the detective saw Jerome and didn't think to look any further. Ellie did seem genuinely surprised when I visited her."

"But why didn't she ever say anything about Jerome?"

Mavis shrugged. "I've given up trying to understand her."

"She left Jerome her house? Is he supposed to pretend he's the butler or the gardener? Imagine him and Trudy trying to move in there. Is that her way of getting him killed?"

Mavis had thought the same thing. "I guess he can sell it, but that's not the issue right now. Obviously, you're going to have to explain how he's inherited a house and a sizeable sum of money from your white employer."

Sliver brooded. "I'm not sure I can do that."

"You don't have a choice. The solicitor said there's a timeline he needs to follow to file the will. You might not have as much time as you want."

"It's just like her, even after she's dead, to force me to do something I'm not sure I want to do. I need some time."

"Sliver, you've had *years* to tell him. Maybe Ellie forcing your hand is a good thing. Jerome has to know. It's just a matter of who will be the one to tell him."

Sliver folded her hands in her lap.

"He's twenty-five," Mavis continued. "He's going to be a father soon. Once you explain things, he'll understand. He knows how much you love him and what you've sacrificed for him. Maybe it'll feel good to let the truth out."

"It's not just Jerome. If I tell him about Ellie, then he'll ask about his daddy. And if I tell him about Charlie, then I'll have to tell Charlie that I lied to him."

Mavis didn't know that part of the story. "How did you lie?"

"I told him Ellie's baby wasn't his and that it was sickly and likely not going to live."

"You've been carrying that secret for a long time. Maybe it will be a relief to tell the truth. You won't know until you try."

Sliver got up and dished the meal onto plates. Besides the chicken, everything came from the garden. Potatoes, corn on the cob, and fried zucchini.

"Who else is coming? You've made enough to feed the building!"

"Like I said, I had extra time on my hands."

They were quiet as they ate and satisfied their hunger.

"I always thought I'd go before she did," Sliver said. "And maybe I wish I had."

"Don't say that."

"And I guess I thought I'd go to my grave not telling Charlie about Jerome or Jerome about anything."

"Not knowing doesn't feel good." Mavis knew that firsthand. She thought about meals she'd shared with Danny in their home and how he parroted his ugly views held up by ugly beliefs and traditions. "Did you know that Danny was the father of Rosetta's boys?"

"Everybody knew that."

"Everybody but me."

"You knew it too. You just didn't *want* to know it."

Mavis started to disagree, but she remembered her instincts to back away from unpleasantries. She had talked herself out of seeing the truth on so many occasions. "Remember when we first left Neelan Junction?"

Sliver nodded.

"You only wanted to borrow some money, and I invited myself along, thinking you'd need my help."

"Yes. I tried to talk you into staying home."

"You could have ditched me at Union Station, but you didn't. You waited for me. For the longest time I told myself that I had helped you and Jerome, but that wasn't the case at all. I needed you to show up and ask for money. I didn't have the courage to leave on my own. It was you and Jerome who saved me, not the other way around."

"You didn't know that?"

Mavis laughed. "Not then, no. But I know it now."

CHAPTER 59

Sliver thought about truth and how it was something everybody had access to. It didn't require money or education or a particular colour of skin. A poor black woman might know truth better than the wealthiest white person. Truth was weightless; lies, by contrast, were a heavy burden to carry, and her knees had been under strain and near-to-giving out for a long time. *One hundred thousand dollars?* The sum was too big to imagine. All her life, she'd counted her coins, knowing each one played a necessary role in her survival. Did taking money from Miss Ellie now make her somehow beholden? Was it wrong to take it if she'd never particularly *liked* Miss Ellie? Was it wrong to take it knowing she had made it from those awful books? And would the money even come? Wouldn't that be a joke for Miss Ellie to get her thinking she could enjoy herself only to find out the will was fraudulent after Sliver had spent all her savings? No sir, that wouldn't happen. She'd believe it if and when the money arrived. In the meantime, she'd make sure to keep much of her own.

She had lied to Old Lady Yates, or had certainly been selective in her honesty, telling her Willis's baby had died, knowing Mrs. Yates was asking about the second baby. But that second baby had been Charlie's boy, so saying Willis's baby had died *was* telling the truth, only it was twisting it too.

As the years passed, Sliver had grown comfortable with the secrets she held. Like most people, she gravitated towards comfort. Jerome was going to be a father soon. He was content with his life. Was now the right time to tell him who his parents were? What would it change?

And what about Charlie? She had denied him a son. That was nothing short of cruel. When was the right time to fix that wrong? Could it be fixed? Yet Sliver knew if people waited until they were ready to do things, nothing would ever get done. Being ready was not a precursor to taking action.

A week passed and Sliver imagined various ways to explain herself. And then another week passed. Before she knew it, two months had gone by since she'd learned the contents of Ellie's will, and her secret was still locked tight.

The November drizzle was cool against her skin as she walked to the grocery store near her apartment. She had to admit shopping was more enjoyable since learning about Ellie's money. Even though a part of her doubted the truth of it, the voice that normally told her she couldn't afford things was quiet, and it didn't tell her to wait for a sale or to put things back. That was a new freedom she allowed herself to enjoy.

She paid for her groceries and left the store with her bags evenly weighted. At the corner, she noticed people huddled together in groups. Many were leaning into cars listening to the radio. Some of them were crying and hugging one another. It wasn't hard to see something terrible had happened. If white folks were upset and crying, Sliver knew she was better off out of sight. It was only a matter of time until they looked for someone to blame. She limped along, eyes to the ground, admiring the weeds growing in sidewalk cracks like tiny, defiant gardens.

She was relieved to reach her apartment. Climbing the stairs, she thought fondly of the days when Jerome had been there to greet her after work. He'd usually be at the kitchen table studying, warming the meal she'd prepared for them the previous night, starting a new meal, or watching the news. And always his face lit up when he saw her. Surprisingly, the apartment felt smaller without him. His enthusiasm for life and belief in possibilities had made the place feel like there were no walls. She'd go back to sleeping on the couch this very night if Jerome needed her to. But he slept beside Trudy now, the woman he loved who was growing their child. Maybe their child would live in the dream world that Martin Luther King Jr. had described. It was a dream worth dreaming.

She put her bags on the counter and turned on the television. The white dot at the centre of the screen grew larger as it warmed up until finally *As the World Turns* came into view. Almost immediately, a special news bulletin flashed on the screen. Then came a man's voice: *Here is a bulletin from CBS News.* Walter Cronkite's voice read the update: "In Dallas, Texas, three shots were fired at President Kennedy's motorcade in downtown Dallas. The first reports say that he has been seriously wounded by this shooting."

Then the soap opera returned.

Shot? Sliver sat heavily on the couch. *Please don't die.* Kennedy had dared to speak about inequality. The scourge of segregation, and he had framed it as a moral issue. A wrong that needed righting. When he'd beat Nixon, Jerome had celebrated, saying, "now there'll be change," In reality, the president had been slow to respond. Still, the president and the preacher were a hopeful team. Jerome was right about that; he even had her believing that change would finally happen.

And now this.

One step forward and two steps back. If the president of the United States wasn't safe, then none of them were safe.

She glanced at the clock. It was 1:40.

But Kennedy still had work to do. He had the best doctors in the world caring for him. He'd be okay.

Sliver got up to put the groceries away. The chicken had partially thawed in the bag, leaving a thin, bloody liquid on the counter.

A bullet was quicker than a noose, she thought. It was more humane. And more anonymous, too.

What kind of a setback would this be for Jerome's group? Where was Jerome now? In September, he had come to her apartment and cried for the four girls who were murdered in the church bombing. *How can I bring a child into this world? How?*

She told him there was no perfect time to bring a child into the world. There never was and there never would be.

She made herself a cup of tea and returned to the couch.

Almost an hour later, Cronkite was back reporting from his news desk. The president was dead.

Sliver surprised herself by crying. All of Kennedy's bright ideas had been shot right out of his head. A vessel was only good as long as it wasn't broken.

An old anger ignited. It was against *the law* to murder, yet the president of the United States had just been assassinated.

It was against *the law* for schools and colleges to keep black students out, but the government had been forced to send in the military to escort negroes inside buildings.

Jerome put too much stock in *the law*, repeating what Martin Luther King Jr. had said: *It may be true that the law cannot make a man love me, but it can keep him from lynching me.*

But that was a lie! Lynching didn't stop when it was made illegal.

Now that her tear ducts had opened, Sliver couldn't close them. There were so many things she hadn't cried for that had deserved her tears, and they all came to mind as she sat on her couch and watched replays of the president's murder.

She cried for her own naïveté in believing things might change. She'd been duped again. Just like she'd probably be duped by not getting Miss Ellie's money. *The law* would likely find a loophole.

She had finally worked up the courage to tell Jerome about the will, but how could she tell him now, when he'd be reeling from this news?

Another voice in her head spoke: *Tell Charlie and get things started.*

Tell him about the son he doesn't know he has, the son he will be proud of.

Tell him about the grandchild that's on the way.

Tell him.

Sliver dried her face and tried to reason with the voice. *I can't. I've waited too long.*

But the voice was persistent and had a rebuttal ready: *Waiting longer won't fix a damned thing.*

It was a familiar voice, soothing as a mother's lap.

Okay.

Then she said it out loud. "Okay."

She got up and found a piece of paper.

She stared into the corner of the room for a while.

Then she picked up her pen and started to write.

Dear Charlie ...

CHAPTER 60

The calendar turned to December and brought temperatures almost ten degrees cooler than normal. Shock remained in the air. Mavis watched news footage of Jacqueline Kennedy and her two children moving out of the White House. Men in suits pushed children's bicycles and carried toys and boxes to a truck that would drive to a new house where the children would grow up without their father.

Mavis knew her daddy and brother would think Kennedy deserved what he got. Get *along* with the negroes? Get *along* with the Soviets? That wasn't leadership. That was waving a white flag, rolling over, and showing your underbelly. Ending segregation would only bring violence.

Sliver was right when she told Mavis that *her* people didn't tell the story straight. To Sliver, Mavis's people were the ones that gathered around the shade tree.

She closed her eyes and imagined she was the tree itself, her blood the sap that made it grow.

Then she imagined picking up her roots like a skirt that was too long, holding them up in the air, and taking long strides to move them somewhere else, planting those roots in richer soil with better light where the tree could enjoy a better life. Isn't that sort of what she'd done, or at least *tried* to do when she left Neelan Junction?

She looked out her kitchen window and watched Sliver walk up and down the garden rows in her rubber boots, a scarf tucked into the neck of her coat. There wasn't much gardening to be done in December, but Sliver had never gotten used to doing nothing.

1963 was winding down. Mavis wasn't sorry to say goodbye to it. Some good things had happened, like the March being a success and Jerome and Trudy announcing they were expecting, but a lot of bad things had happened too. The list would be a long one. Losing Ellie still hurt. It was the death of expectation. Mavis had expected they'd mend things.

She wandered into her living room and stared at the shelf that held Ellie's notebooks. She had read through them all after her sister died, and then read through them a second time, dog-earing pages she knew she'd want to return to. She pulled one off the shelf, and it opened automatically to a spot she'd read numerous times. It was written six weeks after Ellie killed her baby.

July 31, 1936

My dreams keep me awake. Sometimes, I hear a knocking, as if tiny fists are banging on my door. I jerk awake to listen. Then I realize the fists are beating against the inside of my breastbone. The sound is coming from inside my body!

Then, as happens in dreams, everything changes. The baby is in my arms, struggling. I put my hand over his head. It is the size of a cantaloupe and lightly furred. My thumb bursts straight through the baby's skull and into his brain where it lodges so tight that I can't pull it out. It's like what Jimmy said happens to dogs caught in the sexual act—the male's penis swells inside the female so he can't disengage until the deed is done. My baby's skull closes on my thumb, and I imagine dragging a rotting corpse along with me for the rest of my days.

I startle awake, shaking.

I move from my bed to my rocking chair. Eventually, my head dips onto my chest and I nod off. But someone is knocking at the door. I open it to find a burlap sack on the top stair. The stench is awful, but I can't stop myself. I reach

down and dump the contents onto the floor. Rotting babies
spill out in a gelatinous rush.
I jerk awake.

Mavis had read that entry dozens of times. Ellie hadn't walked freely away from her crime. Her dreams, at least, proved she had a conscience.

She reached for the final notebook and turned to the spot she'd marked.

August 23, 1947

Sliver showed up at my door today, out of the blue, as if I'd
called to offer her a job. She said she was alone, but Sliver lies.

September 3, 1947

I knew it! The detective said Sliver's here with a mulatto
boy. He saw them walking together and learned the boy's
name is Jerome. He got a copy of Jerome's school records. He
is the same age and was born the same day as my son Sliver
said had died. I am both furious and relieved. It appears
Charlie is not with her. Does he know about our son? Should
I tell Sliver I know she brought him? What if I told her and
she disappeared with Jerome? What would I have then?

Until reading that passage, Mavis hadn't imagined that Ellie was afraid Sliver might leave. Was it too much of a stretch to think Ellie had kept Sliver around for sixteen years because she knew she was helping Jerome too? Or was that simply Mavis's attempt to rewrite Ellie's motives and character?

She returned to the kitchen. Outside the window, Sliver continued to poke around. It was only 45 degrees, and the ground was damp. It had rained in the night. Her boots would be caked with mud.

Ellie was dead and Trudy was pregnant. A life for a life.

She put the kettle on, thinking Sliver would enjoy a cup of tea after being out in that damp. When it was ready, she called Sliver in.

"I made tea. Will you have some with me?"

Sliver took her muddy boots off outside and left them on the porch.

The tea steamed as it poured from the pot. Mavis pushed the mug across the table.

"He's coming," Sliver said.

"Who?"

"Charlie."

"You wrote to him?"

Sliver nodded.

"That's great!"

Sliver stared at her hands.

"Isn't it?" Mavis asked.

Sliver nodded again.

"Just because you're nervous doesn't mean it was the wrong thing to do."

"Did I say I was nervous?"

"No. You didn't. Sorry." Mavis had done it again, assumed she knew what Sliver was feeling. "I was just thinking that I'd be nervous."

"Well you're not me."

"I know that."

"And you'll never be able to think like me."

Mavis paused. Something in the room had shifted. She wasn't sure how to proceed. "I don't understand."

"That's because you can't. You think I'm free now because of Miss Ellie's money, but that's not true because black folks aren't free in this country. Miss Ellie knew that she gave Jerome a house he can't live in. Why would she do that? Was she just putting him in his place?"

"I don't think Ellie did it to be hurtful."

"But it *is* hurtful. He gets to look at something nice that he can't have."

Mavis took a sip of her tea and let the hot liquid scorch her mouth.

They sat quietly for a few minutes.

Mavis finally broke the silence and asked when Charlie would arrive.

"Tonight."

"Tonight?!"

"His bus is in at midnight."

"Wow. He didn't waste any time. Do you want me to pick him up?"

"He can take a cab."

"I know he can, but he'll likely be tired after all that travelling. I'm sure he'd welcome a ride."

Sliver took a sip of tea and thought about it. "I didn't tell him a ride would be waiting."

"I know what he looks like. I'll just flag him down and say you sent me." It was a short drive from the bus station to her apartment. "Please. Let me help."

"Okay."

⌐ Mavis watched the clock carefully. She didn't often stay up until midnight, so she made sure to keep herself busy. She swept the kitchen floor and mopped it. She vacuumed. She took down the shower curtain that had a hint of mould at the bottom and put it in the wash. She dusted the bookshelf. She'd placed Lillian Smith's *Killers of the Dream* right beside Ellie's books, as if it was an antidote to the poison.

As she worked, she thought of her younger self growing up steeped in segregationist brine before she even knew what it was. For years Samuel had been her childhood friend and playmate, and then one day he was a coloured boy and deemed a threat. He hadn't deserved his end.

She remembered how much space Danny took up in a room and the sheriff's impenetrable confidence it was right to favour people that looked like him. She thought of dinner table discussions when her daddy ranted about negroes and unions and the government. She thought about what Sliver had told her went on at Slew Town and wondered if it could be true and how she hadn't known. And she thought of Mrs. Booth, saying the trouble with people who were good is they couldn't imagine doing things to others that they wouldn't do themselves.

Sliver had pulled Mavis out of that environment by the scruff and set her down where she could make up her own mind about things. Mavis couldn't take credit for her own re-education. According to Ellie, Mavis hadn't seen the racism that was staring her in the face because she'd benefitted from it too much. She hoped that wasn't true but was afraid it might be. Maybe she'd ask Sliver one day if she got up the courage. Or maybe she'd leave Sliver alone and take responsibility for herself.

For now, she knew where she came from, and she knew what she didn't want to be. She couldn't apologize for everything because she'd never stop saying 'sorry.'

It had taken decades for Mavis to learn that she couldn't save Ellie. In truth, Mavis had barely been able to save herself. Her parents had filled their children's heads with notions of superiority, hate, and entitlement well before their kneecaps had formed, well before they could even get on their knees and ask for help. She thought, *Shame on them for what they did, but shame on me if I don't change.*

There was nothing left to clean in the house now. She looked at the clock. It was 11:30 p.m.

Charlie was coming. Jerome's father. Mavis had once tucked notes into his hand. Maybe she had been the one to draw Ellie's attention to him.

I'm sorry.

But Jerome wasn't something to be sorry about.

She put on her coat to meet Charlie at the station.

CHAPTER 61

Outside Sliver's apartment window, the moon had fully waned. That meant the sky was at its darkest and filled with stars. Her daddy had always told her to look to the stars to navigate, and she was looking hard right now, so maybe the new moon was fitting; it was easier to see the constellations in the pitch-black sky.

Thinking the word 'pitch' reminded her of Slew Town, of the turpentine, pitch, and tar, and of the poverty and brokenness of its inhabitants. It didn't have to be that way. It never had to be that way. How far she had travelled. Charlie was making a similar journey, by bus instead of train, but he was travelling the same distance.

They had a big discussion ahead of them. It was unlikely that Charlie would wait for the morning to hear it, that's why she'd agreed to Mavis picking him up. They might as well get started.

Her plan was a simple one: she'd already told him in the letter that he had a son. She figured the long bus ride would dull the hard edge of anger at his not knowing. Once he got here, she'd tell him more about Jerome, anything he wanted to know. Maybe she'd leave it to Charlie to tell Jerome he was his father. She'd ask what he'd prefer. And if Charlie decided to tell Jerome Miss Ellie was his mother, Sliver would let him. That was for him to decide. She'd tell Charlie about Jerome's inheritance and ask how and what Jerome should be told. Keeping a secret for so long made her wonder if it might be right for someone else to tell it. In truth, it was more Charlie's story to tell than hers.

There was no getting around that she'd caused Charlie harm, even when she reminded herself that she'd done what she thought was best. If Jerome had stayed in Neelan Junction, he might have ended up like Samuel, murdered for no reason and left to rot. What might Eugene and his friends have done to Jerome on their way to becoming men or once they'd crossed over? It didn't bear thinking about. Sliver had seen far too many ways white folks made themselves feel superior; she would go to her grave not understanding that low and base need to put other people down.

If she hadn't taken Jerome away, he wouldn't have gone to university and become a lawyer. None of that would have been possible for him. Charlie would at least recognize that truth.

And maybe, if she *did* receive money from Miss Ellie, she could bring Becky and the rest of her family north. All her children and their children too. Maybe she could fulfill Gideon's dream for them. If they wanted to leave, that is; Florida was their home, and some people chose to stay and fight to make their home better instead of starting all over someplace else. There was no such thing as a perfect place, but she couldn't deny the comfort that came from knowing the shortcuts in a place, knowing its people and being known in it. Even now, after sixteen years living in the nation's capital, Florida still felt more like home.

The timer sounded in the kitchen. Sliver pulled two fresh loaves of bread from the oven and did a mental check of the contents of her refrigerator. She had enough food for her and Charlie to talk for days if need be, without having to go out.

She checked the clock. If his bus was on time, he would be here any minute. Her stomach did a flip flop. "He's coming, Giddy," she said out loud. "Charlie's coming."

The boy who had set everything in motion.

She would sleep on the couch again tonight with gratitude.

Outside, a cat walked slowly across the road, not bothering to look both ways because there wasn't a need.

A car rounded the corner, pulled up to the curb, flashed its headlights, and parked.

Charlie climbed out of the back seat. Sliver recognized his movements and her heart picked up speed like a horse being put through its paces. She recalled his entrance into the world and the sorrow he'd been born into. Maybe taking her milk, so filled with heartache, had shaped his special gift, which was wanting to heal things that had been damaged. How else to explain his natural attraction to the three-legged dog, the kitten born blind. And Ellie.

He looked up at her window.

Sliver raised a hand and waved.

He waved back and walked towards the front door of the building.

Mavis drove off.

Sliver's heart stalled and skipped then broke into a gallop. Such a wondrous thing, a heart. How it contracted when it felt pain but expanded when it felt love. She'd never until this moment thought how like a uterus a heart was, and how many births it experienced in a lifetime.

She felt a lift in her belly as if God had just scooped her up, kissed her brow, told her she'd done good, and then set her down lighter on her feet but in a body still stiff with age. She understood that didn't mean everything that had happened to her had been good; it meant she'd done the best she could with the circumstances she'd been given.

Sliver opened her apartment door, walked to the landing, and stood at the top of the stairs. She heard the front door open and then latch. She heard footsteps on the first flight of stairs to the landing, and then the next set.

She didn't call out because it was late.

Charlie rounded the corner.

Her son.

Jerome's father.

Their eyes met.

She raised her arms and opened them wide.

He hesitated for only a moment then took the last stairs two at a time.

EPILOGUE

A **baby with** a dark thumb print on his brain leaves the world by one door and enters by another in a midwife's hands in Florida.

And that child emerges slick with amniotic fluid that's a combination of swamp water and bone marrow.

Gideon never made it out of the swamp.

He tucked himself into the bank for hours, breathing in the sulphuric swamp gas, hoping whoever was at the fishing hole would soon go away. But new voices kept being added to the mix. Some kind of celebration was going on. And drinking. He could tell by the songs being sung and the pitch of the singers' voices.

The breakfast Sliver had made for him had long since digested by the time he decided to make his move. If he went slowly, the water would barely reveal his movement. Fish already disturbed it by coming up for air. Water bugs and marsh treaders too, skidded across the surface. The water didn't always sit placid, and he didn't need to go right by the revellers. He'd keep close to the bank, but he'd press on.

The first bullet skimmed past his ear like a skipping stone. He dived to the muddy bottom and pulled himself along by whatever roots he could grip, cursing himself for not using his time better and finding a reed to breathe through before making his move. Then he could have stayed submerged.

When his lungs cried for air, he anchored himself, lifted the smallest surface of his mouth to the air, and breathed through pursed lips, careful to not let the water flood his nose. His lungs filled and emptied. Oh sweet heaven!

I'll send for you, Sliver. You and the kids. Don't you worry. I'm going North, to the land of freedom. I'll send for you. Yes I will.

With each new breath he grew more calm. He could be patient when he needed to be. Everything was going to be okay.

⌐ Gideon's remains were never identified, along with scores of other bones around him that one day were hauled up in nets when people searched for a missing white boy and discovered a mass graveyard of skeletons instead. Some were chained to heavy objects, others were retrieved in parts. Some were picked clean of flesh, others were still decomposing. A disappointed reporter questioned why there were so many more bodies than missing people reports. *Drifters*, Sheriff Thorpe said. *Migrants and drifters. Slew Town vagrants. Do you see what we put up with here?*

There was no file for a Gideon Lanier.

⌐ A woman cries out in pain, and a midwife rolls up her sleeves, catches the newborn slick from its journey and mottled with memory, and welcomes its howl. She wishes she could take all the learning she's done in life, fit it into a box and pack it tight, and gift it to the newborn eager for the decades of living ahead. But there are no shortcuts. Such a shame, she thinks, that each child swimming towards life through a woman's body must learn the same lessons over and over again. It seems time could be parcelled out a bit better and evolution hurried along. Why did people have to learn and forget and repeat the same lessons and learn and forget and repeat them yet again?

Sliver is old. Sometimes she mixes sleeping and waking. The dream world with the real world. Sometimes Gideon stands beside her, his arm draped over her shoulders, holding her close.

Trudy cries out, a primal sound that comes from a woman breaking open and not knowing if she'll survive the break.

Sliver is there but not there. Working but observing.

Jerome clutches Trudy's hand. Fear dilates his pupils.

Sliver's palms itch. She rubs them together so they're warm when she catches their baby. *Push. Push.*

The baby's head is in sight.

Push.

Crowning and heaving and breaking and crying.

Push!

The newborn warms her hands in the filling.

A boy child, come straight from the soil.

She confirms he has all his parts and hands him to the boy who used to hold her hand and worked so hard to get ahead. The boy who became a man who became a father. The boy who believes the future is so bright that they all squint their eyes when he describes it.

The blood washes from her hands, circles in the porcelain sink and flows down the drain.

It is February, 1964.

Sliver squints into the future and allows herself to believe in Jerome's vision. Why not?

Here is what she knows: There is more tending to be done.

More tending indeed.

And the world needs more gardeners.

ACKNOWLEDGEMENTS

My thanks go to the jurors of the 2020 Guernica Prize for choosing *The Shade Tree* as the winning manuscript. I am also grateful to everyone at Guernica Editions who put time into bringing this book to publication. Michael Mirolla and Julie Roorda for editing, David Moratto for designing the beautiful cover, Margo LaPierre for navigating as publicist, and Dylan Curran for handling marketing and sales.

Prior to submitting the manuscript, it was my good fortune to have Heather Lazare's keen editorial eyes on *The Shade Tree*. Her detailed comments and feedback improved the novel immensely, and her belief in the book was invaluable. I'm grateful to have her in my corner.

To my literary mentor and friend, Merna Summers, who read a much earlier draft of this novel, I can't apologize enough. I'm a fortunate recipient of your generosity.

The Canada Council, the Alberta Foundation for the Arts, and the Banff Centre for the Arts all provided financial support at critical moments in the writing process. Time is every writer's dream, and money buys time.

To my extensive support system who see me through the highs and lows of life in general and artistic creation in particular, thank you. I hope you see yourself here.

Finally, and most importantly, I'm grateful to my husband and three children—no accomplishments in life would be as meaningful or fun without you.

ABOUT THE AUTHOR

Theresa Shea's debut novel, *The Unfinished Child*, was a finalist for the Georges Bugnet Award for Fiction and the Alberta Readers' Choice Award. A word-of-mouth bestseller, the novel remains a book club favourite. *The Shade Tree,* winner of the 2020 Guernica Prize for best novel manuscript, is her much-anticipated follow-up. Born in the United States, Shea moved to Canada as a teenager in 1977. She lives, parents, and writes in Edmonton. Find her online at theresashea.com.

 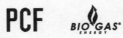